To Peter

Happy 80th birthday
Love from
your sister Brenda
x

THIS TIME AROUND

J.P. Ledwon

Published in 2008 by YouWriteOn.com

Published by YouWriteOn.com

This book is for Amelia

Also dedicated to the memory of Keef and Rog

PROLOGUE

I used to have such an amazing life.

I thought myself the luckiest guy in the world, living with my beautiful girlfriend in our stunning apartment. I had a close-knit social circle, loving parents, a high-flying job and plenty of money in the bank.

Then, over a period of eighteen months, I lost it all.

Everything.

It left me in a hell of a lot of trouble. Time is running out, and here I am only a couple of paragraphs in.

Last week I entered my twenty-sixth year. It was supposed to be a time of celebration, surrounded by friends and family, food, drink and dancing; instead, I spent most of the evening on my own in a hospital, waiting to hear that someone I loved was dead. As you can probably imagine, it didn't rank highly on the all-time, best birthdays list.

My name is Barry Brooks. I am tall and slim, with puppy-dog brown eyes that could once command a hug from four-hundred yards. I am writing this from what remains of my living room. Once a haven filled with a subtle blend of modern technology, abstract art and expensive furniture, it now looks like three monster trucks have released their pent-up rage and frustration on it. The door is off its hinges, bookcases have collapsed, and to make things worse, my fifty-inch widescreen TV is scattered around the room in a thousand pieces.

That hit me hard.

The man responsible for the mess is in the kitchen next door, munching his way through a packet of fig rolls. At first, I wanted to kill him; I wanted to remove his head with a penknife and play football with it, but he wouldn't let me. With his impressive powers of persuasion, he told me in the long run, it wasn't worth it. Why didn't I go and do something constructive instead?

So I navigated my way through broken glass and chipped plaster, pulled up the one surviving chair and began to scribble down my thoughts. Anger management, he called it; the calmer you are, the more rational you become. I was never one for psycho-babble.

As far as I can tell, it all started with Beth. When she left me *that* summer, it kicked off a chain of horrible events; events that would ultimately lead me to where I am now. She may have acted like a bitch throughout - not giving back my *Knight Rider* leather jacket or the money she owed for bills - but I couldn't blame her for everything. The real culprit stood just out of shot, orchestrating my downfall with unsettling satisfaction.

The one who honed my extraordinary ability to destroy anything I put my hand to.

The only man I could bring myself to hate.

Even if I get out of this mess, he'll still be watching me. I'll see the pesky little cretin in the corner of my eye, hanging around like an aggressive fart. For a time, I thought him unbeatable, but I got there in the end.

At least, that's how he made it appear.

ONE

My story begins from a high spot. For those of you big on precision, it begins one-thousand, three hundred and forty-four feet above sea level, at the summit of Ben Nevis, Lochaber, Scotland. It could easily have begun before the ascent, but that would have resulted in this chapter being nothing more than a glorified guidebook. Could there be anything worse?

I'd been sponsored to do the *Three Peaks Challenge*, which involved climbing the three highest mountains in Great Britain: Snowdon, Scafell Pike and the Ben; no mean feat for a man who'd spent most of his formative years running scared from exercise. Having put my politically charged opinions on physical exertion to one side, I decided to do something for someone else for a change, and duly informed a local charity of my intentions to donate.

Seven of us did the climb in total, alongside two extra bodies brought in as designated drivers. If we managed to complete the task in under twenty-four hours, sponsor money would be doubled, so foolishly, we agreed to push for the fastest time possible. I'm not sure the drivers knew they'd be expected to smash the speed limit to pull this off, pelting down country roads wide enough for only one vehicle at the speed of light. It was a miracle the minibus, its occupants and passing ramblers made it through the jaunt intact.

In the run up to the climb, I'd been told by friends who'd previously completed the challenge that Ben Nevis was the most enjoyable of the three. On a clear day at the summit, you could see over one-hundred miles to the hills of Northern Ireland. It would be one of those unforgettable life experiences, when you realise that you're higher than ninety-nine point nine nine per cent of the country's population - a proper *get your mobile phone out and call everyone you know* moment. Just my rotten luck when I miraculously reached the top, huffing and puffing like a chain-smoker well into the early stages of hypoxia, visibility was down to a few metres, and hailstones the size of small cars were dropping down on us from the cloud we just happened to be at the heart of. What a letdown. I'd also left my phone in the minibus.

I don't think I have ever been as cold since. Sitting in my parents' chest freezer wearing only Bermuda shorts and a pair of sunglasses would have given me a tan, in comparison. It was my own fault for thinking the warm weather at the bottom would be replicated at the top. I should have packed waterproofed bottoms instead of relying on jeans and long johns. One thing you will discover about me is that, on occasion, I do have clumsy moments.

At the summit lays a small shelter where climbers can sit, protected from the elements, should they turn hostile. Though not a five-star hotel by any stretch, crawling inside to warm up a little would have been heavenly. To my disappointment, it was already occupied by four shaggy-haired students, huddled together, passing around several fat spliffs.

My first moment of real irritation. At a squeeze, I could have slotted in beside them, but they'd hot-boxed the entire shelter. You could smell the stuff from metres away.

One larger-than-usual intake of breath and I'd be cackling uncontrollably on my back, warbling my way through the *Coronation Street* theme tune in the pub stylee.

Out of options and unable to feel my fingers, I signalled to the group leader that I really needed to keep moving, or risk the onset of hypothermia. Of course, that's not exactly what I said; amidst my frozen body and the noise of the wind, it was more a painful mumble. I had done my research, though, and losing ten per cent of the sensation in both fingers and toes told me it was time to skedaddle back down the hill, pronto.

Dean was well aware of the dangers the cold could bring. We left the rest of the group behind, all of whom seemed unaffected by the Arctic conditions, and started the descent.

I had only met him a handful of times before, but it was clear he knew what he was doing. A seasoned veteran, Dean had successfully completed the challenge umpteen and a half times before, and had been considering the possibility of climbing Everest. I didn't know if he was serious or trying to take my focus away from the cold; nevertheless, it was interesting stuff.

We did our best to stick to the same route taken on the way up, but the fog and ever-increasing bullets of pure ice made it difficult to recognise familiar landmarks. Furthermore, the snow had already covered our previous tracks.

I started to panic, but took comfort in knowing all this was second nature to him. Dean had most likely dangled over a few cliffs in his time; he wore the most expensive hiking boots, acted as a constant source of motivation and carried food and medical supplies Sir Edmund Hillary would have been proud of.

Obediently, I followed.

It wasn't long before the path disappeared and I found myself wading through deeper, virgin snow. I couldn't see the ground. It felt like I was walking downhill.

'Can you feel that?'

'Yeah. Back it up a bit, Baz.'

We stopped and I looked around. The ten or fifteen climbers from another party who started the return journey with us had vanished.

We were completely alone.

Not good. Not good at all.

'I don't like this.'

When Dean turned to look at me, I knew we had deviated off course. This *seasoned veteran* was staring at me with apprehension in his eyes. My first reaction was one of anger and I cursed him under my breath. This was Ben Nevis, not *K2*, for God's sake. What kind of experienced climber with expensive boots and a hi-tech compass gets lost at the top of Ben Nevis?

'We must have drifted off-path.'

Oh, really? Could that go some way to explain why we're standing here like lemons, freezing our balls off?

Climbing up the mountain a few hours earlier, Dean pointed out a cornice a few hundred metres to the left and made a joke about slipping over it. Stood there, lost and confused, it was the only thing I could think about. I didn't know where the hell I was, couldn't see a damned thing and was paranoid I'd end up dropping over the side of the highest mountain in Great Britain.

'We're lost, aren't we?'

'Stay calm, mate. Come on, we'll retrace the steps back.'

Stay calm, indeed. I'll stay calm when you finally get me down this bloody mountain, *mate*.

I was in no position to argue with him, so swung around and resumed my search for the footsteps I'd already made. Straight ahead, all I could see was white; to the left and right, more of the same.

To the hills of Northern Ireland, my arse.

Scafell and Snowdon were both clear climbs. At the top, I glanced out for miles across the Welsh and Cumbrian skylines, admiring the breathtaking views. Although the wind was strong, there was always something to hold on to in case of a rogue gust: a rock, a boulder, a clump of grass. In Scotland, however, I didn't know whether the ground beneath my feet was safe. The drop could have been two metres away. One step forward, back, to the left or right could have seen me tumble non-stop down the mountain. I'd taken for granted the stability of the ground underneath. Living in a country mostly unaffected by large earthquakes, it was something I had the utmost confidence in. To have it yanked away played havoc with my equilibrium.

My internal compass told me to continue straight on, but Dean was heading to the right. Once again, I put my faith in him. What seemed like hours passed, disturbing thoughts flashing through my mind: how would anyone find us in this fog? Would my death take hours or seconds? Would it be painful? Would I ever see loved ones again? Why the hell didn't I bring my phone with me? What does raw human flesh taste like? Who killed J.F.K.?

To my excitement, blinking a few times to make sure I wasn't going mad, I saw movement from the corner of my eye through the blizzard.

I grabbed Dean by the arm and screamed in its general direction. 'Look. Over there.'

Scrambling in less-than-perfect conditions, preparing myself for a drop with every step, we came upon the path directly ahead and climbed up a small incline to reach it. I don't recall the moments that followed, but apparently, I ran too quickly, slipped, fell on my backside and slid like a pillock back down the way I came.

Back into unknown territory.

When I regained consciousness, my head was banging a drum solo. Disco lights of various colours were pulsating behind my eyelids. All I could hear was Dean's voice and a selection of club classics from *Now That's What I Call Dance 2001*.

'Get up, Barry. Come on.'

I didn't want to. I wanted to go back to sleep.

'Half an hour,' he continued to shout, my own, personal motivational man. 'Half an hour and we're beneath the cloud. Come on. Get up.'

That sparked me into action. I got to my feet in a daze, which took a few minutes, and trailed behind him. I kept my beady eyes on the newly-discovered path and made sure I didn't lose sight of the other hill walkers around us. Dean stuffed a chocolate bar into my mouth, despite my protests, and my energy tank received a much-needed boost.

Soon enough, the snow thinned out, visibility improved and the temperature began to rise. With most of the sensation to my fingers and toes restored, I checked my body for cuts and any evidence I'd soiled myself.

No evidence at all. Mother would be pleased.

The remainder of the descent passed without any further incident. Hail turned to rain, rain turned to light rain, and as if nothing happened, I got to within five-hundred metres of the car park and gently jogged the rest of the way, confidence alive and well once more.

I did it.

The whole challenge.

I BLOODY DID IT!

What an adventure. I could see the following morning's headlines:

The valiant Brooks returns triumphant!

Magnificent athlete raises £300 for charity!

Then, I remembered that national newspapers weren't too interested in insignificant people like me, or small-fry hills like Ben Nevis. I stopped thinking about the *Times* or the *Guardian*, and wondered if the *Islington Inksplodge* (circ: 500) or *Nevis News* (3) would run the story instead. In the meantime, I was happy to reach the minibus, take off my boots and get a hot cup of coffee.

Dean joined me in the shower a few moments later and took me by surprise. 'You did well up there, Baz.'

'Err, what?'

'Up there. Well done.'

I couldn't help but notice he was hung like an Arabian stallion. 'Err, yeah, you too.'

What a stupid reply. Stop looking, Barry. Why are you looking at it? You're a healthy, straight, normal male with normal urges. Think about your girlfriend instead.

'Don't you wanna know how we did, time-wise?'

Amidst the drama of almost losing my life, I'd completely forgotten.

'Twenty-three hours, thirty-six minutes. Pretty impressive, huh?'

I finally managed to avert my eyes. 'Fantastic. Sponsor money's doubled, then?'

'Three grand between us.'

He went on to apologise for getting us lost, which baffled me, as he was the one who saved my life. If anything, I should have said sorry to him for being such a pathetic novice. I waved it away and finished up, realising it was the first time in my life I'd raised any money for charity.

It felt good.

I promised myself I'd do it more often.

I dried off, got dressed and ran to the minibus to pass on the good news to Beth and my parents.

TWO

Dad was fiddling with his collection of automobile memorabilia in the garage, so I spoke to Mum instead. Turns out I interrupted her mid-pack. They were getting ready for a skiing holiday to Switzerland and she was sorting through his vast collection of thermal underwear.

'I knew you could do it, son.'

'Raised a lot of money, too. I swear I nearly died up there, though.'

'Don't be daft. Bet you were nowhere near the edge.'

Hmm, yeah, if five metres can be considered *nowhere near the edge*, then no, I guess I wasn't. She was only half-concentrating; in contrast to the abilities of most other women, this one found multi-tasking an arduous chore.

'What time you flying out on Monday?'

'The flight leaves at two o'clock, I think. I'll text you when we get to the hotel. Dad's taking me out for a slap-up meal somewhere posh on the first night.'

'Very nice.'

'Told him it's the least he can do seeing as I've done all the packing.'

'It's a good job you did. Otherwise, you'd have two suitcases full of socks and marzipan.'

She laughed. 'I'm still a bit worried about the flight, though.'

'You'll be fine. Remember what I said? It'll be over before you know it.'

'Hope so. Anyway, I don't want to think about it just

now. How's Dean?'

Dean and his wife were good friends of my parents. Only last week over dinner, Mum made him swear to keep me safe or prepare to endure a substantial amount of pain. She may have been exaggerating, but not by much. 'He's glad it's over.'

'I bet he is. Did you two get on well?'

'Yeah, he's a nice bloke.'

Soapy, lathered wang.

'Knew you'd like him. Look, sweetheart, I'd better go. Am trying to fit everything in these bloody cases.'

'Okay, Mum. Safe journey, yeah?'

'Thanks, love. I'll tell Dad you rang.'

'And bring me something nice back.'

So many times I asked, but the gift would never materialise. I'd always end up on the receiving end of a pack of authentic Belgian playing cards or the finest Egyptian coat hangers. This time she'd come back with a bottle of Swiss mineral water, or something equally as bizarre.

'You know me. Hope Monday goes well.'

I ended the call and immediately hit speed dial two to call Beth. It rang four times before the line connected, then a five-second pause before she spoke.

'Yeah?'

'I did it, baby. The whole lot!'

'Baz?'

'Can you hear me?'

'Err, yep. Congrats.'

She sounded distracted. I looked at my watch to check the time. 'You okay, hon? Were you asleep?'

'No, I'm awake,' she said curtly, 'where are you?'

I reckoned that was pretty bleeding obvious. 'At the bottom of Ben Nevis. You?'

'In the flat.'

Clearly, detailed and informative responses were firmly off the menu today. 'What's the matter? You in the middle of something?'

Another delay. 'Kinda, yeah. Can you call me back in a bit?'

'Right, err, yeah, what time's good…'

The line cut dead. She was gone. Love you too, schnookums.

Dean shouted over that it was time to leave, but I dallied for a moment, deep in thought. She sounded annoyed with me. Had I forgotten a birthday or anniversary? Maybe she'd found a stray copy of *Razzle* under the mattress? No, it couldn't have been that; I got rid of them all after the last argument.

I'd hoped to get some sleep on the way home, but her tone of voice worried me. I knew I'd be distracted until I next spoke to her.

What was she doing that was so important at eight-thirty on a Saturday morning? She always stayed in bed watching TV until at least midday. *She* was the one who insisted I got on the blower to her straight after the climb. *"No matter what time it is, call me, baby, okay?"*, she'd said, only forty-eight hours before. If Beth was in the flat, why did it sound like she was outside? And were those voices I could hear in the background?

Male voices?

It could have been the TV, but I got the nagging feeling it wasn't.

How long should I wait before calling her back? Five minutes? Ten? Twenty? My imagination revved into gear again. Was she with someone else? Had she used the time apart to go shag some other bloke - or more worryingly, blokes - behind my back? Did I pre-empt it with my fascination over Dean's naked form in the shower?

Beth and I had been together for three years by that point. Six months beforehand, we had moved into a newly-built, two-bedroomed flat, having previously lived in what could only be described as a cesspit for two years. It was a stinky, slimy, crap-laden, broken down, festering cesspit with walls; diseased gutter rats would have found the structure and aesthetics unsatisfactory.

She'd received an impressive promotion slash bonus at work and invested it in our new place; one that didn't honk of rotting monkeys and wasn't decorated like the inside of an over-filled colostomy bag. We'd looked for a few weeks in various suburbs, eventually landing dead on the bull's-eye: a perfect apartment in the perfect neighbourhood. I can still remember the estate agent showing us around. Squeezing Beth's bottom discreetly with my hand, my excitement grew as we walked through the clean, neutral-coloured rooms, knowing without a doubt it was the one for us.

Things were on the up.

For starters, it was a blank canvas, and with Beth being an interior designer by trade, she used several contacts to kit the whole place out, cashing in discounts and overdue favours along the way. Vinnie, our landlord, turned out to be one of the nicest people you'd ever meet: generous, friendly and flexible with rent payment dates. The day we got there, he'd given us a bottle of scotch and stocked the fridge with milk, butter and cheese as a moving-in present. What a legend. Overall, it was a faultless apartment. There wasn't a single thing I would have changed. It was simply amazing.

I sat down on the back seat of the minibus and got comfortable for the ride home. Phone still in hand, I checked how long the call to Beth had lasted: a disconcerting nineteen seconds.

Nineteen seconds? I'd climbed three mountains in less than a day. I'd had about twenty minutes of sleep in-between. I was at the peak of physical exhaustion, and the first call to my girlfriend - my stunningly-gorgeous better half - had been less than half a minute? She couldn't have mentioned how proud she was of me, or how much she loved me? Nineteen seconds? I spent more time on the lav. I spent more time vomiting. I spent more time telling cold callers to leave me alone in a variety of insulting ways.

I couldn't remember ever having such a short conversation with her. Even on my way down to the off-licence to pick up groceries, when she'd call to remind me not to forget loo roll or washing-up liquid, our chats were longer. There'd be too many smooches, sucking noises and *I love yous* to count.

I decided to wait fifteen minutes before trying again.

Dean was talking, but my head was in the clouds. Thankfully, he was addressing the group as a whole so I didn't have to make eye contact or lead any contributions. From what I gathered, he was pleased we all made it down in one piece, which was understandable; Dean was the team leader and still managed to get himself lost, having climbed Ben Nevis six million times. No one else from the party ran into trouble, which didn't exactly thrill me, but if nothing else, it was an experience I'd never forget.

He was trying to scout everyone's availability for a post-climb dinner the following week, which is when my concentration returned. How was everyone fixed for Wednesday? Most of the lads were up for it, but I told him I was starting a new job on Monday and didn't want to go into work hungover to hell in the first week. I wanted to make a good impression, so asked if there was any way we could do the week after. The boys checked their calendars, and after eliminating live football nights and romantic evenings forced upon them by their partners, we decided on Tuesday-week.

Sorted. At least my muscles would have stopped aching by then.

I was starting to get nervous about my first day. I'd have to learn a whole new set of procedures and would probably be seen as the less-than-capable new starter for a while, but it was a huge step forward for my career. I was determined to make the most of the job and the remarkable wage that came with it.

Beth had shown me the ad in the newspaper, and after

15

seeing *very competitive salary* printed in such a large font, I decided to apply:

We are seeking a **Data & Info Business Researcher.**
The firm requires a competent, dynamic team player to undertake this demanding, but ultimately rewarding role.
Ideal candidate will be a graduate, with six years experience in a similar environment.
Apply in writing, including C.V. and salary expectations to:
Laura Delgado - Personnel Dept.

It was pitched some way above my skill-set, but you don't get anywhere in this world without ambition, or so I thought. For a start, I never went to university, leaving school at eighteen and opting for a mixture of retail jobs instead of joining the great unwashed. My three years of experience, instead of the six they expressly stated, also meant a certain amount of *winging it* had to be done. I updated my *Curriculum Vitae*, polished a covering letter and whizzed it off to Ms. Delgado, thinking as I slipped it into the postbox I'd be lucky if she sent it back having wiped her arse with it.

After three days, I was astonished to get a telephone call from the same Laura Delgado, inviting me to attend an interview.

Three days? How could that be? The closing date hadn't even passed. I remember thinking I must have made a damn good impression on paper, but on reflection, it was probably that bit my bio about taking first prize in the *Palermo Spunky Hunk of the Year Competition 1999.* I was always told to add a hint of comedy into an application; at least then, they know you have a sense of humour. Of course, this would be a big mistake if the company you were applying to didn't have a sense of humour, but thankfully, in this case, it worked.

I'd gone for an interview, and was asked back for a second. I'd obviously blown them away with my forward-thinking approach, and they'd knocked me sideways with their hi-tech building and free-vend chocolate machines. Two days later, they'd offered me the job.

£29,000.

Up from *£23,000.*

£6,000 more.

I was gonna be rich.

Watching the breathtaking Scottish countryside fly by the bus window, I looked down at my phone again and dialled Beth's number. This time, she answered straight away.

'Hey, Barry.'

Weird. It was always *Baz, Bazza, Bazza-bear* or *baby.* Never *Barry.* Never ever *Barry.*

'Hey. Is now a better time?'

Ponderlust. 'Hmm, yeah. Soz about before. You caught me in the middle of something.'

Something? Caught you in the middle of *something?* Well, isn't that smashing? Did that *something* just happen to involve chocolate-infused whipped cream and another man's genitals? Hmm? 'What were you up to, baby?'

'Oh, nothing much.'

I should have been a dentist. At least I'd have been paid for pulling teeth. 'Nothing much, but enough for you to not talk to me?'

'Yeah.'

I felt a twinge of anger. 'You sound distracted, Bee. What's up?'

'I'm gonna go stay with my parents for a few days.'

'No, I asked you what was wrong.'

'And I said I'm gonna go visit my parents.'

Anger turned to panic. 'Okay, why? Has something happened? Are they alright?'

'They're fine, I just wanna go see them.'

'So you don't want to stick around and wait for me to get back first?'

'I wanna go see them.'

'Why?'

17

'Cos I wanna go see them.'

It was useless; she was avoiding every one of my questions. I was aware that if I kept firing them at her, she'd either get agitated and slam the phone down, or we'd end up having an argument. I didn't want that to happen, not over the phone and not in earshot of everyone on the bus.

'What the hell is with you today?'

'I'm fine.'

'You're obviously not fine, are you? You've been off with me twice now.'

'I just need to see Mum and Dad. Call me when you get back, okay?'

Paranoia came a'knocking. 'Are you with someone else?'

My baseless accusation was enough to make her hang up, but I wasn't finished. It seemed she wasn't prepared to discuss this like grown-ups, so I did what any self-respecting male would do. I began to type a text message:

What the hell is wrong with you? Have I done something to piss you off?

I pressed *send*, got the delivery report a few seconds later, and went straight back into my sent items to re-read it. It sounded rubbish. It went from confrontational to back-off defensive in only fifteen words. I was about the put the phone back in my pocket to consider my next move, when it vibrated.

That was a quick response. I looked down at the screen:

One new message: Beth. Read now?

Unaware of what was lurking beneath the numerous layers of technology, I cautiously pushed the button marked *yes*:

Don't start. Going to parents NOW.

Were capital letters really necessary? Was that her way of letting me know she was shouting? Silly cow.

I stared at the screen for a few minutes trying not to lose my cool. Over and over I read her message, scrolling down for the rest of it that I knew wasn't there. Why was I tiptoeing around her? She'd made it clear she wasn't in the mood to share whatever was bothering her. Against all my instincts, I didn't reply and laid the phone next to me on the empty seat.

But I so wanted to reply. My fingertips were itching to send another one back.

Thanks a bunch, Beth; thanks for enhancing my already-elevated stress levels. Three years together and you can't tell me what's on your mind. You can't even sound genuinely enthusiastic about my achievements on the mountains. I thought our relationship meant more to you; apparently, I was wrong.

I should have been lapping up the view, having cheeky banter with the boys and supping on some well-deserved cold beers; instead, I was pre-occupied. She was going to visit family - NOW - so I'd be stuck in the flat, powerless to sort out the situation, twiddling thumbs and toes, waiting for her to come back, *still* on edge about Monday. What should have been a weekend of celebration would no doubt be one of misery and frustration.

To be honest, I do have a tendency to overreact. My parents said it, my friends said it, and so did Beth. If ever we had an argument or a crossed word, I'd often fear it was the end of the relationship. So many times in its infancy, she told me to accept occasional bickering and disagreements as a healthy part of any coupling, so, in my unique style, I sought to avoid them at every opportunity. Over time, I learned to trust our bond was tight, that we would come through any given confrontation because of our love for each other. And I did love her. I loved her so much I sometimes thought my heart and surrounding muscle tissue would burst out of my chest due to the sheer amount of love there was in there for her, but following her hazy, unfriendly manner on the phone, I was beginning to wonder whether she still felt the same. In my mind, soulmates should never keep anything from each other.

The minibus turned right after Holloway Road station and I grabbed my bag and rucksack. After another thank you to Dean and a *see you next week* to the boys, I rolled the door shut and waved them away. Opening the front door into the communal reception, I grabbed the post from our cubbyhole, stuffed it into my mouth and walked up the steps to the entrance of our place. Dropping the bags on the floor with a sigh of relief, I slotted the key in the lock and opened the door.

Home, sweet home.

As I looked around, the whole wad of post slipped out of my mouth.

The entire flat was empty.

No furniture, no fixtures, no fittings; everything that once had its place there had now been removed.

THREE

Had I gone back in time? The flat looked the same as it had on the day we came to view it.

I didn't know what to do, so stood, paralysed, my mouth wide open. A look at my watch confirmed that I hadn't been the world's only pioneer of time-travel, plus there was no sign of Beth, and I certainly wasn't using my hand to stroke her bottom in any way. The last time we spoke, I got the feeling she wanted me as far away from her and her petite rear-end as possible.

I walked into the lounge. Empty didn't cover it. The television, video, DVD player, satellite receiver, stereo and speakers were all missing; bookshelves, books, magazines, ornaments and curtains had also been taken. There was no computer, or the desk it sat on; no CDs, sofas, chairs, or my favourite beanbag.

It was the clear out of the century.

I knew we were up to date with bills, so it couldn't have been the bailiffs. All the doors were locked, but I guess that meant nothing to modern day burglars. The bedroom was completely bare except for the bed which had been stripped, leaving only the frame and mattress behind. The bedside lamps had gone, as had the framed, black and white print of a young Elvis, sat at a piano, that hung on the wall next to the window.

Bastards. That was my favourite.

Rotten, sodding bastards. How dare they?

I wanted to stay calm and think rationally, but the

thieving shites had nicked the King. Any logic I could have applied to the situation went flying out of the window. Approaching a state of fury, I swung my leg and kicked the edge of the bed with enough force to move the frame a few inches. A couple of minutes later, after hobbling around the bedroom on one foot, cursing everyone who had ever been born, the pain subsided.

Beth would be gutted. It did look like a professional job. They were most likely targetting the more upmarket flats down the road, knowing they'd cash in a bigger profit; two bed apartments started at half a million down there. We had insurance in place, but I knew it would take a bloody long time before getting anything back.

I went into the bathroom, splashed my face with cold water and reached for a towel.

There wasn't one.

The little turds had nicked my towels. And the toothbrushes, face wash, deodorant and bath mats. What the hell kind of criminal does that?

Using my tee shirt to dry off, I noticed a small, cardboard box sitting underneath the toilet bowl. It was the first time I'd seen it. We never usually kept boxes under the lav. I walked over and peeled off the parcel tape slowly with one hand, taking out my phone to call Beth with the other. She'd probably be as freaked out as I was. She'd most likely come running back to the flat and we'd be able to sort out what was bothering her, as well as joining forces to figure out who had stolen all our stuff.

It went straight to voicemail:

Hi, this is Beth. I'm not here right now, so leave me a message and I'll get back to you as soon as possible. Hope I haven't missed your call, Bazza-bear. Love you. Mwah. Byeeeee.

I smiled. It had been a while since I'd heard that message. She usually always answered, except if I caught her in the shower or in a meeting at work. 'Beth, it's me. Look, I know you said you were going to your parents, but

I've just got back and, well, we've been burgled, sweetheart. Everything's gone, and I mean *everything*. You better come back as soon as you…'

The last piece of tape came away and I opened the box. Gazing inside, a wave of nausea passed through me. I dropped the phone on the marble floor, the back and battery breaking off as it landed.

It was my stuff.

Everything belonging to me was in this single cardboard box. It didn't even qualify as a box, really, more a medium-sized container. My toothbrush, deodorant, a pencil case, half a packet of *Earl Grey* teabags, a jar of mayonnaise, six frozen fishfingers (now thawed) and twenty-nine pence in coppers. Laid neatly on top of it all was a note:

Didn't want to do it over the phone, so wrote you a letter instead. I've gone, Barry. I've taken all my stuff with me and I'm not coming back. Don't try to call, text or email me, I won't reply. I'm moving on to bigger and better things, so naturally, I don't need you anymore, Beth. PS: Your clothes are in the washing machine. Have a nice life. PPS: Check under the bed :-)

Err, pardon?

Excuse me, what?

I read it a further three times, then a fourth. Was this a joke? A larger than life prank from the girlfriend with a sick, but mostly harmless sense of humour?

I got up and ran to the utility room to check the washing machine. My clothes were in there. My dirty, sweaty, stinking clothes. Note still in hand, as if part of some sadistic treasure hunt, I went back into the bedroom and looked under the bed. I couldn't see anything apart from what looked a few torn pieces of paper. Reaching under, I grabbed hold of them.

It was Elvis. He was torn into four. The poor, hamburger-munching genius had been senselessly ripped from his frame, most likely tortured and ultimately quartered. Only a twisted, disrespectful piece of infected sputum would do such a thing.

Beth.

It was no joke. So much for thinking through all conceivable funny sides to this supposed attempt at mirth. It was far too late for that now; there were too many distracting factors getting in its way. If she'd left a less disparaging note with our belongings (and Elvis) still intact, it may have been different. I may have even let out a nervous chuckle in appreciation. An involuntary gag of acid reflux into my throat sent me hurtling towards the realisation that she was gone. She'd also had enough contempt for our relationship to depart on truly horrific terms.

I sat down on the edge of the bed. For a moment, I felt nothing. No sadness, no rage, no devilish urge to track Beth down and garrote her with barbed wire; I stared at the bare, magnolia walls and took a deep breath. As the tears began to well, my stomach grumbled and I vomited into my hands, getting up to run to the bathroom as fast as I could.

An hour later, I pulled my head out of the toilet bowl and wiped my face. Everything was sore: my stomach, my throat, the roof of my mouth; for thirty minutes beforehand, all I could do was cry and dry-retch. There was nothing left to throw up. In-between gasping for breath and moaning *"please, God, please stop"*, I started to get paranoid I'd cough up a lung.

As unpleasant as it sounds, you can get a lot of thinking done between vomit surges. I wanted to put my phone back together and call her again, but every time I moved, another bout would hit me. If I was angry, I'd pretend I was vomiting on her; that it was *her* face etched on to the porcelain at the bottom of the bowl. For sadness, she was rubbing my back as I hurled; she used to do that if I'd had too much to drink. By the end, after wiping both fresh and dried tears from my face, I didn't want to cry or shout anymore. I was dehydrated and half my throat had been scraped away already. Light-headed, I got up from the floor and stumbled into the kitchen for a glass of water.

At least the units were still in place. Fortunately, they were part of the fitted kitchen, so there would've had to be one hell of a damned fine explanation for the landlord if she'd swiped those too. Opening the cupboard above the sink, I saw one glass, one mug, one fork, one knife and one spoon.

How depressing. She really was rubbing it in.

Why I peered further into each of them for a permanent, quick fix, I can't explain. There was no puncture repair kit for the soul, a miraculous plaster providing a tight seal to a broken heart, or a *do-it-yourself prise an explanation from the woman who ended your relationship* pack. Just the aforementioned items and a smattering of dust. One thing was clear: I wouldn't be doing any entertaining for a while.

The cold water soothed my sore mouth and I repaired the mobile to call my folks again. They didn't say anything at first, letting me have a good moan instead, listening to me on speakerphone. Dad would chip in with a comment now and then, but it was Mum who did most of the talking.

'I just don't know,' I said. 'One minute we're fine, the next she's gone. What's she playing at?'

'I wish I knew. It's so unlike her. I wish we could be there. It really has come at a bad time, hasn't it? I hate to think you're on your own.'

She couldn't find the right words, which was disappointing as she so very frequently did. From being a child, all the way through my teenage years, Mum would be the one I'd turn to if ever I was upset or feeling lonely. It had been a while since I'd called upon her counselling expertise, but in light of their holiday, I figured I'd be the one who'd have to nurse myself through this rather massive setback. I had a job to start in two days time and needed to keep focused, or risk messing up my career as well as my love life.

'Do you want to come and stay here? Look after the place while we're away?'

'I can't. The commute's too long.'

'Okay, how about asking them if you can start a week later? You could come with us to Switzerland?'

I wasn't in the mood for a holiday. My fragile state of mind would have only ruined it for them. Selfishly, what I wanted was for them to cancel it and come stay with me, but I couldn't bring myself to propose that. Dad had taken skiing lessons and the flights and accommodation were booked. I'd be the worst son in the world if I made them choose an empty flat over a luxurious hotel for the week.

After saying goodbye, assuring them I'd be okay on a friend's couch, and no, I wasn't considering taking my own life, I scrolled through my phone book to see which lucky mucker I'd call.

I narrowed it down to either Frank or Will. I knew they were both around and pictured their sofas, trying to weigh up which one was the most comfortable. It had to be Will's. Although smaller than Frank's, he didn't have a persistent flea problem, and even though I loved the guy to pieces, I thought it best not to go head-first into a new job with my hands shoved constantly down my trousers, scratching all day long. They'd think me a serial masturbator.

I called his number and waited for the rings. It rang, then rang some more. Seven rings in total before he picked up.

'What can I do for you, Barry?' He sounded agitated. What the hell was wrong with everyone today?

I did my best to sound chipper. 'Hey buddy, how you doin'? Things good?'

His response was swift, said without a moment's thought. 'A lot better than they are with you, I reckon.'

'Eh?'

'Heard about Beth ditching you.'

How did he know? Had she called all my friends already? 'Who told you?'

'Beth did, yesterday.'

What? When I was busting my balls climbing mountains? The lousy, cretinous, dishonest… 'She told you before me?'

'Whoops, guess so, budster.'

'What's wrong with you? Are you enjoying this?' The discomfort in my voice must have alerted him to the fact I'd spent a fair amount of time before calling him in tears.

'Calm down, son.'

'Calm down? My girlfriend does a runner with all my bleedin' stuff, and you're telling me to calm down?'

'Woah, steady, no need for the language.' He was chuckling to himself. 'She called around midday and said she was off. Said you were a twat, told me why, and I gotta say, I agree with her.'

What did he say? My best friend of almost ten years - my blood brother dating back to secondary school - agrees with my psycho ex classifying me as a twat? What had she told him? Beth and I had secrets, as most couples did, but none of them were sordid enough to hurl me into such an offensive category. Contracting genital warts was probably the most personal of the lot, but I caught them from her shortly after our third date, the skanky slapper.

'What you did? You think it's a laughing matter?'

'What did she tell you?'

'I don't wanna repeat it. It cut me up to hear it, fella, and I've made up my mind. I don't wanna see you again.'

'Where's your brain? Don't you wanna at least ask me about it? We're supposed to be pals? You're not gonna check with me before taking her side?'

'Don't need to. She's got proof.'

'What proof?'

His tone changed from personable to threatening. 'Just how stupid are you? Call me again, Baz, and there'll be trouble. Got that? Trouble. I'm not messing around.'

This had to be a joke. They must have all gathered to have a big laugh at my expense. The torn Elvis was probably a copy, the real one being still in its frame, hidden away somewhere. Soon enough, she'd call back, ask me to meet her at a random pub down town, and there'd be a big party organised to celebrate my safe return. I wasn't accepting that Beth had called Will to make up some story, which he'd believed so blindly without asking me first. It was so unlike him. More to the point, it was utterly ridiculous. 'You're havin' a laugh, aren't you, mate?'

'I'll kill you, Barry, I really will. I'm not even bluffing. You wanna find out if I'm bluffing? Try calling again.' With that, he hung up.

I wasn't sure how serious to take his threat; we'd known each other our whole lives and Will couldn't have raised his hand to kill a moth. He did sound mad, though. Whatever Beth told him must have been appalling.

I'm not sure whether everyone else I called were out or simply ignoring me, but in hindsight, if their attitudes were in any way like Will's, I'm glad they didn't pick up. I called twelve people in total and didn't get through to any of them. A little shook up, I gave my phone a rest, put it down on the side and stepped over to the window to slow my heartbeat.

Daylight was fading outside and it wouldn't be long before the timers of the streetlights kicked in. It looked the same as it always did: cars continued to drive up and down, a smattering of people stood at the bus stop waiting for their ride into town, and I saw the sickening sight of a loved-up couple, walking hand in hand, laughing and fooling around. It sounds crazy, but I was hoping to see something offbeat, like a legion of morris dancers rapping a *Nirvana* song, or Tony Blair dressed in union jack cycling shorts, waving around a gigantic banner promoting the *Conservative Party*; anything to convince me it was all part of a nightmare or fever. I'd been back for over two hours and was still no closer to solving the mystery of the day's insane events. Beth's phone was off, Will wanted me dead and my parents were going on holiday. Summing up, it had been one hell of a forgettable afternoon.

For whatever reason, I had nothing left; no access to the ones I loved, and to boot, the evil wench had systematically set about alienating each one of my friends. Brilliant. What other delights did the *powers that be* have in store for me? Perhaps later, the oven would blow up, or my toilet would collapse. Those prone to superstition would say that bad things come in threes; I dreaded to think what my third would be. Discounting everything I could, from waking up blind to smashing the only remaining glass in the cupboard, I had a good idea.

A very good idea.

It was the best idea since potato waffle sandwiches.

I'd go out for a breath of fresh air, pick up a bottle of scotch from the shop and get absolutely wasted.

FOUR

I didn't have any cash on me, so prayed hard Beth hadn't cleaned out my bank account. Given what happened to Elvis, a print she knew I adored more than most things in life, I presumed stealing money wasn't beyond her capabilities. Before leaving, I called the bank to check the balances of both my account and the joint we shared.

'Good evening, Mr. Brooks, you're speaking to Daniel. How may I help you today?'

I asked for an up-to-the-minute check on funds available.

'Bear with me one moment.' Pause. 'Mr. Brooks, while the computer processes this request, could I ask whether you have a mortgage with us?'

'No, I don't.'

'And why's that?'

'Because I don't own a property.'

'And why's that?'

I didn't have time for his chirpy hard-sell and it was reflected in my voice. 'Can you just give me the balance on my accounts?'

'I'm only asking you a question while we wait.'

I apologised. It was a tad impatient of me.

'Don't mention it.'

'So, any word on the balance?'

'Almost there, sir.' Another pause. 'Mr. Brooks, do you plan on buying a property in the near future?'

He had to ask, didn't he. He couldn't have just let it

drop after the last time. 'No,' I shouted, 'I don't plan on buying a pissing property in the near future. Look, Daniel, I know you get commission if you arrange an agreement in principle, but you've got the wrong bloke, okay? Can you *please* just give me both balances?'

There was one final pause before he responded. A long one. It was like waiting for the chuffing world to end. Finally, he told me both accounts were in credit. Beth hadn't touched a penny, which surprised me, but I wasn't complaining. I asked Daniel to transfer the cash to my account, effectively freezing her access.

'All done now, Mr. Brooks.'

'Thank you, and no, I don't need anything else.'

'Fine,' he replied, 'but you should know that I have logged an official complaint on to the system regarding your language.'

'Excuse me?'

'Have a nice day, Mr. Brooks,' and he was gone.

The cheeky arsehole. An official complaint against me? I should have filed one on him, the overly-cheerful, hard-selling numbnuts. What kind of sad nobody gets excited about flogging mortgages on a weekend?

Then again, I wasn't really qualified to pass judgment on sad nobodies.

I turned off the phone and left it on the kitchen table. Slipping my wallet into my pocket, I opened the door and took in the evening air.

I didn't pay much attention to anything during the ten-minute walk. All I wanted to do was get rip-roaringly drunk. That way I wouldn't have the aching heart, and if I did make a selection of embarrassing calls later on, the ability to feel guilt or embarrassment would have totally faded. It may not have been the greatest of plans, but I couldn't bear the thought of sitting alone in the flat without something to knock me out.

Before getting to Abdul's, I passed my local pub, *The Alligator*, and glanced through its filthy windows. It was completely empty, not a soul except for the bar staff. Usually, there would be handfuls of people stood outside on the street smoking at this time. Where was everyone at seven-thirty on a Saturday evening?

Why did I even ask the question? They were most likely avoiding me. It seemed like everyone else was.

The Ag was the number one pre-town pub in the borough. From there, drinkers would take a cab into the West End to dance and puke the night away in various upmarket establishments, where designer lavatory ledges were commonplace for the finest white powder experience, and prices started at twenty quid per drink. To complete the hedonistic circle, they'd make their way back on Sunday morning for one of *The Ag's* revered fry-ups.

This was a good thing. I could grab my booze from the offy and kick back there for an hour. At least they had furniture and the tiniest hint of an atmosphere, a feature sadly lacking at home. I could opt for the real cliché by pulling a stool to the bar and crying into my *Jack On The Rocks* for the evening.

I got to the shop and was greeted by the smiling face of Abdul himself.

'Hey, my friend, long time no see. How you?'

A pleasant shock. He wasn't calling me names or chasing me out on to the street with a loaded shotgun.

I stuck my card in the cash machine. 'Not so good, mate. It's been a bit of a crappy day.'

'Yeah? Why so?'

Would telling him make the tears and vomit come back? 'Beth left me.' Saying her name aloud forced the knife inside again.

'What? She gone?'

I nodded.

'Wha'? For good?'

'I think so, yeah.'

'Oh my shit, that's terrible. I really liked her too.'

Was this an appropriate time for bravado? 'Aw, y'know, it happens, pal. Plenty more fish in the sea.'

'Hmm, and they all smell the same, innit?'

No. Bravado didn't help at all. I was on the verge of losing it again and Abdul noticed.

'She catch you with another woman?'

I couldn't tell if he was being serious or trying to lighten my mood with comedy. He'd seen Beth and I together too many times to count, and must have picked up on the glint in my eye whenever we came into the shop. 'You know I'd never do anything like that.'

'I know, I know,' he replied. 'I'm so sorry to hear it though. When did it happen?'

I told him about the climb and the sheer amount of nothing I was faced with when getting back to the flat. At the same time, the machine whizzed into life and spewed out two twenty pound notes.

'I'm sorry to hear, Baz. But is her loss, yeah?'

No, it was my loss, but I knew what he was trying to say. I didn't reply. I wasn't sure how to. I chose my whiskey by pointing to the shelf behind him, placing a note on the counter.

'Is no good getting drunk on your own, my friend. You need company?'

'No, I'll be fine.'

'You sure? We could have mini-party in the shop after closing time?'

'Thanks, but I just wanna be alone. You understand, yeah?'

'I do, I do. Keep in touch, though. Maybe another time?'

I took my change and we said our goodbyes. Abdul told me he was there if I ever wanted to chat, but I didn't think I was ready to share my innermost with the local shopkeeper *just* yet. Maybe after a couple of months when I could finally think of Beth without wanting to extract the beating heart from my chest and stamp on it repeatedly.

Walking out on to the street, I wondered if the sense of loss and rejection would ever go away. I thought about Jemma Smith, who'd split up with me on my fourteenth birthday. What kind of a heartless wench did you have to be to break up with someone on their birthday? She'd whispered in my ear as I was cutting the cake: '*I'm finishing with you.*'

The thought one day the pain would subside was the only thing stopping me from taking four hundred aspirin and washing them down with a bottle of bleach. If I could ride out the next week, I'd go stay with Mum and Dad when they got back from Switzerland. Then, the healing could begin. All I had to do was cruise through the next seven days on autopilot, then run into the protective arms of the ones that created me.

Plan-tastic.

FIVE

I chose beer, and was served by a chubby bloke wearing a grease-stained tee shirt. He looked and smelt as if he hadn't washed in weeks. Smearing his filthy, overgrown sausage fingers all over the pint glass, he plonked it in on the bar in front of me. 'That's two paahnd eighty.'

Would it have killed him to freshen up before his shift? A splash of water would have done; a sanitary wipe, even. God knows what life-threatening medical conditions were breeding on him.

I put three quid down and told him to keep the change.

'Cheers pal,' he said, sarcastically, 'that'll feed the kids this week.'

'Excuse me?'

'I said thanks. Very generous of you.' He shook his head in disgust and waddled away.

I was so tempted to bark back. I wanted to tell him to use the extra twenty pence to buy a cheap bar of soap or shower gel. What did he want from me? Would he have preferred the exact amount in loose change? I could have used a good shouty argument to free up some tension, but in the end, I thought better of it. I'd have only lost and wound up crying again.

Where was the woman I'd seen earlier through the window? Why couldn't she have been the one to serve me instead of *Lieutenant Lard*?

Since my shop visit, a couple had walked in and stolen the corner seat I'd had my eye on. There was no way I was sitting at the bar now ignorant fat arse was behind it, so I took my pint and sat down next to the window.

Halfway down my beer, boredom set in. I pulled out some coins from my jacket pocket and headed over to the games machine. Slotting in the right amount, the console whizzed into action.

Cue: dramatic music/image of the Quizmaster's gormless face.

"Welcome to 'Who Would Like To Be a Gazillionaire'. I'm Kris Tenement. Are you lucky enough to win the jackpot? Let's find out."

Misinformation, really; the jackpot wasn't a *gazillion* pounds, it was a hundred. Nevertheless, I was determined to win it. If I did, it would be the one good thing to come out of such a horrible day.

Five questions in, I was on a roll; I had all my lifelines intact and looked well on course for the cash. The screen continued to tell me how amazing I was, and my confidence grew as I reached the final question:

Which country won the football World Cup in 1986?

Oh, my, sweet, great, grandmother. Yes, yes, yes, how easy was this? Kris, I love you; marry me, you big hunk of unbridled lust. I don't care what anyone says, you're the absolute bloody best. You bring the wine, let's have a romantic evening in together.

Four options were displayed on the panel in front of me:

Botswana; Pakistan; Argentina; Keith

Where the hell was Keith? Was it even a country? Who programmed this bloody thing? Keith? Had Keith grown weary of designing machines to offer sensible answers, inputting his own name wherever he could to alleviate boredom during lonely hours on the job?

It didn't matter. I could smell the notes already, and they smelt good. Hovering my finger over option 'C', I was about to push down with all my might. One nudge of the plastic button and I was victorious. It just goes to show you can always find some good in every situation…

Without warning, the screen flickered. Quizmaster's face disappeared and the console fizzed and died.

'Noooooooooo…'

I didn't know who she was, but on her way to the toilet, she'd tripped on the wire. The plug was yanked out of the socket and my chance to be a *gazillionaire* went flying out of the window.

I punched the blank display. 'Arse.'

My nemesis got up, brushed herself down and walked over. 'Oh, God, I'm so sorry. You weren't on a winning streak, were you?'

I let out a loud, exaggerated sigh of disappointment. The opportunity was there to make her feel really bad, but I didn't take it. She seemed genuinely apologetic and I could see from her eyes she'd been crying. 'Nah, don't worry. I was only one question in.'

'Phew, that's lucky.'

'Yeah, no harm done.'

She stuck out her hand. 'I'm Poppy.'

'Barry,' I said, shaking it. 'Nice to meet you.'

'Are you on your own?'

I looked around the pub. The couple in the corner had left, and behind the bar, big tits was reading the newspaper, shoving handfuls of pork scratchings into his mouth. 'Yep, just me.'

A coy smile. 'Mind if I join you?'

'Err, yeah, sure.'

'Cool. Grab a seat, I'll be back in a minute.'

Poppy re-appeared from the lav moments later, ordered a rum and coke at the bar and took a big gulp. She was quite the stunner: about my age and blonde, she was dressed to kill in a tight, red dress which pushed her breasts beneath her chin. It came to rest just above the knees, showing off the bottom of her tanned legs.

I was staring a bit too much.

Smiling, she walked over and sat down. 'Why's it so quiet in here, tonight?'

Small talk. Never my strong point. 'Maybe the guy at the bar put them off.'

'Wouldn't be surprised. He was staring at my chest the whole time he was serving me.'

I felt guilty; I'd been doing the same. 'So, you got a big night planned?'

'I did. Got stood up by a friend. We we're s'posed to go dancing.'

'Sorry about that,' I said, not sure if I really cared.

She winked. 'Never mind. All's not lost.'

Was that flirting? It didn't happen very often so I wasn't sure of the telltale signs. 'It isn't?'

'Not at all, if you don't mind the company, that is?'

Part of me wished Beth would walk in and see me enjoying a bit of Saturday night confabulation with a pretty girl who wasn't her. How annoyed would she be? 'Be my guest.'

Another wink. 'Alright then, I will.'

Definitely flirting. Yeah, take that, lover, I'm over you already.

She was guzzling the booze in record time, having gone back to the bar for a top up before I'd finished my first pint. Now on to my second, it was obvious she was well on her way, and I took a swig from the bottle in my bag to catch up. Conversation didn't progress into anything deep and meaningful, but I did tell her about Beth. She seemed to sympathise, offering her hand to hold as I let it all out. I didn't cry, thank God, choosing to adopt a more philosophical approach: what's done is done, there's no use crying over spilt milk, and other over-used, meaningless clichés that in the cold light of day would have made me wince.

Her full name was Poppy Popperwell. She caught me mid-sip with that one and I blew bubbles in my beer.

'I know, it's silly.'

'No, it's not,' I lied.

'It's a porn star name.'

'That's not necessarily a bad thing…'

A third wink. She was either really into me or had a nervous twitch. I don't know why I found it so funny. Barry isn't exactly the hippest of forenames. When I told her my full name, she kept repeating it in a variety of funny voices:

'Barry Brooks, Barry Brooks, Barry Brooks, Barry Brooks. Buh, buh, buh, Barry Brooks. Buh, buh, Barry…'

Was she retarded?

'Sorry,' she said, stopping at last, 'I've never met anyone who has the same initial for their first and last name.'

'What about you?'

She thought about it. 'Oh, yeah. I've got it too, haven't I?'

'You didn't notice?'

She sniggered into her drink. 'Nope. How thick am I?'

There was something sweet about her senility. 'Not as thick as I am. You'd think someone would be able to notice the signs that a long-term girlfriend was about to pack up and leave.'

'Well, you're better off without her, I say.'

'How's that?' I sneaked the bottle out again and topped us up.

'All I mean is, what's the point in being down? She made her decision and she'll come to regret it. I know I would.'

I took another gulp. 'You're right. She must have been mad.'

Her phone was ringing on the table. Ignoring it, she put it in her bag and zipped it shut.

I finished my shot and topped up with a double. 'Someone you're avoiding?'

She nodded. 'My ex. We broke up last April. He still can't let go.'

I petrified myself thinking that could be me in a year's time. 'So I'm guessing you ended it?'

'Yep. Found him in bed with my best friend.' She took

the scotch from me and filled her glass half way. 'It was our bed. What a twat, hey?'

'Harsh,' I said, before the killer line, which only came out due to a mixture of beer, whiskey and a broken heart. 'How could anyone do such a thing to a girl like you?'

I didn't fully regret saying it. There was a distinct tongue-in-cheek element to my delivery, but I was still cringing a little inside. My eyes were fixed on the glass I was drinking from and I hadn't built up the courage to gauge her reaction. When I looked up, she was smiling and playing with her hair. That told me everything I needed to know. I was nicely drunk by this point, and even though she was pretty attractive sober, she looked like Eva Longoria in fishnets and pink rubber gloves now.

'You're one of the nice ones, Barry Brooks.'

'We're a dying breed, Poppy Popperwell.'

Giggles. 'You know what? I'm having a really nice time. There was me thinking I'd be all on my own tonight, then you came along.'

'Glad I could be of assistance.'

The clock on the wall read ten-fifteen. I was astonished to realise we'd been chatting for almost an hour. Time does fly when you come out the wrong end of a relationship and meet someone new only hours later. The whiskey hidden inside one of Abdul's flimsy carrier bags was now empty, and we were both slurring our words. I'd run out of cash and had to buy the last round on card, *Rear-Admiral Chip Fat* forcing me to buy two bags of crisps to take the order over five pounds.

'Guess I better be going, then,' I said, stacking our empties.

'Come back to mine for a nightcap, if you want?'

Was that a good idea? 'Where do you live?'

'Islington. Ten-minute drive in a cab. You're more than welcome.' She was smiling again.

'Are you sure?'

'I'd only be going back on my own, otherwise.' More

hair twiddling. 'It's a lot more fun with two.'

I pictured walking into my flat, with only an irresistibly-sexy looking mobile phone I could use to make abusive calls with for company. 'It is?'

'Don't make me spell it out, Barry. All I'm saying is, if you want something to take your mind off *you know what*, come back and we'll have a bit of fun.'

Ha ha, yes, there it was. I'd been single less than twenty-four hours and had already bagged myself a stunner. Get in there, my son. So this is what being on the rebound felt like? There was no resounding wave of pre-coital regret or guilty thoughts of Beth and our time together; I was satisfied to let the rest of the evening play out as fate intended, knowing I didn't have anyone to answer to except myself.

It was a typical man thing to do, I know that. Looking back, I should have declined the invite, but I was drunk, lonely and heartbroken. I needed some attention. Having never been promiscuous at any point in my life, I knew it was radically out of character, but didn't care. This was fun. Poppy was fun. We were two consenting adults enjoying each other's company. What was wrong with that? Beth who?

Grunting at *Greaseface* as I passed the bar, we left the pub and I looked out on the main road for a cab. The odds weren't stacked in our favour at half-ten on a Saturday night.

A couple of minutes went by before a car pulled up beside us.

Poppy got in and gave directions to the driver. I followed her into the back and closed the door.

She seemed to sober up a little during the journey, but it didn't stop her from taking my hand and interlocking her fingers into mine. 'Thanks for tonight,' she said, 'you really cheered me up.'

'I'm just sorry you got ditched.'

'Glad I did. Had a much better night with you.'

We arrived at *King Kutz*, a salon located on one of

Islington's back roads. Poppy rented the one-bedroomed flat above it. Stepping out into the cold, she paid the cabby, adding a hefty tip. All the way back, I'd seen him adjusting his mirror, trying to get a good old squizz up her skirt. She hadn't noticed, which was lucky for him; I'm sure she wouldn't have paid extra if she had. Dirty old man.

Her flat was small, but did have an array of attractive furniture, which instantly made me jealous. It was half the size of where I lived, compact and very homely; she was clearly proud of her place.

Poppy brought some scotch with two shot glasses, and I filled them up. After a three-count, we knocked them back and I refilled straight away. Taking time over the second, she sat down next to me and placed her hand on my knee.

'Nice place,' I said, watching her stroke the patches on my jeans. 'I like what you've done with it.' Everything was cream: walls, carpets, curtains, sofas; it had a relaxing feel to it.

'Glad you approve.' She was using her other hand to play with her hair again. Her skirt had ridden up as she crossed her legs and I could see the majority of her thigh. I had to admit, they were good legs. Even though it was cold, she'd still ventured out without tights, which was a lot more pleasing on the eye from a male point of view. She caught me looking and immediately took her hand away from my knee, placing them on her cheek. I turned to her, about to lean in for a kiss, when she asked if I'd like to take our drinks to the bedroom.

You may find this difficult to believe, but I would have settled for a hug. On the other hand, if she was going to offer herself to me on a juicy, blonde, well-balanced breasts kind of plate, I wasn't really going to say no. When I got to her room, I kicked off every last piece of clothing as she freshened up in the bathroom, jumped into bed and felt the clean, crisp sheets caress my body. It would only be a matter of minutes before she was doing the same.

I'll spare you the grisly details, but every second of the

encounter was mind-blowing. She was by no means a shy girl. I flopped back on to the bed after finishing on top, breathing heavily for a minute or so, before turning my head. 'That was amazing.'

'Hmm.'

Hmm? Is that all she could say? Fill me full of enthusiasm, why don't you? 'Something wrong?'

She took way too long to reply. 'It's okay, Barry.'

'What is?'

'I understand.'

'You understand what?'

'Maybe this was a mistake. It was probably too soon.'

'Poppy, what's going on? What was too soon? Didn't you enjoy it?'

'Honestly?'

'Well, yeah, preferably.'

'Barry, I'm sorry, I just didn't feel it.'

I sobered up in seconds. 'Feel what?' I shouldn't have asked. It was blatantly obvious. 'Never mind.'

'Look, I'm sure it's just a combination of nerves and the shitty day you've had. Nothing to worry about.'

This was my third thing, wasn't it? Beth had gone, the flat had been gutted, and for the first time, I was told by a stranger how crap I was in the sack. 'Oh, right.' I was mortified. Looking down, I saw my penis shrivel to the size of a garden pea. 'Am I... y'know, too small?'

'No, no, not at all, sweetheart. I mean, it's not the biggest I've had, but certainly not the smallest.'

Was that a compliment? I couldn't decide. 'What size do you prefer?'

She dodged the question. 'It's not all about size. Usually, I come at least four times, regardless. It's all about hitting the right places, y'know?'

Places? I knew how to hit places. I was an expert on them. Beth had places too, and I hit them on a regular basis. They got hit, you understand? There were never any complaints from her. Maybe Poppy was just fussy. Or a freak. A weird sex-goblin who only got her kicks by ploughing through the whole of the *Kama Sutra* every time she got jiggy with it.

'You look mad,' she said, 'are you mad?'

'Honestly?'

She nodded.

'Yeah, I'm mad. What do you expect? A little pointer in the area of human relations: wait until the bloke's out of sight before cutting his sexual skills to pieces. Save it for your friends. Don't tell the poor bugger twenty seconds after he pulled out.'

'I was only…'

I hadn't finished. 'I mean, what's wrong with you? Are you twisted? How do you think that makes me feel?'

'I was only telling the truth.'

'Then lie a bit. Lie a lot, I don't care.' I jumped out of bed and put my clothes back on.

'Sorry?'

'Don't say that. You don't think you've done anything wrong, so why apologise?'

'Sorry.'

'Stop it. I'm leaving.'

'Don't be silly. Stay the night.'

'No,' I barked, pulling my trainers on.

'Come back to bed. Let's give it another go.'

'Why? So I can not hit all the right places again? Give me a break, Poppy. I'll see you around.'

She turned on to her side. 'You're being a dick about this, y'know.'

'Whatever.' I zipped up my jacket and left. What a passion killer. How dare she criticise me like that? In the cab on the way home, I thought about previous partners: none of them had ever been as callous, not even Suzie from college, who later admitted she'd only slept with me after losing a bet. It wasn't a reflection on how good I was at all; it turned out to be a pleasantly surprising experience, she'd said.

You see, Poppy? See how it's done? Didn't hit the right spots, indeed. Give me a break. You can take your *four orgasms in one go* and stick 'em where the sun don't shine, love. Some of us are happy with one.

SIX

I woke up, making the most of the second or two it took for my brain to remind the rest of my body and soul how depressed I was, before the pneumatic drill in my head pierced and drained every ounce of sanity remaining. I turned over, stuffed my face into the mattress and let out the smallest of whimpers.

Ten minutes later, I staggered into the bathroom to empty my bladder.

Damn it, Beth. Did you really have to steal the toilet roll as well?

Shaking the last few drops of whizz into the bowl, I wobbled like a one-legged caveman into the kitchen to find my phone. I switched it on and opened the window blinds, the morning sun shining in and blinding me momentarily. Melinda from the flat downstairs was fiddling with a floral arrangement of some sort in the communal garden. I couldn't make out what it was, exactly, maybe a man-sized pint glass or a trimmed afro, but she saw me and waved, before covering her eyes.

What was up with her?

I looked down and realised it was because I was stood, completely naked in front of the window. What's more, I still had the erection I'd woken up with. Moving away quickly, I mimed an apology, which she obviously couldn't see with her eyes covered, and closed the blinds again.

Why wasn't I more careful? She could have reported me

to the authorities for flashing. Later, she'd tell her husband about that weirdo from upstairs who was watching her from his kitchen window with a lob on. There'd be a knock at the door and he'd give me a stern ticking-off for upsetting his missus, warning me if it ever happened again, he'd slice my face off with his orbital sander.

Once the blinds were closed, I took my naked, apparently aroused self back into the bedroom.

I stared at the phone for just under a minute. The network motif was showing and I was in a strong signal area, but nothing happened. No texts, no voicemails.

Balls to it.

Double balls.

Nothing at all? This was terrible. Primed to throw it against the wall in anger, the familiar message tone reverberated around the room. *"Bing-bong"*.

The high-pitched alert worsened the headache.

One new message; Beth. Read now?

Was this the text telling me she'd made a huge mistake and wanted to come back? As my phone was off all night, I didn't know what time she'd sent it. It could have been the evening before when I was out wooing another woman. I felt awful thinking of her sitting there, waiting for a response from me. Why did I leave my blasted phone at home? How much of a chore would it have been to take it to the pub with me? If she sent the message early on, it could have saved all that yuckiness with Poppy. Oh, Beth, it's alright, I forgive you, it was just a blip, wasn't it? Come on, let's go out for a slap-up Sunday lunch and put it all in the past.

Nervously, I push the button marked *yes* to open the message. There was only one word:

Prick

She thought of me at 3.07a.m. and picked up the phone

especially to relay an expletive. I pictured her in bed with another, taking a break from love, hugs and rubs to whip out the mobile and have a good giggle at my expense.

"*Ha ha haaaaar,'* she'd cackle, "*Barry will hate this. I'm gonna call him the one name he hates. The one that makes him proper Hulk-angry."*

And it did. I felt the rage return. Bruce Banner, you got nothing on me, pal. I steadied the phone in my hand and sent my own little ball of hate back:

Hey, has-been. Glad to see you're mastering sentence structure at last. Thought you might wanna know I got laid last night. She didn't squeal like a pig in labour all the way through, and neither did she have a moustache. Love to Mum and Dad. Bye, hairy. Baz xxxxxx

The anger I was feeling took me well into a second message, but it was worth the extra ten pence plus VAT just to get that bit in about the 'tache - the one thing she was paranoid about. I received a delivery report straight away and pictured her face as she read it.

Ha ha ha. Demonic chuckle.

Halfway through a second text about her morning breath, the doorbell rang.

I ignored it.

Do I look like the kinda guy who likes kippers for breakfast? Every morning with you was like waking up inside a dog's arse. I bet you think I'm upset. Well, I'm not. Couldn't be happier…

It rang again. God, take a hint and leave me alone, would you? I'm busy.

One more time. 'Alright, alright, I'm coming.'

I put on the previous day's boxer shorts and made my way to the door. Looking through the peephole, I saw Melinda standing in the hallway.

Crap. Cover your skin, Barry, it's about to be brutally sliced and diced by the orbital sandman's accomplice.

'Hey, Melinda,' I shouted through the door, 'really sorry about before. I wasn't thinking, y'know?'

She rang the doorbell again.

Reluctantly, I opened it a few centimeters and stuck my head through the crack. 'Hi.'

'Hey, stud-muffin!'

'Huh?'

'You gonna let me in?'

'Err, why?'

'You know why.' She pushed the door open and walked into the flat. 'At the window? A few minutes ago? Where's your girlfriend?'

It was the weirdest thing: she didn't seem to react to the lack of anything in the apartment.

'She's not here,' I said. 'Melinda, what can I do for you?'

She went into the kitchen and stood at the window while I hovered by the door. 'Do you make a habit of showing your personals to all the women in the block?'

'Err, well…'

'You could get into a lot of trouble,' she said, stern-faced. 'Are you gonna tell Greg?'

She laughed. 'Not at all.'

Relief. 'Thanks, I'm glad. It was an honest mistake, I swear.'

'You don't have to explain it to me, honey,' she said, peeking inside the cupboards, 'but you gotta know, I only covered my eyes 'cos I didn't want Greg seeing me staring at you.'

Oh dear. I didn't really hear that, did I?

Let me tell you a bit about Melinda. She was around forty, very timid, had short, curly-brown hair and loved gardening. No, she adored gardening. Whenever we passed her on the stairs or outside the building, she always had some kind of gardening implement in her hand. Either that or she was covered in soil. She was a timid, normal, forty year old gardener; so straight-laced it was painful. She sang in a choir, for God's sake. She even baked scones and cakes for book club. She didn't flirt, especially not with the young guy from the flat upstairs.

Shuffling across the floor, she looked me up and down. 'Truth is, I liked what I saw.'

I backed away when she extended a finger and ran it all the way down my chest, stopping at my boxers. She had to be kidding. 'What are you doing?'

'What does it look like?'

'Stop it. I think you'd better go.'

'You don't mean that,' she said, stroking him.

In a higher-pitched voice than usual: 'I do. I really do. I've got a girlfriend.'

She took her hand away. 'Barry, you can't expect me to believe what you showed me at the window was an *accident*?'

'It was, I promise you. I was hungover - half-asleep.'

'Really?'

'Yes, really.'

She looked disappointed. 'So... you don't... want me?'

Be careful, Barry. Play this one carefully. 'No, I don't.'

To be fair, Melinda wasn't bad to look at. If I was closer to her age I may have gone for her, but I wasn't, and she was married. I'd only just come out of a long-term relationship, and to tell you the truth my balls were still aching from the previous evening. 'I'm sorry you got the wrong idea.'

She paced around the kitchen for a few seconds. 'You're sorry?'

'Really, I am.'

She wasn't best pleased. 'Barry's sorry. Isn't that something? I've come all the way up here and made a complete idiot of myself.'

'No, you haven't, it's just a mix-up, that's all.'

She stared through me with psychopathic eyes. 'I think you want me. I'm a good judge of character, y'know. I know what you're thinking. You want it, don't you?'

In amongst the ache, I felt a twitch. No, no, no.

'Have you ever fantasised about a married woman? The taboo, out of bounds side to it?'

Of course I had. Growing up, it was number one on the list, but if I told her, she'd probably have erupted into a huge ball of ravenous lust and sent me into spasm with one glance at my lower regions. 'Melinda…'

Her arms were now wrapped around my waist and she leaned in for a kiss. I pulled away before our lips touched.

'I suggest you go along with this,' she said, 'if you don't want me to tell Greg you tried to take advantage.'

And there it was: blackmail, in its most alluring form. She could have left when I told her to, could have accepted it was all a misunderstanding and forgotten I was even stood at the bloody window, but she didn't.

'What would you prefer, a kicking or a shag?' She clasped my hand, pulled me from the kitchen to the bedroom and threw herself down on the bed.

I was almost pleading. 'You don't have to do this.'

In record time, her clothes were off and she was rolling around on the mattress in a purple bra and panties set.

I wasn't expecting that, I have to say. She wore matching while digging the garden? Impressive.

My head and heart were fighting for supremacy. The former told me to stand firm and say no. Even if Greg killed me, at least there'd be nothing to feel guilty about. 'No. I won't do it. You have to leave now.'

She hesitated for a second then got to her feet. 'Fair enough. If that's the way you want to play it, I'll just run downstairs like this and tell my husband you won't give me my clothes back.'

Head: *'Stand your ground, Barry.'*

Heart: *'Give her one. She's gagging for it!'*

Head: *'Don't listen to him. Think of your morality.'*

Heart: *'In, out, in, out, shake it all about…'*

The next part was by far the most disappointing: an awakening from inside my underwear.

Damn it all to the foul pits of hell.

I tried so hard not to look at her firm breasts and shapely, cellulite-free thighs, but my masculine impulses let me down again. To make matters worse, she saw my rapidly extending tent pole, took off her underwear and walked towards me. She ripped off my boxer shorts and crouched down to perform a variety of not-too-unpleasant things with her mouth on my appendage.

Damn, she was good.

Head: 'It's not too late. The deed isn't done yet. You can still end this.'

Heart: 'Oooohhh yeeeaaaaahhhh, baby. Like that. Yeah, like that.'

It only took a few minutes before I felt the lower half of my body shudder and I knew I was close to letting it all go.

Damn. What a weak, spineless individual I was.

Damn, damn, damn, damn, damn.

Feeling my body tighten, she moved back on to the bed and spread her legs. 'Give it to me, Barry. Give it to me right now.'

My wafer-thin resistance buckled. I closed the bedroom door and climbed on top. She let out a loud moan as I entered her, and I imagined Greg hearing his wife's naughty screams all the way downstairs. They got progressively louder as I eased in and out, and after another two minutes, I climaxed, Melinda shortly after. She dug her fingernails into my back so hard I thought a few veins had been punctured in the process.

Shame, shame, we know your name.

A minute later, with the monster tamed and back in his cage, I slumped back and stared at the ceiling.

Head: 'Too late now, Barry.'

Heart: 'Yeah, dude, I kinda agree with Head.'

The grin said it all. She must have been happy. From nowhere, she lit up two cigarettes and handed one to me.

When Beth and I moved into the place, she'd made me promise not to smoke inside. Having quit a few months before, she didn't want any temptation in her own home. Fair enough, I thought at the time, but I must confess being able to do it freely now she'd gone felt mighty fine. I watched Melinda as she took a few more drags and wondered if it was really over. Was she going to force me to partake in another sordid act in the name of emotional blackmail? Would it involve cornflakes and a wall socket? I waited until she spoke, hoping the first words out of her mouth would be *thank you* and *goodbye*.

'I hope your girlfriend's not due back anytime soon,' she said, coughing. 'What would she say if she found you here with me?'

Beth probably wouldn't give a bucket of dog's piss. 'She'd most likely knee me in the balls.'

'You sneaky little stud.' She stood up, opened the window and threw the cigarette butt out. 'You were pretty damn good, y'know.'

One consolation, I guess. 'Don't you think you should be getting back to your husband?'

She sat on the edge of the bed. 'I suppose so. One thing's for certain, though...' Her hand cupped my length again, but this time, it didn't respond.

'What's that?'

I had to ask. I could have shut my stupid, fat mouth and not given her centre stage.

'I'll be back for more.'

'You'll what?'

'I'll be coming back for more of the same.'

No you won't, you demented cow. 'Why?'

'I haven't come that hard for years, sweetheart. If you were me, you'd be coming back. When I next need your,' she paused to choose her words, 'services, shall we say, I'll come find you. Y'know, when Greg's out. He's out a hell of a lot, Barry, with work and other stuff.'

I didn't look her in the eye. I couldn't. The tone of voice she used was beginning to rouse *Fleet Commander Floppy* again. Please, Melinda, take your hand away before you think I'm gagging for a second helping.

She did, and I rolled on to my front to conceal the rumblings. 'I don't think that's the best idea. What if someone catches us?'

'That's the fun part, don't you think?'

Actually, no, I don't. There's nothing about being caught with another man's wife I consider fun in the least. Greg was by no means a small guy; from what I'd seen, he had muscles everywhere, even on his lips, and could probably floor me with one of his weaker farts. The last thing I needed was to be on his bad side.

'If you don't come running whenever I say, I'll be telling my husband everything. You wouldn't want that, would you, mister?'

Was the schoolteacher tone really necessary?

She ruffled my hair and got dressed. At that point, I was thanking every religious figure I could think of for getting her one step closer to being out of my flat. She slipped on her shoes and said goodbye, leaving a long kiss on my forehead. 'See ya later, gorgeous.'

'Err, yeah,' was all I could manage. The front door clicked, and she was gone.

I laid there, wishing my meaningless life was over. Every inch of my body and soul was throbbing in pain. Not only had the climb stolen every last morsel of energy from my legs and arms, now two women had savaged me, zapping me of the scrap of morality and physical stamina I had left.

I didn't move from the bed for nearly two hours. Looking up at nothing, re-living what had occurred since I got back, I noticed something new: Beth had also taken the ceiling mirror.

Beth.

The girl who'd destroyed me.

The girl who's disappearing act had turned me into an adult movie star.

What had I done that was so bad? I was the perfect boyfriend. I never cheated or looked elsewhere, frequently showered her with gifts and always made sure I was there for her in any way I could. On a scale of one to ten, I hit twelve, boyfriend-wise. There was no way she'd ever find someone as devoted to her as me. From her letter and monosyllabic text, the whole situation didn't seem to affect her in the slightest. Surely when you do the breaking-up there's a tiny bit of emotion and nostalgia somewhere? You can't say farewell to three years of your life without feeling something. What amplified the hurt was that Beth seemed so remorseless over the whole thing. If I only knew what it was I'd supposedly done; what she'd told Will to turn him against me. I was sure it wasn't the warts. There was something else; something so stomach churning that my closest friend - the friend who confided in me about everything - had disowned me.

I put her face and Melinda's threats to the back of my mind, finally got off the bed and had a shower. There was still a new job to prepare for. Maybe if I threw myself whole-heartedly into my professional life, it would shift the attention away from the problems I was facing up to at home.

It was worth a shot.

I really couldn't see a viable alternative.

After drying off, I checked my phone to find a new text message from Mum:

All packed and ready to go. Are you alright? Did you find a friend to stay with? Love you always, Mum xxx

I smiled, then replied:

Yep, all sorted. Have a safe flight. Love you back, B xxx

SEVEN

Having prepped up on the company's strategy, objectives and values the previous evening in an internet café downtown, I arrived at their plush, new offices in the West End thirty minutes early.

With no entertainment in the flat, I'd gone to bed at eighty-thirty, hoping to recover some of the energy that had deserted me over the course of an exhausting weekend. I did my utmost not to think about the personal issues weighing me down; there was no way I wanted to mess up the opening day of my dream job.

I walked through the revolving doors into my new place of employment. It was an absolute palace. It took state-of-the-art and flushed it down the lav with one yank. The girls on reception were dressed immaculately in black, all of them looking like supermodels who mixed in with the upper echelons of Hollywood; *Armani* suits were on show from every single security guard I could see, and the foyer's centrepiece was a stunning, hand-crafted waterfall, spraying jets of liquid into a crystal-clear, marble pool beneath it. These jonnies had a stupid amount of cash behind them. It was an honour just to be part of the experience.

Security handed me a temporary pass and I was asked to make myself comfortable on the sofas provided. What a place. I had suddenly become the luckiest guy in the world, professionally speaking, anyway.

Helping myself to some water from the cooler, I sat

down and flicked through a selection of magazines displayed for light reading on the table: *The Business In You Weekly*; *Achieve Your Potential Or Die*; *Money, Money, Money: Do You Want Some?*

What in the name of sanity were these? Were they meant to relax me in preparation for the day ahead? Would dropping a tabloid in the mix really have caused so much hassle?

I didn't want to risk not achieving my potential and dying so early in the day, so abandoned the reading idea and went back to sipping my water. Shortly after, I heard a familiar voice call my name. Laura Delgado, the exotic-sounding woman from Human Resources, was stood next to reception, clipboard in hand. She saw me, smiled quickly, and walked over to shake my hand.

'Nice to see you again, Mr. Brooks.'

'You too, Laura,' I replied. 'Call me Barry, please.'

She looked down at her notes. 'Now, Mr. Brooks, I'm going to take you through a quick induction, which is a routine part of every new starter's first day with us, and then you're free to join your department. How does that sound?'

Her tone was annoying me a little. I couldn't put my finger on why, exactly, maybe because she refused to call me by my first name. I was twenty-four, she must have been at least thirty. Less of the respect, lady; save it until I've got no teeth and I'm shouting abuse at supermarket staff for not having any *Sterident*. Call me Baz, everyone else does. 'Sounds fine, Laura.'

Nothing. Not a wink or a smile. Not even the tiniest indication she was attune to my little quip. There was no other explanation: she clearly hated men. I cast my mind back to the interview; she was all smiles and jokes, asking me what I liked to do socially and what my favourite music was. It had to be the classic Monday morning blues. Either that or she didn't get any the night before. If dipping your wick was the only thing that dictated whether Monday mornings were destined to fail, my day

would be blessed by the Lord himself. Which remi
me, the thud in my lower regions still hadn't subsided

As I followed grumpy bollocks into a meeting room, I seriously wondered whether Poppy and Melinda had damaged me in some way. They had never ached for this long before; it had been a particularly vigorous workout, that's for sure. I just hoped it wasn't the beginning of a larger problem, like gangrene of the pipes or incurable syphilis.

The meeting room, situated on the fourth floor of this super mega-complex, was unnecessarily large for two people. She kindly pulled the chair from under the table for me, then walked the length of it, parking herself down as far from me as possible. The act alone was so bizarre I couldn't help but smile. I'd showered, applied both roll-on and after shave, and was confident I didn't reek like a corpse left undisturbed for six months. My shirt was pressed to perfection and I'd chosen a tie that complimented it beautifully. Vanity aside, I did look good. If she didn't appreciate my efforts, she could go to hell.

Pouring myself a cup of coffee and taking two biscuits from the specially-printed, firm-motif crockery, Laura slid the induction pack down the table to me. I opened it, darting my eyes across its contents. All the basic information was here: emergency contacts, fire exits, private medical insurance forms and a map of the building. Laura explained the history of the business, what it hoped to achieve and how I could effectively contribute to its development. I'd heard it all before. At my old firm, I'd actually helped design the programme for new starters. My audible acknowledgements to what she was babbling about quickly turned to nods and smiles, before I lost interest and switched off.

It was a promising start. I'd all but fallen asleep within thirty minutes of being on the payroll, but at least I'd be able to meet and start getting to know my new workmates. What I didn't know was I'd be spending most of the days ahead trying not to drop off at my desk. If someone had cared to enlighten me to this crucial bite of information ahead of joining my colleagues, I'd have skipped and sprinted for the door without looking back.

The vibrant department I'd been shown around on interview day now appeared sullen and empty. The blinds were closed, the lights dimmed, and there was a faint smell of stale sweat in the air. Dusty books lined shelves stretching far away into darkness.

Laura cleared her throat for attention as we arrived. 'Hi, guys, this is Barry.'

'Hello, Barry,' two strange-looking men said in unison.

I couldn't remember them from my interview. 'Hi. Are you new starters too?'

'These two?' Laura said, with derision. 'No, they've been here for years. Colin and Clive are the firm's librarians. Can't you tell?'

I gazed over at them. They did look a bit sticky. 'And I'm working here? With them?'

'Yes, of course. Where did you think you'd be working?'

They were trying hard to break a smile. How come I hadn't met them before? 'Oh, right, it's just that when you gave me the tour before, there were others here.'

'Others?'

'Yeah. A girl called Gwen, I think. She sat over there.' I pointed to where I remembered her desk to be. Beige cabinets now sat in its place. 'And another guy... Tony, was it?'

Laura stared straight through me. 'Tour?'

'When I came for the interview?'

'Right,' she said, nodding, 'yes, the tour. Sorry, don't know who you're talking about.'

'Are you sure?'

'Of course. I think I'd remember two extra people. I do work for HR, y'know.'

Smart arse. 'Fair enough.'

'I'm sure they'll look after you, won't you chaps?'

Excited nods.

'Excellent. Well, I'll leave you in their capable hands. If you need anything, do let me know, won't you?'

That's what she said, but I'm sure what she meant was *don't bother me again, I've got more important people to attend to.*

After she left, I sat down at my desk and opened the welcome letter on my chair. 'I think I'd remember two extra people,' I mocked, loud enough for Clive and Colin to hear. 'How about finding my missing colleagues, you scabby harlot?'

Two faint sniggers came back at me.

'I don't think she likes us very much,' Clive said.

That was understandable. At first glance, they looked the archetypal geeks. In their mid-thirties, they wore tank tops, corduroy and sandals, sported late-eighties perms and had *Star Trek* pencil cases. Where the hell was everyone else? 'I wouldn't take it personally,' I said, 'I don't think she's my biggest fan either.'

I unfolded the letter and began to read:

Dear Mr. Brooks,

Welcome to Tinkler & Tinkler. We hope that you are settling in, and have pleasure in enclosing your access details for the firm's computer system. You will be contacted at a further time to make sure everything is in order. On behalf of myself and the partnership, we hope you're employment with us is one of enjoyment, fun, but more importantly, hard work! Best regards, H.M. Tinkler - Chief Executive Officer.

That was nice, wasn't it? A personal message from the commander-in-chief? Obviously, it was all typed and his signature was a JPEG image that the IT department pasted into every document requiring .his autograph, but I couldn't help but feel the head honcho himself was pleased I was on board. Yeah, right, the greased-up multi-millionaire didn't even know I existed. He probably needed the map of the building more than I did, with his seventeen holidays per year in Saint Tropez and private island in the Caribbean. If I ever saw him in person, I'd spit all over his freshly polished, designer shoes on principle.

Waiting for my PC to load all the files and programmes relevant to my department, I tried to make conversation with my new colleagues. Colin was initially responsive, but the banter tailed off when he got a phone call asking him to reset someone's access to a certain database. Clive, on the other hand, was very talkative. You couldn't shut the guy up. He spent the rest of the morning whining about Laura's behaviour towards him.

'I'm not saying that I want her to be my girlfriend, Barry, but we hardly see her. She's the one we're meant to approach with any problems, but I daren't approach her, and that's the problem. It puts me in a really difficult situation.'

'Isn't there anyone higher up you could speak to?'

'I haven't been off this floor in almost two years. I'm not allowed.'

'No, Clive, I mean someone more senior? And what do you mean, you're not allowed?'

He got up, walked over and balanced himself on the edge of my desk. 'The last time I did, people kept tutting at me. They waved the air when I walked by as if I'd farted.'

'Really?'

'Yes, really.'

'That's terrible. Did you tell anyone about it?'

'Only Colin. Same thing happened to him. But we hadn't farted, Barry. We don't do that in public. We were only dropping off some documents.'

I sympathised. If normal-looking librarians got a rough deal, these two were in for a pasting. 'You should say something.'

'It'll happen to you, too.' He walked back to his desk. 'Mark my words, Barry, I know.'

Don't think so, pal. *I'm* the business researcher, *you're* the librarian. Don't tarnish me with the same, unfashionable brush. 'I'll take my chances, thanks.'

'Tell him, Colin. Tell him it's true.'

Colin looked up from behind his screen. 'It's true.'

'There, you see? Colin thinks it too. All I'm saying is, be careful. This place does things to you. Strange things.'

'What things?'

He tapped his nose. 'You'll find out.'

What a peculiar individual. 'Thanks, Clive, I'll remember that.'

He smiled and went back to work.

Overall, my first day at *T&T* wasn't how I'd imagined it to be. I thought I'd be working with modern professionals, contributing my ideas and moving further up the ladder.

That hadn't happened.

Maybe it was the new-ness of it all affecting me. It was perfectly plausible come the end of the week, I'd have settled down, warmed to my professional comrades and grown ready to give it my best shot. After all, I was hardly sound of mind at the time. When the unfamiliarity died down and I could walk the corridors knowing where I was going, maybe I could make a difference and re-integrate Clive and Col into the rest of the building, offering fashion tips for the occasion too. They could even turn out to be my closest buddies.

It seemed doubtful.

I'd give it a week. If things hadn't improved by then, it was probably time to reconsider my position.

Five-thirty came around. I logged off and gathered my stuff together.

'See you tomorrow,' Clive said, with a wave. 'And remember what I said.'

I gave him a half-hearted salute and left the building.

Once outside, I got into an argument with myself over which was the fastest route home.

The bus.

No, the train. The station was closer to home than the bus stop.

I hated the West End. So busy and unnecessary. Too many tourists and camera flashes going off in your face.

Wait, no. The shop was closer to the bus stop, and I needed bread.

So I'd take the bus, then.

Sorted.

EIGHT

The tube was packed. Carriage after carriage of sweaty Londoners stood shoulder to shoulder, *Evening Standards* in the air, all striving towards the same goal: to get home as quickly as possible. Not getting a seat and having to stand with your face in someone's leaking, guffy armpit was a frequent downside of rush hour London, but unfortunately, it had to be done, unless you had the spending power to take a cab everywhere, which I did not.

It wasn't the number of people that bothered me, more the way they insisted on reading their newspapers next to my head, catching my cheek or scraping my eye. How could anyone read that way? Stood up, crammed against a door or wrapped around a pole? Can you really process anything in that position?

Jumping off at my station, I got outside and felt the cooling, fresh air dry the wetter parts of me. Nine hours ago, I slipped into a spotlessly-ironed shirt; it now looked like someone had run a marathon in it.

I switched on my phone for the first time since lunch. A voicemail message appeared almost instantaneously and I pressed the button to connect to my answering service. There were two messages waiting, the first of which was from Mum. She'd called from the airport to leave a sloppy, two-minutes worth of goodbyes, making sure I was coping on my own, asking me to text as soon as I could to tell her how my first day went. It did make me smile; there she was, fretting, about to board a plane for the first time, and could still spare a thought for me and my dweeby department.

Message two: *"Err, hey Barry, it's, erm, Poppy here. Just calling to let you know how sorry I am about the other night. I've had time to think… and, err, well, I was out of line, I know that now. I understand if you don't wanna speak to me, but I'd love a chance to make it up to you. Anyway, hope your new job is good. Give me a call on…."*

How did she get my number? I don't remember her asking for it. Did I go to the toilet in the pub and leave my phone there for her to violate?

I did appreciate the thought. It did sound like she regretted voicing such a negative opinion of my bedroom repertoire, but I certainly wasn't ready to head straight over for another roll in the sack. The early part of the evening went really well; if we were to start again - to chalk Saturday down to experience - it should be for a drink and nothing more.

I held off replying. It was nice to have a bit of positive attention, but I needed some time to think. Poppy did seem like a fun-loving girl, but there was too much going on. It was far too soon to plunge headfirst into another relationship two days after Beth had left, and a dark part of my soul questioned whether I had really heard the last of Melinda and her steaming-hot libido.

After stopping at the shop, I resumed the walk home and thought about Mum again. This holiday was a big deal for her. For years, she'd avoided planes in favour of trains and ferries, until Dad's incessant nagging forced her hand. During the week before the climb, it wasn't unusual for her to call me twice a day, to clarify airport and aircraft procedure: what to take in your hand luggage, whether they still gave you boiled sweets on take-off. It was her way of seeking reassurance, and I was happy to provide it.

'The flight will be relatively short, Mum,' I'd said. 'I know it's daunting, but if you take a load of trashy magazines, by the time you've had something to eat and read about empty-headed celebrities, it'll be time for

71

landing. The time will fly by, forgive the pun.'

It did settle her nerves a little.

Remembering my amateur psychiatry, I checked the time and typed in her number. Knowing Mum, as soon as they got through customs, she'd switch her phone on straight away to wait for my call.

Before I could dial, something stopped me. Turning on to my road, I placed the phone back in my pocket and went to greet the tall, well-built police officer standing by my front gate. Hopefully, he'd come to cart Melinda away to the nearest institution. 'Can I help you?'

'I'm looking for a Barry Brooks.'

I panicked. Had she shopped me for indecent exposure? Was he about to drag my ass down to the cells? 'Yes, that's me.'

Stone-faced: 'Mr. Brooks, I'm Constable Walters, with the Metropolitan Police. Can we go inside, please?'

Not the smartest tactic, dear neighbour. How do you envisage getting your oats with me gone, huh? Didn't think about that, did you? 'If this is about the window thing, it was an honest mistake.'

'Window thing?'

'I'm telling you I didn't realise I was…' I could see from his face that he didn't have the first idea what I was talking about. 'Never mind. Come on up.'

His jaw dropped when he saw the place. 'Having a clear out?'

At least it was tidy. 'No, err, domestic issues. Girlfriend moved out.'

'Right.'

'Took everything.'

'I can see that.'

'Yeah, sorry, it is a bit sparse.'

'Was it theft? You should report it if it's theft.'

I waved away the suggestion. 'It's fine, I'll sort it out.' We moved into the kitchen. 'Can I get you a drink? Tea or coffee?'

'Thank you, no.'

Good. I didn't have either.

He looked around. 'Normally, I'd ask you to sit down, but there doesn't appear to be anywhere...'

If it wasn't the flashing, why was he here? Asking me to sit down, too? That didn't sound good. 'It's fine. What's the problem?'

He took a notepad from his pocket. 'Mr. Brooks, are your parents...' he confirmed the details written down, '...Ian and Yvonne Brooks?'

Oh, God. Please, no. 'What's happened?'

'Are they your parents, sir?'

'Yes,' I replied, impatiently, 'are they okay? Where are they?'

'I'm so sorry, Barry, but I'm afraid I have some bad news. There's been an accident. It concerns flight number eight-six-eight to Switzerland - the flight they were booked on?'

NINE

Mum and Dad's flight crashed on approach to Geneva International, killing everyone on board. When the official explanation finally came it was comprised of phrases like *total system failure* and *unexpected bad weather*, but I couldn't accept that. It was nonsense. Were they really saying that in this age of modern technology, the craft wasn't designed to cope in the event of such an occurrence? How bad does the weather have to be?

They also said that as a result of the *total system failure* and *unexpected bad weather*, the pilot was essentially flying blind and undershot the runway by two miles. He sent the plane down into a built-up area. It burst into flames, leaving a small community devastated in its wake. Doesn't that sound like a big, crusty plethora of nonsense?

'*What about back-up systems?*' I asked.

'*They failed too,*' I was told.

'*So the plane just died mid-air?*'

'*It happens.*'

'*Really? How often?*'

'*Not often.*'

'*Have you lost anyone close to you in a similar accident?*'

'*No.*'

'*Can you understand why I have all these questions?*'

'*Maybe.*'

'*Maybe? What does that mean?*'

'*What do you want from me? I only work here.*'

'*You idiot bastard jobsworth. My parents are dead because of this.'*

'And you think I can bring them back to life? Who d'you think I am, Jesus? I'm not a miracle worker. You want me to feed the five-thousand too?'

'Oh, just go and die somewhere.'

'Don't take your grief out on me. Just because they're dead, doesn't mean I should be.'

See what I mean? Nonsense.

It was a total mess. Lives were lost, homes were destroyed and families of those both on the plane and on the ground needlessly broken in two. Regardless of how it felt, I knew I wasn't the only one affected by the tremendous loss of life. Hundreds of other relatives were no doubt having similar conversations with the so-called *specialists* about why such a tragedy was allowed to happen.

After Constable Walters relayed the bad news, I didn't know what to do or where to go. There was no point travelling all the way to the airport and I certainly didn't have the money to jump on the next flight to Geneva. I wasn't sure it would do any good, anyway. Walters suggested I went to stay with a friend, but none of them were returning my calls. The only thing I could do was hover around my lonely hole of a flat, nothing there to console me except a sadistic, cold-hearted, sex-obsessed neighbour, and a quartered Elvis.

The first thing I did was parade through every room and switch on all the lights. Wherever I went, I had to be able to see. Then, I took my anger and frustration out on Walters. It wasn't his fault, he didn't deserve it, but he stuck around for an hour anyway acting as my verbal punchbag. By the time he left, I was leaning over the kitchen sink unable to keep the vomit down. I wanted him to stay longer, but he was still on duty and had to attend to a disturbance a couple of miles away. He put a business card on the side, apologised for having to dash in the middle of my stomach upset, told me to call anytime and was gone.

I couldn't raise my head to thank him. I didn't even have the strength to move my exhausted frame to the bathroom. With the hot tap running, steam forming moisture on my forehead, I vomited again, and again, and again, and some more, until I couldn't breathe. The burn intensified with every drop of liquid that came up, and I knew it wouldn't be long before I was dry-retching again.

There was no way I could endure another bout; the sharp, twisting pain in my stomach was travelling up my body causing heartburn to take over my chest, and my head was thumping as I pictured Mum and Dad's charred corpses in amongst a sickening field of the dead.

It wasn't happening.

Bad things don't come in threes; only freaks, fortune tellers and the impressionable believed in that shit.

This couldn't be happening.

The water was at its highest temperature; I'd been wasting it for over twenty minutes. Without thinking, I stuck both hands underneath the flow and held them in place for as long as I could. The pain was unbearable, but I didn't move, leaving my scolded hands where they were, desperately hoping the pain would wake me up in another world - a world as far away as possible from this one.

Nothing.

I closed my eyes again, and through the pain, wished myself away.

Still nothing.

I took my hands from the stream, felt a surge of dizziness and collapsed in a heap on the kitchen floor.

The pain from my hands and stomach opened my eyes a few hours later. I ran them under cold water, but the damage was already done. Blisters had formed on the back of my palms and skin was peeling from my fingers. When the chill of the water numbed the pain, I searched everywhere for antiseptic cream and bandages, expecting Beth to have emptied the first aid cabinet too.

She had.

The slut.

She'd even taken the cabinet.

Then, I remembered the climb. Dean told me it was vitally important to take cream with you in case of scratches or grazes. I ran to the bedroom, found my rucksack under the bed, took the half-empty tube from its front pocket and slowly squeezed the lotion over my hands.

I reeked like a hospital ward, but it was worth it. The burn faded a little and I crawled to the bed and fell asleep again.

Tinkler & Tinkler were surprisingly understanding about my request for time off. It was only my second day. I called Laura to explain; she sympathised, apologised and told me to take as much time as was needed to work through this *ever-so difficult period*. I remember thinking she was reading from a script as she spoke; it didn't sound like the kind of sentence you would come out with spontaneously. At any moment, the dozy cow would lose her place on the cribsheet and blurt out *insert disaster here* instead of *loss of parents*. It made sense to me, though; you have to be prepared to console the workforce should unforeseen tragedies arise. Maybe those with an ounce of personality could conjure up condolences naturally, but it didn't matter, I appreciated the sentiment.

I called everyone in the family I could think of, asking them to pass the news on to others I didn't have phone numbers for. After listening to Aunty Claire sob her heart out for almost two hours uninterrupted, I switched my phone off.

Through brief showers of tears, I took some time to think about my next move. Getting the bodies flown back for the funeral seemed to be the number one priority. When I spoke to Walters a second time, he mentioned the *Foreign and Commonwealth Office*. He'd informed them of the crash and told me they would organise for my parents to be returned home. They had all my details and would be in touch shortly. It made zero sense at the time, but I was relieved, as my mind was so traumatised, I didn't have the strength to see any kind of inquiry through from start to finish. It took every last bit of determination I had just to keep it together when thinking about it, let alone running through it over and over again with strangers on the telephone.

Alvin Potter, the chirpy, but respectful man from the *FCO*, kept me in touch with developments over the course of the week. I was impressed with the way he handled everything. His professionalism shone through, and looking back, if it wasn't for him, I doubt I'd have been able to juggle all that was thrown at me. In a way, he was the only friend I had. None of my other so-called buddies had been in touch to offer support or take me out for a pint and a chat. As unusual as it sounds, I actually looked forward to his calls. Talking to him about the accident gave a me a well-deserved release, and even though he was being paid to listen to my devastation, he was listening after all. At that particular time, it was the only thing I needed.

A few days later, I got another call.

'Hi Alvin,' I said, having stored his number in my phone.

'Barry, how's things?'

We went through the usual pleasantries.

'Have you got a pen?' He gave me the number of Northwick Park Hospital. 'This is the switchboard number. Ask for Doctor Miller. If he's not there, tell them to put you through to extension 8279.'

'What's extension 8279?'

'The mortuary. Your parents were brought in last night. You're gonna have to go down and identify the bodies.'

TEN

'Hey, mister spider, what'cha doin'? Fancied a stroll, did ya? Yeah, you did, didn't you? Well, stroll away, my friend. Don't mind me.'

The arachnid in question was crawling up my leg. I'd been watching him scurry back and forth across the open floor, until he deviated off-course, straight into the path of my foot. 'Woo, yeah, the spider got guts, I reckon.'

I was sprawled on the floor, completely naked, with a half-empty bottle of whiskey beside me. I wasn't too concerned about running out, as the cupboard was stocked with lots more scrumptious, *Jack Danielsy* goodness. At last count, there were a further six bottles in there.

Spidey was approaching my knee. 'Is he gonna make it all the way to the top, I wonder? Quiet in the auditorium, please. All eyes on Cliff…'

Cliff was a good name for a spider, I thought. Gave off an air of maturity. I picked up the bottle and had another swig. The liquid got caught in the wrong end of my throat and I erupted into a fit of coughing, the bottle flying out of my hands. Panicking, I rolled over to catch it, but was too late. It landed, bounced, rolled, all the time leaking expensive whiskey on to the hard floor.

'Bastard! Arse, bastard, arse!'

The phone was ringing.

'Piss off.'

It didn't.

'Which scrotal sack's calling me now?'

I shouldn't have answered it half-cut. 'For God's sake, whaaaaat?'

'Barry?'

'Who's this?'

'It's Laura Delgado, from *T&T*?'

Who? 'Ah, yes, hello Loooooora,' I slurred, 'what canneth I do for you this, err, this…'

'This afternoon?' she replied.

'Yes, yes, this afternoon. Well?'

'Barry, is this a bad time?'

I wore my heart on my sleeve, which was impressive as I didn't have any sleeves. 'Goooooood question,' I replied, 'have you caught *Bazza-bastardy-dead-parentsy-Brooks* at a bad time? Well, let me have a think, I don't know.' I began to shout. 'WHAT DO YOU THINK, HUH? WHAT DO YOU RECKON, LAURA NO-SEX-FACE UGLY PANTS? HAVE YOUR PARENTS JUST DIED? HAVE YOU JUST DROPPED YOUR… ARSEING, ERR, WHISKEY BOTTLE? WHERE THE KNOB IS IT?'

A five-second silence. 'Right, I see. Barry, obviously I understand that you're going through a difficult time right now, but we do need some kind of idea when you will be returning to work.'

'Have you got a boyf… a boyfriend at the momentoooo, Laura Delgadooooo?'

'I don't see what that's got to do with…'

'Have yooooou orhaven'tyougot one?' My sentences were beginning to meld together. The fact that she understood more than five per cent of what I was saying was incredible.

'No, I haven't got a boyfriend at the moment. Now, if we could get back to the matter…'

'I could beyourman, Laura. I think you're stunning sexy phwoar. I dream about you at night. You could be my womaaaaaaaaaan.'

She dismissed the compliment, such as it was. 'Thank you. Look, this is a bad time. I'll call back tomorrow.'

'I'll stillloveyoooooooooooooou, Lauuuuuuuuuuuuuura,' I sang.

'Bye, Barry.'

'Oh, Laura, lightof myliiiiiiiiiiiiiiiiiiiiiiiiiiiiiiife. Do you like rimming?'

She hung up.

'Sod ya then,' I said, finding the bottle at last. 'There you are, baby. Come to Bazza.'

The bottle was empty. I was about to launch into another expletive-laden rant, when I saw him on the floor. 'Oh, no, no, no, spidey!' The poor thing had been crushed as I rolled over. 'Oh, spidey-spoo, what have you done? What have you done? You were soooooooo close to the summit. It's my fault. All my fault. I did it, I killed you, just like I killed my dead, rotting parents, sat there with their skinless faces and closed, peeling dead eyeballs.' I belched. 'You should've known better than to climb up my leg of eternal death.'

Wobbling from side to side, I got up for another bottle, dropped back down on the floor and took three more gulps. I thought it would be fitting to perform a funeral ceremony for spidey, but when it came to the cremation - cigarette lighter standing by - I almost caught a mound of pubic hair in the process. 'May you rest in peace, you fifteen-legged mammoth moth.'

Twenty-four hours before my drunken come-on to Laura and the death of Spidey, I'd dragged myself down to the morgue for the formal identification bit. It wasn't the most uplifting twenty minutes I had ever spent. It felt as if someone had shoved the sharp end of a white-hot poker through my chest, at the same time as kicking me in the balls and pouring vinegar in my eyes. I'd psyched myself up for the assistant pulling back the cloth to reveal the lifeless faces of my mother and father, but it was all in vain. I had never seen a dead body in my life, and the trauma was only magnified by the fact that it was the two people on earth I was closest to.

I didn't gain any closure from seeing them that way. How could I? Neither of them were ill or nearing a natural death. They were taken away, senselessly ripped from this world and I didn't even get the chance to tell them I loved them or say goodbye. How can any man draw comfort from such a situation? I would have done anything, absolutely anything at all to be given an opportunity to tie up the loose ends that remained, even if it meant sacrificing my own life. It's not like it was worth much now they were gone.

I signed the forms given to me by the coroner. Yes, these were the bodies of my parents; yes, I could confidently vouch for their deceased status. It killed me to face up to it, but now they were *officially* gone, never to return.

Before the identification, it didn't seem real. I could happily drift off into the welcoming arms of my imagination, believing them both to be still with me, about to call or walk through the door. Now, I was witness to their demise. I thought that picking things up and starting again without Beth would be a daunting enough task. In comparison, she was the equivalent of boiling an egg.

The assistant led me outside for some fresh air. When the nausea passed, I made a promise never to set foot inside a mortuary again. Not this mortuary, or the other one further down town, or any other damned mortuary in London. I didn't know how many there were in total, but was sure as hell never going to see the inside of another one for as long as I had all my scruples. When I died, well, that was a completely different story. Someone else would have to do the honours. What a joy that would be for whoever pulled the short straw. The rate at which I was leaking friends and loved ones meant the poor sod left with the mundane task of confirming my identity would either be my doctor, Clive or Colin.

What a sobering thought.

On my way home in the cab, the smell of bleach and disinfectant clinging to my clothes, I ran through the ever-growing list of things awaiting my attention: funeral arrangements, Mum and Dad's house, unpaid bills and all the other necessary practical tasks that went hand in hand with giving the deceased a respectable send-off.

My new and improved salary gave me extra breathing space, but I still applied for an extension to the already maxed-out credit card in my wallet, to avoid any embarrassment at the transactional stage. The reading of the will would come later, after the funeral; hopefully, there'd be a lump sum with my name on it, so I could drag myself out of the debt I was slumping further into.

Damn you, family. Where was the help I needed so badly? None of them had followed up my calls to see how I was doing. Not one of the useless fools felt obliged to chip in and offer a financial contribution. It was all down to me. I had a feeling the months ahead would help me appreciate how strong I was - how capable I could be under pressure.

The following day would be one for setting goals and making promises. Mum and Dad would get the perfect ceremony; their affairs would be taken care of with no setbacks, because I was on the case now. I was the only one who could make it happen. They brought me into this world and raised me in the best way they could. What's more, they did a stunning job. I owed them one. As a matter of fact, I owed them more than one. I knew them better than anyone else did, and they would want me to do the best I could for them, then focus all my energy on me.

So I stopped by the shop, bought a shed's worth of whiskey and drank myself into oblivion. There you have it: the events leading up to my nude, sit-down protest on the living room floor. Up yours, world. Up yours so hard it comes out of your mouth, covered in guts.

It wasn't possible to see amidst the haze of an intoxicated summer afternoon, but the light would soon come. Not only would it come, it would allow me to leave the twisted reality of mourning behind and amend my outlook on life. The first stepping-stone would be the acquisition of a new home; a totally different blank canvas, with no bad memories or lingering nightmares. Somewhere neutral I could call my own, and start afresh.

II

Moving on…

ELEVEN

Almost a year later…

Remembering the look on Melinda's face when she discovered I was moving out will never cease to make me smile. It was one of those brainless expressions I wished I could have captured on camera and uploaded to *www.whatadozyspazface.net*. The worldwide population would then view and rate on a scale of one to ten; one being not so dozy, ten maxing out the spaz-o-meter. This one could have made an excellent case for extending the scale to eleven.

Christmas had come and gone and it was approaching the first anniversary of my parents' death. I'd spent approximately three-hundred and sixty-five days living alone in an empty flat, with no motivation to go out and replace what Beth had taken. All I bought were toiletries, a laundry basket, a second-hand quilt from a charity shop and some new towels. What was the point? I had no desire to make the place look homely. I couldn't find the eagerness or drive to change things for the better.

I went back to work after three weeks of compassionate leave, expecting to find my position had been filled and I was surplus to requirements. What I arrived back to was a huge pile of sympathy cards sitting on my desk, from colleagues I'd never even met. Astoundingly, Laura's was top of the pile. The note accompanying the verse instructed me to call whenever I needed an ear, and she'd added her landline and mobile number for ease underneath.

It was *Laura* who called me during my alcoholic frenzy, wasn't it?

Over the course of the year, my life and everything in it had stooped to a new low. I'd bled the loss I'd suffered for all it was worth, drowning my sorrows with the aid of a variety of potent whiskeys. However, when New Year's Eve arrived, I experienced what I can only describe as an epiphany - a moment of total clarity - which I gather is quite a rare event. I had to drop the bottle, pick my life up from the gutter and make some radical alterations. I couldn't physically continue on the road leading to self-destruction; my lungs and liver were screaming out for mercy. If I'd carried on at that rate, I'd have been seriously ill, or even dead before long.

I'd stopped counting the number of times Melinda popped round for her sex fix, but it was averaging twice a week. She insisted I called her Mel, as part of our arrangement, which only increased my extreme hatred for her. *"Call me Mel, otherwise I'll tell my husband you keep grabbing my wabs and rubbing yourself up against me on the stairs"* took pettiness to an entirely different level. What could anyone hope to gain from that? Surely, *"Give me what I need, or I'll tell my husband I caught you breaking into our flat to steal one of my bras"* was blackmail enough? Evidently not.

It must have been when I was tied to the bed one time, but the scheming little bitch actually stole my keys and made a copy for herself, giving her ultimate control over when she was able to walk through the door. What did she do when I tried to steal the set back?

"If you take the keys, I'll tell Greg you forced me to have sex with you on our bed wearing his favourite tee shirt."

Or if I threatened to change the locks?

I couldn't change the locks. It was a rented apartment and I needed the landlord's permission before doing that.

I was trapped. When she was around, there was nothing

I could do or say to make it stop. If I had a headache, she gave me aspirin; when I couldn't perform due to the all-consuming disgust I was feeling, she gave me a little blue pill.

Melinda was insatiable. Nothing I could say or do hindered her quest for my loins, which is why I had to come up with a plan. She was a cunning, calculating vixen who had me in the palm of her hand. I knew as soon as I told her I was leaving, she'd be straight downstairs telling Greg I'd suggested we have a threesome or act out the chocolate watersports fantasy. I wasn't about to let her do anything like that, and had the foolproof ace up my sleeve to prevent it.

My pièce de résistance.

Oh yes, it was a good one.

It involved a special item of hardware I'd recently acquired for a discounted price from the internet. Yes, that's the fella; a mega high-tech, anti-blackmail *Dictaphone*, complete with stereo playback.

Take that, wench.

'You're what?'

'I'm moving out. I've found a new place and I'm leaving next week.'

She stopped to consider her position. 'Are you serious?'

'Deadly.'

'But… what about us?' She gave an unconcerned look, believing she'd coil me further around her little finger, despite my revelation.

'Us? There is no *us*. What are you talking about?'

Smiles. 'Have you forgotten our little arrangement?'

I played dumb. 'Arrangement?'

'Come on. Don't make me spell it out to you again. I tell you what to do and you do it, otherwise I make you look like the single most disgusting human being who ever lived. How many times have we done this?'

In order for my scheme to work, I had to let her believe she was having the desired effect, so I pretended to be irritated and slumped down on the kitchen floor.

'You're not going anywhere, my boy. You're staying here for as long as I say. Clear?'

As appalled as I was with myself for thinking it, I couldn't help but admire her for a second. Here was a woman who knew precisely what she wanted and how to manipulate everything and everyone around her to get it. What she didn't know was that her grip on my personal services was about to come to its rightful end.

'Clear,' I said, a few seconds later.

The mischievous grin re-appeared and she held out her hand for me to take. 'I'm ready. Today, you're gonna give it to me from behind.'

We walked into the bedroom, a journey I'd made countless times. She closed the door and propped herself in front of it, motioning for me to undress her. I complied eagerly, starting with her blouse, unbuttoning it and throwing the little black number on the bed as I massaged her breasts. I could hear her breath become heavier as I stroked her nipples in a circular motion, doing my best to make her think I was enjoying myself. My stomach fluttered; it was the final time I'd have to endure the torture.

'So you're staying here with me, baby?'

'I'll never leave you,' I replied, lifting up her skirt. She grunted in surprise as I ripped down her panties and threw her on to the bed.

'You're in a good mood today,' she said, one finger in her mouth. She probably thought it would turn me on. It didn't.

'Shouldn't I be?'

'No, no, I'm not knocking it, I've just never seen you this...'

'Aroused?'

'Yeah, I guess.'

'Are you gonna psycho-analyse me, Mel? 'Cos I'd rather be doing something else.' I wasn't sure if she was taken aback and hiding it, or simply not bothered.

'You don't have to tell me twice.'

I pulled down my boxer shorts and joined her on the bed. Throughout our many sessions, we'd hardly kissed, and if we did, she always instigated it. This time, I threw myself at her face and snogged her as passionately as I could, resisting the urge to gag and vomit. 'Oh, Mel,' I moaned, giving her neck some attention, 'you're amazing.'

She pulled away a little, but not completely. 'Stop talking and give it to me.' She grabbed my buttocks and pulled me towards her.

'Wait,' I shouted, just in time. 'Let's enjoy this moment first.'

She wasn't interested in anymore foreplay. 'I said give it to me now.'

'No.'

'What?'

'I said no, Melinda.'

She was seething. For a start, I'd called her by her full name, which she hated with a passion, and secondly, I'd disobeyed a direct order to have intercourse. 'Do it now, before that man I live with finds out about your sordid obsessions.'

I rolled over, leaving her visibly frustrated on her back, and pulled the *Dictaphone* from under the pillow. 'It's over, Melinda.'

'Beg your pardon?'

'It's over. You and me, us, whatever you believe this revolting activity to be. It's done.'

'How dare you tell me what is and what isn't, you little shit? Who do you think you are? I make the decisions here.'

I pressed play on the *Dictaphone*:

"D'you think Greg would believe you over his own wife? I have him wrapped around my little finger. I control him, Barry. He has no idea what we do here."

"But you're blackmailing me. Doesn't that make you feel the slightest bit guilty?"

"No, it doesn't. He has the money, you have the equipment.

94

What more could a girl ask for? The best thing is he'll never find out about any of it."

I stopped the machine and waited for her to try to snatch it from me.

To my shock, that didn't happen. She didn't even speak, just stood up, got dressed and headed for the door. Before leaving the room, she crouched down beside me. 'Fine. Leave this flat, leave us, but I'll tell you one thing.'

I smiled. 'What's that, you crazy bitch?'

She stuttered a response.

'What is it? What the hell have you got to say that could possibly benefit my life? I've dealt with your shit for the last year, so as you can imagine, I'd really like to hear your opinion right now.'

There was no reply.

'Get out of my flat. I never want to see you again.'

Unable to think of a retort to better anything I'd said, she left, slamming the bedroom door with almighty force. Seconds later, I heard her stomping down the stairs, back to her own place.

'See ya,' I hollered, cheekily in her general direction, 'wouldn't wanna be ya.'

I didn't know whether that was truly the end of it. I still had a week in the flat before moving; plenty of time for her to rethink her strategy and get her claws into me one more time, but it wasn't to be. After that day, I never saw Melinda or her naked body again.

TWELVE

Admitting it would have surely thrown another barrage of unspeakable horror and demolition my way - not that there was anyone to tell - but things were certainly improving. Looking on the brighter side of life became less of a chore, and I'd also established a decent sleeping pattern, instead of an hour here, ten minutes there, until the morning light broke through the window and steered me out of bed. Work may have been evolving into an agonising pit of despair and anguish, but at least it was consistently so.

Thanks be to Mum and Dad. They'd left me enough money to put a deposit on an apartment, with some left over to decorate it the way I wanted. It was a small place with only four rooms: lounge, kitchen, bedroom and bathroom, but it was love at first sight. Located in a quiet, residential part of London Fields, the station, local shop and pub were a five-minute walk in each direction, and bus routes served the road outside, ensuring I was never too far away from all the amenities the area provided.

Spot on. The country's most reputable property gurus couldn't have found a better place. This week's property guide was brought to you by Barry Brooks, who no longer has to endure twice-weekly, brain-frying sex with the resident psychopath, or the lingering scent of his ex-girlfriend.

I explained to *T&T* that I would shortly be moving house. As I didn't have any friends to help me - the scrotes still weren't making or receiving calls - they allowed me three extra days leave to get the job done, which was mighty kind of them. Imagine how speechless I was when Clive and Col caught me on the hop at work, volunteering to help me pick my new furniture up over the weekend. I really did give it some thought too, but having to endure every weekday in their presence was depressing enough for a bloke, so politely, I declined. I was grateful for the offer though; at least there were two people out there who didn't hate the sight of me and believe I was Satan's illegitimate love child.

By the end of Saturday, most of my new home was in place. I'd even bought cushions and covers for the sofas - a traditionally un-male thing to do. I puffed them up and sat down, admiring my handiwork. DIY had never been one of my greatest skills, but I was proud of the job I'd done with the bookshelves. All I needed was some books to put in them. A quick trip to *Oxfam* would sort out that particular problem.

The living room wasn't too large, more cosy and compact. I was convinced I needed the largest television screen available when roaming the store, but once installed, it seemed a few inches too large, but it wasn't that big a deal. The games console and DVD player were due a few days after, and honestly, can a TV screen ever be too large?

I switched on the lamp, allowing the low-watt bulb to pump a carnation glow into the flagship room of my new home.

My first bachelor pad.

I used to dream of my own place when living with my parents, but when Beth and I moved in together, I naturally assumed I'd never get the chance.

What a stupid assumption that turned out to be.

It had all turned out for the best. Here I was, surrounded by all of my things - things I could call my own - that no spineless witch could ever take away from me. Hot damn, it felt good to have possessions again.

I poured myself a glass of wine and began my sixth tour of the place, starting in the bathroom. The big-nozzled power shower more than made up for there being no bath, especially as the head had four different settings, ranging from wide spray to direct flow. Get your nethers caught on the most vigorous option and it was guaranteed to cause you a bit of discomfort down there. In most cases, the middle setting would suffice. I was slightly disturbed at the amount of attention I was paying to the cleaning facilities, but part of me imagined enjoying a nice, warm, foamy shower with a lucky girl sometime in the future. Although an enjoyable fantasy, I knew it would take a while to fully recover from the cerebral humiliation I suffered at the hands of Melinda, so I moved into the bedroom and put that particular reverie on the back burner.

It would be nothing but a pleasure to sleep here. Fitted wardrobes lined one of the walls, a hanging mirror, framed pictures and a window the others. I had chosen my own bed linen, a nice masculine blue that matched the carpet, and was looking forward to climbing in and rolling around like a man possessed in a few hours time. Under the bed, I kept a cream-coloured set should the same lucky girl have the privilege of sharing it with me. Finally, a pair of lavender-scented candles were perfectly positioned on my bedside cabinet, adding a touch of elegance to proceedings.

What a class act you are, Brooks. In one room, I had my high-def, super-tech gadgetry, and in the other, a chick-friendly, chilled out atmosphere, with the *en-suite* option thrown in for good measure.

This place had the wow factor.

A big gulp of wine later, the doorbell rang. For a split-second, my mind couldn't place the sound. The old flat had a doorknocker, but towards the end, the only person who'd ever used it was Melinda, and she had resorted to letting herself in without warning. Glass in hand, I moved to the door and crouched a little to look through the spy-hole. Three figures stood outside - two guys and a girl - waiting for me to open the door. I didn't recognise any of them, but the girl was holding a bottle of wine, so unless she was planning to smash it over my head while the boys ransacked the place, I guessed it was a welcome from the neighbours.

'Hi,' the brunette in hippy clothing said. 'Welcome to the building.'

The three figures introduced themselves and I invited them inside. Miles and Penny were the couple from next door; Teddy was Miles' best friend and also lived next door, only on the other side. Both of them were textbook pretty boys: Miles was tall, with dark, cropped hair, wearing a tee shirt with sleeves so short you could see his perfected, bulging biceps; Teddy, blonde, with a dark tan, had his muscles covered, but from the bulging veins in his neck I could tell he was also partial to the gym now and then.

Penny handed me the bottle and they followed me into the kitchen, gasping in unison when I opened the cabinet to reveal a full set of matching glasses: tall glasses, small glasses, wine glasses, shot glasses, all arranged neatly across three shelves. It was highly unlikely they'd be displayed as perfectly over time, but it was nice to show off in front of guests. First impressions and all that.

When our glasses were filled, I repeated the tour, showing them what I'd done with the place. Teddy was loving the television, I could tell straight away. Whenever he wasn't speaking or being spoken to, his glance shifted in its direction. If I wasn't mistaken, another gadget-boy was in my midst. Bearing that in mind, I pointed out my reservations on the screen size to keep the conversation flowing.

'Do you reckon?' he said, moving in for a better look.

'Don't you think?'

'Come on, Barry, can a TV screen ever be too big?'

'My point exactly!'

He jokingly offered to take it off my hands for half the

price should it turn out to be an unbearable problem. He seemed like a nice guy. I normally decided whether I liked someone during the first ten minutes of knowing them, and Teddy had impressed me thus far.

Miles and Penny were holding hands on the sofa. It didn't bother me that much; at least they weren't necking in my front room, but if you live together, surely the urge to be touching one another twenty-four hours a day fades over time? Then again, Miles could have been marking his territory in front of the new boy. I myself had been guilty of that, years ago with Beth. Not that I was afraid he'd boldly announce his courtship to Penny in a caveman's lilt, more a gesture that said, *"Don't even think about it, sunshine"*. Well, don't worry about it, mate, my humping days are over for the time being.

I was hardly about to put his mind at ease aloud, but as it happened, Penny wasn't really my type. For a start, I prefer blonde women with long hair; hers was brown and she wore it in a bob. Given a choice, I'd go for bigger breasts, whereas Penny's were cute and stumpy. Miles could probably fit one and a half in his hand, which would be no good for me; I like to be able to push them both together to resemble juicy melons during passionate clinches. Anyway, that's enough about Penny's anatomy. I'd only just met the girl and had already been warned off by her boyfriend. If he caught me staring at her stumps, I could see him getting down on all fours and cocking his leg over my new furniture.

I was grateful to have new people to talk and interact with socially, but much of the discussion relied heavily on current affairs: news, weather, the state of the public transport system in London; subjects that didn't really whet my conversational appetite. As the onlooker, it was clear to me that Penny wore the trousers in their relationship. The way she spoke over him as he tried to make a point to the way he sat there and took it from her spoke bundles. I'm positive Teddy was aware of it too, but most likely chose not to voice his opinions fearing accusations of interference.

The atmosphere became less tense as we got through more alcohol. They slumped back in their chairs and I thought it would be a fitting moment to introduce them to my sense of humour. I was rather merry by that point, at the stage where it wouldn't have worried me too much if the tumbleweed flew across the room. Every social gathering has to have a ten-minute period when people throw out one-liners, knock-knock jokes and short-to-medium anecdotes, and I had one aching to be told.

'Okay, guys, how about a joke?'

'Go on,' they all replied.

'It's a bit risqué…'

'Doesn't matter, dude,' Teddy said, 'as long as it's funny. Give it your best shot.'

I launched into it without a second's thought. 'Why did the woman fall off the swing?'

Total silence. The room was locked in anticipation and a sense of dread flooded through me. I'd let it go and there was no taking it back now. I kept my eyes on Teddy; I sensed he'd be the one who'd appreciate a *not-so politically correct* joke the most.

'Because she didn't have any arms.'

I sobered up completely delivering the punchline. All the variables I hadn't considered sat on my shoulder, tutting in my ear: what if Miles' father had no arms? What if Penny's mother had a prosthetic arm? What if both their grandfathers had lost both arms years ago, fighting for King and country? The first decent company I'd had in over a year was about to collectively march out of the apartment in disgust, most probably throwing what was left in their glasses over me in the process.

I didn't think it was *that* horrific. Okay, it wasn't one to tell at Aunty Flo's on a Sunday afternoon, when everyone was gathered around the table eating tiffin, sipping tea from china cups and skimming through the broadsheets. That's probably what would happen if you got on a swing and didn't have any arms. In my mind, it was an authentic spin on the swing/no arms sequence of events. As I was inwardly waiting for one of them to make the first move, the unthinkable happened. Unsure at first, I rubbed my eyes to clarify. Yes, Penny was smiling. Wait, so was Teddy. Miles cracked too and the entire room burst into laughter, quietly at first, but then the volume pumped up for a good sixty seconds.

'Where do you get 'em from?' Teddy said, in-between giggles. 'That's soooooo crass!'

The telly,' I replied. 'Hope it wasn't too much.'

Nah, not at all,' Penny chipped in. 'The dirtier the better.'

Miles looked slightly ruffled by that comment. He shot her a look of *calm down, dear, maybe you've had enough wine*, then picked up his glass and took a long sip. Penny's laugh turned back into a smile and she excused herself to use the bathroom. I could see Miles subliminally telling her to splash her face with cold water. It was entertaining to watch such a blatant tussle for power, but I was aware if I stared at either of them for longer than was polite and necessary, Miles would be cocking his leg up again and I hadn't had a chance to buy any carpet cleaner.

It got to eleven-thirty, and after more wine and jokes, they left for their apartments, telling me what a nice evening they'd had, with promises we'd do it again soon.

Yay me! I'd made some new friends. Just goes to show that with a bit of luck, a corkscrew and a dodgy joke, fortunes can turn in your favour. Deleting the names and numbers of those dickheads who refused to talk to me was first on tomorrow's daily goal list.

I'd previously fretted over the whole *neighbour* thing, taking into consideration the relatively thin walls and my yearlong ordeal with Melinda, but now there was no need to. Taking the empty glasses into the kitchen, I switched off the lights and locked the front door. I let out a self-satisfied sigh and walked into the bedroom to get my head down on those brand new pillows.

THIRTEEN

The hours of nine to five-thirty had long-since devolved into a new species of boredom. On this particular day, at eleven in the morning, I began my fifth self-interrogation session, questioning why I persisted to put myself through the irrelevance that was my job. Foolishly, I expected it to improve along with my revitalised social life, but such good fortune chose not to accompany me to the office.

Pen in hand, I was filling up the complimentary *Tinkler & Tinkler*-branded notepad with numerous lists of pros and cons. So abundant were my lists, the pad was three-quarters full. A swift glance at my calendar told me I'd been jotting down meaningless dross for roughly six months.

Half a year.

One hundred and eighty-two and a half days of life wasted trying to out-do myself on a daily basis with futile scrawl, not counting weekends.

Problem was, the lists had no variation. I flicked back to page one and compared it with page two-hundred and four.

PROS: Salary.

CONS: Everything else.

There was no dilemma here; no deep interpretation required. It was as plain as one of Dad's pancakes. Why was I dissing the environment so carelessly, squandering sheets of paper that could have so easily been put to better use, like covering up Clive's face, for example? To blame lack of ambition on the death of my parents was a valid excuse, to a point, but it was a year since they'd passed. I was in no doubt that if Mum was looking down on me, she'd be urging me to get the hell out, irritated by my reluctance to do so, upset at my lack of productivity.

I had to sort out my professional affairs, dig deep and find a way out. Money wasn't everything, was it? I thought I was the kind of guy who didn't place too much relevance on the acquisition of wealth. Sure, it was nice to have it, but it wasn't the ultimate pinnacle of my aspirations. I'd have happily taken another role for less money to be able to go home feeling I'd really made a difference, instead of contributing to the ever-growing pockets of senior management.

I looked over at Clive, who was picking his nose, then Col, who was staring into space. What a pair of awe-inspiring individuals. I adopted my ever-pleasant tone, hoping to rev him into action. 'Hey, Clive. Do you have a life plan at all?'

'Huh?'

Pray silence, a literary scholar is here. Shakespeare would've been proud. 'Do you know where you wanna be, in ten years, say?'

Col's head emerged from a bland-looking book he was engrossed in.

'Err, probably where I am now.'

'What, here, at *T&T*?'

'Yeah, why not?'

Why not? 'Oh, I see. You must be happy here, then?'

'It pays the bills.'

Whether he was doing it intentionally or not, Col's head was whizzing from side to side as we spoke, like the crowd at Wimbledon. 'I've always wanted to write science fiction,' he said, interrupting.

I had no words.

'Me too,' said Clive.

I should have known. Try to be constructive, Barry. 'Have you written before?'

'A bit.'

'How much?'

'A couple of pages?'

'Doesn't sound like an immediate money-spinner to me.'

Silence.

'Colin?'

'Guess not.'

'I don't wanna discourage you, I'm just saying…'

'You're saying I'm useless. That I'm not good enough to write science fiction.'

'What? I didn't say anything of the sort. Where did that come from?'

'It's what you meant, though.'

'No, it's not.'

'Yes, it is. You haven't read it. You don't know whether it's any good or not.'

'Look, I'm…'

'Why are you dismissing it? Isn't it possible I have a talent for writing and you're pooh-poohing it because of a nasty stereotype?'

Someone was tetchy today. 'Forget I said anything.'

'Wish I could forget you.'

That was unnecessary. 'Yeah, well if I'd known I'd be working with two gobshites who smelt of piss I'd have never taken this lousy job in the first place.'

'I knew it,' Col said, 'you think we're odd too. You racist. You're just like the rest of them.'

Under fire, I backtracked. 'Sorry, I didn't mean that. I was out of line.'

'Too late. You've said it now.'

'Come on, I'm trying to apologise here.'

'Save it for someone who cares.'

'Fine,' I replied, 'I'm going out for a fag.'

Seconds after putting my coat on, the phone blurted into life. 'Barry Brooks?' I said, with a scowl to the other side of the room.

It was Laura.

'How can I help?'

'Barry, I've been trying to get you for a few days now,' she chirped.

'Yeah, sorry, I moved house so took a few days off.'

'Oh, congratulations. Did it go well?'

'It did, thanks. I'm more or less sorted now.'

'Good, good. Anyway, as you probably know, HR has been communicating appraisal results to all members of staff.'

I didn't know, as I never read the firm's bi-weekly bulletin. I deleted it with the rest of the crap that littered my inbox. 'Oh, yes?'

'I have your letter here. It's been sitting on my desk for a while. Feel free to pop round and pick it up whenever you have a moment.'

'Sure, okay, I'll be there in a minute.'

'Thanks, Barry. Bye.'

It was odd seeing her in person. I thought back to that dark day the year before, proclaiming my never-ending love immediately after calling her a series of ridiculous names. Things could have been a lot different had she reported my crazy outburst further up the chain of command.

She handed me the sealed envelope marked *private and confidential*. 'Well done. We hope you've had a good first year with us.'

That didn't bode well at all. Her words of encouragement filtered down my throat and settled in my gut, leaving me needing the loo pretty badly. I could only dread to think what horrifying information was written inside. 'Thanks very much, Laura.'

I headed back, my clammy hands moistening the paper. At my desk, I sat down, braced myself, and after shooting Clive and Col another look of contempt, carefully opened the envelope and began to read:

Dear Barry,

First of all, may I convey my personal thanks to you for your contribution, in what has turned out to be Tinkler & Tinkler's most successful year to date. This time last year, the Management Committee set numerous goals and objectives for the year ahead, and now, one year on, I am proud to inform you they have all come to fruition...

How dull. Part of me wished I still suffered from insomnia; this garbage would send those who'd had their brains altered so they were incapable of sleep, to sleep. More lines about vision, responsibility and respect followed, and I disrespectfully skim-read to get to the part I sensed would shatter me in two.

...It is my pleasure to inform you that your salary has been increased to £59,750 with immediate effect, and also, the firm's annual bonus payment of £9,467 will be incorporated into this month's salary. On behalf of myself and the partners, thank you once again for helping to make Tinkler & Tinkler an overwhelming success. Yours together, H.M. Tinkler – Chief Executive Officer.

I blinked repeatedly, like an armless man with something in his eye. Excuse me, what, pardon, hmm?

...It is my pleasure to inform you your salary has been increased to £59,750 with immediate effect, and also, the firm's annual bonus payment of £9,467 will be incorporated into this month's salary.

Yup, that's precisely what it said, but there was still something in my eye.
Were they mad?
What in the name of heaven, earth, land, trees and wildlife were they doing here?
Fifty-nine thousand, seven-hundred and fifty quid?
It had to be a mis-print. A big, sodding mis-print, that's blatantly what it was. I couldn't even count to that

number, let alone earn it. Wait, no, there was something else inside the envelope; surely a supplementary note telling me it was the first of April, with a smiling image of old man Tink underneath, a crudely-drawn speech bubble coming out of his mouth which said, *"Hey hey, you've been Tinkled!"*

I tipped it up and my pay-slip fell out. Ripping it open, I went straight to the figure on the bottom-right:-

Net pay (Month): £3,405

That didn't make sense. I checked the gross figure:

Gross pay (Month): £4979.167

That didn't make sense either. I got the calculator out and panic-pressed the buttons.

It wasn't a mis-print.

It wasn't anything like a mis-print.

For reasons known only to senior management, the pinstriped ferrets had huddled together and increased my salary by thirty-thousand pounds. Thirty bloody thousand crapping pounds? Did they have me confused with the Barry Brooks who worked on the fourth floor in a solid gold office, responsible for overseeing the entire friggin' world?

I got straight on the telephone to Laura again.

'Laura, it's Barry.'

'Is there a problem?'

'Yes, yes there is.' Should that have been my response? Should I have even called to question it? I lowered my voice to keep Dick and Dom out of the loop. 'Obviously this is between you and me, but my pay increase this year was a little more than expected.'

'It's been a good year for us, Barry. The firm really knows how to retain and look after its staff.'

'So it's not a mistake?'

She chortled. 'A mistake? No, not at all. We don't make

mistakes with something as important as salary details.'

I paused, unable to process anything she was saying.

'Enjoy it, Barry. You've earned it.'

Yeah, bye, whatever. Fifty-nine thousand, seven-hundred and fifty quid. How much was that again?

The dust settled, and four cigarettes later, it dawned on me. It was there as I walked back from Laura's desk with the unopened envelope, only the shock of its contents made me forget. I couldn't leave this place now. The salary was impressive to begin with, but now it was bordering on the obscene. It was more than plausible that I, Barry Benjamin Brooks, was the highest-paid person in the country - maybe even the world - for the role I was in. Market rate was twenty-eight thousand, I was on thirty before the raise. Now, I was pushing sixty. The firm was literally throwing its cash away. Which was fine, y'know, I did have bills to pay like everyone else. The added bonus being that if I was so inclined, I could also have paid everyone else's.

In light of that, how could I leave? The acquisition of wealth - the whole concept I'd abandoned in favour of making a difference - was now the dominant factor in my life. Was there a chance in hell I'd turn my back and walk away from almost sixty grand a year?

Err, no.

After another twelve months, if the pattern continued, I'd be earning a six-figure salary. Could I willingly up and leave with a delicious prospect like that on the horizon?

Again, no.

Even the great Lord himself, armed with a list of reasons to choose job satisfaction over financial gain the length of a super-deluxe bog roll, wouldn't have convinced me otherwise. Laura said I'd earned it; she obviously hadn't spent more than five seconds in the department since introducing me to Clive and Col. I hadn't earned it in any fashion. My entire day was filled with stupid amounts of nothing. I had no projects, ongoing tasks or continuous odd jobs that required maintenance; I sat at my desk, surfed the internet, checked my email, sniffed, farted and did lots of little things not connected in any way to doing work. Earned it, indeed, Laura. You stupid woman. I'd earned nothing – zip - but it wasn't for lack of trying. The overseer of our group, a bigwig, hooray Henry who hardly ever came down to check on us, didn't distribute ideas and ways to increase productivity. All he did was sit in his office, flout the firm's *no smoking* rule with his cigar habit and count the pennies he was raking in from a series of massive deals from wealthy clients. We didn't mean a thing to him. He wasn't bothered about us in the slightest, and in turn, we didn't evolve or seek to improve output.

I imagined what Clive and Col's reaction would be if we had to attend brainstorm sessions to maximise effectiveness. They'd be flummoxed; totally out of their depth. What about daily timesheets designed to let senior management and HR know exactly what we were doing during the working day in our ignored corner of the building? I'd have nothing to write down. Would going to the toilet class as a valid entry?

Thankfully, the chance of such things materialising was unlikely. A normal employee wouldn't have settled for it. A normal employee would have called a meeting of those responsible, explained the issue and sought a resolution to benefit everyone. What was the point in doing that? My salary was astronomical. Only ambitious people eager for a healthy pay rise did that kind of stuff. I didn't need to. I didn't need a pay rise. Didn't you read the review letter? What did I have to gain by trying? *T&T* had me by the balls.

All that money, each and every month, and all I had to do was come to work and sit down a bit. How mind-numbingly depressing.

FOURTEEN

In the middle of one of my frequent attacks of the morbid on the way home, I was counting the number of funerals I'd attended during my twenty-five and a bit years as a citizen of planet Earth.

Barry's Bleak Hour, as I affectionately nicknamed it, began at five o'clock. I'd been wishing away yet more time at work, half-heartedly surfing the internet for news stories I hadn't spotted during my previous rummage, impatiently waiting for the day to end.

There was never any good news. It seemed to me this country didn't thrive on inspiring developments. I'd rather have read about a dancing sheep or talking jellyfish than snippets concerning the dirge of society and their drug-related robberies, murderous instincts or road rage. What kind of impact does that have on the millions who pick up the daily newspaper or scout the web? Couldn't there be a divide between uplifting and soul-desecrating? A teensy-weensy little button you could click to block out the dregs? Was it any wonder one in four of us suffered from depression at some point in our lives?

After the bombshell that was my salary increase, I accepted I was bound to *T&T* until death. There was probably something in the small print binding me to them after the event, as well. At 5.25p.m. I was idly combing through a report on the average cost of a funeral - pretty gloomy reading - and started to plan my own farewell ceremony: type of coffin, music, the buffet/no buffet quagmire, but quickly got bored and resorted to a mental counting game instead.

The grand total came in at nineteen.

Nineteen funerals?

Most people only had the good fortune of attending four or five in their lives, unless they happened to work as a minister or pallbearer.

Mum, Dad, Grandma, Grandad, other Grandma, other Grandad. That's the standard, isn't it?

My grandparents on both sides were dead, numerous aunts and uncles had bitten the dust thanks to cancer and dementia, and for some reason, when I was ten, Mum and Dad dragged me along to celebrate the lives of Bob and Judy, two fairweather friends mowed down by a psycho drunk-driver outside their home.

Taking a ten year old to the double funeral of people the poor child didn't even know? What was the matter with them? Were they official mourners? Had they gotten wind of a Michelin-starred buffet, donned their blackest attire and turned up for exquisite pastries and the heavenly, mini line-caught turbot fishcakes?

Nineteen funerals.

One-nine.

The majority of them had been dismal affairs lavished with *Kleenex*, stifled whimpers and organ music. Uncle Jack's, on the other hand, had been a revelation from the minute we entered the crematorium and realised no family members would acknowledge our presence.

Tensions had been rising a week beforehand. On his deathbed, Jack had expressly stated that he wanted to be cremated, instead of having the traditional Brooks' burial. Dad's side of the family couldn't abide the notion of the deceased occupying an urn on someone's mantelpiece; it cheapened the integrity of the dead, or so they said.

When he finally bowed out, Aunt Ivy and my father sorted through his affairs and organised the memorial. Remaining faithful to her beloved husband post-mortem, Poison Ivy tried to persuade Dad to arrange a burial, regardless of his dying wish. She claimed it was an uncharacteristic request, probably said in a moment of senility. To compound matters, she also said he wouldn't find out anyway because he was dead.

That was nice of her, wasn't it?

She may have been the one who coined that verbal nonsense about cremation cheapening integrity.

Fortunately, and rightly so, Dad respected Uncle Jack's preference and booked the crematorium. This left Aunt Ivy and her close allies so enraged, they refused to fork out any money towards the send-off. When he found out he and he alone would be picking up the tab, my late father didn't say a word. Not one word. Ever the diplomat, I knew he'd wait until the proceedings were over, then deal with the fallout. A wise choice; it was Jack's day, and the issue of family politics wasn't high on the agenda of crises to resolve.

We weren't to know, but sadly, Dad's mentally disturbed side of the family would find the biggest spanner they could and whack it right in the middle of the works. I wouldn't have been surprised if the spanner itself was stolen from Jack's toolbox.

The day of the funeral came and we'd sat down in the crematorium as a three-pronged family unit, ready to pay our respects. The collective rendition of *Amazing Grace* passed without incident, as did the minister's dedication and prayers. I was starting to lose the butterflies, when the fireworks I'd half-expected were well and truly lit. Aunt Ivy decided to scrap the pre-planned order of service and approach the pulpit to say a few words. I winced as she spoke and looked over at Dad; his face was the deepest red I had ever seen and there was a madman's glare in his eyes, the thought of which still unsettles me today.

'My beautiful, beloved husband has come to the end of his earthbound journey.'

Cringe. Not the best opening line.

'He had been ill for such a long time, as many of you are no doubt aware. I feel a tiny morsel of relief now the pain he suffered so bravely has finally ceased.'

Yeah, right. It was slightly larger than a morsel, I'll bet. Jack was so frugal he had a bank balance that would make a Premiership footballer blush. Ivy now had access to the lot.

'Thank you all for being here and supporting me today. I'm sure Jack is smiling down on us all from the precious Lord's side in heaven, grateful to you all for making the effort to say goodbye.'

If she was embarrassing to begin with, the poisonous one was venturing into the excruciating.

'Life will never be the same again. In Jack, I have lost my best friend, my lover, my soulmate.'

A fresh batch of wailing came from the intellectually challenged side of the room.

'I sincerely hope, with the Lord's guidance, that he along with everyone here today can forgive my brother for not giving him the burial ceremony he'd especially asked for on his deathbed.'

The cries of grief and nose-blowing had stopped. Everyone inside the room turned to look at my father, including the minister.

'The Lord will deal with you on judgment day,' she said, pointing. 'You have disgraced this family. How can you live with yourself?'

Oh, Ivy, no. How bad was this? This was really bad. This was badder than Michael Jackson's *Bad* video. Feeling the burn of a hundred and fifty pairs of eyes, I hid my face inside my hands and looked down at the floor.

'He trusted you, Ian. He trusted you and you let him down.'

What a coward I was, planning my escape through a crack in the floor. I should have sat boldly at my father's side, sticking up for him throughout this public humiliation. Eventually, I looked up and stared at Ivy behind the pulpit. This wasn't a grieving widow pining for her lost love; it was a twisted individual, thriving on confrontation and recognition, disgruntled because she hadn't got her own way.

Dad was a sensible man, most of the time. He wasn't the kind of guy to lose the plot totally without provocation. I was more than confident he had the ability to diffuse this fracas peacefully, but Ivy's baseless insults continued. No man should ever have to sit and take such abuse, especially from a family member at another family member's funeral. Every nerve ending in my body was boiling with fury and I yearned for him to retaliate, for his own self-respect if nothing else. Seconds passed and all he did was sit there and absorb her venom. The disappointing, dozy minister didn't know where to look.

'You're a mess, Ian. We all know it. We've known it for years. How you had the audacity to even turn up today is beyond me. You're pathetic, you spineless idiot. Is it any wonder our parents hated you?'

I couldn't believe what happened next. I was sure I heard something snap in my father's head, like an elastic band stretched too far. Even Ivy knew she'd gone overboard with that last comment. He coolly placed his order of service on the floor and stood to his feet, smiling as he did so, which I'm sure pissed her off to intense proportions. I saw Mum grab his hand quickly, a show of solidarity before he spoke.

'Just who the hell do you think you are?' he bellowed. It wasn't a question he wanted her to answer.

'I'll tell you who…'

'Shut your mouth, you disgusting witch.'

That startled me. Aunty felt much the same and covered her mouth in shock.

'You love being the centre of attention, don't you, Ivy? Stood up there on your soapbox, in view of everyone?'

This was nothing. The best was yet to come. I reached over and took Mum's hand.

He addressed the congregation. 'Everyone, I'll let you into a little secret about Ivy, shall I? Take a good look at the woman standing in front of you. You are staring at the most foul and obnoxious creature ever to walk the earth.

You are staring at what the devil himself would consider beautiful.'

Nice one, Dad. A bit strong, y'know, but never mind. In the moment and all that.

'On numerous occasions before his death, I spent time with my brother-in-law and considered him to be a good man - a trusted friend. He confided in me, sharing his fears of death - fears he refused to share with his wife. In fact, during the last two years of his life, when the illness consumed him and he was at his most vulnerable, he didn't share anything with his wife, did he, Ivy?'

Realising she was no longer in the spotlight, Aunt Ivy did something I wish I could have filmed. It was so over the top, such a ridiculous plea for attention, it overshadowed every contestant who had ever appeared on *Big Brother*.

'You're lying,' she screamed, then ran from the pulpit and threw herself on to Jack's coffin, clinging on with one hand and banging her other fist on the casket's wooden lid. 'Come back to me, Jack. Please, come back to me. I love you, Jack.'

Everyone in the room had stood to their feet. The cries intensified and a couple of old ladies I'd never seen before fainted in the aisle.

'Stop the charade, you heartless fool.'

'Don't tell me what to do.' The echo of hollow wood bounced around the crematorium. 'You didn't know him like I did. You don't know what we shared.'

Dad ran to the front, effortlessly pulled her away from the coffin and threw her into the nearest empty seat. 'Sit down and shut up,' he shouted, directly into her ear. For a minute, I thought he was going to punch her out. 'Jack knew you were having an affair. He found the letters.'

This was brilliant. I had no idea she was playing away. Dad kept his counsel well. Ivy's faced bleached as she stuttered through a response.

'He knew you were only with him for the money, waiting 'til he died so you could take everything and start a new life.'

Busted.

Aunty was well and truly gobsmacked, the congregation aghast.

'Well I've got news for you, sister of mine.'

Oh, pray tell, Daddy dear, what is this news you speak of?

'A month ago, when you were off gallivanting with your bit on the side, Jack asked me to take him on a little trip.'

Respect, father. Play it for as long as you can.

Ivy looked up at him. 'What? Impossible. He hadn't left the house in months.'

Dad went on, ignoring her. 'Do you know where he wanted me to take him, sister of mine?'

Silence.

'He wanted me to take him to see Mr. Johnson.'

'What?'

'You know Mr. Johnson, don't you? Of course you do. He's Jack's solicitor.'

The crowd had no idea what he was talking about, let alone the scene he was setting. I doubt they could even have spelt *solicitor*.

'He spoke to Mr. Johnson about changing his will. You see, Ivy, if there was one human characteristic Jack despised, it was dishonesty. He knew you were screwing someone else, but kept quiet, clinging on to the futile hope you'd somehow come to your senses and right your wrongs. But you never did, did you? Every time he asked, you denied it. You couldn't even look your dying husband in the eye and tell him the truth.'

'You expect me to believe you? You really think I'd take your word for all of this?' I could see the spit flying from her mouth as she spoke.

Dad stepped on to the stage and stood behind the pulpit. 'No, I don't, sis. You've made your feelings for me pretty damn clear today. You can take it up with Mr. Johnson yourself. He'll be delighted to confirm Jack's authorisation to have *me* look after his finances.'

Incensed, she stood up with arms outstretched and ran towards my father, intending to grab him by the throat. Instinctively, I rushed to the front to help out, but it turned out I wasn't needed. As she was about to make contact, he lifted up his arm and she ran head first into his fist, hitting the floor a second later, spark out.

Dad had decked Aunty Ivy.

In a crematorium.

There were tiny birds flying around her head and everything.

Good old Dad. He never stood for any crap, not even at a funeral. That's one of the things I loved so much about him. Not that he deliberately meant to knock her out, you must understand, he simply raised his hands in self-defence. The silly cow didn't have time to duck out of the way.

She came to a few moments later, the beginnings of an impressive shiner appearing below her left eye. It was a minor miracle she didn't call the police and have him carted away to the cells on assault charges. Dazed, she sat still and allowed the minister to stammer his way through the remainder of the dedication, before leaving the building wobbling, mourners in tow. Mum, Dad and I stayed in our seats until the entourage left, before walking in silence to the car and driving home.

Predictably, we lost touch with Aunt Ivy and the rest of Dad's plebby side of the family after that. He never received a contribution towards the cost of the crematorium, coffin or minister, and worst, we didn't eat any of the finger food Mum had slaved over for the wake. Personally, I'd have loved to have seen *Round two: the food fight*, but there had been enough unplanned violence for one day. Consequently, I didn't even call and let Ivy know my parents had died. Word must have got back to her via the family grapevine, but there was no contact. Can't say I was too mortified about it. I never wanted to see her putrid face or listen to that coarse, *Berkeley Red*-induced laugh ever again.

I reached my front gate, conceding the celebration of my own demise would come a measly second in entertainment value. I'd be lucky if anyone turned up at all.

Walking up the path, cursing the decision not to have my parents stuffed, I saw Penny sitting on the doorstep.

FIFTEEN

'Penny?'

'Hi, Barry. I left my keys indoors. Would you mind letting me in?'

'Where's Miles?'

'At night school, and Teddy's working late.'

I opened the door to the communal hallway and picked up the mail. Amongst the pile, I saw the gas bill, water bill, phone bill and council tax bill.

All on the same day? Was this the latest government drive to send everyone below the bread line? Four simple steps to secure your own space in cardboard city? Having recently acquired a fifty per cent pay rise it didn't really concern me, but four bills? I'd have to wait a bit longer before getting those surround-sound speakers I had my eye on.

'You don't mind me hanging out at your place 'til he gets back, do you?'

To be honest, I did a little. It was my weekly *wallow in self-pity* evening, but I couldn't tell her that. 'Of course not. You haven't got a spare key?'

She smiled. 'It's on my keychain. Kinda defeats the object, doesn't it?'

'Guess it does a bit, yeah.' Politeness aside, who puts their spare key alongside their main key? I'm not being antagonistic, I just want to know. 'Don't worry about it, *mi casa, su casa* and all that. Make yourself at home.'

And that's precisely what she did. She went straight for

the lounge, leaving her black, high-heeled shoes at the door, sat down and put her feet up on the sofa. She was dressed differently to the other night; instead of the hippy look of long, baggy trousers and distressed tee shirt, she was wearing a tight, white blouse and smart, black trousers.

'You look very official,' I said. 'Important business meeting?'

'Job interview. Just something part-time for a bit of extra cash.'

I offered her some wine and went through to the kitchen to pour. I couldn't help it, but thoughts of Melinda preoccupied me. Penny seemed so nice; I prayed she wasn't a tapper. It'd be nice to have a female friend, especially after the saga of Beth and the aforementioned neighbour from hell.

The bottle was full, but I left it in the kitchen and told her there was only enough for one glass each. It was a precautionary measure to keep the drunken beast that may have been lurking within her at bay. Also, I didn't much like the idea of Miles coming home to find his girlfriend had spent the evening getting sozzled with a bloke she'd only met once. No man would ever be comfortable with that, even if they managed to convince you otherwise.

Penny was a full-time student - which more than explained her haphazard approach to organisation - in the second year of studying psychology at London Met. Knowing less than nothing about the subject, she did most of the talking. It was fascinating to begin with, but I found myself drifting off, only coming back to reality when she uttered attention words such as *sex*, *violence* and *criminal profiling*. Firing appropriate questions her way was unbelievably difficult, but it kept the conversation away from my vocation, surely a topic dreary enough to send her to sleep. As she was outlining the part of the brain which controlled long-term memory, I emptied my glass and looked over at hers.

It was still full.

Excellent. Keep talking, love, your beau will be back soon.

I so wanted a refill, but knew my plan would be rumbled if I topped up. Could I get away with finding another bottle I didn't know I had? As I mulled over the wine/no wine conundrum, she fell silent and looked over at me.

Damn. She'd asked a question. She'd asked for my take on something, but deep in alcoholic contemplation, I hadn't heard what it was. I did pick up on the inquiry inflection in her voice, but was at a loss how to respond. My mind replayed the conversation as best it could: she was jabbering on about the brain, human perception, then what? Maybe she'd elaborate if I didn't say anything. Taking the risk, I stuck out my bottom lip and stared upwards to make it look like I was mulling it over. I'm sure it made me look retarded.

'I'm sorry, I shouldn't have said anything,' she said eventually, clocking my dense expression. 'He'll be back soon. Forget it.'

It wasn't a psychological question, that's for sure. Who did she mean by *he*? Miles? Teddy? They were the only guys I knew who'd be back soon. 'No, Penny,' I said, 'my mind slipped away for a second, can you ask me again?'

When all else fails, be honest.

'Do you think Miles is cheating on me?'

Pause. What did she say? Miles cheating? From describing the cerebral cortex to Miles cheating? How did that happen? 'What? Penny, I don't think I'm the right...'

'Aren't there meant to be give-away signs?'

'Err, well, I'm not too...'

'Things have turned stale lately.'

Enough with the butting in, already. Oh, and by the way, too much information. 'Penny, listen to me. I don't think you should be sharing these kinda things with me. I'm not fobbing you off, but this is only the second time I've met you...'

'There's no one else I can talk to.'

'What about Teddy?'

She looked at me as if I'd just stabbed her beloved childhood pet through the heart. 'What? Miles' best friend? I can hardly go to him in confidence, can I.'

Good point, well made. 'Okay, what about friends at uni, or your parents?'

'Look, I'm sorry, Barry, it was a mistake. I should've kept my mouth shut.' Picking up her wine, she gulped it down in one and stood up. 'I better go.'

Now there was a good idea if ever I heard one. 'Are you sure?'

'Yeah.'

'But Miles isn't back yet.'

'Hmm, I wonder where he could be.' She was most likely picturing him thrusting between the legs of another.

'Come on, you don't know that. Why don't you try calling him?'

'I did, before you got home. His mobile's off.'

The choir of voices in my head told me to let her leave and not push it any further. I still had to be polite, though; I couldn't just say "fine, thanks" then push her out before she had a chance to button up her jacket. 'Where are you gonna go?'

'For a walk. He might be home by the time I get back, unless he's lost track of time and…' She stopped. 'Never mind. See you later.'

I let her leave and watched her walk down the street from the window. Minutes later, the doorbell rang. I ran to answer it, not before peeking through the spy-hole once more. It was Miles.

Shit. How do I play this?

'Hi mate.'

'Hey, Barry, is Penny here?'

He seemed chirpy enough. 'Err, she was, yeah. She forgot her spare key. She went out for a walk about a minute ago.'

'Oh, I see. Mind if I come in for a bit?'

Arse. Why did he want to come in? And how long was a bit? Did he want to check for quantities of wine consumed, or items of Penny's underwear she could have left behind?

I don't know why was I so nervous. According to his other half, Miles was the one having an affair. He should've been the one trembling in his super-cool trainers. This was my flat, damn it; my domain. I was King of this particular castle, matey-boy. 'Sure, come in. What can I do for you?'

He came through to the lounge and sat down. 'It's about Penny, actually.'

Sweat was forming. 'Yeah?'

'Thing is, I'm planning a surprise birthday party for her and wondered if you'd be up for it?'

A birthday party? A surprise birthday party? Act surprised, Barry; surprised, not relieved. 'Great idea, mate. When is it?'

'Next Saturday, at our place.'

'Cool, definitely. I'll be there.' Even though I'd done nothing wrong and had no reason whatsoever to feel guilty, I was off the hook. Off the hook for something I hadn't done. Even better.

'Fantastic, cheers mate.' He stood up and rubbed his eyes. 'I'd better go find the trouble and strife. I've hardly seen her in the last few days, what with all the planning.' He snorted with laughter. 'She'll be accusing me of having an affair next!'

I laughed. It was a loud one. It was too loud, but thankfully, Miles didn't notice. 'She went in the direction of the shop.'

'Cheers, pal.'

I opened the front door and he walked through. 'Oh, one more thing,' he said. 'Next Saturday, I need to get her out of the flat to put the decorations up, sort the food out and all that, know what I mean? Would you mind entertaining her here for a few hours? I'd ask Ted, but he's working all day.'

'Not a problem, dude,' I said, not fully digesting the

small print of his proposal.

'Legend, cheers, Barry. I'll catch you later.'

When the door closed, I fully digested the small print of his proposal. He wanted me to entertain his girlfriend for a few hours? How the hell does he expect me to do that? The crazy woman had only just stormed out after I snubbed her request for a confidant. A few hours? I'd be surprised if she came back at all. She must have been so embarrassed. If only I could track her down and explain: "Penny, it's okay. Come back and finish your wine. Miles isn't knobbing some other chick at all, he's out planning a surprise birthday party for you. Everything's fine."

Wrong, on at least two levels.

A few hours? Does that mean two, three or four? God, no, not five? Whatever the length of time, I'd be unable to let it slip about the party, as that would ruin the whole evening and possibly my face. I'd also have to avoid a discussion of any sort regarding her and Miles' relationship. I couldn't be roped into domestic affairs so soon after meeting them.

With a bit of luck, she'd bypass my place completely and go out for another walk instead.

I'd be off the hook again.

SIXTEEN

9.47a.m.

Waitrose was rammed. Hundreds of Saturday morning shoppers milled through the aisles, fighting over freshly-baked croissants and warm loaves. Didn't these upmarket royalists know how to sleep in? I only went for a bottle of whiskey and the newspaper. I should have gone to the corner shop instead.

9.52a.m.

I decided to get a crate of beer too. My contribution should have been babysitting Penny for an unspecified amount of time beforehand, but those who turn up to a party without alcohol are frowned upon more than *Superman IV: The Quest for Peace.*

9.56a.m.

It really is a terrible film.

9.57a.m.

I hate supermarkets. Always have. I hate what they do to people. I especially hate them during busy periods. Supermarkets can transform the most kind-hearted soul into the Antichrist in less than two aisles. All it takes is a clash of trolleys or someone picking up the last bag of carrots and all hell breaks loose: trolley rage, arguments, petty theft from another's groceries - it's a domestic nightmare. I could fully understand why so many shoppers chose to place orders online and have them delivered for an extra charge; it takes away having to navigate your trolley through a minefield of more trolleys. Also, if you choose to take a cab back, it saves having to push through people determined to take the first one that arrives - usually your own - regardless of what name the driver calls out.

Cab man: 'Brooks?'

Random shopper: 'That's mine.'

'Are you Brooks?'

'No, but that's mine.'

'This one's for Brooks.'

'I was here first.'

'You're not Brooks?'

'No.'

'Who's Brooks?'

'I WAS HERE FIRST!'

I picked what appeared to be the shortest checkout line, cemented my place in it and waited. A large fellow was standing one down, and without thinking, I rudely gaped into his trolley. In it, and I kid you not, were ten litres of full sugar cola, seven baguettes, six packs of bacon, eighteen eggs, ten packs of lard, enough cheese to feed the southern hemisphere, four bottles of red wine, three jars of mayonnaise, three bags of frozen chicken and mushroom pies, eleven (count them) bags of frozen chips and a small packet of lettuce.

My mouth was wedged open in horror. He caught me staring as if I'd watched that surreal videotape from *The Ring* in full and my seven days were up.

'Finished gawping?'

'Sorry, mate,' I replied, fearing a confrontation. 'Didn't mean to…'

'No problem, pal. Most people wish they could eat as

much as me without putting the weight on.'

He laughed. I laughed. Ha ha ha ha, relief. How refreshing it is when folk don't take themselves too seriously. There was I thinking a fat punch was coming my way.

'One thing's confusing me, though,' I said, pointing at the packet of lettuce: the one angel stuck in the middle of Satan's hoards, if you will.

'It's for my budgie. He got a bit sick the last time I gave him lard.'

More laughter. He got served, said goodbye and pushed his heaving wagon of cholesterol towards the exit. My turn came and the checkout girl was shaking her head, mumbling something under her breath.

'Morning, Kelly,' I said, clocking the name badge.

She was still looking at the guy. 'Fat bastard. Idiot's gonna have a heart attack pushing all 'dat shit.'

And they say customer service is dead. What was her problem? I was annoyed as he seemed such a nice man. 'Steady on. Each to their own, love.'

'Oh, piss off,' she replied, manhandling my items, 'and don't call me love.'

I stayed calm. 'No need to swear. And be careful with the beer.'

'Do you want me to serve you or not?'

How dare she, the glorified lav cleaner? He may have been a bit on the large side with a penchant for fatty foods, but it was his choice. There was no need for her to take her minimum wage frustration out on him or me.

I toyed with the idea of shouting for a manager, but looked at the queue behind me. It was growing at an enormous rate. My act of morality would be less of a victory for the use of manners and more an invitation to have abuse hurled at me from those wanting to pay for their stuff and go home.

Keeping quiet as she scanned my items, I committed her name and appearance to memory before taking my whiskey, beer, newspaper and receipt.

'I don't appreciate the way you just spoke to me,' I said in an official tone, walking away from the till. 'I'll be writing a letter to the store manager about you.'

She stuck her middle finger firmly in the air. 'Do what you want, twat.'

The cheek of it. I couldn't resist one final insult. 'Up yours, bitch.'

Unfortunately, my closing contribution to *The Barry and Kelly Show* was one I'd immediately regret. From further down the queue, two men with shaven heads, wearing identical tracksuits, broke the line and ran in my direction.

'What did you say, bruv?'

Kelly stood up from behind the till and laughed. 'Mistake, twat. You're thick as shit, innit.'

I could have been the only man in history to insult a checkout girl, when her chav boyfriend and even chavvier brother were in the same queue purchasing items of their own, or at least hankering after a discount. There was nothing I could do but face up to them and pray security split us up quickly. The two guys were prodding my chest, questioning why I had chosen to disrespect their *girl* and *sis* so cheaply in front of the whole supermarket.

'You'll regret this, blud,' skinhead one said.

Skinhead 2: 'You're fuckin' dead.'

Stand your ground, Baz. Do it for your own integrity. I put my shopping on the floor and uncharacteristically pushed them both back, one with each hand. 'Get your filthy hands off me, slags.'

Slags? Now there's an insult I hadn't used in a while. Applicable at that point? Could've been better, could've been worse.

Skinhead 1 didn't look happy. 'What the fuck, man?'

Skinhead 2 was equally insulted. 'Get the fuck off me. Who the fuck d'you think you are, *batty boi*?'

'I'm the one who's gonna take you both down if you keep pushing me.'

They both tittered and were well within their rights to do so. It was two against one. The odds weren't exactly stacked in my favour. 'You're a fucking dick,' they said, in unison.

'Finish him, bruv.'

One of them reached inside his pocket and I started to panic, expecting a blade or gun.

There was never a security guard around when you needed one. Enough time had passed for a small group of shoppers to gather round and rubberneck, so where the hell were they? I was about to get *mash up bad* by these common hooligans, and the guards were most likely puffing on a cigarette out back.

With time running out before he pulled out whatever was in his pocket, I bent down quickly and grabbed my bottle of whiskey. Kelly, the checkout demon from the pus-filled pit of Hades, or possibly Slough, was stood on her chair, encouraging them both to take me down, innit.

I got to my feet, bottle in hand, as he removed a knife from his pocket. Why did it have to be a knife? Why couldn't it have been a mobile phone or a packet of chewing gum?

I lunged towards him before he could get the blade anywhere near me, dropping the bottle with force on to his head. It smashed and sent jets of *Jack* flying everywhere.

I felt a twinge of déjà vu.

The chav dropped the knife and fell to the floor, as security finally made their way to the scene. The other guy, shocked at the sight of his mate face down in a pool of his own blood, surrendered to the guard immediately. Just when I thought it was all over, I felt something cold hit the back of my head, and passed out.

Kelly had swung for me with a bottle of *Lucozade*. It was the first thing she'd found after witnessing me club her boyfriend into next week. The bottle may have been plastic, but it was full, and the force she applied when swinging was more than enough to send me sprawling into unconsciousness.

10.47a.m.

'I saw what happened. I saw the whole thing.'

'One at a time,' the copper said. 'Name, please?'

'Barry Brooks.'

'Address?'

'Flat 10, Winterford Mews, 12 Vineyard Road.'

'Age?'

'Twenty-five.'

'Can you tell me what happened?'

I felt like my head was about to rupture. 'He had a knife. He was about to go for me.'

'So you struck him over the head with a glass bottle, is that correct?'

'Yeah.'

'It's true, officer,' the voice said again, 'that's definitely what happened. He would have been stabbed otherwise. I saw it.'

'Thank you, sir,' he snapped, 'can you let me deal with this?'

'The guy I hit, is he okay?' I needed to know. I was acting in self-defence, but didn't want to kill anyone.

'As far as I know, he's fine.'

Relief.

'Mr. Brooks, as a precaution, I think you better get yourself to the hospital for a check-up. This gentlemen has offered to drive you there. He says he knows you?'

I looked up and saw the fat man from the checkout smiling down at me. 'That's fine, yeah.'

'We'll be in touch. Please let us know if you intend to leave London.'

The fat man's name was Kev and he helped me up and led us out to his car. There was no sign of Kelly or the two thugs. I couldn't imagine such a well-respected supermarket chain allowing her to continue working there after what had occurred. As for the Krays, one was surely off to hospital under police guard, the other cuffed, on his way to the station.

'How are you feeling?' Kev said, opening the boot of his

car to put what was left of my shopping next to his.

'A bit shaky, but I'll live.'

'This city's full of monsters. No matter where you go, you can't get away from them.'

That much was true. What was the world coming to when you couldn't stick up for someone without the threat of being stabbed? I wasn't a wuss by any means, but the whole experience left me with a sour taste in my mouth. Knowing this country's judicial system, they'd be out in a few months, terrorising someone else who didn't happen to have a bottle of *JD* on them to double as a weapon. But what could I do about it? How could I change the system?

God bless Kev. I'm sure he had better things to do with his Saturday than run a total stranger to A&E, but I appreciated it nonetheless. As he dropped me off, I thanked him for his help, and although he offered to wait around, I told him I'd get a cab back home. We swapped numbers and I said I'd give him a buzz the following week to meet up for a pint. Regardless of what some might say, there were decent human beings out there; you just had to go out and find them. Most of the time, I couldn't be arsed.

1.26p.m.

After flicking through old editions of *Z-Lister Monthly* and making friends with a guy who had blu-tack stuck up his nose, my name was finally called out. Five minutes post-my name being called out, the doctor told me I had a concussion.

Surprise, surprise. The unexpected hits you across the head with a bottle of revitalising energy drink.

If I had any dizziness or nausea in the following twenty-four hours, I was to report back immediately.

How much do these people get paid? I could have worked that out. The entire waiting room could have worked it out. All he did was confirm my name, stroke my head once and flirt with the duty nurse. It was a complete waste of both our time.

"That's a lovely smock you have on" is not a good chat up line. It never has been, never will be. As a line, it couldn't dream of being anything but a poor attempt at getting your leg over. I hope he treated his career with a bit more respect.

It was also a crap smock. Regulation hospital attire, it was white, cream and orange. Who designed that? Are you seriously telling me a group of people got together and signed off on such an insult to fashion? Were they blind?

'Can I go now, Doctor?'

He wasn't even looking at me. 'Yes, yes, of course. Rest up, take it easy and remember what I said.'

Oh, I will, pal. *"That's a lovely smock you have on"*. That little gem will stay with me for some time. 'Thanks a bunch.'

He grunted back, eyes still on the nursey. When I'd gone, he'd probably tell her the smock would look better on his bedroom floor.

2.17p.m.

The cab dropped me off and I staggered into the building. Switching on my phone, it buzzed into action, telling me I had voicemail.

Message left at 9.47a.m.: *"Hey Barry, it's Miles. Just checking you're still on for this afternoon, y'know, watching Penny for a bit? Let me know, dude. Bye."*

Message left at 10.30a.m.: *"Barry, Miles again. Did you get my earlier message? Call me back."*

Message left at 11.27a.m.: *"It's Miles, where the hell are you?"*

Message left at 1.13p.m.: *"For God's sake."*

I called him to explain.

'I've been trying to get you for friggin' ages, where've you been?'

'Sorry, I had to go to hospital.'

The line went quiet. That shut him up.

'Oh, I see. Are you okay?'

'Some trouble at Waitrose. Got a knock to the head. Just a concussion, according to the Doctor.'

'Oh. Right. Sorry to hear that, mate.'

'No big deal, am fine now.'

'Err, well then. Err…'

Oh, Barry, put the guy out of his misery, why don't you?

'Am still up for tonight though. Everything going to plan?'

'Fantastic, that's great. Wonderful news.'

Calm down, man, it's only a party. I haven't given you a million quid or anything.

'Feel a bit cheeky asking this now, but are you still around to look after Penny?'

Oh yes, that. I still hadn't seen her since she bolted from my flat over a week ago, but I did promise him. 'Sure, mate,' I said, inwardly reluctant.

'Aw cheers man. Okay, this is the plan.'

Then, he told me the plan, and I'm not being melodramatic when I say that every millimetre of my body shivered. Not just my spine, or my arms or legs - everywhere. It wasn't a good plan. There were literally zillions of other plans in the world to top this one. Surely he was aware of the fact. Why on God's green earth did he choose this one? Because he left it too late and couldn't think of a better one in the time he had left.

He was going to start an argument with Penny over something small and irrelevant. They would shout and scream at each other about this small, irrelevant thing, until she stormed out of flat, looking for a place to cool down. As Teddy was at work, Miles was hoping she'd knock on my door.

It was by far the shittest, crappiest, most half-baked plan anyone had ever invented. Only spackmoids would create plans like that. He was a fully-fledged member of the spackmoid community. He was spackmoid-in-chief, to boot. Penny clearly hadn't mentioned anything to him about our conversation last week; there was no way he'd have thought up such a pathetic idea otherwise.

Who's to say she'll storm out at all? Who's to say she won't go to her room and cry uncontrollably instead? Alternatively, she could choose that moment to accuse Miles of sleeping around, which in turn would lead to a heated exchange about trust and commitment. Even if she did storm out, why would she knock on my door, having embarrassed herself in the same place a week earlier? It would make much more sense to leave the flat entirely, choosing fresh air over Barry's comfortable sofa.

My itchy feet got itchier. Why did I have to be involved in such a sham? The party was shaping up to be a complete disaster, but luckily, all I had to do was sit in my flat. Given the fact I was concust and had a headache approaching the pain threshold world record, I couldn't see it being too big an issue. If she came round, fine, I'd pop twenty aspirin and do my best to avoid the obvious topic of conversation. If she didn't, even better.

Miles thanked me for my help and ended the call. Why were some members of the human race so indescribably dense? What would their argument be about? If he insisted on going ahead with it, it had to be something non-serious, but serious enough for her to leave the flat. There were so many better plans. There was most likely a book entitled *Better Plans Than The One You've Just Had* sitting on a shelf in *Waterstone's* or a local library somewhere, waiting for Miles to pay a visit and have a read.

2.29p.m.

Raised voices began to seep through the walls.
It was time.
Quarrels were not his forte. If, by some unfathomable stroke of luck, he had been invited to join the *Question Time* panel, Sir Robin would have taken one look and discharged him immediately. While human nature dictates that co-habitation is bound to cause disagreements, one of those disagreements should not

140

concern an empty jar of oregano. Under normal circumstances, the lack of a particular herb in the cupboard should not be the catalyst for a war of words.

'Damn it, I wanted to cook spaghetti bolognese tonight. Where the hell is it?'

From what I could gather, Penny used the last of the oregano two nights ago for her legendary tomato sauce. As you would expect, her response was one of surprise. How was I hearing this so well? I had a cup to the wall.

'Miles, for God's sake, do you want me to go out and buy more oregano?'

'Why do I bother? Tell me why?'

'What the hell is wrong with you? It's a herb!'

'It's not just that. You used the last of it without telling me.'

'I can't believe what I'm hearing.'

Neither could I. Come on, Miles, think about what you're doing here. She was more likely to go to the shop and stock up on bloody oregano than pop next door to say hello to Barry.

'Oh, piss off, Penny. Piss off and leave me alone.'

Silence. I heard heavy footsteps and the sound of crying. If I'd spoken to Beth that way she'd have knocked me flat on my face.

'I'm going out,' she screamed, 'let me know when you've calmed down.'

'Whatever.'

The front door opened. 'Pussy,' she shouted, and slammed it shut.

I imagined Miles rubbing his hands with glee, running to the storeroom to bring out the party decorations, while she stood in the hallway balling her eyes out. I looked through the spy-hole and saw her. She had tears in her eyes and make-up was running down her face. She was absolutely devastated and my heart went straight out to her.

What could I do? Good intentions aside, his girlfriend was now heartbroken, numb and looking over the stairwell in a way that really unsettled me. She wasn't going to throw herself over, was she? That would be lovely; topping herself over oregano. On her birthday too.

I couldn't take it any longer and opened the door. She looked at me, ran over and threw her arms around me.

'Can I come in, please?'

'Yeah, of course. What's happened?'

'It's Miles,' she said, in-between sniffles, 'he's being a shit.'

'I thought I heard raised voices. Are you alright?'

'No, not really. Do you have any wine?'

We went inside and I closed the door. 'Sit down, I'll pour you a glass.'

My phone beeped as I was in the kitchen. It was a text message from Miles:

Cheers, pal, good work. I'll buzz you when it's time for the party

Although I was sure he was a nice guy at heart, he'd put me in a position where I had to lie. *OreganoGate* may have been planned, but her tears were not. What would she think of me when discovering the truth? What if Miles had gone too far and Penny refused to attend the party? Guess I'd have to wait and see how events unfolded.

She was drinking very quickly. 'I'm sorry to lay all this on you. I didn't know where else to go.'

I joined her on the sofa. 'Don't worry, you can stay here for as long as you like.'

'Thanks, you're a star.'

Was I? Really? Don't think so, sweetheart. I was a dirty schemer working in tandem with that *pussy* next door, that's what I was. 'Anytime.'

I filled her glass and she took two more big gulps. 'He's got to be seeing someone else.'

'Penny, don't…'

'Okay, okay, I'm sorry.'

After a few minutes, the tears stopped. 'So,' she said,

wiping her eyes, 'putting *my* relationship issues to one side, is there a future Mrs. Brooks on the horizon?'

'Not really. My last relationship ended badly so I'm taking a bit of a break. Don't want to rush things and wind up getting hurt again.'

She smiled. 'Best way. Take it nice and slow. The right woman will come to you in time.'

'Yeah,' I said, wondering if the eight bottles of wine I had in the cupboard would be enough. I couldn't let her get too plastered otherwise she'd be asleep before the party started. Bet Miles didn't factor that into his super-amazing plan, did he?

'I'm sure Miles will calm down eventually,' I offered, not wanting my love life, or lack of, to act as a conversational centrepiece.

'I don't care if he does.'

'You what?'

'I've had enough.'

'Huh?'

'I told you last week, and I'm sorry for leaving like that, by the way. I'm sure he's having an affair.'

'How can you be sure?'

'He's been so secretive the last few weeks - out 'til late, hiding things.'

'What things?'

'He won't tell me where he is when I call him. I'm finding receipts in his pockets from places I've never heard of. It's obvious.'

Receipts from party-organising places? Hiding things like a surprise get-together? 'Have you asked him outright?'

'No. He'd just deny it.'

I needed to calm her down, but she was getting tipsy and it wasn't helping. I finished my second glass and turned to face her on the sofa. 'Listen to me. You have to be sure of this before you do something you might regret later.'

'But the communication's gone, Barry,' she said,

grabbing my hand and bashing it against my leg to reinforce her point. 'That's the most important part of any relationship.'

'True, but you said yourself you haven't tried talking to him. Why not do that instead of waiting for him to speak?'

She let go of my hand and looked to be deep in thought. 'Maybe you're right.'

'I'm always right.'

'Yeah, whatever,' she joked, slapping me on the leg. 'Can I have another glass, please?'

I sat back, satisfied with my advice. I should have had my own column: *Love-life problems? Ask Baz. Tuesdays and Thursdays.* Could be a nice little earner.

Penny was staring into the television. It wasn't on, so I don't know what was so enthralling. She turned to me. 'It's weird.'

'What's that?'

'You're not a typical man, are you?'

'Meaning?'

'Meaning, you give advice. Good advice too.'

'Thanks.'

'I've only known you for a few weeks and I feel like I can tell you anything. You're a good listener.'

They were nice compliments to hear. 'Glad I was here to help.'

'And you did.' She was slurring ever so slightly. No more wine after this one.

'I did what?'

'Help. Most guys would try to take advantage of a woman in this situation. Argument with boyfriend, too much wine. Isn't there an unwritten rule when you mix those two together, a groping of the breasts must follow?'

I laughed. 'I must be part of the one per cent of guys who don't think women are there purely to ease our aching lust. As for breasts, they are groped by invitation only.'

'Smooth reply, mister.'

Yup, it really was.

She put her glass down on the table. 'I invite you,' she said, twiddling her chocolate-brown hair with one hand, and stroking the buttons on her shirt with the other.

'Huh?'

'I invite you, Barry.'

Oh, crap. 'Penny, no, you've had a bit to drink. It's not a good idea.'

'Go on,' she said, sticking her chest out, 'don't you want to feel them?'

After three glasses of wine, I'd have happily fondled Margaret Thatcher's. I was a single man, after all. 'Penny, stop it.'

'It's my birthday today. Did you know that?'

Did I? Was I meant to? Oh, damn my bad habit of getting into uncomfortable predicaments. 'Err, yes, no, no, I didn't.'

'Miles forgot. Can you believe that? My own boyfriend forgot my birthday. How would that make you feel?'

I didn't answer.

She leaned in closer. 'It can be your present to me.'

'What can?'

'Touch me.'

Oh big, sweaty balls. I was losing the battle and about to dive in. Common sense finally prevailed and I stood to my feet and backed away. 'Penny, Miles is next door.'

'Fine,' she said, getting up.

'Fine?'

'Yes, fine. Can I freshen up, please?'

Phew.

Double phew. She'd go to the bathroom, sort herself out and that would be the end of it.

I knew I'd done the right thing. She made a play for me, I said no. She got the message and left to compose herself.

Me equals no blame.

Penny was upset. She needed care, attention and a shoulder to cry on. I'd do my best to make sure she got those things, just not in the form of sex or any other kind of activities that involved rubbing and grinding.

I couldn't understand why she felt the need to come on to me when her other half was only a few meters away; she had everything to lose and nothing to gain. In hindsight, I should have said no when she asked for a glass of wine. I shouldn't have opened the door when seeing her upset in the hall, and introduced smut with that bit about booby invitations.

3.37p.m.

I sat, panicking on the sofa, waiting for her to emerge from the bathroom. What was taking her so long? She'd been in there for almost twenty-five minutes. How much time did it take for women to complete their toilet routine? Was she having a psych one-on-one with the bog seat?

Reluctantly, I decided to check how she was. 'Penny? Everything okay in there?'

'Fine. Be out in a minute.'

The flirty tone in her voice had disappeared. As I finished the bottle of wine and threw it into the recycle bin, the bathroom door opened and she made her way into the kitchen. Her face looked remarkably fresh. The first thing she did was give me a hug, following it up with an apology.

'I'm sorry, mate.'

Excellent. She called me mate. A great sign.

'I don't know what came over me.'

There was a joke there, but it was hardly the most appropriate time to share it. 'It's fine, don't worry about it.'

'I'm so embarrassed. You must think I'm a complete lunatic.'

I didn't. 'Don't be daft.'

'I just don't know what to do about Miles.' She let go and pointed to the sink. 'Mind if I grab some water?'

My heart was now beating its normal rhythm. Water would sober her up. What a splendid idea, Pen. You have as much water as you like. Give me a six-figure water bill, it really isn't a problem. I nodded a yes. 'I still think you need to sit down and tell him how you feel.'

'What if I don't think it's worth it?'

Personally, I believe if it's not worth it, then you have to walk away. Easy for me to think, less so to say out loud. I eventually did, after a few seconds, and it was met with a blank look of acceptance from Penny, which I didn't anticipate. I expected her to backtrack and realise losing her boyfriend would be too heartbreaking to contemplate. It was then I understood there was a lot more to this than oregano. It had been playing on her mind for a while.

I was on shaky ground, in a no-win predicament. Why did Miles have to bring me into this in the first place? What was wrong with a plain and simple party invite? A few beers and a stint by the buffet would have slipped down perfectly.

It was a mistake to go out to her in the hallway, but I always had a soft spot for crying women. I also dropped an unspeakably large clanger being so blunt when asked for my opinion. If God could have smiled down on me, I'd have asked him for an immediate change of conversation and a stress-free party that evening.

Alas, neither wish would come to pass.

'I better get back,' she said, glugging the water. 'Gotta face up to it sometime. No time like the present.'

What a steaming pile of dog mess this day had turned into. I almost got stabbed, spent unnecessary time in the hospital and ruined the evening ahead. Penny deserved a birthday party. It wasn't her fault Miles was a thoughtless pranny when it came to plans. For that reason, I had to make her want to go back. I needed to change her mind from *Miles is a complete dick* to *Miles is the most wonderful man alive*, but how? Pretend I'm gay and tell her I'll make a move on him if she leaves? Invent a beautiful lie about him asking my advice on how to name your own star in the sky?

'Don't go,' was my ground-breaking starter for ten.

She looked confused and I can't say I blamed her. Two minutes ago, I told her to march over there and tell him how she felt.

'You just said…'

'I know. I know what I said, but don't you think you need to cool off a bit first before going over there? If you face up to things with a clear head, the situation will most likely resolve itself peacefully. Don't you think?'

I had absolutely no idea what I was talking about. I was bound with a sense of obligation to Miles and the party, counteracted by my personal thoughts on maintaining a stagnant relationship. The six glasses of merlot had obviously weakened those psychology skills of hers.

'You should be a counsellor, you know that?'

Hmm, I'm not sure the course syllabus had a section entitled *How to Spot a Scheming, Vicious Liar at Five Paces*. 'I'll keep that in mind if I ever consider a career change.'

'Fancy another drink?'

What the hell; I needed one and she seemed to have stopped slurring her words. What harm could another glass do? 'Go on then. There's another bottle in the bottom cupboard.'

Which turned out to be another idiotic gaffe, because ninety-seven minutes later, in a multi-coloured haze of extreme satisfaction, I was lying on my bed, post-concussion, having just had the five most powerful and mesmerising lovemaking sessions of my entire life.

SEVENTEEN

5.47p.m.

'Well,' was all I could muster.

'Yeah,' was all she could muster.

'Yeah,' I added.

'That was incredible.'

'Really?'

She was gasping for breath. 'Oh, yeah.'

No one had used that word to describe my lovemaking skills before. *Great, cool, fab* and *again?* were common, if you didn't count Poppy, but never *incredible*.

Beaming in the afterglow of her compliment, I too was electrified by the experience. There was good, there was bad, and then, there was phenomenal. I, Barry Brooks, had participated in the most phenomenal ninety-odd minutes anyone was likely to participate in. I didn't care that I couldn't feel any part of my groinal area or find the energy to move, all that mattered was lying here with the woman who had comfortably installed herself as my best ever.

I coughed to clear my throat. 'I don't know what to say.'

She rested her head on my chest. 'You don't need to say anything. You talk in other ways.'

'And you call *me* smooth?'

Giggles. 'I didn't realise how alike we were.' She kissed me and held it for a few seconds.

'You're very good at that.'

'That's what I was gonna say. See how alike we are?'

She felt great in my arms; a nicer fit than anyone I'd been with. I wasn't doing it to boost my own prowess, but as I lay there, I drew comparisons with ex-girlfriends, trying to recall whether any of them had made me feel this good.

They hadn't.

And I wasn't just thinking about the sex, either.

What did that mean?

My heartbeat began to accelerate and she noticed. 'What's wrong?'

'What?'

'Your heart's racing.'

'Nothing,' I blagged, unsuccessfully.

She lifted her head to look my in the eye. 'Come on, you can tell me.'

I glanced around the room for an excuse, focusing on the clock. 'The time,' I said, pointing, 'look at the time. Won't Miles be worried?'

'Don't change the subject. Something's bothering you. What is it?'

'Honestly, nothing, I'm fine,' I said, more convincingly that time. 'I mean it, though, what about him?'

'Who cares?'

'You?'

'Do I look like a girl who's worried about her other half right now?'

Wrapped up in each other, our feet entwined, me massaging her scalp affectionately, feeling the warmth of our bodies together - no, she didn't. 'What you gonna do?'

'I don't know.'

'It's not really fair, though, is it?'

'I feel like going round there and telling him it's over, y'know? Getting out of his life for good.'

Was that what I wanted? It was too confusing, and everything was moving so fast. My gut started to twitch, a sign I'd grown to trust over the years. If my stomach wasn't happy with something, it told me by grumbling and invoking the diarrhoea directive. *"All hands to the pumps. Give Barry the trots. Let him know I'm not best pleased with this arrangement."*

'Let me stay with you tonight,' she said. 'It feels like the right thing to do, don't you think?'

I did think, which bothered me for a whole variety of reasons, but that was beside the point. My mind was focused on Miles. And my stomach. 'So, you're just gonna stay here? You're not gonna let him know you're safe?'

'Do you want me to go?'

Was there a right answer to this question? If I said yes, that'd be it - the end of everything with my new best ever. She'd go, never to return. If I said no - the truth - well, I had no idea where it would leave us. 'No, not at all. I don't want you to...' I was about to say *go anywhere ever*, but that would have freaked her out, I'm sure. 'Just let him know you're alright, yeah?'

She sighed, letting the moment carry her away. 'Okay, I'll call him.'

Penny slipped into her panties and went into the lounge to get her phone. I couldn't stop looking as she walked out of the bedroom. Her small, firm breasts and toned stomach caused my loins to throb once more. I was glad when she finally disappeared; inappropriate thoughts bombarded my head, and if I was confused when attempting to work out the technicalities of how to keep her in the flat as Miles did his thing next door, I was completely brain-dead now. I no longer cared about the party. I no longer cared about Miles and the hours of preparation he was putting in. All I wanted was for Penny to come back to bed and make me feel the way I had moments before.

She switched on the speaker and called him. 'Miles? It's me.'

'Penny, I'm so sorry about the oregano. I overreacted.'

'Right.'

'Are you coming back?'

'No, Miles, not tonight. I'm going to stay with friends.'

'I thought you were at Barry's?'

She looked at me as if to say *how did he know*? I shrugged

my shoulders blankly, like the foul liar I was.

'Yeah, I was, but I left ages ago.'

'Oh. Right, then.'

'You seem surprised. Did you really expect me to come back after you flew off the handle like that?'

I was finding it hard to concentrate, smiling as I tugged at her panties. She slapped my hands, playfully.

'Penny, I know you're with Barry.'

I froze and began to panic, losing my erection in the process.

'What?'

'I'm outside the front door. I can hear you talking on the phone.'

If he could hear her speaking in what was a relatively low tone, had he also heard the passionate grunting of our lovemaking a short time earlier? If so, what was he doing hanging around outside my front door anyway? Was he a peeping Tom?

'Oh, whatever, Miles, yes, I'm with Barry,' she shouted, in the general direction of the front door. 'Did you get that?'

'Just come to the door and speak to me for a minute, love, please?'

'Why should I?'

'There's something I need to tell you. Please, Pen.'

She thought about it for a minute. 'Okay, gimme a sec,' she said, before getting dressed and asking me to do the same.

There I was, struggling to pull on the garments Penny had recently ripped off, flattening my hair so as not to give the game away. Thankfully, she chose to speak to him outside the flat, which bought me a little more time. I went to the sink and splashed my face, putting the toilet visit on hold before checking my hair in the mirror.

I looked acceptable. Did I smell acceptable?

No, of course I didn't. I reeked to high heaven of passion, thrusting and sweat. It's one of those unmistakable smells almost anyone can pick up on. Even if they can't put their finger on what it is straight away, they can smell it. I only hoped Penny didn't reek the same way.

But of course she did. It takes two to tango, after all.

Out in the hall she was, listening to what Miles had to say, emitting the sweet odour of sexual emissions directly up his nostrils. I sprayed deodorant everywhere, fearing that within seconds, he'd be in my room, pinning me to the wall, demanding to know why I violated both his property and trust.

It was time for me to go out there and stand by her side. I didn't know why, I just knew it had to be done. I marched to the front door and violently yanked it open, only to see Penny with her arms wrapped around Miles, in what seemed to be a passionate embrace. When she noticed I was there, her face flushed and she ended the hug.

'Barry, can you give us a few minutes, please?'

A few minutes? Outside *my* front door? You want *me* to vacate my own space outside *my* front door so you can pash around in it, you hug-friendly, sex-mad… 'Err, yeah, sure,' I grunted back, 'be inside if you need me.'

My balls of steel deserted me once again. They took an unplanned, last minute trip around the world and left the rest of me wandering around the hallway trying to eavesdrop. *My* space outside *my* front door? Had I not a tough bone in my body? Occasionally, I'd hear an *Oh, Miles* or a *Miles, you didn't*, leading me to believe the party secret was now out in the open. I have to say she sounded extremely happy about the whole thing. You wouldn't believe it was the same person who was re-thinking her entire relationship moments earlier, wanting to stay with me because I'd given her the satisfaction she'd craved for so long.

Or it could have been an act; a deliberate deception whereby she'd endure the evening's events for the sake of her friends, then let Miles down gently come back to bed with me. That would be nice. I would like that very much.

It wasn't long before I found out which choice she made.

EIGHTEEN

6.15p.m.

There was a spark; a mutual attraction preceding our almost primal encounter between the sheets. Yes, alcohol did play a part, but it happened nonetheless, leaving me drained, but reflective. Outside, as they continued to chat about whatever they were chatting about, I was forced into time alone with my thoughts. It gave me the opportunity to be brutally honest about what we had done, and how I felt now the excitement had died down.

I had to be a grown-up about the situation. Penny was attached, and it didn't matter how mind-blowing our intimacy was, she was out-of-bounds. Even if she was *the one* - and I was nowhere near determining that - there wasn't a damn thing I could do about it, because she was involved with another. Back in the bedroom, swept away in the moment, I'd have packed a bag and run away with her if she'd asked, which was extremely out of character for me. Even the world's most emotional man, swept away in a series of moments, would have to stop, back up and question whether that was a good career move. What was this girl doing to me?

It was clear I was letting Stan, my penis, call the shots. To extend or to stay flaccid, to pee or not to pee should've been the highlight of his repertoire; whether or not to elope with a woman you only met two weeks ago was a big no-no. Bad Stan.

6.27p.m.

I could no longer hear voices through the door. Either they were talking quietly, doing some more hugging, or they'd pissed off into their flat without telling me. I couldn't bring myself to peek through the spy-hole for fear of disappointment. Eventually, I heard the click of the door as Penny let herself back inside. Miles had gone back to their place and I looked up to see her standing there, head bowed, looking feeble.

'How'd it go?' I asked. From her expression, I knew what the reply would be.

'You never mentioned the party.'

'It was supposed to be a secret.'

'You kept it well.'

I balanced myself on the arm of the sofa. 'I promised Miles. I didn't expect what happened to happen.'

'Oh.'

'I'm sorry, Penny. It's hasn't really gone to plan, has it?'

She tried hard to not to cry, taking time before she spoke. 'I told him I'd be there tonight.' Taking a tissue from her pocket, she blew her nose.

I wasn't surprised. 'Thought you might.'

'Are you angry?'

'No, not at all. Why?'

'Because of what we did.'

'I'm not an idiot, Penny. I know what's at stake here.'

'I'm so sorry,' is what I thought she said, but through blowing her nose and all the sniffing, I missed it. 'This is such a mess.'

I didn't reply. Instead, I tried to come up with a definitive spin on what I was feeling. If I could arrive at a firm conclusion regarding my emotional state, it would be much easier to say the right things and move on, in whatever direction that was. I could say with certainty I wasn't in love with her - two weeks isn't enough time to commit to something so strong - but could I have been falling for her? My actions in the bedroom seemed to indicate it was a possibility. Or maybe I was approaching all of this from a purely physical perspective, content I was finally getting some again from a woman who wanted me without any hint of blackmail or betrayal.

Nope. After weighing up the options, I still had no idea. 'So, you're gonna stay with him?'

She looked at me as a doctor would a patient when relaying bad news. 'For now, yes. I've got to.'

From the second she replied, whatever I was feeling became irrelevant. I could hear the voice of sanity in my head telling me to back away to avoid any heartbreak. 'I understand.'

'What else can I do, Barry?' she asked, aggravation trickling into her voice. 'He's gone to all this trouble for me, y'know? Sent out invites, decorated the flat. I'd be the world's most heartless bitch if I ran out on him now, wouldn't I?'

I winked at her. 'Yeah, you probably would.'

She smiled back.

'Pen, you don't have to explain it to me. Like I said, I understand.'

She sat down. 'God, this is so confusing. Why did this have to happen today?'

'It's my fault,' I whispered, 'I should've stopped it.'

'How's it your fault? I'm the one who asked you to grope me. And anyway, it's a two-way thing. I wanted it too.' She paused. 'I still want it.'

'You do?'

'Doesn't matter. Can't have it, can I.' She stood up and walked to the door. 'I really like you. What I'm feeling now, y'know, it may even be something more, but I've got to go back to him. It's the right thing to do. Maybe if things don't work out…'

'You can't say that. If you've made your decision, you've got to go now.'

'I do have feelings for you, y'know.'

Oh, feelings. Yes, I have them too. How are *you* doing

with the interpretation? 'It's fine. Like I said, I understand.'

She apologised and burbled into the tissue once more. 'The last thing I want to do is hurt you, you know that?'

'I know.'

'Come on, at least try to convince me.'

Did she want me to hire the red arrows to spell it out across the sky in multicoloured smoke? Even with my new wage and bonus, it was a bit out of my price range. 'What else can I say? I'm fine. I wouldn't lie to you.'

'Sure? We're good, then?'

'Yeah,' I said, but hadn't given much thought to the effect our jet-powered rocket humping session would have on any blossoming friendship. 'I just think we need to forget about today, for both our sakes.'

She nodded and took my hand. 'This afternoon was really special, but I have to go back and at least try to make it work again.'

Of course she did, I knew this. Miles had obviously said and done all the right things outside during their chat. Having seen her so upset and frustrated, he'd focused on everything she was unhappy with and promised to rectify it. She had done the right thing in giving him another opportunity to prove himself worthy of her. 'I hope you two can work it out.'

'Thanks.' She turned to leave. 'One more thing?'

'Yeah?'

'I completely understand if you don't want to, but it would mean a lot to me if you were there tonight.'

Oh, fartcakes, the party. I'd almost forgotten. And I'd already RSVP'd to Miles too. 'Err, yeah, sure, I'll be there.'

'Thanks, Barry. You really are one of the nicest guys I've ever met.'

And with that, she was gone. A few meters away, give or take a wall or two, Penny and Miles were reunited, leaving me to reflect on the afternoon's experience. I took a small blanket from the cupboard, threw it around me and dropped down on the sofa, allowing my head to justify the guilt I was feeling. Chances were the process would take a while to complete.

If I was to attend the party, I had to decide how to act to avoid anyone coming to the correct conclusions. Avoiding her would look strange, given Miles knew where she'd spent the afternoon. Teddy was most likely aware of this too, being his best friend, so there would be two people I'd have to behave impeccably in front of. Every inch of me wanted to get trashed and forget it all, but that would've been dumb. I'd no doubt spew up all the intimate details of the tryst, including the twiddly thing Penny did with her fingers, to all guests present, which would result in Miles sending me to hospital for the second time in twenty-four hours.

I would not drink to excess. Only one or two glasses would pass my lips, then I'd pretend my straight cola had a triple vodka in it. With a morsel of luck, Penny would do the same.

My phone rang as I was flicking aimlessly through the channels. It was her.

'Hey, just wanted to let you know the party's kicking off at eight.'

I could hear Miles whispering something to her in the background.

'Get off,' she giggled, away from the earpiece. 'Oh yeah, and Miles says bring alcohol.'

'See you at eight, then,' I said, before hanging up without a goodbye. Was there any need for the happy-go-lucky tone of voice? I could tell it was there to soothe the atmosphere with him listening over her shoulder, but did she have to call at all? Couldn't he have done it?

7.45p.m.

I was still channel surfing, on the lookout for a last minute glimmer of wisdom or inspiration from the *Home & Away* omnibus, polishing my prepared behaviour protocols for the hours ahead.

7.50p.m.

I took a shower, chose clean clothes that didn't smell of Penny, picked two bottles of red up from the kitchen and slowly walked down the hall to their flat.

8.10p.m.

I pressed the doorbell once. I was fashionably late.

NINETEEN

'Wahey, come on in, pal. How's the concussion?'

I shook Miles' hand and gave him the wine. 'Hey buddy, not too bad, thanks. Bit of a headache, but nothing life-threatening.'

'Cheers, mate.' He read the label on one of the bottles and put on a posh voice. 'I say, old boy, I cannot wait for the aromas to pleasure my nostrils.'

'That they will,' I replied, playing along. 'It's a mighty fine year and quite an astonishing grape.'

'*Oddbins*?'

'*Tesco*.'

He slapped me on the shoulder. 'Nice one, mate. Come through, let me get you a drink. Tell you what'll help the head? Lots a'booze. The more you neck, the better you'll feel, I promise.'

Not on your life, sunshine, I'm sticking to my pre-planned two glasses max.

'Show me the stash!' I replied. What a hypocrite.

Miles had done his best, quick slap job on the place, given the limited time and unforeseen bust up with Penny. Being a bloke, it wasn't tastefully done at all: multi-coloured, flashing lights were strewn wherever there was a plug socket close enough to accommodate, and hundreds of balloons with *Happy Birthday* branded on to them were stuck to the ceiling. It would only be a matter of time before some idiot climbed up, let one down and began the standard helium half-hour. To round off the cobbled job, yellowy-blue streamers were either hung or stuck to every fixture imaginable, including the microwave.

The microwave?

It was a total chav-fest.

All it needed was a stampede of youth with peroxide-blonde hair, imitation sovereign rings and off-white tracksuits, smelling of bleach, together with their happy hardcore compilation CDs to complete the theme.

Miles whispered in my ear. 'Look, man, thanks for looking after her today. I'm just sorry you had to play counsellor.'

'Not a problem,' I said, showing off my impressive improvisational skills. 'It's none of my business, but I'm glad everything's fine now.'

'Indeed, it is,' he beamed, and walked into the lounge to introduce me to unfamiliar faces. 'Barry, meet Paul, Kate, Alan, Sean, Adam, Jill, there's Graham and his girlfriend, Babs. You know Teddy in the corner.'

I smiled and said hello. Teddy winked and gave me an army salute back.

'Penny's getting dressed. She'll be out in a minute.'

My pulse rocketed. The mention of her name was all it took. What was going on? I was getting soppy in my mid-twenties. It was going to be a very long evening.

Miles threw me a can of lager and left the room to get Penny. I went over to Teddy who was studying the CD selection.

'Bazza! How you doin'? Heard about the concussion. What happened, bro?'

I told him about the incident in Waitrose and he burst into laughter when I got to the *Jack Daniels* bit.

'Can't believe you did that. Classic!'

'I can't remember what was going through my head at the time.'

'Great story for the ladies, though, isn't it?' He leaned in closer. 'Definitely one to get them out of their knickers.'

If only he knew.

'Anything decent in that lot?' I asked, pointing at the CD collection, pretending I cared.

'Mostly shite,' he laughed, brushing the curly-blonde hair from his eyes, picking one out and showing it to me. 'Folk music. Can't stand the stuff.'

This was going to be a short chat. I loved folk music. 'What's wrong with it?'

'It's so depressing, man. Poncey blokes playing guitar in the countryside, banging on about milking cows and divorce settlements? Nah, you need something with a beat and a groove.'

Reaching in, I chose a disc at random. 'How about this, then?' I asked, showing him a jazz/funk mix.

'That's more like it. Put that bad boy on.'

Someone tell me why I *put that bad boy on*. Even at a young age, I had such an embarrassing taste in music. What the in-crowd considered cool and of the time I thought was mindless trash, so to avoid swimming upstream, faked my enjoyment of this assault on the eardrums. It wasn't creative or genre defining; it invoked images of some drugged-up teenager, fiddling around with waveforms on a computer. It was nowhere near real music, played by real instruments. In a word, it was crap.

I was about to tell Teddy just how crap I thought it was when his head spun around quickly to face the doorway. 'Woah, bloody hell,' he shouted. 'Pen, you look fantastic!'

Oh my. Penny. She had entered the room. She was here, greeting her guests, but I daren't look. Not wanting to turn around and risk my cheeks flushing, I kept my gaze firmly on the CD player. Everyone else was whooping and cheering as she entered, and if I didn't follow suit sharpish - if I was the only one not drooling over the star of the show - I'd be ousted pretty quickly.

Prepare yourself, Brooks. Think about Uncle Cyril applying the hemorrhoid cream, face twisted in concentration. Anything to take your mind away from lustful thoughts of your best ever.

Head: Uncle Cyril, Uncle Cyril...

Heart: Penny, naked, Penny naked…

I turned my head to see what was wowing the room.

I shouldn't have.

Penny, naked, Penny, with me, in my bed, together, next to me, on me, kissing me, wanting me. Be gone, Cyril.

The outfit was so stunning, Valentino himself would've found words hard to come by. The black dress clung to her every curve. The low cut around her breasts left little to the imagination, with small, sparkling diamonds encrusted into the thin straps. The long, translucent chiffon material of the skirt made her look as if she was gliding through the air. It was all I could do to prise my eyes away. Surveying the room, I saw most of the men were having the same problem, girlfriends looking on in envy.

I waited for the compliments to die down and made my way to the bathroom to splash my face with cold water. Passing Penny at the doorway, I made eye contact and smiled. She saw me, but there was nothing there; no response, no emotion. She was clinging to her boyfriend, who, from the glint in his eye, was clearly thinking about ripping that dress off later when everyone had gone home.

Well, damn you, Penny. What happened to *it would mean the world to me if you were there tonight*?

I only turned up because of her. How easy would it have been to decline the invite and use concussion as the excuse? What a two-faced, heartless cow. Stuff the bathroom, I felt like thanking my hosts for a pleasant evening (which wasn't true, but it never pays to tell someone you've had a crap time at their party), saying my goodbyes and striding home to catch the Saturday night film.

I locked the door and leaned over the sink, studying my reflection in the mirror. For a second, I didn't recognise him. Who was this stranger?

'What happened to you? Is this really the kind of person you are now?'

'What's that supposed to mean?'

'Consider yourself, Barry, but consider others too.'

It was a valid question. What was happening to me? All I wanted was a quiet life. No matter where I went, trouble and heartache always seemed to track me down. So much shit had been thrown my way. I didn't always have control over events, but that afternoon, I had a choice: I should have said no to Penny, but I didn't. I caved in and messed up. Why wasn't I more careful? Why didn't I consider the consequences?

I prayed with all my heart I wasn't destined to constantly find myself in compromising situations, where someone was always in danger of getting hurt. Was the solution to sever all connections with the world, hide beneath the radar and shy away from human contact?

It was time to leave. This was a lot bigger than me; Penny and Miles were at risk too. There was also a large queue forming outside the bathroom.

Out of habit, I flushed the lavatory without filling it and opened the door. Sean was stood outside, cupping his crotch. I smiled as he ran inside, slammed the door and let out the most over-exaggerated sigh you've ever heard when the liquid began to flow. If I was in a better mood, I would have collapsed on the floor in hysterics. As it stood, I just wanted to be alone.

I went back into the lounge and spoke to Miles. 'Listen, buddy, I think I'm gonna call it a night. My head's still a bit fuzzy from earlier.'

'No, I forbid it,' Teddy chimed, bouncing over from his chat with a scantily-clad blonde. 'You can't leave now, man, the party's just getting started.'

'I dunno, guys.' Part of me was hoping for a reaction from Penny, but she was already chatting with someone else.

'He's right,' Miles said, looking at his watch, 'you've only been here ten minutes. We've got paracetamol in the kitchen. Go grab a couple, have a sit down and you'll feel better in no time.'

Was there a solution for all of life's problems in his

head? Normally, paracetamol did help get rid of headaches, but they were useless when it came to getting your head around a shag and snub scenario. Against my wishes, I followed him and Teddy into the kitchen. He dropped two solubles into a glass of water and added a shot of rum into the glass.

'Rum? I'll be on my back.'

'Don't be daft, it'll be a nice kick.'

'Doooo it, mate,' Teddy said, 'but hurry up, will ya? I reckon Jenna's a dead cert for me tonight.' He high-fived Miles and they both cackled.

Like an idiot, I waited for the tablets to dissolve and knocked it all back in one. He was right, it did have a sharp kick, but when I put the empty glass back on the table, I didn't know if I wanted to throw up, pass out, or dance the fandango. I sat down, hoping common sense could choose which one I opted for.

'There you go,' Teddy said, grinning. 'How does that feel, dude?'

What did he want me to say? That the guilt of boning Penny had now passed, along with my headache? That I was now fully restored and ready to boogie on down until the small hours? 'Good, I think. Yeah, that was good.'

'Another one?'

No thought required. 'Hell, yes.'

11.26p.m.

Four paracetamols and nine rums later, I was sat in a circle on the floor of the lounge, playing the game no house party would be complete without: truth or dare. One of many empty wine bottles was spun, and whoever the neck pointed at when it came to a stop had to choose one of two options: answer a question, truthfully, or perform a dare chosen by the one who initiated the spin.

By concept alone, truth or dare is one of the most demeaning, degrading and embarrassing games ever invented, but when all participants are drunk, it takes stupidity and libido to new heights.

After the pills, Miles and I stayed in the kitchen for a while longer while Teddy went back to the party to continue his schmooze of Jenna. Though initially unsettling, we chatted about football, music, hairstyles and comedy, before re-joining everyone else. Luckily, I managed to avoid referring to the oregano incident, and as the rum hit my senses, I relaxed.

Penny still wasn't talking to me, although she did manage a nod of the head in acknowledgement as we assumed the circle for the game. The *no alcohol* vow had been broken, my inhibitions softened, so I plonked myself next to her as we all sat down. Teddy sat down on the other side of me, Miles next to him.

What was I worried about? Breaking hearts and causing uproar? That wasn't going to happen. Drink makes all those nagging feelings of guilt and shame disappear. I was having a great time. Miles didn't suspect a thing and Penny didn't seem to care one way or the other. There was no realistic chance of her coming clean to him about her infidelity, so I was off the hook, right? I was drunk, enjoying the company of new people, and about to play spin the bottle. All cool. If I spun Penny or vice versa, we'd both ask each other tame truths, or dare either one to drink a shot, and, oh yeah, those pills had got to work. The pain in my head had soothed.

I was off the bloody hook!

Who cares if I had feelings for her? I've had feelings for people before, and they went away. What are feelings anyway? What good did they ever do anybody? Wayhey, where's that bottle of rum?

The game began, Alan kicking off proceedings. He must have had a wealth of upper-arm strength as the bottle spun at least twenty times before settling and pointing at Jess, a relatively sober latecomer. The poor girl appeared timid, having only been acquainted with one or two of us, before being forced to join the game. From what I overheard, she was on Penny's psychology course.

'Truth, please,' she said.

Alan, out of his skull, didn't pull any punches. 'Ah, Jessicah,' he slurred, emphasising the *ah*. 'Tell me, how often…' he paused, '…do you masturbate?'

Kate, his other half, tutted and slapped his arm. 'Alan, shut your mouth. Jess, honey, you don't have to answer that.'

'Yeah, come on, Al,' Miles said, 'give the girl a break. Why don't you kick off with something sensible?'

'No one said anything about sensible questions,' he shouted, above stifled laughter from the boys.

'Ooh, at least three times a day,' Jess said, out of the blue, seemingly oblivious to the personal nature of the question. 'I'm a single girl, Alan. We've got to keep ourselves entertained somehow.'

I reckon all the boys were instantly aroused by her answer. If I were a betting man, I'd have put my flat on it. Kate didn't look too pleased. I'm sure there was nothing in it, but the lusty tone Jess used to reply sent her straight on to the defensive. 'Shall we get on with the game?' she said, shuffling to get comfortable on the floor.

'I can't believe you just asked that,' one girl said.

'Maybe we should lay down some ground rules,' Teddy chipped in. 'We don't want anyone freaking out.'

'What's the point?' Alan replied. 'We'll end up asking people what their favourite food is, or film or TV programme. That's bloody boring.'

Everyone muttered amongst themselves, until it was decided that if a question was deemed too personal, whoever it was targeted at was under no obligation to answer. Finally, the game resumed and Jess whizzed the bottle around the wooden floor. I sensed it would land in my direction, so wasn't surprised when I saw all eyes focused on me, waiting to here what my choice would be.

'Yeah, Barry, come on, son,' Teddy said, reaching over to give me a high five.

'Truth.'

From her previous offering, I figured Jess was a bit of a

171

dirty girl. Anyone unfamiliar with a group of people, willing to admit to daily acts of self-love, the details of which true or otherwise, had to be a bit of a goer. Thoughts of hitting it off with her, followed by drunken, steamy, *forget about Penny* sex in my beautiful power shower flickered through my intoxicated subconscious.

'I'm Jess, by the way. Nice to meet you.'

Penny accidentally nudged my leg.

'You too, Jess. So then, what's the question?'

'I'm presuming you're a straight man?'

'Is that the question?' I asked, flirting a little, keeping one eye on Penny's reaction.

She nudged my leg again, harder this time.

'No,' Jess replied, coyly, 'my question is this: who, out of every girl in the room, would you most like to sleep with?'

Ah, the classic question. I felt Penny stiffen up next to me. It was the one question always asked at some point during every game of truth or dare, ever. I'd played it a number of times before, and not a session passed without some tanked up, sex-obsessed nymphomaniac letting this pearler loose on a much-suspecting crowd.

'That's not very original.' I winked at her, careful to take time before answering. With couples in the room, I didn't want to piss Alan off by saying I'd most like to hump Kate, though from the state he was in, he'd have probably suggested we all get it on with a liberal-minded goat if I had. 'Well, Jess, that's an easy one.'

'Really?'

I can't fully recall, but I'm sure after saying that, she licked her lips.

'To answer both your questions, yes, I am a straight man, and out of everyone here, I'd most like to sleep with you.'

It was the safest reply and she seemed to appreciate the compliment.

A third nudge from Penny. What was with her?

'Get in there, my son,' Teddy shouted, whoops and cheers coming from the rest of the boys. I didn't take my eyes away from Jess, dishing out playful punishment to her for asking the question in the first place. She crawled across the floor, politely ousting Penny from her position and occupying the space next to me. I didn't know what effect all this was having on today's earlier conquest, but if her nudges were anything to go by, she wasn't happy at all.

Tough titty, love, you made your choice.

She whispered in my ear. 'Wanna go somewhere a little quieter for drink?'

Score. Super score. Prepare yourself, power shower of mine, we've got company tonight. 'The kitchen?'

'After you.'

'Excuse us,' I said to the room, 'we're, erm, gonna get another drink.'

'Oh, really?' Miles said, with a wink. 'Knock yourselves out!'

I wasn't playing fair here. Jess was an attractive girl, but when I answered the question, it was said for effect, and didn't represent my true feelings at all. Penny was the girl I wanted, but you all know what happened earlier in the day, so I wasn't about to give her any indication I was hurt or distracted.

We stepped into the kitchen and I poured a vodka and orange for her, finishing off the bottle of rum myself. We sat down at the table and shared a bowl of nachos.

'So, Barry, what do you do?'

'Business researcher.'

'Sounds interesting. What kind of stuff do you research?'

'Oh, y'know, companies, individuals - it's really dull. What about you?'

'I'm a student. You know Penny, right?'

Oh yes, intimately. I nodded.

'I'm on the same course.'

'Psychology, right. How do you find it?'

'S'alright.' She picked up a straw from the table and stuck it in the glass, swirling the ice around. 'We didn't really come in here to talk about research and psychology, did we?'

'We didn't?'

'Well, I didn't. Why don't we talk about your answer to my question?'

She was gagging for it. Make your move, Brooksy. 'Fair enough, if you like, but you know that talking's boring.'

That's all it took. As soon as I finished the sentence, her face flew across the table and attached itself to mine. She shoved her tongue down my throat and roughly ran her fingers through my hair. Two or three slurps later, she pulled away, giving me back the use of my mouth. There was also a vague look on her face.

I was still catching my breath. 'What's up?'

She stood up and walked towards the door. 'Err, nothing. Look, I don't appreciate you treating me that way.'

'What?'

'I didn't ask you to kiss me. You took advantage of me.'

Seriously, what the hell was she talking about? 'Jess, you were the one who kissed me.'

'Don't think so. I was half-way through a sentence and you threw yourself at me.'

Good Lord, she was completely insane. 'What the hell? Are you mad?'

'Don't insult me. I'm being candid with you and you're getting annoyed.'

'I'm getting annoyed? You drag me in here after licking your lips, tell me you wanna talk about what I said during the game, now you're saying I forced a snog on you?'

'I'm leaving.' She opened the door.

I shouted after her. 'Wait, Jess, look, I'm sorry if you got the wrong idea.'

'Too late. You're scum, you know that?'

I may have had a few outstanding issues, but scum was a bit strong. 'Jess, please.'

'Get away from me, rapist.'

Right, now that was totally unacceptable. I rushed back

into the lounge to find every pair of eyes, except for one, gazing at me in disgust. 'Where is she?'

'She's gone,' Penny said, as the front door slammed shut.

'Dude, what did you do?'

'Nothing. We were chatting. She kissed me, then ran out. She accused me of trying to force myself on her. What's her problem?' My heart was racing. What if she was on her way to the authorities to accuse me of something sinister?

Penny stood up. 'Barry, can I have a word, in private?'

'Erm, yeah,' I replied, looking at her, then Miles.

She took me into the bedroom and I sat down on the bed. 'Penny, look, about today, I'm so…'

'Don't, hon, that's not what I want to talk to you about.'

'No?'

'No, it's about Jess.'

'Crazy woman? What about her?'

She sat down next to me. 'Didn't you feel the nudges earlier?'

'Yeah, what was all that about?'

'I couldn't say anything, not with her in the room.'

'Say what?'

'I invited her tonight, so it's probably my fault. She's got a bit of a reputation at college.'

'Reputation?'

'Rumours are flying around she's a bit mad.'

You don't say? Really? How could anyone come to such an unfair conclusion? 'What are you saying? She's done this before?'

It turned out Penny only asked Jess to the party because she felt sorry for her. During recess and after class drinks, fellow students had spread mindless gossip about her, mainly guys who had allegedly succumbed to her advances. Penny befriended her, thinking it was the work of spiteful males who didn't have a kind word to say about anyone.

'I think I know you well enough to believe you wouldn't

try something so perverted only yards away from a large group of people.'

It wasn't the most ideal situation, but at least she was talking to me again. 'I hope so. I was really scared there for a moment.'

'I could hardly say, "Barry, don't go into the kitchen with her, I've heard whispers she's a nutter", could I?'

'Guess not. You don't think she's on her way to the police, do you?'

'I doubt it, hon, don't worry too much.' She placed one hand on my leg, sending a shiver through my body. 'What was that?'

'What?'

'You flinched.'

'Sorry. You have that effect on me.'

No reply.

This was my chance to confront her about tonight's behaviour. 'Penny, why have you been ignoring me all evening?'

She took her hand away and walked over to the dresser, staring at her reflection in the mirror. 'I'm sorry. I hated every minute of it.'

'Then why did you do it?'

She turned back to me. 'For Miles. Because he organised this entire thing, that's why. When he told me what he'd planned, I couldn't just walk out on him. How heartless would that've made me?'

Very heartless, no doubt about it. She would have been viewed as the biggest bitch in the land; the cold, uncaring slapper who'd shamelessly boinked her next door neighbour while her boyfriend was hanging up streamers and making fruit punch.

There had been enough danger and excitement for one twenty-four hour period. 'Look, I'm gonna head home, call it a night.'

'You sure?'

'I'm sure. Thanks for the invite. Up to a point, I had fun.'

'Thanks for the honesty.'

'You're welcome.' I was distracted by her magnificent dress. Distracted by her in general.

'You gonna go straight to bed?'

'Yeah. It's been a long day.'

'You gonna think of me when you're there?'

'Yeah.'

'You gonna imagine me riding you slowly, screaming out your name? Telling you you're the one and that I wanna spend the rest of my life with you inside me?'

Hang on a minute. What? Wait a second... what? 'Penny, what?'

'Barry? You okay?'

'What did you say?'

'I asked if you were gonna go straight to bed. What's wrong?'

'Then what?'

'Then, I said it's a good idea. What did you think I said?'

'It doesn't matter. Sorry, I lost concentration.'

I asked her to say goodnight to the party on my behalf, before giving her a small kiss on the cheek and leaving the apartment. I must have been knackered, as there wasn't a single grumble from my private parts when getting close to her.

11.57p.m.

The only thing on my mind when I stepped through the front door was sleep. Exhausted, I climbed straight into bed and switched off the light.

TWENTY

The thud woke me instantly and I rolled over to check the time.

The alarm clock read one-fifteen.

There it was again. A dull bang, followed by a click that sounded as if it was coming from inside the flat. Half asleep and still unable to move, I listed all the possible explanations: a burglary in progress, the wind, a very big rat, a burglary in progress; whatever it was, I had to find the courage to get up and investigate.

I had to do this right away.

Climbing out of bed, I pulled on a pair of boxer shorts, reached into the cupboard to arm myself with…

A coat hanger? What the hell kind of weapon was that? Where was the baseball bat?

No time. The situation required immediate action. On tiptoes, I switched to stealth mode and made for the door. Reaching the hallway, I saw a darkened figure facing me. 'Who's there?' I asked, hanger prepped and ready to swing.

'It's me.'

I knew that voice. I knew it very well. 'Penny? What are you doing here? How did you get in?' I lowered the weapon, such as it was, and walked towards her.

'The door was unlocked. I had to see you.'

'Where's Miles? What about the party?'

'He's asleep. The party's finished.'

'Really? So early?'

She flicked the light switch down, and when my eyes adjusted, I was faced with her and *that dress* once more. Even in the early hours, she still looked as fresh as she did at eight o'clock. 'Barry.' She rushed over to me, 'I had to come over. I tried to forget about it, but I couldn't.'

'What is it?' The dress was mesmerising. Feeling her hands all over me again sent my body into spasms.

'I love you.'

Woah, lady.

'I love you and I want to be with you.'

Back up, please, back up now, Penny, before the diarrhoea strikes again. 'You what?'

'You feel it too, don't you?'

I felt something, that's for sure. After two weeks of knowing who Penny was and a smattering of intimacy, I couldn't put all my money on it being love. 'Why are you saying this?'

'Because it needs to be said. I made a mistake ignoring it earlier. I shouldn't have put this off.'

There she stood, announcing her affections to me. There I stood, sleep in my eyes, listening to her announce her affections for me in my boxer shorts. I felt considerably under-dressed.

'Pen, it's late. Are you sure it's you talking and not the booze? You know Miles is next door, don't you?'

'I know what I'm doing and I don't care. This time I mean it. After you left, I sat on my own in the kitchen, sobering myself up. Look at me, I'm not even drunk. My mind is clear.'

'On your own?'

'Everyone else was having such a good time. I didn't want to ruin it for them. By the time I sorted my head out and headed back to the party, half of them were asleep. The other half had gone home.'

I hadn't heard anyone leave. I must have crashed harder than I thought. 'Penny, I don't want you to screw your life up for me. I haven't got the best record when it comes to women.'

'What happened between us, you felt it too, didn't you?' Apparently, she was unfazed by admissions of my pathetic love life. 'Don't deny it, I know you did. You didn't want me to leave, I could sense it.'

Damn. Now she was thinking clearly, those bloody psychology skills had re-emerged. I couldn't lie to her. 'I don't deny it.'

'Then let's do it.'

'Do what?'

A door slammed, but it wasn't mine. Both of us jumped and turned around, even though I knew realistically it could have only come from one place: Penny's apartment.

'What was that?' She ran out of the flat towards her place and tried the door. It was locked. 'Damn,' she cursed, 'I haven't got my keys.'

'What's going on?'

Before she could answer I heard shouting coming from inside.

'Dirty bitch! Dirty fucking bitch!'

It was Miles. What was he talking about? Who was a dirty bitch?

As if the suspense is necessary.

The door opened again and he was standing there, crimson-faced, holding a suitcase. A bleary-eyed Teddy popped his head around the door and asked what the all the commotion was about.

He threw the case on the floor. 'There. Take it and get away from me.'

'Miles, what the hell are you doing?' Teddy said, yawning.

'Miles, what...'

'I heard every word of it,' he shouted. 'I heard you tell Barry you loved him.'

'What?' Teddy said. 'She what?'

'Mate, hang on a sec,' I said, 'it's not...'

'You, shut your mouth,' he said, pointing at my face. 'Come any closer and I'll make that concussion ten times worse than it is.'

Low blow, son. I didn't ask her to come around and stop short of proposing to me.

'Miles, I can explain,' she said, picking up a selection of clothes he had gathered together. It wasn't the time for humour, but four swimsuits? Come on, pal.

'Can someone tell me what's going on?' Teddy shouted.

'I'll tell you what's going on. I woke up and went to find Penny, but she wasn't in the flat. So I went out into the hall, and… well, you know the rest, don't you. You slept with him, didn't you?'

She didn't answer.

'Didn't you, you slag?' His voice echoed throughout the building.

'Is it true, Pen?' Teddy asked.

She raised her head. 'For God's sake, yes, it's true. I slept with him. Five times. If you must know, Miles, I'm in love with him.'

Miles wiped the spit from his face. 'In love with him? How can you be in love with someone you've only just met, you cheating bastard?'

'You're calling me a cheating bastard? If you must know, it was pretty easy. This afternoon's argument was the final straw. You made me do it, you idiot. It was you!'

'The oregano argument? I made that up to get you out of the flat. I'd never have done it if I thought you'd go next door and shag my neighbour.'

'Can't you see? The very fact that you needed to start an argument to get me out of the house says it all. Couldn't you have asked me to go to the shop, or arranged for one of my friends to take me shopping? Do you know Barry wished me happy birthday before you did? Our next door neighbour, who we've only known for a few weeks, wished me happy birthday before the man who supposedly loves me?'

'Penny, wait a minute,' I said, attempting to diffuse the tension, not overly pleased with her for turning his and Teddy's attention to me.

Miles cut me off. 'Shut up. How could you do this? I

trusted you to look after her. What kind of dickhead are you? You're scum, Barry.'

There was that word again. I wasn't scum, I was far from it. I'd made several mistakes in my time, but I wasn't a bank robber or murderer; just a guy who'd made a couple of poor choices in life. 'I'm sorry, Miles,' was all I could think of to say.

'You're sorry? I suppose that makes it all better, does it?'

'No, it doesn't, I'm just saying…'

'Get out of my sight.'

He was right about one thing, I did need to get out of his sight, before suffering a broken nose or punctured lung, or whatever torturous plans he had for my body. Things were threatening to turn ugly, and I just wanted to be away from it all. 'Right, I'm going,' I said, turning away. This time, I'd be locking the door.

Ten minutes later, they'd all gone back inside and I had no idea what was going on. Miles could have been slapping her up and the down the place for all I knew. He could have made Teddy hold her down while he beat her around the head with a frying pan.

What a horrific image.

There was a loud knock on the door. Taken by surprise as my mind had wandered, I opened it, expecting to see Penny standing there. Sadly, she wasn't. I didn't even have time to bring my hands up in self-defence. Teddy clouted me full in the face with a clenched fist. I hit the floor, stunned, the taste of blood in my mouth.

'You bastard,' he said, bending down to check if I was dead.

'Teddy, wait,' I pleaded, but his mind was made up. He landed another blow on my left ear.

Steady on, dude. Since when has kicking someone when they're down been a legal move? The second punch offended me more than the first. He was well within his rights to come around and have a go, I just wish he'd given me some kind of warning.

'You don't do that to your mates,' he continued, in

mono. 'That's not what you do.' Closing the door, he sat down beside me. 'Feels bad, doesn't it?'

'Coward,' I burbled, blood dripping on my new laminate floor. 'You couldn't wait for me to get up? You had to hit me again when I was already down?' It wasn't the best time to antagonise him, but my hatred of fighting, along with the fact he was the one having a go and not Miles, made me very angry.

'You don't deserve any friends.' He swung his leg back to kick me.

I rolled away before he made contact, moving my leg backwards and catching him on the knee. He lost balance and joined me on the floor, groaning as he fell. I crawled on top of him to make sure he couldn't inflict any further damage on my already busted face. Taking his arm and locking it between my own, I bent it back until he cried out. 'Do you want me to break it, Teddy? Do you?'

'Do what you want,' he replied. 'Break it, I dare ya.'

'Are you gonna calm down?' I twisted it further until the pain became too unbearable for him to argue. 'I don't want to hurt you.'

'You bastard,' he repeated, not proving to be very original with his insults.

Penny burst into the flat. 'What's going on?' she screamed.

'He tried to break my face is what's going on.' I was still holding Teddy's arm firmly behind his back.

Miles followed her, saw us both and pulled me off him, catapulting me across the floor. 'Come on Teddy, we're leaving.'

'What?'

'We're going. I don't want to see either of these dickheads again.'

'But, Miles...'

'Leave it, Ted. They deserve each other.'

He helped Teddy to his feet and they left, Miles slamming the door with unbelievable force behind him. 'Slag,' he roared, desperate to have the last word. I stopped myself from storming out there, picking him up and dropping him down the stairs.

Penny checked my face and made sure I was alright. Physically, I was. A small cut was leaking from below my eye and the ringing in my ears was beginning to fade. Emotionally, however, I wasn't too sure. I felt totally out of sync, like the world was spinning normally on its axis, but my timing was out, leaving me dragging woefully behind. She led me into the living room, sat me down and wiped the blood from my face.

'Does it hurt?' she asked, kissing my cheek.

'A bit. It's more numb than anything.'

'Teddy's not normally like that. I don't know what got into him.'

Great. I'd brought out a side of him never seen before. 'Don't apologise. I got what was coming to me.'

'That's not true. If anyone should have got hit, it's me.'

I wasn't an advocate for men beating up women, but she was right. She was the underlying cause. I didn't make a single move on her. 'Did you lock the door?' I didn't want Teddy getting his breath back and popping over again for round two.

She nodded, snuggling into me. 'Yeah, and I put the bolt across too.'

I felt slightly exposed, sat next door from a guy who clearly wanted more of my blood on his hands.

Where did we go from here? There was no going back to Miles now, so what was her plan? To move in with me or go stay with friends? Would we be effectively starting our relationship only yards away from her ex? The more I spun and re-modelled every available option, the more twisted it became. 'What now?'

She thought about it. 'What do you think?'

'Have you got any family you could stay with?'

'Yeah, but I wanna stay with you.'

'Is that a good idea? I mean, with Miles next door?'

'Okay then, why don't we go together?'

'To stay with your family?'

'I'm sure they wouldn't mind. I've got a sister in Edinburgh,' she said, 'but the country's a big place.' Her face came to life. 'I've got a great idea. We could go on a road trip! You can drive, can't you?'

'Are you serious?'

'What's stopping us? We're both young, free spirits. How exciting would that be? You and me together, driving to loads of different places?'

A road trip? Talk about rushing into things. I thought back to my conversation with the man in the mirror. I had a certain element of control over this; I had to be strong, rational, at the same time as considerate over her situation.

'Pen, I gotta be honest with you. I don't want to make any rash decisions and mess things up because of them.'

'Who says that's gonna happen?'

'We've only known each other a few weeks.'

'Isn't that enough time? It is for me. I know exactly what I want.'

'You do?'

'Yeah. I wanna be with you. It's all that matters to me now. In my mind, there's nothing else to worry about.'

Was it that simple? 'What about my job? Your course? Are you saying we should just quit?'

That's precisely what she was saying.

It was a plan she'd thought up weeks previously, only now had modified it to incorporate yours truly. Following a rather unsavoury fight with Miles almost a month ago, Penny went online and bought a one-way ticket to Edinburgh to stay with Kat. She changed her mind and got a refund when he apologised a day later, an offering of roses and bottle of her favourite red in hand to soften the unrest. It turned out to be yet another run of the same sequence: disagreement, storming out of the flat, guilt, remorse, flowers, alcohol. Once she realised the pattern was repeating itself yet again, Penny was resigned to leaving. From then, she waited for his next mistake, which came in the shape of an empty pot of dried oregano.

'Do you really wanna be stuck in an office for the rest of

your life?'

Being brutally honest, I didn't want to be stuck there for the rest of the week. 'Well, no, but…'

'There you go! Come on, it'll be so much fun.'

'Can we talk about it in the morning? I'm not feeling too good.'

She sighed and relented.

I tilted back my head and tasted more blood. Can someone tell me how agreeing to babysit a friend in preparation for her surprise birthday party brought me to this point? A road trip? What were we, American students?

The numbness in my face evolved into a deep throb and I held an ice pack to it, having popped another two tablets.

Six in the space of twelve hours.

If I went by the label - not that anyone did - I should have been unconscious, or at least well on my way to the land of snooze. Instead, I was wide-awake. Every time Penny asked me if I wanted to go to sleep, I let my head mould its shape into the cushion, only for the throb in my face to worsen, forcing me upright again. I was waiting for the pills to kick in before giving it another shot, using the time it took to give serious thought to her idea.

Did I want to pack a bag and see where the road took us? Did I feel the desire to say goodbye to my flat, city and job, to become free spirits on the long stretch of highway called life? Honestly, I was unsure. I'd spent the last two hours weighing up the plan's positives and negatives, at the same time wanting to crawl into bed and give my head overly needed respite from the waking world.

I wanted to be with her.

Yes, I did.

Drama aside, along with my initial qualms over the size of her breasts, I knew we would be good together. I could see us both riding out the current predicament, but my head still cautioned me over the rapid time it had taken for us to get to where we were. What if, perish the idea, it all fell apart? A week or so on the road, living in each other's pockets, and one of us could realise we'd made a mistake. Where would that leave us?

An hour later, the aspirin took effect and we went to bed. Cradling her in my arms, Penny was out quickly, and it wasn't long before my eyes grew heavy. I stopped worrying about whether Miles was trying to pick the lock to my front door, and gave into the need for sleep.

TWENTY-ONE

I felt so sorry for Mum. She wouldn't have thought twice about giving her life to ensure her son's happiness. She would have given Dad's too, without feeling the need to consult him. Such was the confidence she had that he felt the same way. If parenthood ever came knocking on my door, I promised myself I'd display the same love and warmth towards my children, because it worked so well when I was growing up.

I'd come home from school one day with a bloodied nose and torn uniform. The top-dog bully from hell had stolen my lunch money, thrown me into the school allotment and stamped on my head twice, all because I wouldn't share the last half of my blackcurrant beverage with him. Me and my squashed face made our way back, covered in sludge, to find Mum standing by the door with open arms. She scooped me up, tended to my injuries with a warm, damp cloth and a bucket-full of love and attention. I nuzzled into her chest, crying out the agony and humiliation of a public beating.

I vividly recall the way she spoke. Soft, gentle words flowed from her mouth, making me feel safe and protected. 'Come here, my baby, come sit on my knee. Let me have a look at you.'

'Th, th, there was this boy,' I said, fighting back the tears. 'He, he, he hit me and kicked me. Mama, it really hurts.'

'It's okay, Barry, everything's okay now, I'm here.'

'I don't ever want to go back to school ever again.'

'Shh, there now, sweetheart. Mummy's here.'

But come the following day, I'd be back. Complete with memento bruises from the scuffle, the previous day's events would be more or less forgotten – for both me and the bully - and I'd run into the schoolyard, join in with friends and their frantic game of army, before the bell rang and we all made our way into class.

It was all thanks to Mum. She had been there at the right time, said the right things and comforted me as only she could. At twenty-five years of age, re-visiting a fifteen-year-old memory was effortless. It was a moment I could never let slip away. How could I? It defined part of who I was.

But Mum wasn't able to help me now, as much as I believed she wanted to. I could see her, sitting above me on an elevated ledge, a crowd of people, mayhem in their eyes, surrounding it. Her lips were moving, she was doing her very best to be heard, but the message was lost on me amidst the background noise. I waved my arms frantically, screaming for her to shout louder, but it didn't work. She wouldn't do it. She couldn't do it. Why wasn't I able to lip-read? What was she banging on about that was so important? How much effort would it take for her to jump off the ledge and relay the information to me in person? Come on, Mum, you can do it. After three, jump. One, two, three: nothing.

'Why won't you come down? It's me, Barry, your son. Am I not worth it?'

I saw the figure again. A static after-image of something you may or may not see from the corner of your eye, but when you face it head on, it disappears. It felt shiveringly familiar. Keeping my head still, I slowly diverted my eyes to build up the best picture I could, before curiosity took over and the echo faded.

It may have faded, but it never truly left.

Then, something else. Another moment of clarity. The mysterious, vanishing figure from the corner of my eye was always there. I could sense him wherever my dreams took me, but when I awoke, my mind was wiped clean. It wasn't until he appeared to me again in my sleep, that the memories flooded back. How long would it be before the depiction of my mother and omnipresent shadow were erased from the canvas? How long before I found myself tumbling back towards what the waking world had in store for me? Screw it, I wasn't going anywhere. I was going to stay where I was, real or otherwise, until I found a way to reach her. The urge to decipher what she was trying to convey was impossible to ignore.

Every effort I made to climb up seemed to increase her agitation. I began to jump, higher with each attempt, and as I lifted myself off the floor for the sixth time, my fingers brushed the underside of the ledge, splinters digging themselves in with every swipe. I was almost there. A little higher and I'd be able to grab on and pull my body upwards to her. It took until the tenth go; I used what was left in the tank for a final leap, and my hand gripped on to the sharp wood. It wasn't enough. I didn't have the strength to hold on. I was about to drop once more, until I felt her soft fingers gently cover mine, giving me the chance to steady myself and pull the rest of my body up.

I sat alongside Mum on the ledge, looking down on a multitude of bodies I hadn't seen before, waving their arms and pleading to be heard. They were doing exactly what I was only moments ago. To each side of me were more benches, suspended in the air, occupied by more people. I was now a part of the mayhem I had observed on the ground. Is this what really went down when you were asleep? Was it a gigantic mass of people wishing to contact loved ones who were no longer around? Why were said loved ones perched on air-born swings? Did they have seesaws, football pitches and other park-related accessories up here too?

I looked at Mum, who was still bent over, as if unaware I had joined her. 'Mum, it's me. I'm here. Can you hear me?'

She turned around quickly and I saw her serious face.

'Do you know who I am?'

She must have done. She'd been shouting directly at me. I was about to start shaking her out of the silence when I saw her smile. She took my hands in hers, looked deep into my eyes, but still didn't speak.

'I miss you so much, Mum. Everything's falling apart without you. Can you come back? Can you bring Dad back too? Please?'

A solitary tear formed in her left eye, and with force, she pulled me close and sobbed uncontrollably on to my shoulder.

'What is it? What are you trying to tell me?'

The crying didn't stop and I could feel myself going too. As if it wasn't unsettling enough to be balancing on a park bench in the middle of the sky with your dead mother. 'You have to tell me before I wake up.'

The wailing stopped. She composed herself and looked me straight in the eye. Beneath and above, I felt the ground shake with increasing force. The bench began to sway steadily.

'If you're gonna say anything at all, make it now.'

I felt the wind pick up, its pincers prepped to grab on and propel me back to my bed. In a few seconds, I'd be conscious. Holding her shoulders, I shook them violently, but suddenly, everything stopped. There was no wind, no commotion below, the whole place and everyone in it was still.

I was in the final stages of waking up. I could almost taste the morning breath and feel the ache in my stomach informing me of my need to pee. Only split seconds remained before I was routinely sucked back to reality. Finally, her mouth opened and she spoke:

'Not long now, Barry. Be careful and take care, my son, it's coming for you.'

III

And more, much more than this, I did it his way...

TWENTY-TWO

'Pardon me?'

'I'm leaving.'

'Excuse me?'

'I said, I'm leaving.'

'Huh?'

Was she deaf? Normally, as a rule, a company shouldn't employ you to answer telephones if you're deaf.

'My letter of resignation is in the internal mail to you.'

'You're leaving?'

What an irritating human being. 'That's correct.'

'I see. You do realise you have to give us written confirmation?'

Funny, I could swear we'd just been through this. 'Which is what I've done, as I *just* said? The letter is on its way to you as we speak.'

'Oh.'

Oh? What did that mean? Had she processed this simple nugget of information, or was she ploughing through the dictionary, looking up the meaning of resignation in the 'P' section, thinking it was spelt with an 'F'? It was a huge conversation stopper. 'Have I made myself clear?'

'Erm, yes, alright then. Bye.'

The line went dead. Enraged, I was about to redial her number, but sensed it would be another five minutes of my life I'd never get back. Laura was busy in meetings, so I was stuck with Kelly, the new girl; the latest deaf, manner-less YTS we acquired by making the crucial error of placing job advertisements in *Spaz & Gurn Weekly*.

About to curse quietly into my coffee, the phone rang. I recognised the name on the display straight away. It was Marion, the head-honcho, queen of the Human Resources department, Laura's immediate superior.

'Barry Brooks?' I said, picking up the receiver.

'Hello, Barry. Marion Fruglesmith, here. How are you?'

She was using the formal approach, which I returned with ease. 'Hi, Marion. Well, thanks, you?'

Introductions aside, she began to grill me over my decision to resign. 'Kelly relayed the details of your telephone conversation to me, and I have to say, I'm quite surprised and shocked by your outburst.'

It wasn't an outburst, it was a choice made. 'Outburst?'

'Yes. I presume this is some kind of sick joke?'

'A joke?'

'Yes. You can't be serious.'

'I'm very serious.' Deranged cow, what was she thinking?

'You're telling me you really want to leave the firm?'

What was going on? Had Kelly infected everyone in the department with stupiditis? Was there a five-point plan doing the rounds on how to turn intelligent people into nonsense-spewing, brainless cabbages? 'Yes, I really want to leave the firm. Why is that so difficult to accept?' Frustration crept into my voice and I instantly reined it in to avoid a potential shouting match.

'You have seen your pay slip this month, haven't you?'

'Yes, Marion, I have.'

'This company has been very generous to you, wouldn't you say?'

'Yes, it has,' I said, rage begging to be let back in to my responses.

'So, what's the bloody problem?'

She swore. She actually she swore, at me, down the telephone, during working hours. It was totally unacceptable. 'Excuse me, Marion?'

'You're behaving like a dick, you know that, Barry? Any

normal person would give a limb to be in your position.'

That tipped me over the edge. Already seething from her failure to grasp simple instructions, I snapped. I didn't even try to control it. With a long, deep breath, I harnessed the world's anger into my tiny, unsuspecting throat, and spat it all down the line into the ears of this dopey, gutter-mouthed tramp.

'The problem, including you and your stupidity, is that in all my life, as far back as I can remember, I have never been as fucking bored.' I started to shout. 'The work is shit, do you know that? Absolute shit. And anyway, who the hell do you think you are? How many times do I have to say something before you idiotic cretins get it through your head? I am leaving, do you understand? I am leaving. I didn't ask the firm to give me so much money, I don't give a flying felch. My letter is in the internal mail, as I told that brainless retard earlier. I'll work my month's notice and then go, okay?'

Silence.

'Okay?' I screamed. 'Did you get all that, you stupid bitch?'

'Fine, you ungrateful tosser, whatever,' was her reply.

'Ooh, great comeback, Marion, well done with that.'

'Ungrateful arsehole,' she hissed.

'Smelly knob.'

I slammed the telephone down. The final insult was completely inappropriate, and didn't even make much sense, but I couldn't care less.

I could feel Clive and Colin's eyes burning a hole in the back of my head, but chose to pick up my cigarettes and head out for a smoke instead. I didn't have to justify my behaviour to those two. I'm sure if I had tried, it would only have escalated into another altercation about why I disliked science fiction.

Whenever I heard someone talk about his or her blood boiling due to a certain situation, I never understood the concept until that moment. The ability to think rationally had gone, and during the thirty-five minutes it took before

I headed back inside, I must have punched the wall ten times due to red-hot frustration. It sounds incredibly macho, but although my knuckles were blistered and raw, I couldn't feel a thing.

Tinkler & Tinkler finally accepted my resignation, and I even managed to avoid being dragged into the Chief Executive's office to explain my lewd discourse with Human Resources. It was a plus; they had every right to do it. I was just glad to be gone, and swiftly talked myself out of penning a strongly worded letter outlining my post-employment opinions.

What startled me was the reaction of Clive and Col as I was packing up my things. They dropped the attitude and asked me about future plans, where the trip would take us and how long we'd be away, without one reference to starships or matter/anti-matter devices.

Maybe they were just glad to get rid of me. As pleased as I was with their apparent social progress, my decision stood. I just hoped my replacement would be able to do a better job with them than I did, but honestly, I pitied the sad, old fool who took up the role.

Having said goodbye to Luke and Darth, I threw the rucksack over my shoulder and stopped by security to hand in my pass.

'Barry,' a female voice shouted, 'wait.'

I turned around to see Laura walking towards me.

'Marion told me you're leaving?'

'Yeah, I tried to call you…'

'I know, I'm sorry, I've been in meetings all day.'

I nodded. 'Kelly said.'

She took my arm and led me to one of the sofas next to reception. 'What brought this on?'

'You're not gonna go all Marion on me, are you?'

'What?'

'Never mind.'

'There's nothing I can say to change your mind?'

'Afraid not.'

She opened the folder she was carrying, pulled out a

business card and handed it to me. 'Here, take this.'

On it was her name, job title, a selection of numbers and her email address. 'I don't understand.'

'Between you and me,' she whispered, 'the meeting I was in earlier was actually a job interview.'

'An internal role?' I asked.

'Marion's job.'

'She's leaving?'

'Yeah. They're not announcing it yet, but you're looking at the new head of Human Resources.'

'Congratulations, but what's that got to do with the card?'

'It's just to let you know that if you ever change your mind and want to come back, give me a call or drop me an email, okay?'

Bloody hell, how generous of her. Unlikely as it was I'd ever take her up on the offer, it was a nice fall back gesture. A fall back, fall back, fall back gesture. 'Thanks, Laura.'

'All the best, Barry. Thanks for all your hard work.'

Hard work? She really had no idea.

We shook hands and I went back to security, pass in hand. Paul, the daytime guard – a short, ginger-haired man with bad breath and a three-day growth – looked up from his clipboard. 'What can I do for you, Barry?'

I handed him the pass. 'It's my last day. I've come to hand it in.'

'What? You're leaving?'

Not this again. 'Yep. Onwards and upwards.'

'I had no idea, mate. Nobody tells me anything.'

'Why would they?'

'I should be kept informed of staff developments. It's muggins here who activates and deactivates security passes.'

'Right,' I said, hoping he'd finished so I could leave.

'What do you think would happen if someone left the company without me being told, then came back with their active pass and stole computer equipment from the storage lockers?'

I didn't care. 'You'd get it in the neck?'

'Oh, I'd get it in more than the neck, son.'

'It only happened this afternoon.' I was surprised word hadn't filtered down about my tirade of abuse on the telephone.

'I see. They obviously haven't had time to send me the email yet.'

'Can I go now?'

'Wait a sec. Be patient.'

After tapping for a little bit longer, Paul froze in his chair. His fingers stopped what they were doing and his eyes glazed.

'Paul? Mate?' I said, waving my hand in front of his face. 'You okay?'

'Fine, Barry.' His reply was almost robotic. 'Nearly there. Just a few seconds...'

'Seriously, what's with the voice?'

He continued to speak with increasing volume. 'All done. Best of luck, Barry. Hope it all works out for you.'

'Why are you shouting?'

His eyes were still fixed on the monitor. 'Meet me by smoker's corner in twenty minutes,' he whispered.

'What?'

'Don't look at me. They're watching. Turn around and run. Run to smoker's corner.'

Who was watching?

'We're in the same place. It's too suspicious. Go now. I'll be there in twenty minutes.' His normal voice returned. 'Your pass has been deactivated.'

It had to be a wind up. What had gotten into him? Since my very first day, Paul had manned the entrance desk with excruciating formality. He never smiled and hardly spoke. The most I'd ever extracted was a *yes* or a *no* when quizzing him on the firm's procedure for organising a courier pick-up. Up to this day, our total word count was around ten; he had doubled that in less than a minute.

'Wait a minute,' I said, staring around reception for

these supposed inquisitive eyes. 'You can't just say something like that without explaining. Who's watching? Why am I supposed to run? Is someone after you?'

The whispering was back. 'Smoker's corner. Twenty minutes.'

'Why there?'

'Go!'

'Not until you tell me why.'

'Go!'

'No. I'm not moving until I get some answers.'

'There's a packet of fags in it for you.'

Twenty minutes passed and there was no sign of him. Rain started to fall, and after chain smoking six cigarettes, I was feeling damp and nauseous.

Twenty-four and a half. Normally, I'd have left by that point, but something intrigued me about the way he spoke inside. Rain was now dripping down my cheek, so I picked up my bag and started to walk away, only to feel an unsettling tap on my back. Paul was standing there, fag in hand, sweating and shaking.

'Mate, what's wrong? You look awful.'

'Cheers,' he replied, taking another drag. 'Look, I haven't got much time. I've gotta tell you something really important.'

'Make it quick, it's pissing it down.'

'You have to become aware, Barry.'

'Aware of what?'

'Aware of this, everything, the stuff around you.'

Was he on day release? 'What are you talking about?'

'I'm not Paul.'

Terrific. I got damp and smoked out for a certified nut-bar. 'You're not?'

'No.'

'Okay, I'll bite. Who are you then?'

'You might want to sit down for this.'

I looked down at the puddle next to my feet. 'I'll stand if it's all the same to you.'

'Very well.' He took a deep breath. 'I'm your grandfather.'

I couldn't hold the laughter in. 'My grandfather? Whatever you say, mate.' Sliding open my phone, I dialled *T&T*'s switchboard.

'Who are you calling?'

'Look, err, whoever you are, stay calm. Someone will be out in a sec to look after you, okay?'

'You don't understand,' he barked, grabbing the mobile and throwing it in the puddle on the floor.

To say I was angry didn't even skim the surface. 'What the hell? That's my phone, you idiot.' But what came next shocked me to the very core of my soul.

'Wilfred Benjamin Graham Brooks. Born, 17 April 1926 in Poole; died, 8 November 1992 in Hammersmith. Cause of death: heart failure.'

His eyes were focused on me through every syllable. Glued to the spot, I wondered how a chubby security guard could have so much information on my family.

'My wife was Emily. We were married for forty-five years…'

'Shut up,' I said, picking the phone up, 'that's enough. How do you know all this? Who the hell do you think you are?'

'I already told you. Now listen to me, because what I have to say concerns you.'

I wasn't in the mood for practical jokes, but this went one step further. It was sick, disturbing and made me want to take hold of his throat and strangle him to death. 'I'm leaving now, Paul. This is your chance to shut up and go back inside.'

'Barry, wait.'

'Fuck off. I mean it. Stay away from me.'

'You have to listen. What's wrong with you?'

'What's wrong with *me*? I'm not the one pretending to be someone else's dead relative. Do you think it's funny?'

'I'm not trying to be funny, I'm trying to get through to you.'

Another two security guards I didn't recognise appeared and took Paul by the hand. Resisting, he tried to struggle free, slapping one of them in the face. When the guard recovered from the shock, he returned the favour, knocking him to the floor with one punch.

'Get off me,' he yelled, holding his face, scraping his knuckles across the ground.

'What's the matter with him?' I asked.

'Nothing to worry about, sir,' one of the guards replied, 'he hasn't taken his pills today. You can go now.'

'With pleasure.'

The demented fool cried out to me one last time as I walked away. 'Your parents are alive. They didn't die in the crash.'

My last nerve was torn. I marched over, took a swing and landed my foot into his stomach. He squealed in pain and hit the floor again. 'If you say one more word about any members of my family - just one - I'll find you and kill you. Understand? Nobody makes a mockery of anyone I love, got it?'

'Take care, Barry,' he said, as they dragged him away. 'Not long now. It's coming for you.'

Then, I remembered.

TWENTY-THREE

Miles was not a happy man. He was on the edge, distraught, inconsolable, and I could more than relate to the bottomless pit of heartache he was spiralling deeper into. It was a no-win situation whichever way I looked at it, and the inevitable confrontations - the petty, throw away remarks we traded on occasion in the hallway - did little to comfort either of us.

I shielded Penny from it wherever possible, even insisting at one point we arrived home separately to avoid awkward moments. After all, we were shortly to leave to start our cross-country road trip; we wouldn't be making sacrifices forever. Soon, the three of us could move on and forget the atmosphere of pain and destruction hovering over our heads.

I never planned for events to pan out the way they did. I wasn't the kind of guy who took pleasure in wrecking someone else's world. Being with Penny did make me happy, but I couldn't shrug the feeling that karma would one day sneak up and tear a hole in my world, leaving me alone again in the arms of my old friend alcoholism. I took comfort knowing in spite of it all, I was a good man. One who had been unfairly portrayed as a fiend by the cosmic order. That would be my tagline. If anything, it sounded a hell of a lot better than *that bloke who stole that bird away then rubbed her ex's face in it by moving her in next door to where she used to live with him*. It was less of a mouthful too.

On a more uplifting note, there were other aspects of my

life less depressing. I'd left the corporate day to day with a minimum amount of hassle, my bank balance was very healthy and a foxy woman wanted to spend a lot of time with me. It wasn't hell, by any description.

What I did find troubling was Penny's decision to quit uni. She gave it a lot of thought, coming to the conclusion Travelodging it with a car and me was exactly what she wanted. If she felt the urge, she could always revisit the course later.

It had been a week since I walked out of *Tinkler & Tinkler*. My P45 and various items of tax-related information arrived - none of which I read or cared that much about - so I stuffed the papers into the same drawer as Laura's business card, allowing my turgid experiences of the company to pour out of my head.

During quiet moments, I'd smile to myself when thinking about my dramatic escape. Only a few months ago, I firmly believed I'd be there forever, cashing the gigantic pay slip each month and enduring the mundane pace it offered. Worst of all, I was probably getting one step closer to caving into Clive and Col's persistence and actually watching an episode of *Star Trek*. I had flashes of being in fancy dress, accompanying the brothers' geek to a science fiction convention. I'd stand in line for hours on end, waiting for an autograph from my favourite actor, then after obtaining the much-anticipated scribble, would run across the auditorium like an electrocuted pig on speed, waving it around in front of three-hundred other mentalists, eager to get it framed and stuck on my living room wall.

It was a lucky escape.

Now, I'd crossed over into normality again. I had a girlfriend, and as long as I did, I could never be the winner of Sci-Fi Magazine's *Dalek Costume of the Year* award.

It was just after seven o'clock and Penny was on the telephone to her sister. She was letting her know we'd most likely be up for a visit in the next few weeks, and told her to prepare the spare room. Kat had passed on the news that she was pregnant, and after the excitement died down, I could tell she was getting a grilling over the Miles fiasco. I could only hear Penny's side, but presumed it went something like this:

'He's amazing, Kat, he's everything that Miles isn't.'

'Are you sure? He's not a psycho killer or anything?'

'No, not at all. I'm happy.'

'Have you checked under the bed for knives or nipple clamps?'

'No. Nothing like that.'

'Rats and tubes?'

'Don't be silly.'

'Glad to hear it.'

'Do you want to speak to him?'

Don't you hate it when people do that? Automatically assume you want to speak to a total stranger on the phone?

'He's here, hang on.' She cupped the receiver as I was shaking my head. 'Come on, Barry, she's really nice. She wants to say hello.'

I pleaded with her, but she turned away, holding the phone in the air. Miffed, I took it under protest and cleared my throat. 'Hello?'

A soft Scottish lilt flew down the line. 'Barry! I'm Kat, Penny's sister. How are you?'

She sounded very friendly. 'Hi, Kat. Yeah, I'm well. Nice to finally speak to you. I hear congratulations are in order?'

'Yes, of course, thanks. I hope you're looking after my little sis?'

'Always,' I replied, the nervousness fading, 'she's pretty amazing.'

'Glad to hear it. Look, Barry, I didn't want to say anything to her, but I'm glad she's found someone she's happy with. I never liked that Miles, y'know.'

'No?'

'Something about him didn't sit right with me, but from what she says, you sound great.'

Penny nudged my shoulder, a silent inquiry as to why I had a beaming smile on my face.

'Well, I'm looking forward to meeting you in a few weeks.'

'You too, hen.'

Hen? Is it customary in Scotland to liken those you're fond of to poultry? 'Bye, Kat.'

'Ooh, one more thing before you go.' Then, it came. It came with venom. 'Do anything to hurt her and you'll be dealing with me.'

If she'd said it playfully, I'd have understood, but she didn't. She practically spat it out, which I wasn't expecting. My smirk disappeared. 'I don't think I'll be doing that, Kat.'

'Then all's well,' she said. 'Put Penny back on, will you?'

'Err, yeah, here she is.' Distracted, I gave the phone back and sat down, waiting for the call to end. What was that last bit about? It was a bit more than a friendly warning, that's for sure.

They said their goodbyes. Penny sat down in the chair opposite me, idly flicking through a magazine. 'What were you smiling about? What did she say?'

Should I have said anything? Was it worth it? 'She told me to treat you right, or else.'

She sniggered. 'Typical Kat.'

'Is it?'

'What?'

'Is it typical Kat? She didn't say it in a jokey way. She sounded almost...'

'Almost what?'

'Psychotic?'

'That's just Kat. Looking out for me like she always does.'

Penny's attempt to laugh it off didn't convince me. 'You sure?'

'Course I'm sure.'

'Really?'

'Yeah.'

'Pen, look, is there something you're not telling me? I'd really like to know if there is.'

'Nothing, honey.'

'Yeah? Look me in the eye and say that.'

She wouldn't.

'Penny?'

She closed the magazine and moved on to the floor. It took her a few seconds, but she did finally look at me. 'I was kinda hoping I wouldn't have to tell you this so soon.'

I knew it. 'What?'

'About a year ago, when Miles and I went to visit, something happened.'

Pause. Talk about dangling the bait. 'What happened?'

'Well,' she let out a long breath, as if about to read the Bible aloud in one sitting, 'we went up to stay with her one weekend. On the Saturday night, I went out with Kat and some of her friends, and Miles hooked up with one of his mates who lived locally. It got to about ten and Kat wasn't feeling too well. She decided to catch a cab home. When she got there, she caught Miles and another woman in her bed.'

'You what?'

'Miles was using her bed to get his rocks off.'

'He cheated on you?'

'Yeah. Kat kicked the girl out and started laying into him. She actually gave him a couple of pretty decent black eyes.'

'What a twat,' I muttered. 'I'm really sorry, but I have to ask: why the hell did you stay with him after that?'

She looked uncomfortable. Maybe I should have kept my mouth shut. 'I wasn't gonna,' she replied, biting her lip. 'In fact, I stayed up there for a bit and he came back to London, but all the time he was calling, apologising, promising it was a one-off and that he'd never do it again. So, I did my best to forgive him and came home. It all started to go downhill from there.'

What a cretin. Nothing but a scummy, two-faced no hoper. 'So now, Kat hates Miles?'

'You could say that. She wouldn't come visit because of what happened. She told me the next time I went back up to see her, he wasn't invited.'

'I don't blame her.'

'That's not the worst of it, though.'

'There's more?' This was turning into an episode of *Springer*.

'The girl she caught him with was my other sister, Shaz.'

A few years ago, Shaz, the oldest of the three, started to date a chap her family didn't much like. They sensed he was a bit of a dodgy character - drug running and pointless acts of violence all part of his repertoire - but she refused to listen, completely besotted with him. When he found out about the family's disapproval, he threatened Penny's father in his own home with a crowbar. He told him if anyone interfered with their plans to be together, put simply, he'd do some of his trademark violence and dispose of them in the River Clyde. Undeterred, Dad told Shaz about it, thinking direct threats against him would open her eyes to the kind of man she was with.

Surprisingly, it didn't.

Instead, she went further on to the defensive. She refused to speak to anyone, choosing life with him over those who loved her. The day finally came when Shaz caught *Nobby Kneecapper* with lipstick on his collar, having bedded yet another broad - one of hundreds - behind her back.

But the prodigal daughter didn't return.

She despised the thought of crawling home and admitting the errors of her lifestyle choices. She severed all ties with Mum, Dad, Penny and Kat, continuing the spat whenever and wherever she had the opportunity. At one point, she even blamed her own father for driving a wedge between them. Imagine her glee on finding out the man she had pulled in a seedy, backstreet club one night was dating her estranged little sister. Picture the look on her face when an outrageously drunk Miles didn't even have the common sense to choose a neutral venue for their sordid affair. She must have thought it was Christmas, her birthday and another Christmas, all rolled into one.

I offered my opinions and comments as she continued with the story, adding supportive noises of agreement where appropriate. Veering off topic and on to fidelity in general, I realised it was the first serious discussion I'd had with Penny unrelated to the break-up with Miles and current relationship with me. It felt like we were getting to know each other better. My half-conscious fear of running out of things to say on the road trip and accepting we had nothing in common began to steadily fade. Maybe we could be in it for the long term. Maybe I was steadily falling in love with this girl. Maybe she was *the one*. 'Well, I can safely say I'm never gonna behave that way with you.'

'I know, baby. You're completely different to him.'

'Yes, I am.'

'Anyway, I was thinking,' she said, changing the subject, 'we should start having a look around for a cheap car.'

'Definitely.' Yeah, money's in abundance, let's get a brand-new *Porsche*.

'We could probably pick something up for a grand or so,' she replied, bringing me back to earth.

On second thoughts, maybe not a *Porsche*. 'Fancy a quick drink down the pub? I could pop into Sunil's for the *FreeAds* on the way back?'

She leaned over a planted a kiss on my lips. 'Done deal, Mr. Brooks, I could murder a G&T.'

TWENTY-FOUR

'Barry Brooks, are you drunk?'

I was. I was totally annihilated. 'Me? Nooooo, no, no. I'm not *junk*, you cheeky lady,' I said, staggering aimlessly across the pavement.

'Yep. I think you're a bit drunk.'

'Nope, no way, no, no, I am absolutely fine. How dare you imply such an un...' Pause. 'A false... a non-truth?'

A quick gin and tonic in the pub became a drawn-out, fifteen gin and tonics in the pub, and seven hours later, Penny and I dragged ourselves away from the lock-in and made our way home.

'Then why are you wobbling?'

Bit of a giveaway, really. 'Okay, you win missy. I may be a teensy-weensy bit squiffy.'

'A teensy bit? You were dancing with the jukebox!'

'That jukebox got rhythm, girl,' I replied, in an American deep-south twang, before repeating the dance, sans partner, in the street.

'Very good, baby!' She was clearly petrified I'd lose my balance and fall flat on my face. 'Let's just get you home, hey?'

'You know I love you, don't you?' I asked, staring into the two faces of Penny.

She giggled. 'Now I know you're drunk.'

Since the day I found out how excessive alcohol consumption could affect your senses, I also discovered unlike many people, no matter how blasted I got, I always had total recall of what I got up to under the influence. Yes, I staggered around, raised my voice unnecessarily, had an insatiable craving for doner kebabs and vomited, but I remained aware at all times. It may have taken a little longer for the memories to surface the morning after, but surface they did, in their entirety.

My mistake was to boast about this spectacular ability to friends. I thought it to be a trend-setting characteristic, but little did I realise at the time I would never be able to use the *I don't remember* excuse.

"What? I don't remember snogging that transvestite."

"I dry-humped a dog? I don't remember."

"I called a nursing home at three in the morning and asked for the all you can eat meal deal, including deep fried, fat nursey thighs and catheter combo? I DON'T REMEMBER!"

Which is why I can accurately retell the story of bumping into Miles on the way back to the flat.

As soon as Penny saw him step from the garden path on to the pavement, she pulled my sozzled frame across the road to the opposite side to avoid him. For a minute, I thought her tactics had worked; he spotted us, but chose not to make a scene and carried on about his business. Giving him a minute to put distance between us, we crossed over again and Penny dipped into my jacket pocket for the door keys. All I can think is that his anger and bravado levels momentarily peaked; as I opened the gate, he turned around and fired a bucket of verbal abuse in her direction, loud enough to wake the street. I won't repeat the tirade in full, but he did use the words *prostitute* and *hole* at least twice. You can probably work out the rest for yourself.

I would have been fearless and ready for a confrontation if I'd heard him speak to a complete stranger in that way *sober*, but this was Penny. No one, not even a world-class ninja or a genetic experiment melding *Jason Bourne* and *Jack Bauer* together, was getting away from this without a beating.

Oh, and did I mention I was pissed?

The last thing I remember was another shouty episode with lots of swear words. I regained consciousness ten minutes later on the front doorstep. Penny was slapping my face: right cheek, left cheek, right cheek. 'Woah, hang on. I'm awake, I'm awake.'

She stopped slapping and began caressing. 'Baby, are you okay?'

'What's going on?' I had sobered up and was trying to work out why my ears were ringing.

'You were out for a while. He hit you.'

'Who hit me?' My whole body was shivering. I thought hard, and then it came back to me.

Miles.

'How did he…' I stopped, massaging my face, 'how did he manage that?'

'It was a lucky punch, sweetheart.'

But it wasn't. In my stupor, I'd charged down the street waving my arms frantically, tripped on approach and my nose had landed on his elbow. After that, it was lights out. Penny freaked, screaming back at him, but Miles continued unrepentant, to wherever the hell he was heading to in the middle of the night. She'd then collared a passer-by who'd also left the pub, and he helped carry me back to the flat.

'Who was it?' I asked. The pub wasn't too packed that night. We'd been sat at the bar chatting to a lot of people. Chances were I'd spoken to, or at least seen the guy.

'Dunno,' she answered, 'didn't catch his name. Big bloke. He's gone to the shop to get some ice. Hope you don't mind but I invited him in for a cuppa as a thank you.'

'Big bloke?' Did I see a large chap in the pub? Was I too wrecked to remember? 'Don't mind at all, I'd like to thank him myself.'

'Come on, let's get you inside.'

Installed on the couch with a large scotch and two long pieces of toilet paper up each nostril, the doorbell rang.

'That'll be him,' she said, rushing to the door.

I tilted my head back and felt a stream of blood roll down my throat. The strong taste of iron made me want to throw up.

She opened the door and greeted my saviour. 'Great, you got cigarettes too. He'll be happy.'

'Had a feeling he might need one,' a very familiar voice said.

Where had I heard it before?

'Barry? Where are you, mate?'

It was on the tip of my tongue.

'In the lounge,' she replied, 'go on through.'

I couldn't believe my eyes when he walked into the living room. 'Kev?'

'What are the chances, hey?'

'What the hell are you doing here?' I said, with a smile.

Penny was confused. 'You know each other?'

'We go way back,' he joked.

'You don't live around here, do you, mate?' We shook hands and he studied the fresh bruise manifesting itself on my face.

'Nah, came to visit a friend. I was on my way back to the station when I saw you out for the count. Lucky I passed by. You copped it sweet there, pal.'

'Bloody is lucky,' Penny said, 'I couldn't have carried him on my own.'

I told her about the supermarket incident.

'He stuck up for me at the checkout.' He smiled and tapped me on the shoulder. 'The girl serving didn't approve of me buying so many so many fatty foods. Takes balls to do that in this city.'

'No bother at all,' I said.

'You what? Nearly getting stabbed then knocked out?'

'I didn't see you in the pub,' I said, changing the subject.

'We were in the back room for a private party.'

'That's why, then. We were in the main bar.'

Penny poured him a drink and wrapped some ice in a towel for my face, before letting out a series of yawns. 'I'm

gonna call it a night. Give you two a chance to catch up.'
She bent down to give me a kiss.

'You sure?'

'Yeah. All the excitement's tired me out a bit. Will you
be okay?'

'Leave him with me,' Kev said, 'I'll look after him.'

'Thanks for everything, Kev.'

'More than welcome. Night, love.'

Penny went to bed and the first thing I did was
apologise to Kev for not arranging a beer out as promised.
He didn't seem offended, especially when I told him what
had happened recently with the job, Penny, Miles and
planning the road trip.

Tonight was the first time he'd been out in a long time.
An anniversary party invitation from an old friend
brought him to my neck of the woods, and after enjoying
himself so much, was starting to feel the pull of a healthy
social life again.

'Gotta say, Penny seems a really nice girl. You've done
well there.'

'Yeah, she is. It's just a shame about all the shit still
going on.'

'Doesn't matter, son,' he replied, 'that'll all calm down in
time. You can't expect to go through life without hurting
people. Could've been better, could've been a lot worse,
y'know?'

'Guess so,' I said, adjusting the tissues up my nose.

'And anyway, isn't she worth taking a beating for?'

I hadn't thought of it that way. Given a choice, I'd have
taken *no beating* over *beating*, but he was right - she was
special. I was starting to realise I'd have happily endured
daily acts of violence if it meant keeping her in my life.
'Sounds like you've given this kind of advice before.'

'A few times, yeah,' he said, 'and I won't lie to you mate,
I've seen couples fall apart because of all that shit. But if
you're careful, y'know, concentrate on each other instead
of the bad stuff, you've got a better chance of success.' He
raised his glass. 'That's the gospel according to Kev. What

do you reckon?'

'Wise words.'

He excused himself to go to the bathroom, leaving me on the couch. With Penny asleep, it was the first time I'd been alone in days. Leaning back, I forgot about the mindless punch up with Miles and started to think about what was really troubling me: the dream about Mum, the elusive shadow in the corner of my eye, what Paul the security guard said outside *Tinkler & Tinkler*. I hadn't mentioned a word of it to Penny. I didn't want to scare her half to death in the early stages of our relationship. I wondered if it was something I could share with Kev. He'd been full of good advice moments earlier, was there a chance he could be objective and constructive again? I could have done with a sound opinion on the matter.

I thought about how to begin. Was he the kind of guy who was partial to intense discussions, or was he of the ilk who thought any topics covered except girls, cars, food, booze and sex was for wimpy little pussies? There was no way to tell. The only thing I could do was approach it lightheartedly. If I gave the impression it was an idle topic of discussion, as opposed to a recurring issue eating away at me, maybe that could make launching into it a little bit easier.

He came back from the bathroom, sat down and took a few more sips from his glass. It felt like the best time to say something as we were between conversation.

'Meant to ask you something,' I said, with an unnecessary cough.

'What's that?'

I took my time.

'Something bothering you?'

My mouth was open but the words wouldn't come out.

'Spit it out, son.'

Eventually, it came. 'Have you ever had a recurring dream?'

He put his drink down and looked at me. 'You mean like turning up for work starkers? Yeah, I've had that one a few times.'

I faked a laugh. 'That's a popular one. No, I mean scary ones. Ones you don't really remember until half-way through the day.'

Confusion. Damn, I'd lost him after two sentences.

'Can't say I have. Why, have you?'

I nodded.

'Really? What about?'

'This is gonna sound weird,' I said, keeping an eye on his facial expression, 'but even though I'm dreaming about different things, it always feels the same because of this shadow in the corner of my eye.'

He still looked interested. 'Shadow?'

'Yeah. Can't explain it, but it's always there. When I turn to face it, y'know, head on, it disappears.' Watching his face trying to work it out, I got cold feet. 'But never mind, hey? Everybody has weird dreams some time…'

'No, no,' he said, interrupting, 'I think I know what you mean. Kinda like if you're tired and see a flicker, then you blink or rub your eyes and it's not there?'

'Yeah, right.' My excitement grew. Perhaps he did get me, after all.

'Does it say anything to you?'

I thought back to the last dream. 'Don't think so, but a couple of nights ago, I looked at the shadow and it didn't fade away.'

'And…?'

'And what?'

'You looked at it, it didn't fade away, then what? What did you see?'

'Well, not much. It was just there, checking me out.'

'Sounds a bit freaky if you ask me.'

'I know. Annoying thing is I woke up before getting the chance to speak to it.'

Any fears I had about Kev laughing in my face had gone; he really did seem eager to listen. Most people I encountered through life had an irritating wish to be heard at all times. They'd talk openly about themselves, and lose interest as soon as you said something to switch the focus away from their ego-obsessed limelight. 'I don't expect you to understand, 'cos I'm not sure I do.'

'Have you told Penny?'

'I didn't wanna bother her. She's been through a lot recently.'

'It's hardly been a month in a Swedish brothel for you either, going by what you told me. Ever thought it might be connected?'

'What? You mean stress?'

He nodded.

'I dunno. It's possible, I suppose.'

He stretched his knuckles until they cracked. 'I reckon next time, if it doesn't disappear when you look at it, you should run and jump on it, y'know, take the bastard down and get a better look at it.'

Decent advice, I'd try that, assuming I remembered his suggestion next time I dozed off. 'Cheers mate,' I said, 'maybe you're right.'

'I'm always right,' he said cheekily. 'Fancy a top up?'

'Always.'

'How's the nose?'

'Can't feel it.' I pulled the red, crinkled tissues from inside my nostrils and tore off a couple of new strips from the roll on the table. Ice was helping; the blood flow had slowed and my nose had gone numb.

When he came back from the kitchen, something was different. For a start, he hadn't brought any drinks with him. He sat down and fixed me with an eerie stare.

'Everything alright, mate?'

No answer.

'Earth to Kev,' I quipped, but he wasn't playing. Suddenly uncomfortable, I moved to the edge of my seat. 'Mate?'

'I don't feel too good, Barry.'

'Shit, really? You want some tablets? I think we've got some in the cabinet...'

'Hang on. The pain's going away.'

'Pain?'

He crouched on to the floor, and with a loud grunt, spread himself across the carpet. Seconds later, he was laying flat on his stomach, arms above his head, stretching his body. I heard shoulders, knees and feet crack, before he got up and sat back down in the chair, with a grin that looked like it was stuck on upside-down.

'What are you doing?'

'That's better,' he said, 'I know where I am now.'

'And you didn't before?'

He shuffled on the chair. 'Barry. I'm so glad I found you again.'

Was he having some kind of seizure? 'Kev, what was all that about?'

He was squinting and sucking his teeth. 'They tried to take me away before I could finish what I needed to tell you.'

'Eh?'

'You don't recognise me, do you? You didn't before, but that's alright, all I need is for you to listen.' All the colour had drained from his face.

'Have you been smoking something?'

His crisp, blue eyes came to life. 'Yes, that's it, smoking. Smoker's corner.'

'Okay, you're starting to freak me out now.'

'Barry, do you remember smoker's corner?'

I said no, but it was a lie. I could sense what he was getting at, but didn't want to face the possibility he was going crazy on me, as Paul had outside *T&T*.

'Yes, you do. They dragged me away, but I'm back, and I don't have long.'

I sensed trouble. 'Oh, God, not this again.'

'So you do remember?'

'What I remember is some nutter telling me he was my Grandad. I also remember kicking him in the guts.'

'That's right,' he said, on his feet again, 'you've got one hell of a swing on you.' He picked up a framed photograph of me and my parents from the mantelpiece.

'Oh my,' he said, grinning, 'I haven't seen this one in a while.'

'This is insane.' I shot off the couch and snatched it back. 'I think it's time you left, don't you?' I opened the door and waited beside it.

'Take it easy, son.'

'No, I won't take it easy. I want you to leave now. I don't wanna hear this shit anymore.'

'It's not shit. And anyway, I can't leave until you hear me out.'

Was I dreaming again? Had I flaked on the couch when Kev was in the bathroom? 'Just go.'

He wasn't listening. Instead, he went back to the mantelpiece. 'I know you think they're gone,' he said, pointing to the photo of my parents on their wedding day.

'They *are* gone,' I shouted, 'they died last year in a plane crash.'

'That's what you think.'

'What do you know about it?'

'More than you realise.'

'Well, whatever. If you don't get out now I'm calling the police.'

He laughed. 'You were always hot-headed, even as a child.'

'What?'

'I could tell you some stories.'

I lifted the receiver and dialled 999. 'You can tell 'em to your cell mates.'

He ran over and grabbed the handset from me so fast I didn't see him move. 'Charade over, Barry.'

He was borderline livid. His reaction reminded me of Mr. Cox catching Katie Wells and me in our underwear at school, smoking weed in the girl's toilets. 'You're gonna stop all this nonsense and hear me out now, otherwise it's all over for you, son.'

'Fine, Kev,' I replied, a shake in my voice, 'say what you gotta say. Just promise me you'll go afterwards.'

He rubbed his face in frustration. 'How many times? I'm

not Kev.'

I wasn't going to argue anymore. 'Okay, sorry. What should I call you?'

He sighed. 'This is turning out to be a lot more difficult than I expected it to be.'

'Oh, well, I am sorry to inconvenience you so,' I said sarcastically.

'We're covering old ground. You already know what I'm getting at so why are you wasting my time?'

Hesitation. 'Grandad?'

'Correct.'

'Bollocks.' I walked out, slamming the door in anger. 'Absolute bollocks.'

I closed the kitchen door and bent over the sink to swill my face. When I opened my eyes, Kev was standing directly in front of me. The door was still closed. No one had come in or out. 'How did you get in here?'

'I haven't got much time.'

'You haven't answered my question.'

He clasped my shoulders with both hands and shook me. 'You have to become aware of what's happening here.'

'Aware of what? What does that mean?'

'It's all going wrong for you again, can't you see?'

'What is?'

'Your parents died a few years ago. They died a few days after your girlfriend left, stripping your flat, leaving an empty shell and turning all of your old friends against you.' He took a deep breath. 'You started a job you hated and they kept giving you more money which stifled your ambition to leave and better yourself. For God's sake, you were born on 16 March; a Pisces baby. When you used to visit your grandmother and me, your favourite meal was either vegetable stew and dumplings or hamburger and chips. You were a newspaper boy between the ages of fourteen and sixteen. Our house was the last stop on your round, so at weekends, you'd come in for a slap-up breakfast. Is there anything else?'

I couldn't speak. There wasn't a reply in the land that wouldn't have sounded like stuttering, nonsense dribble. I was willing to accept Kev could have been suffering from some form of split-personality disorder, but to know so much about my life? What was he, the fucking *Rain Man*?

'So, are we finally on the same page?'

The same page? Not a chance in hell. It wasn't even the same novel in the same bloody genre. He was content browsing the display window for groundbreaking modern thrillers, while I was meandering slowly at the back through pre-Victorian romance.

'Barry?'

'What?'

'Are you with me?'

'No. I'm not even close to being *with you*. How would you feel in my position?'

'Well, I'd be confused, but I'd also give me the chance to tell you what I know.'

'Fine. Fire away. Say what you gotta say, but I can't promise I'll take it all in.'

He smiled. 'Awareness, Barry. That's the key.'

'Yeah, yeah, you've said that already. Elaborate.'

'Face value isn't an option in your life. You feel it, don't you? You feel it falling apart again.'

My responses were quick and dismissive. 'Things have been better, but I wouldn't say things were falling apart. I've got a girl, money...'

'It's never been about those things, though, has it?'

'There you go with the cryptic comments again. Why can't you tell me in plain English?'

'It's difficult,' he said, scratching his head. 'I'm not really in control. I have to think for two people, so occasionally the words get muddled.'

'Why?'

'Why do you think? Kev's still in here, buried beneath *my* consciousness. It's taking everything I have to break through his strong wall of resistance.'

'Right, because that makes sense,' I mocked.

I felt the palm of his hand strike my cheek. 'You cocky little shit,' he said. 'You think you know it all, don't you? Think you've got it all sorted in your head? You're not even close, son. I can't tell you how far away you are from recognising it.' He marched past me and opened the kitchen door. 'I did my best, Barry. If you're too proud to even try to accept what's going on here, there's nothing else I can do.'

'So you're leaving?' I asked, my face stinging.

No reply. He shook his head, let out another sigh of frustration and walked out. Cursing his audacity, I stayed behind in the kitchen and waited for the front door to close.

The click of the lock never came. In its place was the almighty thump of something heavy colliding with the floor. Opening the door, I saw him sprawled, stomach-down on the carpet. He was wheezing and his left leg was in spasm.

'Kev?'

The noise woke Penny and she ran from the bedroom. 'What happened?' she asked, kneeling down beside him. 'Kev, can you hear me? Kev? Barry, help me get him on his side.'

Both his nose and eyes were bleeding heavily when we turned him over. 'My chest,' he said, a rasp in his voice. 'It really hurts. Call an ambulance.'

'Stay with him,' Penny said, running into the lounge.

Kev was wincing through the pain. 'Barry, how did I get down here?'

'You fell. Try not to talk, okay? Help is on its way.'

He tried to get up, realised it was unlikely and slumped back down. 'No, no, I mean down here from the armchair.'

'Kev, we were in the kitchen.'

'When?'

'Before you fell. You freaked out on me.'

'When?'

Even in distress he was insufferable. 'All that stuff about being my Grandad?'

He stared at me like the school dunce would a quadratic equation. 'I swear I don't know what you're talking about.' Specks of blood were flying from his mouth. 'One minute we're talking, the next I'm here.'

Penny would be back any second, so I took the opportunity to ask. 'Look, I know I'm being blunt, mate, but have you got... I mean, do you suffer from... schizophrenia?'

'You what?'

'Just answer me, before she gets back.'

I could see the pain was intensifying. He was clutching his chest, moaning with every breath. 'Don't be daft, Barry.'

'You were coming out with some pretty weird stuff back there.'

'What are you talking about? I'm not mental.'

Penny emerged from the lounge. 'Ambulance is on its way. How's he doing?'

'Hurts like hell,' Kev said, 'and your boyfriend's talking shit at me.' His eyes began to close.

'No, you don't,' she said, rushing to him. 'You're not passing out on me. Stay awake.'

'Easier said than done.' With fresh blood oozing from his mouth, he let out a final cry of agony, and lost consciousness.

'Kev!'

'Is he okay?'

'Hang on.' She pressed two fingers to the side of his neck.

'Pen?'

'Give me a minute.'

Brain reduced to the consistency of soft cheese, I paced up and down the hallway, utterly disgusted with myself. Spat aside, the guy was in a tremendous amount of pain, and instead of keeping him calm and comfortable until help arrived, I insisted on pushing the inappropriate questions. From the bewildered look on his face, I could tell Kev had no recollection of our quarrel in the kitchen.

He was the one who thought I was mad. Why did I have to take it too far with the schizophrenia thing?

A moment later, I heard Penny swear quietly under her breath. She looked up at me. 'Oh, God.'

'What?'

'I… I'm not a hundred per cent sure, but…'

'But what? What is it?'

'I think he's dead.'

TWENTY-FIVE

The ambulance arrived and I talked the paramedic through most of the events leading up to Kev's collapse. Sensibly, I omitted the specifics of our tête-à-tête in the kitchen, in case they thought I was a complete lunatic. I'd met him after midnight, so wasn't sure if he'd taken any substances; also, I could only tell them how much he'd had to drink at my place, not knowing how much he'd guzzled in the pub beforehand.

Despite their best attempts at resuscitation, Kev was pronounced dead at the scene. I overheard them say initial signs pointed to a heart attack, which, due to his size and age, was understandable, but I couldn't shrug the uncomfortable feeling there was more to it. Why would he rescind everything he'd said with such conviction on his deathbed? Seconds earlier, he'd stormed out, branding me a lost cause. A sudden change of heart? It didn't sit right.

On the other hand, who can accurately predict what happens towards the end? Do we receive an advanced gift of wisdom and enlightenment in preparation for the higher plain? I could only be sure of one thing: if Kev did have the answers hidden away in his psyche, it was too late now to play *Give Us A Clue*.

Or so I thought.

Penny emerged from the kitchen pale-faced, and the paramedic asked if there was anything she wanted to add. She shook her head, then sat down and tried to scrub Kev's blood from the carpet.

With his body in the ambulance, they left. 'Thanks, Mr. Brooks. We'll call you if we need to.'

I closed the door behind them, crouching down beside Penny. 'Leave it, sweetheart. It can wait.'

'It'll never come out if it's left,' she replied, not looking up, 'you'll never get your deposit back if the carpet's ruined.'

I forced the sponge from her hand. 'It's my flat, hon. I own it. Come and sit down.'

It took a moment or so before Penny stood up. The tears she was holding back began to roll down her face and she threw her arms around me.

'It's okay,' I said, stroking her hair.

'I've never seen a dead body before.'

A corpse should never be high on anyone's *to see list*, unless you're a funeral director, doctor or serial killer. 'I know, it's horrible. Try not to think about it.'

I took the duvet from the bed and we snuggled on the sofa, the television on in the background. Our whiskeys were stronger than usual, and after a few sips, tiredness took her. She slept soundly as I half-watched the end of *Arsenic and Old Lace*.

I should have told her. I wanted to tell her about the Grandad thing; how Kev had reeled off my life history as if we were brothers. If there was anyone in the world I should have told, it was her. But I didn't. I chickened out and kept my mouth shut. Why? Because I was scared of losing her too. I opened up to Kev about my dreams, told him about the dark figure lurking out of sight, and the next minute he was dead in my flat. What if that happened to Penny too? What if I turned the honesty lever and she keeled over in agony after claiming to be the spiritual embodiment of Mum?

For a moment, let's say Kev wasn't stark raving bonkers. Let's say Grandad was trying to communicate. Why couldn't he use a more orthodox method? Like email, for example? I'd even have a bloody séance if it meant people would stop dying. His floaty soul could pass on words of wisdom all night without needing a host, or however Kev put it.

I needed sleep. I was so tired my brain had casually accepted the implausible. It wasn't easy to put Kev's pain-stricken face to the back of my mind, but eventually, I was asleep, and faced with the mysterious after-image once again.

TWENTY-SIX

Whether he was aware of it or not, Kev pushed my number of funeral attendances into the twenties. Not long after he died, his elderly parents called to pass on the invite, and thank us for being with him at the end.

The post-mortem confirmed the heart attack, but my guilt-o-meter was off the scale. His condition must have been exacerbated by our row in the kitchen - I continually provoked him with my defiance - but it was over now. Kev was dead. There was nothing I could do to change it for the better.

I couldn't let anyone know about the spat. Would coming clean have resulted in some kind of investigation? Would there be accusatory fingers pointing directly at me? I didn't have the necessary proof to vindicate myself. I'm not sure such a thing existed. All I could do was keep the intimates of that eventful night buried deep, and somehow learn to live with the guilt.

The funeral was very low-key. Only a smattering of friends and relatives attended, which said a lot about Kev's social life. The minister shared his carefully-scripted thoughts on life, death and the afterlife, before asking the congregation to stand and join with him in a united prayer. So beautifully understated, Penny was left with a lump in her throat, despite hardly knowing the man. Guilty conscience aside, I was happy to share the goodbye with those who loved him. It seemed unlikely I would ever discover what he was really trying to say to me.

We passed on the wake, offering condolences to his parents on the way out of the crematorium. Out of politeness, I told them to call should they ever need anything, but thought it unlikely they would; a queue of family members were blocking the entrance waiting to do exactly the same.

Earlier in the day, Penny had packed a picnic and we decided to celebrate my birthday by taking the new car out for a trip into the country. She offered to drive and we crept slowly out of the car park, acknowledging fellow mourners on the way.

The sombre after-effects of death have a tendency to linger long after the deceased's affairs have been wrapped up, but there was more to it with Penny. She had been unusually quiet since the night Kev died, choosing one-word answers instead of sentences, only speaking when spoken to. I didn't want to appear pushy and risk pissing her off, but I had to know if there was more to it than him.

After three poor efforts in the week leading up to the funeral, I took advantage of the silence in the car. Bracing myself, I gave it another shot. 'Are you alright, sweetheart?'

'Fine, baby.'

'Sure?'

A grunt. Her eyes stayed focused on the road.

Stand your ground, Barry. You have something to say, so bloody say it. 'Pen, I don't mean to keep going on about it, but you've been really quiet lately, and…'

'God, Barry, how many times?'

'Don't yell. I'm right here.'

'Kev died in the flat. Remember Kev?'

I didn't like her shouty voice; a thunderous noise coming from such an adorable face wasn't natural. 'Yeah, course I do.'

'I watched him die. How do you think that makes me feel?'

'Okay, okay, I'm sorry. I didn't expect you to take it so badly. I thought there may have been something else.'

'It's a pretty big deal, don't you think? I'm not good around death. I haven't had to deal with anything like this before. I'm sorry if I've been quiet, but stuff like this plays on your mind a little, y'know? Can't we just enjoy your birthday without having to think about it?'

It was playing on my mind too, but not for the same reasons. 'I'm sorry. I didn't mean to upset you. Forget I said anything,' I reached over to the back seat and opened the picnic basket. 'Fancy a sandwich?'

I saw the beginnings of a smile and she placed her hand on my knee. 'I didn't mean to snap at you, sweets. The last thing I wanna do is ruin the day. It's just been a strange few weeks is all.'

'No worries,' I said, passing her a cheese and pickle. 'Get this down you.' I was glad about one thing: it'd been a while since I'd heard her utter more than two sentences at a time.

We pulled into a picturesque country park an hour later and Penny guided the car across the gravel, parking up in an available space. Once out of the car, I took the picnic basket from the back seat. She caught me by surprise by grabbing my waist and gently kissing the back of my head.

'Hey, you,' I said, playfully.

'Hey,' she replied. 'You know I love you, don't you?'

I felt her warmth breath on my neck. 'I do now. What brought this on?'

'Just wanted to tell you. Happy birthday, gorgeous.'

The early afternoon sun was beating down as we strolled through the woods towards the reservoir. It was a popular haunt for visitors to unwind with a bottle of wine, far away from the pollution and anarchy of the city; couples with dogs, couples with kids, couples on their own, hand in hand, laughing and joking with each other. I even spotted a couple who appeared to be mid-argument. We listened as they traded petty insults for a few moments, throwing out a few choice, explicit names. She then dramatically declared it was over and ran crying in the direction of the car park. Her forlorn boyfriend was left gazing around the reserve, hoping no one was witness to his humiliation.

'She doesn't look very happy,' Penny said.

I bit my tongue. There was a cutting remark about her less-than-vocal last few weeks aching to come out. It wouldn't have been a nice thing to say, especially as she'd just declared her love for me.

Compliments aside, I couldn't shrug the feeling Penny was having second thoughts about going away. We were due to leave the following day for her sister's place in Edinburgh, but she seemed less than thrilled at the prospect. I was anticipating her calling the trip off as soon as we sat down on the blanket, using excuses like *it's too soon*, or *could we wait a bit longer before committing to something so huge?* Dwelling on it did nothing for my appetite, so I filled our glasses with wine and stared out across the lake, waiting patiently for her to let it all out.

After a few moments, she did. She started to cry and I instinctively moved over to hold her.

'It's okay,' I said, pre-empting her announcement, 'we can wait a while longer if you like.'

In a heartbeat, the floods stopped. 'Huh? What do you mean, we can wait?'

'The trip,' I said, stroking her arm, 'I know you don't wanna go, but it's fine. We can postpone it.'

She gave me the classic, *you don't understand women one bit* look. 'Shut up, Barry. That's not why I'm crying.'

'It isn't?'

'No, you dick.' More crying, but this time she wouldn't let me anywhere near. My attempts to further stroke her arm were met with firm slaps. 'God, talk about jumping to conclusions - the wrong conclusions.'

'Then why the tears?'

I passed her the wine, but instead of drinking it, she knocked the glass clean out of my hand. It flew and smashed on the grass, spilling expensive, *Oddbins* Chardonnay all over her bacon, egg and salad cream selection. A ten-second uncomfortable silence later, she let out a snigger, which quickly turned to laughter.

'It smashed on the grass? Good quality glasses, Baz. Where did you get 'em from?'

My favourite sandwiches were ruined, but it really didn't matter. 'The pound shop.'

She laughed, I laughed, and before long, we were rolling on the blanket, kissing, cuddling and groping. I wasn't bothered; at last, she was laughing again. Even if I had to do the full works in front of a group of Christians having an open-air prayer meeting to keep the smile on her face, I would.

Seconds short of whipping out Mister Solid for a bit of fresh air, she stopped and pulled away. 'No, Barry, not here. We shouldn't.'

'Come on honey, it's my birthday,' I said, tugging at her skirt.

She chuckled. 'No. We can't.'

Though slightly frustrated, I didn't persist with the complaints. A disabled couple on matching mobility scooters had rolled into view and were thundering towards us. If they were to see my white arse bobbing up and down at a pivotal moment in the proceedings, the shock would probably send them crashing into the reservoir. 'You're right,' I said, getting my breath back. Taking another wine glass from the basket, I filled it up. Out of habit, I went to top Penny's up too, but she covered the glass with her hand. 'You're not drinking?'

'No.' She was arranging her hair back to the way it looked before I jumped on her.

'One won't hurt, will it?'

'Barry, there's, erm, something I need to tell you.'

'Yeah?'

'It's kinda the reason I'm not drinking.'

My heart raced, because there was only one way to explain that comment. 'You're pregnant?'

Slowly, she nodded, looking at the grass. 'Yeah.'

Was there a textbook way to react? If so, I didn't know

what it was. 'Are you sure?'

'Yep. Took the test last week. The doctor confirmed it yesterday.'

Which explained the three-hour trip to *Tesco* for pitta bread and houmous.

'I didn't know how to tell you,' she continued. 'So many times I was going to, but I lost my nerve.'

I was beaming, but wanted to determine her reaction first. 'I'm glad you did. How're you feeling?'

'Not sure,' she replied, eyes still down. 'It's been on my mind for the last week and I still don't know.'

I gave her a soft peck on the cheek. 'Actually, babe, I meant physically.'

She smiled. 'Oh, right. Not too good first thing in the morning.'

I sat back, buying some time to make sure I said the right thing, whatever that was. 'I can't say I was expecting it, but it's good news, isn't it?'

She was chewing both lips. 'I guess, but I'm only twenty-two. Isn't that a bit young to have a baby? I mean, do you think I'm ready?'

'Only you can really answer that, Pen, but if you want to know how I feel, I think it's amazing.'

'Really?'

'Yeah, I do, but there's one thing you'll have to get used to.'

'What?'

'Drop the 'I'. If we're gonna do this, it's about *us*, not *you*.'

Was she impressed with my maturity? I'm sure I saw her cringe. 'What's up?'

'Are you saying you want me to go through with it?'

Hadn't I made that clear? 'Well, yeah, why? Don't you want to?'

'Don't get me wrong, I do want children, but I also want to be able to make the decision myself, not have it forced on me by a dodgy pill or broken condom.'

'Pen, we're talking about a child here.'

'I know that, but I'd hate to bring a child into the world when I don't feel I can give it everything it needs.'

It sounded like she'd made the decision. 'But we could give it everything it needs. We've got a nice place and money behind us. I know we haven't been together long, but I love you. The timing might be off, but we'd get through it.'

'Really?'

'Yeah! Plus I think I'd make a pretty decent Dad, don't you think?'

She ran her fingers gently across my face. 'You're serious, aren't you?'

'Of course I'm serious.'

'You really think it could work?'

She was coming around, I could feel it. 'Why not? I could see you as a yummy mummy…'

'Part of me thought you'd push me to get rid.'

'You really think I'd do that?' I sounded more offended than I actually was. 'I'm going to be a Daddy!' I swept Penny off her feet, quickly remembered her condition and placed her gently back on to the floor. 'Who'd have thought it? Me, Barry Brooks, shortly to be a Dad? This is great. The best birthday present ever.'

'God, I'm so relieved it's out in the open. I was having nightmares about you freaking out and leaving me.'

'As if. You know I'd never do anything like that.'

'I'm glad.'

I picked up the wine and took an uncouth swig from the bottle. 'I know you're not allowed, but this is a special occasion.'

'Drink away, lover, I'm fine with mineral water.'

I had everything planned. I'd take care of her through every step of the pregnancy and she'd want for less than nothing. I could even sell up and find a bigger place to accommodate the little one if we found ourselves short on space. I'd have to get a job at some point as the cash wouldn't last forever, but I could think about that closer to the time. The most important thing was we were going to be together as a family. This was my chance to pass on what Mum and Dad gave to me: a sense of belonging and unconditional love. Since the death of my parents, losing Beth and having friends and relatives turn on me, those qualities had been cruelly stolen. Now, we had a chance to recreate it again.

I knew everything was happening far too soon, but I said nothing to Penny. Given the choice, I'd have waited a few years before having children, but there are times when life throws you conundrums you have to work through spontaneously. Not everything can be as straightforward as we'd like it to be, but I couldn't stand the idea of giving up on a living being, especially one we'd created together. It went against every last moral I had.

The journey back seemed to pass in an instant, which could have been down to my ecstatic mood or the bottle of wine splashing its way around my insides. Penny had put up with me pressing my ear to her stomach and ranting at her in baby-speak the whole way home. By the time we pulled up outside the flat, I'd convinced her it was going to be a boy, though she wasn't too keen on my never-ending list of ridiculous names.

'What's wrong with *Penarry*?'

'It sounds stupid.'

'Clever though, isn't it? A combination of Penny and Barry?'

'No, it's not clever at all.'

'Well I think it is.'

'You're missing the obvious one.'

'Huh?'

'If you want a combination of our names, then how about *Ben*?'

Apparently, I didn't understand. It must have been the wine.

We postponed the trip to Edinburgh. It made sense in the short term, as Penny could be close to the doctor for regular check-ups. It also gave us the time to work out a plan for the months ahead. Kat and Penny were on the phone for hours talking about it. Her sister was having the same symptoms, so shared stories and advice was inevitable. No doubt Kat voiced what we were both thinking about the timing of it all, but Penny did her best to reassure her we were totally committed to each other and the baby.

I turned the volume up on the television when I heard them talking about afterbirth and trapped wind. She'd have reacted the same way if I rambled on about football and strip clubs. In nine months, I would deal with such things with impressive maturity, but in the meantime, I'd make the most of watching *America's Stupidest Stuntmen*. It would all be fine. In a few years, Junior would be watching it with me, pissing Mummy off in the process.

In the middle of the segment where a fat, silver-haired fool in a purple leotard failed to jump over seventeen monster trucks riding a girl's pushbike, Penny threw a paper aeroplane over to me. I unravelled her passable attempt and read the note:

Sweetie, could you nip down the shop and get me some eggs, onions, cheese and Lucozade, please? Love you love you love you love you love yoooooooooooooooou xxxxxxxxxxxxx

How could I resist when the *love yous* and kisses almost outnumbered the rest of the message? Screwing up the note and pretending to be annoyed, I stormed out of the room with a smile on my face. I picked the right moment to do so, as I'm positive I heard her say *discharge* as I was putting my shoes on.

I took the mobile with me, as she had a habit of calling me on the way to add more items to the list. As long as it wasn't girl-type stuff, I didn't mind; last time she asked for tampons, I came back with cotton wool.

'Congratulations, my brother,' Sunil said, reaching across the counter to shake my hand. 'You must be very happy man, no?'

'Over the moon, mate,' I replied. 'Can't tell you how much.'

'You have name for it yet?'

'I'm thinking about *Barry, Jnr*. What do you think?'

He laughed out loud. 'Is good name, definitely bruv!'

'I thought so.'

'You wait,' he said, bending down, 'I have gift for you.' He checked there was no one else in the shop, then took a plastic bag from beneath the counter and showed me its contents. Inside was a massive stash of cigarettes. 'For you, my brother.'

I gazed in awe. So much for those voices in my head urging me to quit. 'Where'd you get all those from?'

'How you say? Bootleg, innit.' He winked. 'You take all of them, no?'

'Sunil, there must be three-hundred quid's worth here.'

'So? I got tons in the back.'

Penny hated the fags. Only last week I promised her I'd stop smoking indoors. She hated the way it made her clothes reek. 'Are you sure?'

'Of course. You take. Me, I stop years ago. Wife tell me, "Sunil, you making the house smell". I not touched one since.' He laughed so hard it brought out a chesty cough. 'This brand good for you?'

Okay, so I may have said I wouldn't puff away *inside*, but that didn't stop me from doing it *outside*. Outside was a very large place. I was free to utilise any part of the outside for my dangerously addictive habit. 'Yeah, this is my brand.'

'Then I done good, no?'

I could have kissed him, but thought better of it. 'You done great. Spot on. Thank you so much.'

'Pah, not a bother, my brother. Now, what else you have here?'

I showed him the basket. In it were the items on Penny's list, along with some girly-smelling shampoo she'd added via the medium of text.

Sunil mumbled incoherently, counting the items in his head. 'Okay, that come to grand total of…' Then came his best *ta-dah!* face, 'nothing, my brother. You free to go now. Tell your lady-friend hello from Sunil and Pinder at shop.'

'Don't be daft,' I said, handing him a tenner.

He folded his arms. 'Don't want your cash.'

After a couple of *are you sures* from me and some *stop asking me if I'm sures* from Sunil, I shook his hand, thanked him a further twelve times and left the shop.

What a guy.

What a haul.

Sunil and I often had banter, but I had no idea he thought so highly of me. He didn't *have* to give so much stuff away, unless the police were looking for the fags and the food was out of date.

I turned the corner on to my street and lit up the first of many import cigarettes. Within seconds, I was dizzy, propping myself up against the nearest lamppost.

God, they were strong. After one drag, it felt like I'd smoked seven cigars.

I felt a buzzing in the groinal area and reached into my jeans pocket for the mobile. It was Penny. I was still coughing when I answered. 'No, you can't have any vodka,' I joked, 'think about *Barry, Jnr!*'

She didn't laugh. Why didn't she laugh? I thought it was funny. Was *Barry, Jnr* such a terrible name for a child?

'Where are you?' Sounded like the last thing she needed to hear was my wayward sense of humour.

'Couple of minutes out. What's up?'

'Just get back as soon as you can.'

She sounded distressed and I started to panic. 'Pen, tell me, I'm almost home.'

'Just get back,' she shouted, 'I don't know what to do.'

'Do about what?'

The line went dead. I couldn't be certain, but I thought I heard a second voice talking in the background? Was it Miles? Had the son of a bitch come round for another game of elbows?

I threw down the partially-smoked cigarette and upped the pace back to the flat, bags clattering against my legs as I ran. I couldn't find my keys due to all the rubbish stuffed in my jacket pocket; receipts, Cornish pasty wrappers and stones (stones?) all prevented me from getting inside and finding out what had spooked her so much. Littering the path, I opened the door and clambered up the stairs, barging through the door I'd left open when leaving. On seeing Penny in the hallway, I dropped the shopping and went to her immediately. 'Babe, what is it? What's wrong?'

'I'm so glad you're here.' She was clinging to me as if her life depended on it.

'It's not the baby is it? You want me to call the doctor?'

'No, no, it's not the baby. The baby's fine. In the lounge,' she said, pointing to the living room door.

'What? What do you mean?'

'Look.'

'Is it Miles?' I'd more or less convinced myself that it was. 'What a bastard. He's got some nerve coming here.'

'For God's sake,' she screamed, 'please just get rid of it.' In tears, she backed away and steadied herself against the wall.

What? Get rid of it? It? Cautiously, I approached the door and turned the handle, the creak of the wearing hinge doing nothing for the irregular speed of my heart.

'Can you see it yet?' she asked, destroying the silence.

I flinched. 'No, not yet.'

All the lights were on and the volume of the television was up loud. Once inside, I quickly spun around on my feet to face the rest of the room, expecting the onslaught of another fight.

There it was.

Sitting on the arm of the chair.

The most gigantic bumblebee you've ever seen in your life. A huge bugger with nothing better to do than scare the living crap out of a mum-to-be.

I caught my breath. 'It's just a bee.'

'How did it get in? All the windows were closed. I hate

'em, Barry, get rid of it.'

I took Penny in my arms and kissed her forehead. 'You want me to kill the poor thing? What has it ever done to you, huh?'

'Nothing, I just don't like it.'

'It's only a poor widdle bumblebee, sweetie!'

'I don't give a shit. I don't want it in the flat.'

All it took was for me to open the window, grab an old newspaper and softly shoo the unsuspecting madam out of the room. No big deal, really. 'You can come back in now,' I hollered through the door. 'The huge bee has left the building.'

'You sure?'

'Positivo, m'lady, it can't hurt you anymore. What you waiting for? Come in.'

'You really mean it? If you're lying, Barry Brooks, I'll rip your balls off.'

Of course, that's what would have occurred if I'd been living anything close to a normal life. Some people don't get on with bees, wasps, or any other kind of flying, stingy, bitey-type creatures. They hate them, and would prefer to avoid a confrontation at all costs. On occasion, these people would rather leave said creature alone with only its thoughts, in one of the rooms in the house. They'd wait, for millennia if need be, for someone who doesn't have that much of an issue with stingy, bitey-type creatures to come and heroically save the day.

Oh, how I wish that was the case. When I eventually got home from the shop, the problem wasn't something as minuscule as a bumblebee. Penny was in a state of shock; shivering, shaking, unable to control the excess saliva dribbling from her mouth. It was a sight I'd have given all the money I had never to see again. When the one you love is genuinely petrified, overtaken with fear, it cuts you in half, then quarters. When I discovered the nature of her fear, I felt like curling up in a tight ball until it was time to die.

When I walked into the brightly lit lounge, sitting on the

armchair wasn't a bee.

It was Kev.

TWENTY-SEVEN

'Kev?'

How the hell are you supposed to react when a dead man appears in your favourite armchair? Offer them a beer? Enquire as to how the afterlife is treating them? No, that's not what you're supposed to do at all. The first instinct is to run; run like an Olympic sprinter. Get the hell out of there and pretend your brain is playing a devilish trick on your eyes. You then give it some time to convince yourself what you saw was nothing more than an illusion; you think pure, happy thoughts about puppies, chocolate biscuits and spaghetti carbonara, before re-entering the room to find the dead person gone, with no indication they were ever there. Finally, you accept it was just a wacky hallucination born out of tiredness and stress.

I didn't do that. I didn't do it because I'd always been legendarily slack at taking my own advice. Truth is, I was in no way shocked to see him sitting there; it appeared my mind had grown accustomed to disturbing visions.

'Kev? Can you hear me?'

Looking into his lifeless eyes, I thought back to the night he died. Had my stubborn attitude cost him his life? For all I knew it would have happened anyway, even if I was more receptive. Had he popped in from the other side to give me a bollocking for being humanity's worst listener? As a rule, I didn't believe in ghosts; I thought them tricks of light or cruel moneymaking schemes aimed at grieving loved ones. This one, however, caused me to have a bit of a re-think.

'Answer me, Kev.'

Since that night, I'd found it difficult to focus on anything but the reams of unfinished business between us. Selfishly, I saw this as an opportunity to get the answers I was so desperately searching for. He had them, I wanted them.

'I'm glad you came back.'

Unresponsive, he sat, staring straight through me, the bleached jeans and white dress shirt he was wearing now faded. I moved closer; several buttons were missing, fat rolls bulging from between the gaps. Crusty, dried blood discoloured the collar and I also caught a whiff of stale alcohol.

'When you died, it wasn't right, was it?'

His mouth began to move, but there was no sound. I heard the door open and saw Penny hovering nervously, looking at me for some kind of explanation.

'What's happening? Is it Kev?' She twisted her head in disbelief, eyes fixed on his mouth.

'I don't know, Pen,' I said. 'I really don't know.'

'It's him, though?'

'Looks like it. What happened?'

'I dunno. One minute I'm watching TV, the next he's stood by the door. I tried to talk to him but he ignored me and sat down. I got scared and ran into the hall.' She took a few steps in our direction. 'He looks like he's in shock. Should I call someone?'

I wasn't sure what was going through Penny's head. Did she think Kev was still alive? In all honesty, that is how it looked. If her mind was somehow shielding her from the harrowing alternative, then I would do nothing to dispel that. 'Sweetheart, how about you go make us a cup of tea. I'll try to talk to him.'

She protested at first, but agreed when I told her it would probably make him feel better.

If he was going to say anything to me, now was the time; she wouldn't be in the kitchen forever. 'Talk to me,

Kev,' I said. 'I know I didn't wanna listen before, but I'm ready now.'

The speed of his mouth movement increased, but there was still no volume.

'I know you want to talk.'

The kettle was boiling; I had a few minutes, maximum.

'Come on, Kev, I can't hear you. What are you saying to me?'

Finally, he spoke. 'I'm… trying…'

'Trying? Trying to do what?'

'Pushing… through… difficult.'

He seemed to be in pain. His eyes were scrunched and his cheeks blushing.

'Keep talking,' I said, so close I was almost sat on his lap. 'I'm listening.'

'Barry… Brooks.'

'Yes, mate, I'm here. It's me.'

'Nearly… there now. A few more…. seconds.' He pointed to his breast pocket. 'There. Look, Barry.'

From what I could see, it looked like a scrap of paper. Forgetting all the movies I'd seen about the transparency of the dead, I reached over and pulled it out.

He was solid. My hand didn't pass through him. Ha, take that, Hollywood.

It was a folded-up note, torn messily from a cheap notepad. I hadn't noticed it before as the paper and his shirt were the same colour.

Kev was silent. His mouth had stopped moving. I opened the note and started to read:

Barry Brooks. Hungry, thirsty, occupied. This is the only way I can comuniccate. Diseased, unparaleld nonsense. I was found, but I rote. They found me, but I still rote. Imogen their frustration. Aware for it will all unravell in front of you. Can you sence it! Sixteen thousand, five hundred and counting. Be well, WBP.

I read it a second time. It made less sense.

Thanks for that, W.B.P., whoever you are. There I was expecting it to be nothing more than a sheet of indecipherable drivel.

Kev was smiling; a cheeky smirk as if he'd dropped one and was really pleased with himself.

Frustrated, I put the note in my front pocket and flopped back on the couch. 'What are you smiling at?'

'You, Barry.'

I shot upright. His speech was clear and effortless. 'What? Me?'

'Yep. You.'

'You're talking?'

'Yeah. I haven't got long.'

'What are you on about?'

'Just wanted to say thanks for being there with me. Y'know, at the end and stuff. I'll never forget it.'

'Kev, what's going on?'

'I was used for an echo. You wouldn't understand.'

He was probably right. It wouldn't stop me from trying, though. 'Explain it to me.'

'This body was used to send a message.'

'A message from who?'

'I think you know.'

The kitchen door opened. Penny was almost upon us with the drinks. 'Who?' I shouted.

'Tell Penny not to be frightened. It's safer here.'

Now what the hell was that supposed to mean? 'What are you saying? She's gonna die?'

He winked.

'You leave her alone, you fat bastard.'

'Beware the stairs. Catch you later, pal.'

The tray rattled with the sound of cups and Penny appeared. 'Here we are,' she announced, 'this should make you feel better, Ke...' She stopped mid-sentence. 'Where did he go?'

I turned around quickly, but Kev had disappeared. 'Fuck!' I cursed.

'Huh?'

I thumped the sofa cushions twice with my fist. 'Bastard!'

'Are you alright?'

I growled in frustration. 'I'm fine.'

'Did he leave?'

'Err, yeah,' I ad-libbed.

'Without saying goodbye?'

'He, err, didn't say much in the end.'

'Why was he here?'

'I don't know, babe. Maybe he wanted to be around friends?'

'But it doesn't make sense. Why would he come here?'

I shrugged.

'You think I should call his parents?'

'No,' I said quickly, 'I'm sure he'll be there soon enough. Best not to interfere.'

She wouldn't let it go, firing question after question at me about his appearance. I continued to reel off more lies, hoping my logic remained strong enough to convince her.

What Kev said really shook me up. It didn't take a particle physicist to work out what he was getting at. Should I have taken him seriously or chalked it down to disorientation? I couldn't decide, so opted to stay vigilant. I wasn't going to lose Penny as well. No way. Not a chance. She meant far too much to me.

"Beware the stairs."

I wrapped myself around her and kissed the top of her head. She seemed a little shaken, but the questions soon stopped and she resorted to thinking out loud. After the theory about Kev faking his own death to get out of debt, I'd had enough and asked her to quiet down, for her own sanity as much as mine.

"Tell Penny not to be frightened."

After a moment's silence, she piped up again. 'You seemed so calm about it all.'

'Calm about what?'

'About him being here. Weren't you surprised?'

'Yeah, course I was. The last thing I expected to see

sitting on that chair when I got back from the shop was Kev.' I let out a nervous snigger. 'Can't imagine how you must have felt.'

'My heart stopped,' she said, with a smile.

I didn't answer. That was too close to home.

'I thought he was a ghost at first.'

'No such thing as ghosts, hon, you know that,' I replied, assuredly.

'I know,' she said, stealing my tea for a sip. 'I'm just being silly.'

"It's safer here."

I promised myself it would be the final lie. 'Like you said, sweets, he'll be back home in no time. Hopefully, we can go for a drink with him soon.'

'I'd like that.'

I watched her get up and head for the door. 'Where are you going?'

"Beware the stairs."

'Bathroom. Is that okay?'

'Sure,' I said, getting up to follow her.

'Where are *you* going?'

'Nowhere. Just stretching my legs. Can I get you anything?'

'No, I'm good,' she said, closing the bathroom door.

I opened the front door and stepped out into the corridor, peering down the double winder staircase. Was it *these* stairs Kev was talking about? Was he somehow implying she was going to take a tumble down them?

I heard Penny's muffled voice from the bathroom. 'Barry?'

'Hmm?'

'Are you outside?'

'Yeah.'

'Why?'

I couldn't think of a decent explanation. Come on, Baz, think back to those episodes of *Whose Line Is It Anyway*; polish those improv skills, laddie. 'I thought I saw a rat.'

'A rat?'

'Yeah.'

'Four floors up?'

Four floors = lots of steps. Lots of steps to fall down. 'There's nothing here. Must have been a shadow.'

Sarcasm. 'I reckon. Last time I checked, rats couldn't fly, honey.'

'Maybe you're right, but last time I checked, neither could humans.'

'What's that supposed to mean?'

Shit. I didn't mean to say that out loud. 'Never mind.'

I went back inside after double locking the door, wondering if my bank balance could stretch to a communal lift for the building.

I wasn't that rich.

'Baby, you're hovering,' she said, interrupting my financial calculations.

'Hmm?'

'I can see your shadow under the crack in the door.'

'Oh,' I said, mid-thought. 'Sorry.'

The toilet flushed and she opened the door. 'You okay? You look a bit worried.'

'Oh, y'know, just thinking about Kev.'

'I know, me too, but I'm sure he'll be fine.' She gave me a hug. 'Fancy another cuppa?'

Before I could answer, the doorbell rang.

'I'll get it,' she said, walking to the door and having a look through the spy-hole. 'Eh? That's weird.'

'What?' I answered, lingering outside the bathroom.

'There's nobody there.'

'What?'

'Can't see anyone?'

Weirdness. 'It's not Miles arseing about, is it?'

'Dunno, hang on.' She opened the door and stepped out.

I panicked. 'Penny, watch the stairs.'

She didn't reply.

I pulled her back in by the arm. 'What did I say?'

'Barry, what are you doing?'

What does it look like? I'm saving you from a one-way,

257

high-speed trip to the ground floor. 'Be careful. Don't want you having an accident in your condition.'

'Don't talk rubbish. I can look after myself, y'know.'

Can you? Really? I just don't know, Penny. 'Stay away from stairs and big drops. No point taking unnecessary risks.'

'For God's sake, settle down. What did I just say?' She tugged free of my grip and bent down. 'Look, it's a new pizza menu.'

'Fine,' I said, 'bring it in and shut the door.' Keeping Penny away from potentially hazardous situations was turning out to be a lot more difficult than I originally thought.

'They're doing good deals on mega-sized deep pans.' She was about to close the door when yet another thing caught her eye on the floor outside.

Inside I was screaming. *Get back in here, woman!*

'You don't play golf, do you?'

What was she talking about now? 'No, why?' I looked over her shoulder and saw a golf ball perched on the first step, but didn't have time to figure out why it was sitting there. What happened next sent every vital organ hurtling towards my mouth. Carelessly and with speed, Penny rushed over to pick it up.

'No!' I shouted. 'Penny, no!'

She made a grave mistake by not listening. Her right foot caught on a kink in the rug, and with a dark inevitability, the sole of her left rolled over the golf ball. Completely off-balance, she held out her arms in a last-ditch attempt to steady herself, but the bannister was too far away. I watched helplessly as she hit step after step, each one with a painful moan, trying to grab on to something to stop her flight.

By the time my legs kicked into gear, she was more than halfway down the staircase. I threw myself after her, five steps at once, hoping I could catch up, but quickly ran out of time. She landed with a bone-splitting thud on the marble floor. Seconds later, I reached the bottom and collapsed beside her unconsciousness body. Her right leg was badly twisted and a pool of blood had formed from a gash on the side of her face.

'Penny, can you hear me? Penny?'

I heard a voice from the top floor. 'What's going on?'

It was Miles.

'Call an ambulance,' I shouted.

'What's happened?'

'Penny's fallen. Call a fucking ambulance.'

A few other residents heard the commotion and were now standing by their doors. Not one of the heartless bastards offered to help.

I was choking back the tears. 'Is anyone a doctor?'

Silence. Were they all deaf?

'What's wrong with you? What are you staring at? Help me.' I checked Penny's wrist for a pulse. It was there. Still beating, still strong.

'Miles? Tell me the ambulance is on its way.'

A voice boomed from one of the flats. 'Can you keep the noise down? My kids are trying to sleep.'

It sent me straight over the edge. If I could, I would have marched up there and clubbed him to death. 'Are you blind? Can't you see what's happened, you stupid prick? I don't care about your kids. Get down here and help, or go back inside and shut your fucking mouth.'

'No need to swear,' he replied, before slamming the door.

'Please, somebody help me,' I cried.

Miles launched himself down the stairs. 'What happened? Is she okay?'

'I don't know, she just fell. Tripped on the rug. I tried to warn her but she wouldn't listen.'

He grabbed her wrist. 'Ambulance is on its way.'

'Thanks. I've already checked that.' If Miles had a scrap of decency, he'd keep our ongoing rivalry separate to all this.

I did my best to stop crying. I couldn't fall apart now, not when Penny needed me the most. From the outside, it didn't look too serious, maybe a broken leg and a concussion. Hopefully, in a few days she'd be well on the way to recovering. Unfortunately, I didn't have the same optimism for the baby.

She came to. 'Barry,' she choked, 'where am I?'

'Sssh, try to stay still. You've had an accident.'

'An accident?'

'Yeah, but you're gonna be fine, okay? Just fine.'

'My leg hurts.'

'I know, sweetheart, I think it's broken. Keep still.'

'I'm so sorry. I should've listened to you.' She squinted and saw Miles sitting next to me. 'Oh, are you two friends now?'

Miles chipped in before I had a chance to wow her again with my poor acting skills. 'Course we are. I couldn't stay mad at this dude for long.' It was complete bullshit, but if it kept her calm, that's all that mattered.

'Miles called an ambulance. They'll be here anytime.'

Her nose began to bleed. 'The baby?'

'Honestly, I don't know.' From the corner of my eye, I saw the look on Miles' face. He wasn't completely taken aback.

'Oh, God,' she said, before passing into unconsciousness once again.

Ten minutes later, the ambulance arrived. They carefully lifted her on to a stretcher as I went over what happened. Miles wanted to accompany me to the hospital, but I told him to stay where he was.

'I didn't know there was a baby, Barry. I'm sorry.'

'You weren't to know.'

'Call me when you have some news?'

I appreciated his concern but still wanted to drop kick his pointless face into next year. 'I will.'

I sat patiently in the back of the ambulance as the short, grey-haired paramedic hooked Penny up various devices.

'Penny,' he said, adjusting the oxygen mask, 'Penny, my name is Derek. Can you hear me? Do you know where you are?'

She was unresponsive and it seemed to concern him.

'Is she gonna be alright?'

'All we can do is make her comfortable. We'll know more at the hospital.'

Thanks, Derek, your confidence is most inspiring. What was the point of a fully kitted out ambulance? Surely they had a techie, whizzy device on board that could help? Something to give me a tiny bit more than, ooh, I don't know, fuck all?

It was frustrating. I couldn't do anything but wait. I prayed hard they knew what they were doing.

Penny was still out twenty minutes later when we pulled into Homerton Hospital and finally came to a halt.

TWENTY-EIGHT

I've always hated hospitals. It has a lot to do with the ever-present reek of disinfectant. I know it's there for a reason, but it still reeks.

It smells of illness and death, which essentially, is what a hospital is all about.

Of course, it doesn't *actually* smell of illness and death; it's more a sterile, uncontaminated odour designed to mask the stomach-wrenching alternative. Unfortunately, it has become synonymous with unpleasantness.

Penny was wheeled through to intensive care and I watched the hospital staff tend to her injuries through the glass. There were seven in total, quick stepping around the room, doing everything they could to save her life.

One of the nurses brought me a coffee, which didn't calm the nerves at all. It was a shame the hospital shop didn't sell alcohol; I could have done with a wee nip. I thought about asking the ward sister if she kept an emergency bottle somewhere, but that would mean leaving Penny, and I wasn't going to do that.

I wouldn't have been so worried were it not for the head wound. Sure, a broken leg is serious, but providing it gets the correct attention, is quickly treated. Aside from exceptional occasions, it's not usually life-threatening. A leg break combined with a severe blow to the head, however, puts a completely different spin on things.

It was horrifying to see her lying there so helpless. She appeared conscious, though unable to speak or move. Part of me wished they'd sedate her so those petrified eyes would close. They told me to wait, but every part of me wanted to get in there and hold her hand.

She would never leave my sight again; I didn't care how difficult it would be. I'd gaffer tape myself to her if I had to.

Kev knew this was going to happen all along, and that made me feel sick. He wasn't at all delusional when he told me. If I ever saw his pointless, bloated face again, I'd rip it off.

Close to an hour passed. I'd been ushered into a small room by an unsympathetic nurse, had slurped my way through five coffees and was still waiting for an update on Penny's condition. The caffeine aided my restlessness, and I was close to firing off at the next ICU employee who walked passed the open door. Not one of them had thought to update me on how she was doing. It didn't have to be much; a nod or a thumbs up would have sufficed. What were they doing in there?

The nurse keeping me in coffee walked by and I took my chance. 'Excuse me?'

'Yes, sir?' she replied, popping her head around the door.

'Can you tell me how Penny's doing?'

'Penny?'

'Yeah. Is there any news?'

'Surname?'

'What? Don't you remember? You brought me a drink.'

'Not me, sir, I just started my shift.'

Was this a practical joke? 'Very funny. Can you tell me how she is?'

She shook her head and walked out. 'Hey,' I shouted, 'wait a minute.' By the time I got to the door and peered down the corridor, she was gone. I slammed the door in anger. 'Bitch!'

'Who's a bitch?'

I spun around immediately. Sitting in my chair was the

same nurse. 'Wha…? How did…'

'Everything okay, Mr. Brooks?'

'You just… I mean, I just saw you…'

'Do you want me to get you another coffee?'

'How did you do that?'

'Do what?'

It was late and I was tired. 'Look, I don't know what's going on…'

She stood up, gently placing her clipboard on the seat. 'You know more than you think.'

'What?'

'You've known from the minute you walked in. Look around, Barry. Can you smell the death? Can you hear the sound of your girlfriend in agony? Lying there all alone with no one to hold her hand? You did that. It's all your fault.'

'I didn't. I didn't do anything.'

She laughed, opening her mouth so wide I could see down her throat. 'Beg to differ.'

'Fuck you,' I said, bolting out the room. I ran with speed down the corridor, determined to get some answers.

'Wait,' she screamed, running after me, 'I haven't finished. There's so much more left to do.'

I didn't reach Penny's room. I didn't even get to the door. I slipped on the shiny, recently-mopped floor, landed on my arse and skidded out of control into the wall.

I was awake again. The nurse was hovering over me.

'Mr. Brooks?'

Momentarily startled, I rubbed my eyes to focus. 'Yeah?'

'A bad dream, was it?'

'Huh?'

'You were screaming.'

'Really?' I looked around. I was in the same room. It was just a dream, but I couldn't remember resting my head on the cushion. 'Sorry about that.'

'Don't worry. I'll bring you another drink, okay? The

doctors are still in with Penny. Hopefully, we'll have some news soon.'

I looked at my watch: ninety minutes since she was admitted. 'Thank you.' The overwhelming tiredness faded and I sat up. My mouth was dry and I could taste old coffee. 'Could I get some water too, please?'

'Of course, my love.' She smiled and left me to twiddle my thumbs for a bit longer.

I stood up to stretch my legs and walked over to a noticeboard hanging from the wall. It was full of thank you cards sent by families of patients admitted over the years. Some were only a few lines long, others a lot more detailed.

Reading a selection, I started to pray. I prayed I'd have the chance to send one of my own. I wasn't even sure I believed in God, but did it anyway. If he really did exist, surely he'd want Penny to pull through; God would hate to sit back and watch a young woman die before her time, wouldn't he?

I thought about Mrs. Winter, my religious education teacher at school. A committed Christian, she always used to prattle on about *living God's way*, meaning try not to use God as an excuse whenever you want something. Form a personal relationship with him; talk to him, tell him how your day was and the new things you discovered. It would be the same as having an imaginary friend, only one who has the ability to save your soul and bring promise of a divine afterlife. I thought it an amazing concept back then, spending fifteen minutes talking to God each night before I went to sleep. I'd tell him how good Mum's shepherd's pie was, reel off playground stories and point out which girls I fancied. He never spoke back, no matter how loud I shouted. I figured he was busy sat up in heaven, listening to the thoughts and prayers of millions of children. Older and a little wiser, I realise sending a copy of my glowing exam results via *Royal Mail* addressed to *God, Heaven*, was a bit daft. Expecting him to magic Sally Williams into my bedroom as a reward was also never likely to happen.

My prayer was not a complicated one. First, I asked him to look after Penny and the baby; to bring them both through this ordeal so we could be a family. Secondly, I asked for peace. My head was so full, unable to process any new information; it was spilling out the excess in the form of disturbing dreams. I didn't know which way to turn or what to think, but I knew I needed peace. What was that song Mrs. Winter taught us?

Peace I leave with you, my peace I give to you,
Not as the world gives peace, do I give.

I wanted to cry every time I heard it. No other song affected me in that way, unless you count the original theme to *Emmerdale Farm*.

With my head in my hands, I started to whisper: 'I don't know if you're listening, God, but things are a bit shit... sorry, bad, at the moment. I'm sure you already know how bad they are. I haven't spoken to you since I was a kid, but I'd really appreciate any help you could give right now...'

The door handle turned and a tall, white-coated man with a beard stepped inside. 'Mr. Brooks?'

'Yes?' I said, putting the good Lord on hold.

'I'm Doctor Phillips.'

'How's Penny? Is she gonna be okay?'

He smiled. 'Well, the leg break has been set and we've managed to stabilise her. She has a bad concussion, but all signs point to a full recovery.'

Elated, I jumped up and shook his hand. 'Thank God. Thank *you*, Doctor.' I caught him off-guard when the handshake led to a bear hug.

'You're welcome, but I'm afraid I do have some bad news.'

'What is it?'

He asked me to sit down, then confirmed what I was suspecting. 'I'm so sorry, but we were unable to save the baby.'

Jubilation turned to disappointment. Running fingers through my hair, my voice choked as I tried to reply. 'Are you sure?'

'Unfortunately so. Penny fell with such force it never looked likely we'd save him or her.'

I was glad he didn't refer to the baby as *it*.

'If it helps at all, I can relate to how you're feeling.'

I didn't think so, but according to Phillips, his wife went through a similar trauma a few years back.

'It was a shock, but the most important thing was she got better.'

Maybe he was right. Although I was devastated, Penny was out of danger, and we'd have plenty of opportunities to try for another baby.

'Can I see her?'

'Not just yet, we're still running some tests. They should be done in fifteen minutes, so you're welcome to go in after that.'

I let out a long sigh. It was coming up to two hours since we arrived.

'Try to be patient, Barry.' He pulled out a packet of cigarettes from his coat. 'Here. The shop downstairs doesn't sell them.'

'How did you…?

'I'm a doctor. I can tell.'

I thanked him, grabbed my jacket and headed for the door.

'Be careful, though,' he shouted after me, 'those things will kill you.'

TWENTY-NINE

The smoking area was obviously designed to reflect the medical profession's opinion on the habit. Situated outside the mental health ward next to the clinical waste dump, it consisted of two overflowing ashtrays with no shelter from the rain. A display of anti-smoking propaganda was also stuck to every available inch of wall space.

Alongside me stood Julian, an eccentric man who thought my name was Charlotte, and insisted on asking me ridiculous questions. I told him I wasn't sure what the weather was like this time of year in Minnesota, but could confidently vouch for the fact that women found incontinence attractive.

'Why are you here, Charlotte?' he asked, lighting up for the sixth time in as many minutes.

'Actually, it's Barry.'

'Right, right. Sorry, I get confused sometimes. Barry, Barry, Barry. I won't forget that again.'

'No problem. My girlfriend had a fall.'

'Oh dear, that is a shame. A bad one?'

'Afraid so.'

'Not what you need.' He scratched his head and thought for a moment. 'So, does that make you one of those lesbians?'

'Eh?'

He chuckled. 'You don't have to be coy with me, Charlotte. It's widely accepted nowadays.'

'What is?'

'Being a lesbian. Years ago you may have got beaten up for it, but now people are used to it.'

'But I'm not a...'

'Funny though,' he interrupted, 'my wife's called Charlotte. Isn't that weird?'

'My name's not...'

'I don't think you're related though. Do you have bladder trouble?'

'No, you're not listening to me...'

Another laugh, this time heavier, from the stomach. 'Then again, my other wife's called Barry. What a coincidence. We have so much in common, don't we, Charlotte?'

I gave up. He was clearly as mad as a gallon of sausages. 'Incredible,' I said, stubbing my cigarette out. 'Well, I'd better be getting back. My girlfriend needs me.'

'Of course, of course,' he said, 'you go, son. Make sure you give her a hug from me, won't you?'

Unlikely. 'I will. Thanks, Julian.'

'All the best, Keith.'

I rushed back inside and caught up with the nurse. She was in a panic, flicking through the admissions file. 'Are you okay?' I asked, getting her attention.

She turned around and immediately took my arm. 'Mr. Brooks, thank God. We've been looking for you everywhere.'

'What's going on?'

'Doctor Phillips needs to see you right away.'

'Oh? Where is he?'

'In Penny's room. You have to go see him now. Hurry!'

That didn't sound good at all. I sped down the corridor and burst through the door. Phillips was scribbling something down on a clipboard through the glass, and I tapped on the window. He saw me and immediately rushed out.

'Barry, where have you been?'

'Out for a smoke, like you said. Is everything alright?

The nurse said you needed to see me urgently?'

He removed his glasses and set them down on the window ledge. The intense look he gave told me he was upset about something. 'I don't know how to tell you this, but while you were gone we, err, encountered some complications.'

'What? With Penny? What kind of complications? I thought you said she was gonna be fine?'

'According to preliminary indications, she was, but after you left, she went into cardiac arrest.'

My heart sank. I knew little about medicine, but those two words put together sounded horrendous. 'Is she okay?'

'I'm sorry.'

'Sorry? What's that supposed to mean?' I brushed him aside and ran to Penny's bedside. 'What's wrong with her?'

'We did everything we could.'

I stared at her lifeless body. 'She's dead?'

'There was nothing we could do.'

'How can she be dead? Fifteen minutes ago she was gonna be fine. *You* said she was gonna pull through.'

'I don't know what to say.'

'Try something that makes sense.'

'Sometimes things happen unexpectedly. I can't justify it to you, all I can tell you is that I'm sorry and we did our best.'

I slumped down beside her and started to cry. 'No. Come on, tell me this isn't happening.' Penny's lifeless eyes stared up at me. She looked in pain. Gently nudging my face into hers, the warmth was still in her cheeks. 'I can still feel her.'

He approached her and placed the palm of his hand on her neck. 'It's just residual body heat,' he said after a few seconds. 'It lingers for a while.' Phillips moved his hand from her neck to my shoulder. 'Mr. Brooks… Barry, I really am so very sorry for your loss.'

'She died suffering, didn't she?'

'Try not to think about…'

'Answer me.'

He picked up the clipboard again and skim-read its contents. 'We gave her medication for the pain…'

'But it wasn't enough,' I said, finishing the sentence. 'I can't believe you let her die. I loved her so much. How could you?' I felt a rush of blood to the head. How dare he stand there and tell me the complete opposite of what he told me moments before? The red mist took over and I broke away from Penny and launched myself at him. We fell to the ground and I squeezed my hands around his throat. 'You were meant to look after her, you useless bastard.'

'Barry, stop,' he said, fighting for breath.

'You were wrong,' I said, in-between sobs. 'Admit it. You… were… wrong.'

'We did all we could. Stop this now. Hurting me won't bring her back.'

Maybe not, but it'd make me feel better. Eventually, I relented and let him go, rolling on to my side.

He coughed and wheezed his way out of the room for some water, returning a moment later to find me face down, wailing uncontrollably.

'I know it's horrible,' he said, joining me on the cold floor. 'I lost my sister in a car crash five years ago. It hurts, but taking it out on me isn't gonna solve anything. I wanted to save Penny. You have to believe that.'

'Who dies of a heart attack after falling down the stairs?' My tears were forming a pool on the floor. 'She only had a broken leg and a concussion.'

He didn't reply.

I got to my feet and walked to the bed. I wished her eyes would burst into life. 'Penny, I love you. I love you so much. Wake up, I know you want to. Please wake up. What am I gonna do without you? Why did you have to go?'

I felt his hand on me once again.

'Bring her back. Can't you use those pads that give you

an electric shock, y'know, start her heart again? I'll pay you. I don't care how much it costs. Can you do that?'

A quiet reply. 'We already tried that. I know it's upsetting, but brain death has occurred. Even if we could start her heart, Penny wouldn't be there anymore.'

I imagined her hooked up to numerous devices, unconscious and in care for the rest of her life. 'Not even a small chance?'

'No.'

'Are you absolutely sure?'

'Absolutely.'

'She's really gone?'

'She's gone.'

'What do I do now? Just a few hours ago we were starting a family. How am I supposed to carry on after this?'

'I know it's not easy to get it all straight in your head - that's only natural. If you like, I could arrange an appointment for you with one of the counsellors here on site...'

Not a chance. I didn't want a total stranger scraping inside my head for a non-existent cure. 'That won't be necessary,' I said, caressing her face.

'Fine. It may be too soon now, but you have to think about these things later. Promise me you will?'

I hesitated. Since he told me there was no way to bring her back, I just wanted him gone. 'Fine, whatever. Can you give me a few moments?'

As he left, I wasn't giving too much thought to my behaviour. I would come to regret assaulting him that night, and never got the chance to apologise. It was surely a sign of good character he didn't report me for assault.

Looking down at the bed, I gave it one last shot. 'Penny, please wake up. Don't go.' I held her and cried some more, emptying my eyes over the torn, blue and white shirt she was wearing.

A voice from the corner of the room brought a halt to my

mourning. 'It's unravelling, isn't it?'

I nearly shot through my own skin. Swinging around, I saw Kev in the corner of the room. 'You,' I spat, 'what have you done?'

'Unravelling. Just as I said.'

'I want an answer.'

'Me, me, me. Can't you see? This has nothing to do with *me*.'

'Really? Look at her.' I turned to Penny. 'Look at her face. Can you see that? Looks awful, doesn't it?'

Silence.

'You said it before. Back at the flat, you said she'd be *safer here*. You knew about all of this and I want to know how.'

'She is safe, Barry. Safer than she's ever been before. You wanna know why?'

Kev having the upper hand annoyed me more than reality television. 'I don't care what you think.'

'Oh, but I think you do, Barry. Inside, you're intrigued as to what I know. Your little brain's working overtime trying to get one over on me, but it won't work.'

Score: one to Kev. 'Enlighten me, then.'

'She's safer here because she's not with you.'

Incredible. Only a few hours ago he was thanking me for being with him at the end; now, the overfed dog's arse was slagging off my qualities as a human being. 'So I was bad for her, is that what you're saying?'

'Exactly, but not for the reasons you think.'

Enough was enough. Kev's motives for randomly turning up were still unknown to me, but in light of Penny's death, I was determined to find out why I had to endure his dim-witted face at a second's notice. 'I've had it with the bullshit. Did you kill Penny?'

He seemed a bit irked. 'Pardon me?'

'Did you push her down the stairs?'

'You're not hearing what I'm saying.'

'Because what you're saying is complete shit. You're not making any sense, don't you realise?'

To fuel my rage, he started cackling.

I squared up to him. 'Do you think this is funny? Do you think I want to laugh when I'm looking over my dead girlfriend? I'm not laughing.'

'It just gets worse, doesn't it, mate?' He was still giggling.

'Don't call me mate. You're not my mate. What gets worse?' Why couldn't he show a little respect? What could anyone find so amusing about a senseless death?

'Your life and every aspect of it. It started bad, took a wrong turn and finished a crumbled piece of dust in your hand. That's your life.'

'What do you want from me? Tell me what I have to do to make you disappear.'

'Told you before. You have to become aware.'

'Aware of what?'

'Aware that you, Barry Brooks, are living a life of complete failure. Your existence, everything around you, lies meaningless now. As soon as you can truly accept your abject pointlessness in this life, only then is there hope for you.'

'Shut your mouth, fat arse.'

He patted his bloated stomach. 'I've heard worse.'

'Leave me alone.'

'Have it your way, buddy boy. There's only so much I can do.'

'Only so much? Don't you think you've done enough? How is it that since I met you, everything's gone wrong? It's fine for you to stand there and tell me how crap my life is, but you're the cause. If I hadn't defended you in the supermarket - no, if I hadn't joined your lard-infested checkout queue - none of this would have happened.'

'My presence there and now is irrelevant. It would have happened even if I was never born. There's nothing I can do but lead you on to the right path, but your stubborn attitude is making it impossible for me.'

It sounded like something from *The Twilight Zone*. 'Here's something you can do which shouldn't be too taxing: piss off. Let me grieve in peace.'

He grunted. 'As you wish, but remember, it's coming for you. The only way to avoid it is by taking my advice.'

'I said piss off!'

The image of Kev evaporated into thin air.

One of the nurses crept quietly into the room. I saw her reflection in the mirror above Penny's bed. 'Is there a problem, sir? I heard shouting.'

'No problem.'

'We really need to clean up in here, if that's alright?'

'Okay.' My voice had cracked somewhat from shouting at Kev. 'Can you give me another minute?'

Leaning over Penny, I brushed her eyes closed with my fingers. 'I let you down, baby. I'm so sorry. I promised to look after you and I couldn't even do that, but I swear I'll be there with you soon.'

Was there anything worth living for anymore? My parents had gone, Penny had gone; what delights were keeping me attached to this grotty planet? An apartment riddled with memories? Her favourite perfume lingering in every room? Echoes of my family that never had the chance of life? It was the last place I wanted to be, but I didn't know where else I could go. I had the money to check myself into a hotel for a few nights, but it would only delay the inevitable. Add to that *Giant Haystacks* inviting himself unannounced into my head, begging for my awareness; I was starting to think life wasn't worth the effort. It was a shitty plane of existence that had kicked me in the balls too many times.

I really thought Penny and I had it figured out; our relationship, the baby, the money - it all seemed to be coming together. Now, all of it was gone and I had nothing left to hold.

I made the easiest decision of my life right there: I was better off dead. If anything, topping myself would be a rigid, middle finger to society. At least there'd be one less person to take a dump on from a great height. I wasn't about to give this life the satisfaction of squatting above my head ever again.

Not for anyone. No chance.

Kissing her on both cheeks, I covered Penny's body with a blanket. Saying goodbye wasn't difficult, as I had every intention of being with her before the night was out. Glancing up at the clock, I left my girlfriend behind and made my way to the main entrance. It was almost two in the morning.

THIRTY

'Five seventy-five, boss.'

I handed the shopkeeper a tenner, took my cigarettes and left the shop. The rain had stopped and a biting wind had taken its place. I zipped my jacket and lit one up, blowing the smoke through my nose.

Leaving the hospital took far too long. If it wasn't doctors racing after me with forms to sign, the nurses were coming at me for a hug from all angles, trying to force me to take up Phillips' offer of professional counselling. I managed to shrug them off by lying, telling them I'd be fine in the hands of my parents, then bolted through the main entrance and into the night.

Happy birthday, Barry. Did you really expect to enter the twenty-sixth year of your life under these circumstances?

The streets of east London were buzzing, surprisingly so for the early hours. Most of the hedonistic drunkards I came across were in fancy dress, so figured there must have been a party nearby.

At least they were having fun. I'd have done anything to swap places.

Avoiding pools of puke in the street, I thought back to the last time I was totally carefree. It must have been in the week leading up to the climb. Beth left, shattering everything, and from then on, it was one long sequence of devastation. No matter where I turned, there was always something waiting for me, hovering just ahead to catch me on the hop. Just out of shot.

What kind of a disgusting human being do you have to be to deserve such treatment? Was I Jack the Ripper in a previous life? Had karma decided to open its arsecheeks and fire its judgment straight at me?

I failed to see how it could get any worse, but remained cautious. I may have run out of people to lose, but there were still things that could be snatched away: my flat, the car, my huge stash of cigarettes, to name but a few. No matter how much effort you put in, it isn't possible to conjure every feasible scenario. To try would surely lead to insanity.

I picked up the pace, my decision reinforced. I no longer cared about the material things. My life would end that night.

It wasn't the safest part of town for a post-midnight stroll. It pays to stay alert in the capital, especially at night, but to be honest I'd have welcomed a fatal stabbing or shooting. At least it would all be over quickly. Then again, my run of luck wasn't great; I'd probably find an inventive way to balls that up too. Half-way through the confrontation, I'd tell them to hurry up and shank me, and the silly bastards would think it a waste of time and take off with what money I had and my trainers. Either that or they'd shoot me in the hand, or some other non-life-threatening area.

Idiots.

She had only been dead for an hour and I missed her so much. How the hell could I carry on without her? Wherever I looked across the darkened street corners, I saw her from the shadows. Her face was imprinted behind my eyes like a permanent scar, and all I wanted to do was lay my head down peacefully on her lap. I could drift to sleep knowing she was with me, leaving the harrowing images and endless conundrums behind. My luck had run out when it came to life, but at least she believed in me. Even if there was no afterlife, just a dark abyss of everlasting black, at least the heartache would be gone. I had no clue what to expect, but was willing to give it a shot for her.

Twenty minutes later, I found the all-night pharmacist the shopkeeper told me about. Once inside, I made for the counter and looked around for strong painkillers.

The shop assistant looked up. For a second, she didn't speak, as if trying to place my face. 'Can I help you?'

'I can feel a migraine coming on. What have you got?'

I answered the standard questions: had I taken this kind of medication before? Did I suffer from a range of illnesses that could be encouraged by taking this medicine? Was I pregnant? Answering where appropriate, I thanked her, paid for the tablets and headed for the exit.

'Wait,' she shouted, 'hang on a moment.'

I turned back. 'Yeah?'

'Sorry, but is your name Barry?'

'Do I know you?'

She smiled a beautiful set of shiny, white teeth. 'Oh my God, it is you. Barry Brooks. I can't believe it.'

Maybe she had me confused with another man who looked like me with the same name. Or maybe the stress of the day had caught up with me. 'I'm sorry, I really…'

'Ayesha?'

The look on my face screamed out for a surname.

'Ayesha Harris?'

The name did sound familiar. 'Err…'

'We went to school together? Years ten and eleven?'

Finally, it clicked. 'Ayesha,' I said, walking back to the counter, 'my God, how are you? Sorry, I'm, err, not really with it tonight…' I looked at the clock on the wall and corrected myself, 'this morning.'

Ayesha and I sat next to each other in all the classes we took in the final two years of school. She was seeing the most popular guy - amazingly, that wasn't me - and I was her best friend. I was the one who gave her advice on how to deal with female classmates who regularly threw themselves at him. We had a connection for a while, but predictably, lost touch. I started to like her a bit too much, she found out, didn't reciprocate, we left school and that was that. Unfortunate, really. She'd turned into a Grade A stunner over the years.

She looked concerned. 'Are you alright? You seem a bit distant.'

'Err, yeah, no, I'm good, thanks. A rough night is all.'

'I'll say,' she said, smiling again, 'have you sobered up already?'

'What?'

She pointed to the headache tablets.

'Oh, right, the pills. No, I haven't been drinking. I've, erm, just come from the hospital.'

'Really?'

'Yeah. It turned into a bit of a late one.'

She probably thought I was an addict, sloping through the streets with insomnia, tracking down the nearest dodgy dealer for my next fix.

'Right,' she replied, backing off, 'well, it was lovely to see you again.'

I didn't want her to think me a no-hoper; it'd be all over *Friends Reunited* in a matter of hours: *"Remember that Barry Brooks? I saw him at three in the morning, gurning his tits off."* I'd never touched drugs in my life, except for that one time someone slipped an LSD tab into my coffee and I spent the weekend in Narnia. I blurted out the events of the day, from Penny's fall to how I found myself taking in the early-morning air.

She looked at me in horror. 'Oh, God, I am so sorry,' she said, swinging open the security door and coming out to give me a hug, one of many I'd had that evening.

I held on to her. 'It's alright.' I replied. But it wasn't. It was far from *alright*. It would never be anywhere near *alright* again. 'Look, Ayesha,' I said, after a moment's embrace, 'it's been really good to see you again, but I should be getting home. I'm not feeling too good.'

'Should you be on your own? I mean, after such a shock?'

'I dunno, I'm not…'

'I finish in ten minutes. We could grab a coffee or something?'

No, I don't want to have coffee, thank you. I'd very much like to find a secluded alley somewhere and neck all of these pills. 'It's pretty late, y'know.'

'I don't care. You shouldn't be alone. There's an all-night cafe near my place that could fix you up with something a bit stronger. You look like you need it.'

Something stronger, you say? 'Where do you live?'

'About half a mile that way,' she replied, pointing to her left. 'A cab could get us there in a few minutes.'

The alcohol sold me, and even though my top-secret plan was put on hold, at least I wasn't going back to the flat. I may have said otherwise, but it was never an option.

Behind the counter was a mirror I guessed was the same kind of thing you saw in American cop shows; they could see you, but you couldn't see them. Ayesha banged on it with her fist and a few seconds later, a small man with brown, thick-rimmed glasses and a truly awful toupee popped his head around the door.

'Yeah? What?'

'I'm knocking off now, Simon,' she said, taking her coat from a peg behind the door. 'Got something I have to deal with.'

'But you've still got ten minutes left,' he said, looking at his watch.

'For God's sake, take it out of my pay if you're gonna be like that.'

'Fine, I will.'

'Come on, Barry,' she said, linking my arm.

We left the pharmacy and flagged down a cab. No sooner had I sat down in the back of the car it was time to get out. I saw the coffee house she mentioned at the side of the road.

'You take a cab all the time? You could walk it in five minutes.'

She gave the driver the fare, plus tip. 'I know, but you

see that kebab shop?'

I'd missed it, but six or seven doors down, a large group of men, surrounded by an even larger plume of smoke, were taunting every woman who passed with coarse chat-up lines.

'Woah, come 'ere, darlin', I got summink for ya,' said number one.

Number two: 'Want summink hard to chew on, sweetheart?'

'Get yer tits out, bitch,' number three added.

'You've had to deal with that?' I asked.

'A few times. I went out with one of 'em for a while.'

I didn't say anything. It wasn't my place to question her taste in men. Not anymore, anyway.

'Turns out he was taking money off his mates.'

'What for?'

'They'd give him a tenner if he could get me to do certain stuff, y'know, in the bedroom, and film it on his mobile.'

'What a bastard,' I said, following her inside.

'Innit. When I dumped him he threatened to put in on the internet and send copies to my Mum and Dad.'

'So I guess it's safe to say you're not friends anymore?'

She laughed. 'Yep, definitely. I got him back, though. Asked a friend to pretend to come on to him, y'know, like she fancied him and stuff? He took her back to his place and when he went to the bathroom, she grabbed his mobile and made a run for it.'

'Nice work.'

'Large latte for me,' she said, 'and could you do a double scotch and ice for my friend, please?'

'How do you know I like scotch?'

'Remember at school? You said in year ten that when you were old enough, you'd always order scotch, 'cos it's what all the cool people in films drink.'

'You've got a good memory.'

'There's more where that came from.'

We took the drinks and headed a few doors up to her

place. Ayesha lived above the newsagents in what I could only describe as the anti-bachelor pad. Everything was pink, from the furniture to the wallpaper. Teddy bears were positioned on the sofa and armchairs, and the pink, plug-in air fresheners were pumping out a combination of flowery scents I associated with pink. There was every chance I'd go home having altered my sexual preference and views on pot pourri.

It was three-thirty, and although late, I wasn't in the slightest bit tired. Ayesha should have been, but she was happy to ask me unending questions about Penny and our relationship that I didn't need any encouragement to answer. She giggled when I told the story of how we got together, chipping in to tell me when it's true love, it doesn't matter, as things have a way of working in your favour. It was nice to hear, but all too soon I began to dwell on Penny's numbed face at the hospital. Her distressed eyes were burning a hole in my head and I couldn't finish the story. I was crying once again.

'You poor thing,' she said, handing me a tissue, 'I'm sorry. You don't have to talk about it if you don't want.'

I tried to smile. 'No, I do. I mean, I really want to, I'm just not sure I can.'

'Tell you what, why don't we change the subject for a while? As soon as you feel better and wanna carry on, just let me know, okay?'

'Okay.'

She opened the chest of drawers pushed against the wall and handed me a photo album. 'Have a look at these. They're from a beauty pageant I did a couple of months ago.'

'You were a beauty queen?' I said, with more surprise than intended.

She feigned shock. 'Thanks very much. As a matter of fact, I was.'

'No, I didn't mean...'

More teasing. 'I know, I know, you don't think I'm pretty enough, but that's fine.'

They were stunning. 'You look amazing,' I said, knocking back the whiskey.

'Thanks. Dressing up like that made me feel amazing too.'

I noticed a tall chap with his arm around her in one of the shots. 'Who's the lucky guy in your life?'

'Jordan,' she said, less than enthusiastically.

Jordan was the guy she'd been seeing on and off for the last year. He was a salesman, always away on business, travelling up and down the country. Occasionally, he'd go abroad, leaving her for weeks on end. She wouldn't tell me exactly *what* he sold, choosing only to describe it as *various bits of shit*.

'You must miss him.'

'Not really. When he comes back, he gives me presents, takes me shopping and out for posh dinners, all that girly stuff, y'know? The rest of the time I just go to work and come home.'

'So you don't love him?'

She didn't answer straight away. 'Nah. He's a nice guy, though, he really is. A lot better than most of the men around here.' She was clearly referring to her blackmailing ex with a penchant for mucky videos. 'Anyway, what happened to your migraine?'

I didn't have the heart to tell her there never was one, given the fact I lied to cover up a suicide attempt. 'It eased off. Just a dull throb now.'

We talked for a few hours about me, about her, about Jordan and whatever he was selling, before re-living school days. Her face lit up when I told her how much I liked her and felt sick every time she mentioned the most popular boy in school's name.

'You're sweet,' she said, reaching over for another hug, 'I can see why Penny fell for you.'

By the time daylight began to seep through the curtains, I'd more or less forgotten about my plan to end things. On taking me in and giving me alcohol, Ayesha succeeded in keeping me alive a little longer.

She took the cushions from the sofa and laid them out on the floor. With three duvets from the bedroom, we spread them out and set up temporary camp. At seven o'clock, she pulled me close and allowed me to fade away in her arms.

'You can stay here for as long as you like,' she whispered. 'When you decide to go home, I'll come with you.'

'You wouldn't mind?'

'Least I can do.'

'Thank you,' I said, closing my eyes.

Hovering on the edge of consciousness, I wondered how long it would take before something wrecked our friendship. I'd managed to alienate almost everyone I'd come into contact with thus far, so why should she be any different? Maybe she'd do a Will and threaten to kill me over an unspecified act, or die in a tragic accident like Penny.

Having been re-acquainted with an old friend, I'd have done anything to keep her safe. Seeing her smile gave me the impetus to get up and work through the heartache. Being with her could have aided me through the bad times, her bright, innocent smile helping me believe the world wasn't such a decaying, cess-covered latrine.

But other forces had other plans. Less than a week later, her opinion of me would change drastically. I'd be standing over a dead body, blood on my clothes with a knife in my hand.

THIRTY-ONE

Dear Terry,

I don't know if you'll ever read this, but I just wanted to say how I much I love and miss you. It's so hard with you not around. I wake up every morning, roll over and expect you to be there, but then realise you're not. It sounds silly, doesn't it? Whenever I look in the mirror, I see my reflection and pretend you're talking back to me, hearing me from wherever you are. I hope you're happy there, and although you never write or call, a part of me hopes you still think of me as much as I think about you.

If, by some strange twist of fate, you do get to read this, please let me know. Get in touch somehow. I'll always be waiting for you - we all will. The oven's on and the cookies are almost done - be nice if you joined us for afternoon tea.

Love always, your lemon puff, Kath x

'What does it say?'
  'It's a bloody love letter.'
  'What?'
  'Yeah, to someone called Terry.'
  'Why was it addressed to you?'
  'It wasn't, well, not really. The envelope had this address, but there was no name.'
  'Who's Terry?'
  'No idea. Never heard of him.'

'Shit, Barry, it must be the last thing you need right now.'

We walked up the same stairs Penny fell down. Approaching the door, I chose the right key and placed it in the lock.

'Are you sure about this?' she asked.

'To be honest? No, I'm absolutely shitting myself, but I've gotta do it. The sooner, the better.'

I had been at Ayesha's place for four days by this point, every day putting off the inevitable trek back home. It would have happened a lot sooner were it not for her insisting I stayed there and used the washing machine to avoid running out of clothes. I washed the same set twice, using her pink dressing gown to hide my modesty while they dried.

To put up with me for so long in such a small flat made her an angel in my eyes. There were no moments of uneasiness, or arguments over who used the last of the hot water. She took some time off work and we spent the nights drinking, chatting, watching films not in the least bit soppy or romantic, ordering take-away food and sleeping on the floor.

I called Kat on the second day to let her know about Penny. Understandably distraught, she didn't say much, only that she'd alert the family and liaise with the coroner to organise the funeral. I'd heard nothing since and hoped to God she wouldn't cut me out of any arrangements she was making. We'd only been together a few weeks, but in my eyes, that was time enough. Now that I was back at the flat, I'd have my mobile again and be able to follow up on any plans made.

The door opened without me turning the key. In the mayhem of getting Penny to the hospital, I'd forgotten to lock the damn thing. Half-expecting the place to be in ruins, I was surprised to find everything in its right place. I cursed my stupidity; I could have been totally ripped off.

'Gorgeous place,' she said, admiring the décor, 'I could definitely live somewhere like this.'

'You can have it if you like.'

She walked into the lounge and went straight for the photograph of Penny on top of the television. 'Is this her?'

'Yeah,' I answered, quietly.

'Barry, she is so beautiful.'

'Was so beautiful.' It just came out. I regretted it at once. 'Sorry.'

Ayesha looked uneasy.

'She's a stunner, isn't she?' I took the frame from her and ran a finger over Penny's digitally-enhanced face. 'This is all that's left. The only photograph of us together. I haven't got anything else.'

'I have,' a voice said from the door.

It was Miles. In his left hand was a small, wooden box.

'Door was unlocked, mate.'

I immediately went on the offensive. 'Door's been unlocked for a week. I'm surprised you didn't help yourself.'

'Come on, Baz, it's hardly the time to be arguing, is it?'

I was a bit out of order with him. 'Maybe you're right. How'd you find out?'

He shuffled inside. 'Your phone was switched off so I called Kat. She told me.'

I bet that was a brief conversation. 'I see.'

'I'm sorry. I know how much you cared about her.'

He was the last person I wanted to reminisce about Penny with. 'What's in the box?'

'Yeah, look, I know we not exactly best mates or anything, but there's a ton of photos in here. They're yours if you want them.'

Was he about to hand me a stack of pictures of them together to spite me? Look how many photos I have compared to your one and only snap?

'I've taken a load out. The only ones in there are of Penny on her own.'

At a push that could be considered gentlemanly. 'Err, cheers.' I took it from him and peered inside.

He noticed Ayesha and gave me a suspicious look, as if

Penny was a distant memory and I'd gone out to bone the first girl I clapped my eyes on. 'I'm Miles, I live next door.'

She shook his hands. 'Ayesha. Barry and I are old friends.'

He looked at me as if to say *give her one for me, pal.*

At that moment, I lost my temper and threw the box on the floor. 'You don't have to explain anything to him. She's not my rebound, if that's what you're thinking. I'm not slipping it to her to soothe the grief.'

'Barry, I…'

'You had to get cheap shot in, didn't you, you bastard?'

'Calm down, Baz,' Ayesha said, taking my hand, 'I'm sure he doesn't think that at all.'

'I haven't got time for this,' Miles said, turning to leave. 'I was only trying to offer some support.'

'I don't bloody need it,' I shouted, as the door slammed.

I sat down in the armchair to rest my head. After a few deep breaths, my composure began to return. The room was quiet except for the sound of my brain; a soft, rushing noise, sweeping me away as if I was holding a sea shell next to my ear.

Ayesha broke the silence. 'So, that's her ex?'

'In all his glory.'

'Not blessed in the looks department, is he?'

'I thought he'd be every woman's wet dream with all those muscles.'

She put the photo frame back and sat down. 'Doesn't do it for me, really. Everybody's gotta have a bit of flab, otherwise there's nothing to hold on to. Once they start sweating your hands just slip off.'

'Oooh, I know, there's nothing worse.' I felt qualified to empathise after so much time in the presence of all that pink. 'Thanks, you've made me feel a lot less self-conscious.'

'They've gotta be well equipped, though, y'know, down there?'

'Really? How well equipped?'

'Nothing extravagant. Ten inches is about right.'

A withering feeling in my crotch. 'Really?'

'Oh yeah.'

'You serious?'

'Yup.'

'And most girls feel this way?'

'Those that I know do.'

Hoping she hadn't noticed the look of sheer terror on my face, I desperately tried to remember my own measurements. 'Really? Ten? Wow. That's, err, not very much, is it.'

Teasing laughter. 'Relax, Barry, I'm only joking.'

'What?'

'I'm winding you up.'

I waved a playful fist. 'You had me worried for a minute.'

'Can't believe you fell for it. Ten inches? What do think I am, hollow?'

She went into the hallway to lock the door. 'Are we gonna make a start, then?'

I appreciated Ayesha keeping the conversation light. It helped take my mind away from the task at hand. I wasn't sure if packing Penny's things so soon after her death was the right call, but how much time should you allow in these kinds of situations? How long is too long? I guess it's personal preference, but for me I couldn't stand the thought of her things being within arm's reach. What if I lost the plot and started to parade around the flat in her underwear, listening to her *Dido* CDs on repeat and crying uncontrollably into her favourite teddy bear? It didn't bear thinking about.

We went through to the bedroom to round up Penny's things. Ayesha sorted through the clothes as I stood at the doorway, holding my nose to dodge a variety of perfumes I'd come to associate with my late girlfriend.

Half-an-hour later, we finished. Penny's clothes were sorted into bin bags and Ayesha offered to take them down to the charity shop.

'I'd really appreciate that.'

'Consider it done.' She dropped the final bag alongside the pile. 'Are you okay?'

'I'm okay. Wasn't as bad as I thought it would be.'

'That's good, isn't it?'

'Guess so. You did most of the work, though.'

'That's why I came along. We'd have been here hours if you were the one in charge.'

I smiled and put my arms around her. 'Thank you so much. You've been absolutely fantastic.'

'Least I can do for my new best friend.'

'You're my only friend.'

An affectionate ruffle of the hair. 'Baz, I've been thinking. Why don't you stay at my place a bit longer?'

I felt relieved. The thought of closing the door and being alone in the flat for longer than five minutes gave me chest pains. Having to sleep in *our* bed again? I'd have preferred genital warts. 'You don't mind?'

'I'm not daft. I can see you'd rather spend the whole of Christmas Eve on Oxford Street than stay here.'

True, but it wasn't a case of *give it a week then come back stronger*. I never wanted to spend another night there ever. All she was doing was delaying the time it took me to put the flat on the market. 'Isn't Jordan due back at some point?'

'Not for a few months, but even if he was, he's got his own place. He can stay there.'

It gave me some breathing space. 'If you're sure?'

'No problem. I'll take the bags now, you pack some things and I'll come back to pick you up. Will you be alright here on your own for an hour?'

I nodded. 'That's fine. I need to make a call anyway.'

She left with the bags and I picked up my phone from the kitchen. There were no messages, so I scrolled through the address book and dialled Kat's number.

It rang, but diverted to voicemail. 'Hi Kat, it's Barry. Just calling to catch up. Hope everything's okay, under the circumstances. Speak to you later.'

I hung up.

Ten seconds later, she returned the call. 'Barry? It's Kat. Did you call?'

'Yeah, I left a message.'

'Sorry, I haven't had a chance to check.'

'I just wondered if anything had been decided about the funeral.'

'The what?'

'Penny's funeral? Do you know if it's gonna be down here or up there? I'm thinking about travel arrangements and…'

'What are you talking about?'

Did she really want me to take her through the grisly details again? I did that once and almost lost my entire stomach contents. 'What are *you* talking about? I'm talking about Penny's funeral.'

'Penny's not dead, you loon. What's wrong with you?'

She sounded annoyed, as if I was playing some kind of warped trick on her. Could it be classic denial due to stress? 'I know it's difficult to accept. I'm having trouble myself.'

'Have you got a fever, hen?'

'I'm not the one with the fever.'

'Are you sure? I think you might need to see a doctor.'

'Stop messing around, Kat. The last four days have been bloody horrible for me. I understand you're probably in denial, but…'

'In denial? What's there to be in denial over?' Her patronising lilt was making my teeth itch.

'Listen to me. Penny's dead. You have to accept it and move on. We're both in the same boat, here.'

Silence on the line. 'If this is your idea of a sick joke, let me tell you it's not funny.'

'A sick joke? I called you the other night and told you Penny had fallen down the stairs. I took her to hospital, but she didn't make it. She died, Kat. Penny lost our baby and died. You told me you'd tell the family and arrange the funeral.'

'Get some sleep, hen. You sound like you need it.'

'I don't need sleep. And stop calling me *hen*.'

'I know what this is about, y'know.'

'Yeah?'

'Yes. You don't have to pretend with me. Pen told me about the argument. It doesn't sound like a biggie, she needs some time is all.'

What the hell was this dumb broad drivelling about? 'What argument? When did she tell you about an argument?'

'Last week, when she arrived.'

'Arrived where?'

'At my house, dopey.'

I meant to sit down on the chair in the kitchen, but slid down the wall and hurt my arse on the floor. 'So you're saying Penny's at your house? With you? Now?'

'Where else is she gonna be?'

I was about to say *rotting alone in a fridge*, but thought better of it. 'She's alive?'

• She laughed. 'Of course she's alive. She's sitting opposite me. Doesn't want to speak to you, mind.'

How could Penny be alive? I held her limp body in my arms less than a week ago. 'Don't mess with my head. If you're telling me she's alive, you've gotta let me speak to her now.'

'No, Barry. She came here for a break. A break from you. I told her she didn't have to talk to you if she didn't want to.'

'You don't understand. This isn't right. Please put her on the phone.'

'No.'

'You're such a bitch.'

'Barry, come on,' she said, adopting a more serious tone, 'there's no need for that.'

I was on the verge of shouting. 'She's not there at all, is she? You're lying. You're making it all up because you can't stand the thought of her gone.'

'I'm hanging up.'

'Tell me I'm wrong.'

She cupped the receiver and I heard mumbling in the background. 'Who's that?'

'I'm hanging up.'

'No, no, don't hang up.'

'She told me you've been through a lot recently. That's the only reason I'm still giving you the time of day. If you're gonna carry on insulting me, this conversation's over.'

Penny said what? A rough time? Why would she tell her that? There was no argument; certainly not one which led to her packing a bag and heading to Scotland. I lowered my voice and promised not to call her any more names. 'Let me speak to my girlfriend.'

'Can't do that, Barry.'

I tried a different approach. 'At least tell me why she's up there? What was the argument about?'

'As if you need me to tell you.'

'Yes, I do.'

'She wanted to keep the baby, you wanted her to get rid of it. Does that sound familiar?'

I wanted her to do what? That wasn't the way it happened at all. We'd both wanted the baby and spoken about it at length. I'd even danced a silly little dance and sung *I'm gonna be a daddy* in a variety of funny accents. How could she tell Kat I wanted her to have an abortion? More importantly, how come she was suddenly alive? 'No, it's not coming back to me. I wanted the child, I never said anything about getting rid.'

'Not what she said.'

'I wanna speak to her now.'

'No, Barry.'

'You're lying. This is all bollocks.'

'What is?'

'All this about Penny being alive, the argument between us that never took place. It's bollocks.'

No reply.

'Kat?'

Static. Lots and lots of static on the line.

'Bitch!'

'No,' she replied.

'No, you're not a bitch? Well I disagree.'

'Not what she said.'

It let the bulk of my surpressed rage out, but firing insults and smart-arse replies north of the border wasn't overly productive. I did find it relaxing in a macabre way, though. 'She wouldn't, would she? She's your sister. She loves you. She's not gonna tell you you're a bitch.'

'No.'

'No. Precisely what I just said. Let me speak to her.'

'Not what she said.'

'Let me speak…' I stopped. That didn't make sense, did it? I said *let me speak to her*, and Kat replied with *not what she said*. 'Kat?'

'No.'

'Katrina of Scotland, sister of Penny,' I continued.

'Not what she said.'

'Listen to me.'

'Not what she said.'

'Ding-dong, flange, Scotland smells of piss.'

'She's not here, Barry.'

Penny's sister had stopped acknowledging my questions. 'Mopping the floor is quite therapeutic for epileptic rabbits, wouldn't you concur?'

'She's not here. Stop asking to speak to her.'

'*Land Rover*, dog crap, bus ticket, bouncy ball.'

'She's not here. Stop asking to speak to her.'

Her voice appeared to be on a loop. Thinking back, it had been that way since all that static on the line seconds earlier.

My heart was racing. All of a sudden, the apartment felt bitterly cold. Shivering and a little spooked, I hung up and rushed out, without packing a bag or picking up the car keys. I slammed the door and sprinted on to the street to hail a cab. Once inside, I gave the driver directions and texted Ayesha:

Am coming 2 ur place.Sumthn weird happnd in the flat,freakd me out.Go strait home.Bx

A quarter of an hour later, the cabbie pulled up outside her flat. I threw all the cash I had at him and shot out of the vehicle at Olympic speed. Using the spare key she gave me, I opened the door, ran up the stairs and burst into her front room.

'The weirdest thing just happened…'

She was reading a magazine on the sofa, and when she saw me, jumped up with a fright.

'Oh, God,' she squealed, pinning herself against the wall. 'Take whatever you want. Take it all.' Her arms were in the air as if I had a gun pointed at her.

'Calm down, it's only me.'

'Please don't hurt me. You can have it all.'

'Ayesha? It's me.'

'Please don't hurt me,' she sobbed.

'I'm not gonna hurt you. Come on, don't mess around.'

She took a good look at my face. 'Wait. Hang on, I know you.' She squinted from across the room. 'Barry Brooks?'

'Yes.'

'Why are you here? How did you get in?'

I jingled the spare key-ring. 'With this.'

'When did I give you that?'

'This morning, remember?'

'What? No, I don't. Barry, I haven't seen you since high school.'

THIRTY-TWO

An icy-cold jet of water hit my face.

'Barry, wake up, can you hear me?' It was the voice of a middle-aged woman.

I let out an uncomfortable groan.

'That's it. Come on, son.'

Son? I opened my eyes and there she was. 'Mum?'

'There, that wasn't too difficult, was it?'

I blinked a few times to focus. 'What's going on?'

She placed a warm cloth on my forehead. 'This should help with the pain.'

'Mum, how are you here?'

She was grinning. A smile from Mum used to make everything better. 'You poor baby. You're lucky mama's here to make it all better.'

I didn't recognise the room at first. It was large, bright and airy, with magnolia walls and tea-light candles burning on a mahogany table next to the sofa. A mellow citrus aroma flooded my nostrils. 'Where am I?'

She tilted her head. 'They must have hit you hard this time.'

'Who?'

'The boys at school.'

A familiar painting hung next to the open window and it all came back to me. This was our house. I was in my childhood home. We lived here years ago, before I moved out and Dad sold it for a smaller place. 'How did I get here?'

'You really don't remember?'

I shook my head. 'No. I was at Ayesha's, then I woke up here.'

I walked to the window and stared out. It was such a beautiful day. The sun was shining into the front garden; Dad's lush, green, immaculately maintained lawn as vibrant as it had been all those years ago. Not a cloud in the sky, smoke patterns from the engines of passing aeroplanes stretched as far as the eye could see. They collided, criss-crossing in the distance, alongside the jolly chirp of birdsong wafting gracefully through the open pane.

'Ayesha? Who's that? A friend from school?'

It was time to think rationally. My parents were dead; this had to be an illusion. I was either dreaming, hallucinating, or losing my mind.

'Was she there when they attacked you?'

'Who?'

'This Ayesha you mentioned.'

'Err...'

'You should invite her over for tea so I can say thank you.'

'Mum, are you real? I mean, are really here?'

'Of course I'm real, Barry. What do you mean?'

If this was all a fabrication, my mind had re-created our old place exactly. Everything was spot on, down to the intricate pattern on the cushions and multi-coloured throws Mum used to cover the chairs. It didn't feel fake, like dreams or hallucinations often did. I wasn't frightened or in a panic, as I would be if sensing deception. 'Don't you remember? You died in a plane crash.'

'If I died, how can I be here?'

I should have thought more about the question before asking. 'That's what I'm trying to figure out. It's all so alive here.'

'Alive? What do you mean?'

'Real.'

'What were you expecting, blossom?'

What should one expect to see when travelling back in time? I caught my reflection in the mirror above the fireplace. It was me, only with a younger face. I couldn't have been older than nine or ten. 'Before the ruining lines took over,' I whispered to myself.

'What lines?' she asked.

'Hmm? Oh, nothing. Just ignore me.'

'Come sit down, it's safer here. I don't want you to get all dizzy and have another fall.'

"Safer here". I'd heard that before recently. Fingers crossed the triple cheeseburger on legs wasn't about to make an appearance. 'Where's Dad?'

'He's gone to get pizza. He'll be back soon.'

My childlike instinct kicked in. 'Pizza? With baked beans?'

She smiled. 'Thought that might perk you up a bit. You feeling any better?'

'Yep. Thanks, Mum.'

'The swelling's gone down a bit. You should be back to your old self in no time.'

No. I don't want to. Please don't let me be him again. That poor bastard is stuck ten or so years in the future, dealing with immeasurable grief, floating through his dreary life from disaster to disaster, dirtying his hands with scandals and life-shattering controversies. I don't want to go back. Please, don't make me go back.

'Go wash your hands for dinner, sweetheart. Dad'll be happy to see you up and about after the accident.'

'Mum, what did happen? How was I knocked out?'

'Beats me. I went to answer the door and there was a man standing there. You were unconscious in his arms. I asked him what happened, but he didn't know. Said he found you laying there.'

'What man? Laying where?'

'In the schoolyard. A very large man, didn't catch his name. Do you know him? He was wearing a white shirt? It had a funny, red design on the collar.'

I knew it. I thought I caught a whiff of something frying

in the kitchen. 'Err, no,' I lied, 'can't remember.'

'I was just thrilled he brought you back to me. You took a nasty knock to the head. God knows how he knew where we lived.'

A door slammed and Dad's booming voice echoed throughout the house. 'I'm home. Yvonne?'

'In the living room, love,' she shouted back.

'Can I see you out here for a minute?'

She got up and I followed her. 'Where d'you think you're going, mister?'

'I wanna see Dad.'

'And you can, in a moment. Sit down and relax. I'll dish up and bring the food through.' She left the room and closed the door behind her.

I grew suspicious. We never closed the living room door. Through all my years in that house - and there were many - I'd never once seen it closed. 'What's going on?'

'Be there shortly, hon.'

'What's so important that I don't get to hear?'

'Be quiet, Barry,' Dad said. I could hear the impatience in his voice, and spent a few moments trying to decipher their mumbles through the door. Finally, it opened and he appeared. He was youthful and fresh-faced, as he had been all those years ago. Overcome with emotion, I threw my arms out and jumped up to grab hold of his shoulders.

'I missed you, Dad,' I said. 'I missed you so much.'

He didn't hug me back. Clambering desperately to take hold, I eventually ran out of grip and slipped on to the floor. 'What's wrong?'

'Barry, I don't want you to be afraid,' he said, crouching down.

'I'm not afraid.'

'Your Mum and I have something to tell you.' He put his mouth to my ear and began to whisper. Over his shoulder, I saw Mum hide her face.

'You're not really here. Do you understand?'

'Why are you whispering?'

'Did you hear what I said?' His voice was back to its

normal volume.

'I heard you. I'm not really here. That's what you said, isn't it?'

Mum looked as if she was about to cry. 'We're so sorry, love.'

'What for? I knew all along.'

Dad got to his feet. 'You can't stay here.'

'Why not?'

'You're needed elsewhere.'

Insolence. 'Am I? Really? Why's that?'

'Don't backchat me, young man. This doesn't give me any pleasure.'

Then I realised why he didn't hug me back. His arm was behind his back, but when it came into view there was a baseball bat in his right hand.

'What's that for?'

'It's for the good of everyone and everything, Barry.'

A baseball bat? 'Are we going for a game of ball?'

He wasn't partial to sarcastic me. 'Don't be silly. This is the hardest thing I've ever had to do in my life.'

'I'm not being silly. Why have you got a bat? Are you gonna hit me with it?'

He looked at Mum, who in turn looked at the floor. It was then I realised he wasn't planning to hit me at all.

He was planning to kill me.

'Dad, why are you doing this?'

'No choice, son.'

'There is a choice. You don't have to do it.'

'I do. You're running away, Barry. Your grandfather told me.'

Here we go again. 'Why does everyone keep harping on about him? What's he got to do with anything?'

'He said you have to face up to your own reality. I can't allow you to stay here.'

What a disappointment this illusion had turned out to be. My diseased mind didn't even have the decency to let me rest in the most secure environment I'd ever known. My fictional father from the past was about to swing the bat and send me hurtling forward in time to face what was left of my scummy life. 'I don't want to go back there. It's too hard.'

'We believe in you,' he said. 'You have the ability to dig yourself out of this. It's inside you, Barry, it always has been.'

'What is? I don't get it, Dad. So many times I've been told to become aware, but I don't know how.'

He wasn't even prepared to reconsider. 'It's getting late. Be well, son. You should know by now that it's coming for you.'

'What's happening to me?'

'You're sick. Very sick indeed, but you have to keep fighting. You have to break through quickly before it all dissolves.'

'Before WHAT dissolves? How come you know so much but I don't?'

'I'm so very sorry.' He took a deep breath, then an almighty swing.

'I love you, Mum.'

THIRTY-THREE

I came to on Ayesha's floor, forehead throbbing white-hot as if someone had continuously kicked and punched it. There was no sign of her, but the copy of *Woman's Own* she was reading when I stormed through the door was sitting open, facedown on the sofa.

'Ayesha? Are you here?'

The blood rush hit me as I soon as I got to my feet. Steadying myself against the wall until it passed, I saw my reflection again in the mirror on the wall.

Back to normal.

The gormless, pale face looking back at me was present-day Barry Brooks, no longer in the all-absorbing comfort of his childhood body.

What love Dad had shown choosing to send me back, forcing me to make use of a brain desperately needing its rest. Did he really think I could join the dots and figure this out? I wasn't sure there was anything *to* figure out. If I accepted the trauma of the last eighteen months had sent me mad, would that be enough? I could admit to having a mental illness, couldn't I? I mean, my dignity wasn't really at stake. A few pills and a stint in a rubber room? Easy street.

A phone was ringing, but it wasn't mine. I always set my phone to vibrate, an old habit I'd picked up after years of using public transport. Like most passengers, I didn't want to hear poor re-creations of popular chart hits, cobbled together by some stoned, techno-freak abusing a

Bontempi keyboard. On vibrate, it's a lot simpler: you can feel it, others can't hear it. Everyone's a winner.

This was your basic *ring-ring* tone, coming from somewhere in the kitchen. I rummaged through unopened post and empty crisp wrappers, eventually finding it hidden inside an empty foil container, covered in leftover curry sauce.

I mean why?

It was flashing to indicate an incoming call.

Call: Kev. Answer?

Great. The return of the salad-dodger. I hit the green key. 'What now?' I felt four-day old chicken madras seep into my ear.

'Bet you think you're going mad, don't you?'

Maybe a little, yes. 'Nope. I'm just fine, ta.'

'You sure, pal?'

Not sure at all. 'As sure as you're fat. Where's Ayesha?'

'Are you *really* bothered about her? Is that what's *really* worrying you?'

'As it happens, yeah. I'm sure you know I frightened her half to death recently.'

'You know I'm not Kev, don't you?'

'I don't care who you are. My brain's not in the least bit interested anymore.'

'You still don't want to believe. Do you know how irritating that is? It means I can't break through. As soon as you open your head up to me I can help.'

'That's what you keep saying, but how exactly do I *open up my head*?'

'Just stop battling with me and face up to it. All the crap you've been through, go home and face it.'

'I'm willing to admit my head is damaged, but in the light of all the *crap*, as you so delicately put it, can you blame my head for that? What I need is some rest, Kev. Maybe a psychiatric evaluation later on, but mainly rest.'

'Go home. Go home and face up to it.'

A brief musical skit signalled the end of the call. The screen told me there was one text message waiting to be read:

Meet me at home. Go home and meet me there. I've found a window. See you there, W.B.P.

W.B.P. again. I didn't recognise the initials on the text or the note slipped inside ghost Kev's pocket. Did it stand for *Whopping Big Paunch*?

'He's in here.' A woman's voice was shouting from outside the door. It was Ayesha, and from the sound of it, she'd brought a stampede of people with her. Whoever they were, they were bounding up the stairs to the flat. In her mind, I was clearly disturbed, so realistically, it could only be the police or a group of men in white coats.

I had to get out of there, but they were blocking the only exit. If only to delay it for a few precious seconds, I ran into the bedroom and looked out of the window. There was a small ledge on the outside, but I wasn't sure it would take my weight.

The door to the flat opened. I had to go for it.

Sliding the window open, I brushed the curtain out of the way and crawled through the gap on to the ledge. The drop below was around fifteen metres - large enough to sustain a nasty injury - but I kept reminding myself a twisted ankle would be better than the freedom-stifling toilet bucket of incarceration.

Ayesha ran into the bedroom and clocked my bid for freedom. 'Barry, no. Where are you going?'

'Sorry,' I said, 'I didn't mean to scare you, but I can't let them take me.'

She started to move towards me. 'You haven't scared me and no one's taking you anywhere. What are you thinking?'

'Get back. If that's true, then who's outside?'

'Miles. I brought Miles. You passed out on my floor. I didn't know what to do so I took your phone and called him. Teddy's here too.' She took my mobile from her bag and held it up. 'Look, see?'

Miles stuck his head around the door. 'Baz? You alright, mate?'

'Why did you have to bring him?'

'What else could I do? Come back inside, hon.'

'How did you know to call him?'

'I met him earlier today, remember? We went to your place to sort through Penny's things?'

Way too confusing. 'Are you messing with me?'

She looked at Miles. I couldn't read minds, but she was clearly questioning my sanity.

'Of course not. We only want to help you. Come back inside.'

'No. You're tricking me.'

They exchanged glances again. She was fresh out of ideas.

He tried a different tact. 'Come on, pal. Why don't we go down the pub and talk about it? A few beers can solve most problems, y'know.'

Did any part of him actually think I would agree to that? Having each one of my toes amputated was a more thrilling prospect. I edged further out of the window. 'Is Penny dead?'

Confusion. 'I don't understand.'

'I spoke to Kat. She told me Penny was there with her. Told me she was alive. How do you think that made me feel? Know how that feels?'

'That can't be right,' Miles said.

'It's what she said.'

Ayesha took a few steps forward. 'I know this must be upsetting, but can't you at least come inside? You're making me nervous hanging out the window.'

She was nervous? I was the one about to drop and land on the bone-shattering concrete below. To jump or not to jump; that was the question, I just had to make the decision.

'Is Penny alive or not?'

'No, she's not,' Miles said, 'she died last week, you know that.'

Something caught my attention. I could hear footsteps beneath me on the ground outside. 'Where's Teddy?'

'Teddy?'

'Yeah, you know, the guy who almost beat me to death?'

He stuttered. 'Err, he's here, outside the door.'

Like hell he was. He hadn't said a word the entire time. 'Don't lie to me.'

'I'm not, mate.'

Politicians were more convincing. 'Give me a break. Teddy? Where are you? Come on, let me have a look at you.'

Silence. What a surprise.

'Oh, so he's outside the door, is he? 'D'you think I'm stupid?'

'No, Barry, I'm down here.' Teddy was outside, close to my landing point. 'We got you covered each way now.'

I had to look twice, but the crazy idiot had also found a mattress, from a nearby bin or skip, to cushion my fall.

'You've only got two choices, so choose the easiest one.'

My rage level peaked. I hated losing arguments with people, especially those I'd also lost fights to. 'You think you're so smart,' I said. 'Such a big man now you've got the upper hand. Know what, Teddy? I'm gonna do twice as much damage to you as you did to me.' My whole body shook with anger, sending my mouth into overdrive. 'I'm gonna smash your face in with a bloody crowbar, you piece of shit.'

Miles muttered something from the door. It was along the lines of *"yeah, I'd like to see you try"*.

Ayesha rolled her eyes.

'What did you say?'

He looked at me in the same way a schoolboy would the headmaster, impudently denying responsibility for the graffiti on his *Volvo*. 'Nothing, buddy. Nothing at all.'

'How've you even got the nerve to come here? You don't give a shit about me, so why?' I looked at Ayesha. 'Did you fancy your chances with her?'

'Don't be silly, Barry,' she said.

'Yeah, that's it. I bet you and numbnuts down there fantasised about taking turns.'

She had every reason to look mortified. 'It's nothing like that and you know it.'

'Do I? I'm not sure about anything anymore.'

'I brought them here because they were the only people I knew connected to you. I didn't mean to make things worse.'

With my mouth shut for longer than five seconds, I realised how out of order I was. I looked into her eyes and felt terrible. She was only looking out for me. 'You don't understand what's going on. Weird things are happening and I can't explain it. I need you to let me go and figure it out.'

'Can't do that,' Miles said, 'you're a liability to yourself and everyone around you in this state.'

Except for threatening to throw myself out of a window, in what way was I a threat? I was hardly running down the high street, waving my genitalia to the elderly, shouting, *"get a load of this, Grandma"*. 'Please let me go.'

'No,' Miles said. He rushed towards me at light speed, scooped my body away from the window and sent us both tumbling to the floor. My head cracked as I landed - not an unfamiliar experience - and the throb of another headache kicked in straight away. 'What the hell are you doing?'

'What I've got to. You can thank me later.'

There was no need to turn it into a Hollywood action scene. 'Don't make me laugh.' I sat up and dusted myself off as he leant out and signalled to Teddy the siege was over. 'So you stopped me from jumping. Doesn't change anything.'

'Think you'll find it does.' Out with the chipper, in with the serious. 'I've wanted to do this for weeks, ever since Penny left me.' He moved over and crouched over me with deep-red, bloodshot eyes. 'How does this feel?'

He had a six-inch blade lightly pressed against my jacket. I gazed at him in disbelief. 'Miles? Where'd you get that? What are you doing?'

'I'd have done anything for that girl - anything at all to protect her. Then you came along. You were always there, Baz, d'you know how annoying that was?'

I pleaded with him. 'Think about this. You don't wanna do it.'

'Is that what you think?'

'Yeah.' Shortly before meeting Ayesha, I'd thought about ending things my way and felt no fear. Now Miles was in control, things were a lot different. Self-preservation kicked in. I didn't want to die. I didn't want to be killed. Not like this.

'You're wrong, man. She's dead now, and I can do whatever I want. Might as well start with getting rid of you.'

Ayesha was terrified. 'Don't do it, Miles. Don't hurt him. We can work this out. It won't solve anything.'

He was beginning to sweat, the knife shaking in his hand. 'You don't know what he did. Penny and I were together for years. This piece of shit moved in, and the next thing you know, *she's* moving out. He took it all away. He took Penny, and now she's dead.'

'I can't imagine how that feels, but this is wrong. Are you really a killer?'

As he tightened his grip on the handle, I saw the pain in his eyes, and it became apparent to me Miles wasn't a killer at all. He was angry and upset, understandably so, but not capable of taking a human life.

I took controlled, shorter breaths to try to veer my stomach away from the tip of the blade. 'I know you're upset, Miles, but this isn't gonna bring her back.'

'It'd make me feel better.'

'In the long term? I don't think so. You'll spend the rest of your life regretting it.' I saw a flicker in his eye. Was I getting through? 'We can forget about all of this if you put the knife down. As far as I'm concerned, it's done and gone. What do you say?'

Ayesha picked an object up from the floor and drew closer to us. She was holding a large, hardback book and had raised it to chest height.

'Put the knife down,' I repeated, watching her gain ground.

'I loved her, Barry.' He loosened his clutch on the handle. 'You stole her from me.'

'It's all in the past now, mate.'

She was almost looming over him.

'No. It's not in the past, 'cos I'm still feeling it. How does that make it in the past?'

'I'm sorry, mate. I'm so, so sorry.'

Ayesha was primed for the blow.

'Not good enough,' he screamed.

'Now!' I shouted.

She swung the book from behind her head, but Miles was too fast. He anticipated the move and dropped the knife, lifting his hands to soften the impact, responding with a firm jab to her stomach. She yelped and dropped to her knees, crippled in agony.

I picked up the weapon and gave him a solid push. He lost balance and landed on his back with a horrifying crunch. I straddled him, using the strength I had left to secure his arms and legs. 'Who's got the upper hand now?' I asked, holding the knife to his throat.

Winded, Ayesha crawled across the floor to me. 'Don't. He's not worth it, Barry.'

She was right. I never intended to do anything but threaten him as payback. 'You're such an idiot. Is this the way you solve all your problems? Someone pisses you off in life and you wanna kill them?'

'Do it,' he said, 'get rid of me. I'm nothing without Penny. Put me out of my misery.'

'You loved her so much, did you?'

'You know I did.'

'Didn't think about that when you were playing away with her sister, did you?'

'That was a mistake,' he shouted, trying to break free. 'It's none of your business anyway.'

'Penny's happiness was my business. She was having

my baby. We were gonna be a family. You were out of the picture, you cheating bastard.'

I heard a rustling noise behind me. With Miles safely in custody, I didn't want to turn around unless he took advantage of a shot at freedom. 'Ayesha? What's that?'

She didn't get chance to answer.

'Get off him, Barry.'

It was Teddy.

'What the hell? How did you...'

'I said put the knife down and get away from him.'

'Okay, okay.' I eased the pressure on Miles' body, 'I was never gonna...'

'I said now.'

At that moment, Teddy made the biggest mistake of his life. Instead of letting me get up, he threw himself at me. I don't know how he imagined it ending up any other way, but when the force of Teddy hit me - within the nano-second that felt like a lifetime - his added weight on my arm plunged the blade deep into Miles' throat. I rolled away and watched the blood begin to flow.

'Oh, God. What have you done?'

I didn't know which one of us Ayesha was talking to.

'You fucking idiot,' I screamed, 'I was getting up. Shit, Teddy, are you mad?'

In shock, Teddy fell to his knees. 'Oh, God, no. Please, please, no.'

The mystified look on Miles' face will haunt me for as long as I have breath. 'It wasn't me. I swear I didn't want to do it,' I cried, desperate for his forgiveness.

Teddy ripped a sheet from the bed and held it to his throat. 'You're gonna be alright, I promise. Call an ambulance, somebody, please.'

Ayesha ran through to the lounge for her mobile.

'What are we gonna do?' Teddy sobbed. 'What the fuck are we gonna do?'

In less than a minute, the plain white sheet had completely changed colour and Teddy took another from the bed. Until the ambulance came, there was nothing we could do except make sure he was comfortable. How comfortable one can be when there's a six-inch knife sticking out of your neck is a totally different question altogether.

My reply wasn't the most inventive. 'Try to stay calm. Help'll be here soon.'

Teddy stood up and paced around the room. 'This is all your fault. We wouldn't be here if it wasn't for you and that dumb bitch.'

'Why don't you do something useful and keep holding that bloody sheet?'

He did as I said. 'You're such a dick, man. You're going down for this.'

'You're the one who pushed me. If anyone's going down for this, it'll be you.'

But I knew that wasn't entirely true. I was the one with the knife. I shouldn't have been holding it to his throat in the first place. What was going through my head?

Miles was coughing, blood trickling out of his mouth. 'Don't blame him, Ted. Everything happens for a reason.'

'Hush, man,' Teddy said, 'try not to talk.'

'I know the reason.'

'Miles, be quiet,' I insisted.

'You know the reason, Baz?'

'Not now, okay? You're hurt. You need to be quiet.'

'I'm gonna die.'

'No, you're not. You're gonna be fine.'

'I can see it coming, but it's alright. Do you know why?'

Why wouldn't he shut up? I thought something as serious as a blade in the throat would give the hint that talkies wasn't the best idea.

'Do you know why?' he persisted.

'You don't know when people are trying to help you. Go on, then, tell me why.'

'Because...' A jet of blood hit my cheek as he coughed once more. 'Because, I get to see Penny first. We can carry on where we left off. How d'you like that, eh?'

'Don't ever say her name again.'

'Penny, Penny, Penny,' he jeered, 'I guess that means I win. Up yours, Barry.'

I wanted to stand on his neck with all my weight, but I couldn't. I couldn't even reply to his taunts. It wasn't because I had nothing to say; I had insults on the tip of my tongue that would have made Bernard Manning blush.

Time just ran out.

For Miles, that is.

THIRTY-FOUR

I killed a man.

Barry Brooks had taken a human life.

In a moment of insanity I had pushed a blade to the throat of my neighbour and plunged it in deep. It may have been an accident - an act of violence totally unplanned - but it had happened anyway.

And it was my fault.

There was no one else to blame but me.

Trying to implicate Teddy to exonerate myself was pointless, and also made me feel like a charlatan; why would he want to kill his best mate? He was the one shouting at me to put the knife down. No, that wouldn't work. All fingers would point at Baz: the heartbroken guy with severe mental issues, still reeling from the death of his girlfriend who just happened to be the ex of the man he'd killed. That would be the tagline. A convoluted one at that. If only I'd thrown the blade out of the window instead of threatening Miles with it, things would have been different. But no, that would have been too easy. Barry Brooks had long since abandoned the path of simple solutions.

How could I have changed so much in eighteen months? From being a man on the up with everything going for him, to a nutcase about to be up on a manslaughter charge? Dad was right; I was sick. A sick individual who had lost his way and his life, both in spectacular fashion.

I had two options: stick around and face the police, or leg it.

The latter sounded more appealing. He may have been less than complimentary about my state of mind, but Dad also said I had the capability to dig myself out of the mess I was in, whatever that meant. I knew I'd have no chance of finding answers if I was stuck in a prison cell.

Effectively, I'd be on the run. That being the case, I'd need money and clothes, and that meant going home as both those things were there. I couldn't stick around for long, though; Teddy would give the police my address and they'd catch up with me faster than it took an *X Factor* reject to fade into obscurity.

It would be a very quick visit.

I'd have to leave Ayesha's first without being followed, which sounded like hard work. I could probably outrun her, but Teddy was ripped and regularly worked out, giving him the fitness advantage.

Nothing else for it. I'd knock them both out, and then make my move.

The book Ayesha used to attack Miles was laying on the floor. With Teddy distracted and still cradling Miles in his arms, he didn't see it coming. I hit him as hard as I could across the back of the head. He lost consciousness and landed on Miles' body. 'So sorry, Teddy, no choice,' I said, then walked out and closed the door.

Ayesha was stood by the fridge, phone in hand. 'Is he okay?'

'For now, but he needs attention soon. Did you call 999?'

She started to bite her nails. 'On their way. They said fifteen minutes. God, Barry, what if he dies?'

Holding the book behind my back, I used my free hand to hold her. 'It looks like a flesh wound. I reckon he's gonna pull through.'

Her face lit up. 'You think? There's so much blood.'

I'd seen enough episodes of *Casualty* to blag my way through a passable medical explanation. 'There's always a lot more blood with serious injuries. It's hardly a stubbed toe or a paper cut.'

'I hope you're right. How are you doing?'

'So so.'

She turned around and opened the fridge. 'We'll get through this…'

'I'm so sorry, Ayesha, you've been a good friend.' I didn't mean for her to turn around again, but she did, and I was caught off-guard. With force, I shoved the book up into her face. It connected with her nose and I winced at the sound of it cracking. A thin stream of blood ran from her left nostril and gently, I laid her body down, taking care to avoid banging her head against anything solid. Before leaving, I went to the bathroom to wash the blood from my hands, and zipped up my jacket to cover the stains on my shirt.

I left the flat and ran across the street in a muddle, not entirely confident I was going in the right direction. I could have tried my luck and jumped on a bus, but couldn't risk attracting any kind of attention, so followed my nose and hit the backstreets, keeping an eye out for familiar landmarks.

My bearings returned throughout the forty-five minutes it took to get home, and I came across a familiar road. It ran for over a mile, with Sunil's shop located right at the end. As much as I appreciated all the cigarettes, it wasn't the best time for a chat, so I ran straight passed and turned the corner on to my street.

Out of breath, I swerved into the garden and up the path. I turned the key, pushed the door and bolted up the stairs. The plan was simple: *get clothes, get money, get gone.*

Inside the flat, I got a shock: the whole place was in complete darkness. It wasn't just dark with the right level of background illumination required to see, it was black.

Pitch black.

What was going on here?

I ran my hand across the wall to find the light switch and flicked it down.

Nothing.

Enough already. What kind of sick, twisted stunt was this? Why was I convincing myself I needed psychiatric care when it was right there, staring me in the face? I had not made the darkness up. This was not an hallucination. Under the circumstances I felt surprisingly sane and clear-headed. It wasn't me this time. Something or someone was playing games. Jeremy Beadle wouldn't go this far, would he? He wouldn't sit idly by and watch a person's life crumble to dust without intervention, before switching on the floodlights and taking off the mask?

I went back to the front door and opened it to allow light from hallway inside.

Why was my flat in total darkness when it housed an array of very tall windows? Why couldn't I see inside my well-equipped, windowed-out apartment at four-thirty in the afternoon?

The light from the hall made little difference. I could only see a few yards in either direction.

Why was there never a torch around when you needed one? There should have been one in the electricity cupboard, but it was missing. When you didn't need one - when a torch was the household item you least required - you could bet your last *Rolo* there'd by hundreds lying around, begging to be used. Where did they go? Was there an international flashlight convention that always clashed with those times you needed a torch?

I took the mobile from my jacket pocket and clicked on the camera icon. The handset had an in-built light for taking photos in darker-than-usual situations, and there was enough battery left for partial illumination.

Twenty-six seconds later, I discovered all the windows in the flat had been covered, top to bottom, in black masking tape.

Every last inch of window space.

Is this what Kev meant by *go home and face it*? Face what? A whole lot of nothing? Was Kev really *Beadle* in disguise?

The light on the phone wasn't designed to be on for such

a long period of time. I rushed into the kitchen before it gave out, emptying every drawer to find candles. I anticipated using them for wine-filled seductive evenings with pliable women, not this.

I lit ten tea-lights in total and placed them on a tray, holding it in front of me to light the way.

The rest of the kitchen was clear, aside from my thoughtless rummaging. It was as I'd left it that morning when packing up Penny's things, only with black tape blocking my view of the garden.

I moved into to the lounge. The whole *clothes, money, gone* idea was taking longer than I planned. Teddy and Ayesha would surely be conscious and co-operative, and the authorities would soon be forcing down my door. There was no time left at all, definitely none to waste. I couldn't let them find me and take me away.

Unless it was all a set-up. But how would that explain the shadow?

I could hear a telephone ringing. My mobile had died so it had to be the cordless, but I couldn't see well enough to find it. The ring volume was on its highest setting and seemed to be shifting quickly around the room; ahead of me, to the left, right and directly ahead. I placed the candles on the floor, and with both hands clear, carefully felt my way around.

The tape on the windows in this room hadn't been applied with the same care as those in the kitchen. This allowed several tiny flecks of light to pierce through.

The noise of the telephone continued to resonate for a few seconds in different parts of the lounge. The chill of an icy breeze rushed by me, the drilling, digital ring of the handset closely behind it.

It was when I saw the shadow that I realised there was something in the room with me.

It dashed around with speed, but my eyes were too slow and I couldn't make out its shape. Frozen on the spot, the breeze intensified, and within seconds, had turned into a mini-gale. Magazines were flapping on the table, and to add to the noise of the phone, a high-pitched whistle rattled the window frame. Ornaments and photo frames on the mantelpiece fell to the floor and I heard the sound of glass and porcelain crack as they landed.

'Who's there?'

The wind stopped and I saw it again. It was standing just out of shot, laughing at me from the corner of my eye; a perverse screech you'd expect from a serial killer celebrating his hundredth kill.

How was that possible? I was wide-awake.

The hooded figure from my sleep was mocking me when I was wide-a'bleedin'-wake. That wasn't allowed, was it? Who's in control here?

It seemed the rules had changed. I wasn't consulted beforehand, but didn't get the impression that whatever had latched itself on to me was too interested in around-the-table negotiations. If I stared at it directly, would it disappear? That's how it worked when I was asleep.

It circled itself around me once more and my ears popped under the pressure. 'Answer me.'

It picked up more speed.

'Show yourself.'

The candles had all blown out and the room was in total darkness once more. 'Who are you?'

I had an idea. The window was three or four yards ahead of me from where I stood. It was possible I could use the tray to smash the glass and allow natural light back in. Having the ability to see again would certainly give me a better shot at solving the riddle. Then again, it was also possible it wouldn't work at all. Whatever the outcome, it was a better idea than staying put, but I'd have to time it perfectly. If I didn't choose the precise moment of execution, I could risk being swept up in the tornado forming around me.

Lifting the tray to shoulder height, I waited for a gap in the circle and threw myself into the window. Sadly, my calculations weren't very accurate, and the full force of my body hit the wall instead. The tray dropped to the floor and I violently twisted my shoulder on impact. The pain was unbearable at first; a burning sensation tore down from around the neck to my back, pushing its way underneath my rib cage. Picking up the tray, I urged my body to move across to the left until I could feel the rough exterior of the masking tape.

After three heavy whacks on the glass, a sharp claw gripped my shoulder. It exacerbated the pain and I screamed out for mercy until it pulled me back, away from the window. Determined to finish what I'd started, I wriggled forcefully, eventually breaking free. Another four blows on the glass freed the majority of the pane, and my living room – now resembling a small building site - came steadily into focus. The television was to my right, shelves and a chair to the left; all I needed to do was turn and face whatever was here with me, and finally answer that bloody telephone.

Gradually, I looked around, a mixture of excitement and apprehension taking hold.

The room was completely empty.

I stepped carefully over the broken items and found the telephone on the computer table. 'Yes?'

I was half-expecting to hear the words *smile, you're on Candid Camera*, but this was a new voice.

'Have you seen it?'

'Jeremy? Seen what? Who's this?'

'The shadow. It's there, isn't it?'

'It was.'

'You mean it left?'

'Yes. Who are you?'

'Excellent, it's probably looking for me.'

'Why would it be looking for you? I think it was here for me.' I had to ask again. 'Tell me who I'm speaking to.'

There was no hesitation. 'It's your grandfather, Barry. Now don't argue with me this time. I'm not in the mood and I don't have time.'

The fact that it wasn't Kev's voice made me think twice about slamming the phone down. 'If you're really him, talk to me some more.'

'What?'

'Tell me what you used to say when I trod mud from the garden all over your carpet.'

'Barry, I told you, I haven't got time for this.'

'Do you want me to believe you?'

'Don't you recognise my voice? Can't you tell it's me?'

He did have the faint Yorkshireman's lilt, but that wasn't enough. Anyone can put on a northern accent and talk about lard and whippets; I needed him to answer the question. 'Make it easier on yourself and say it.'

He paused. 'Barry Brooks,' he shouted, 'Come on, bugger-lugs, let's get you in t'bath.'

My stomach did an Olympic somersault. 'Grandad?'

'Yes, now listen. It wasn't after you, it was looking for me. It must have overheard our previous chat.'

'Eh? When did we last speak?'

'Try to keep up, Barry. You were at Ayesha's place.'

'I thought that was Kev?'

He blew a sigh and it crackled down the line. 'And what did Kev tell you? Who did he say he was?'

I didn't answer.

'I'm going to come to you. Can you stay where you are?'

'No, don't,' I said, 'I can't stay here.'

'Why?'

'There was an accident. It wasn't my fault, I swear, but someone I know got killed.'

'Don't worry about that, it's not important.'

That didn't sound like something Grandad would say. Killing Miles wasn't important? It was a pretty big deal to me. He wasn't the one who'd sat through the whistling and burbling of his throat during the final seconds, watching thick, dark balls of blood splash and stain a brand new carpet. How would he have felt if I'd bludgeoned Grandma to death with the iron while she slept? *"Never mind, she was knocking on a bit, wasn't she? Silly old tramp. Fancy a sandwich? I think there's some butcher's ham in the fridge. I'll bury her later"*.

'I think it is. He's dead. I knifed him in the neck and the rozzers are probably looking for me.'

'They're not.'

'They are.'

'Believe me, they're not.'

'How the bloody hell do you know?'

'Watch your mouth, lad.'

I only swore at Grandad once when he was alive. Jeff Spooner taught me the word *shit* at primary school, and convinced me it was a term of endearment. Grandad wasn't impressed when he cooked me dinner a few days later and I told him it tasted really shit. Word soon got back to my folks and I was grounded for two weeks.

'Look, he's going to find me soon. If I can get to you, we can escape him. It'll save you having to go through all this again.'

'Through what?'

'Stay where you are. He's tracking me closely, but if we're fast, we should be able to elude him.'

The call ended.

'Oh, great move,' I said, frustrated, 'and how long do I have to wait around here like a sitting duck?'

'Not long,' said the elderly man from the doorway. 'Long time, no see. How are you, Barry?'

THIRTY-FIVE

Was it him?

The man died when I was eleven. I suppose it could have been my mind showing me what I wanted to see, or *Beadle* again in a very convincing suit.

He stepped forward. 'You recognise me?'

'I'm not sure...'

'I know this must be upsetting, but we have to leave.'

'Grandad? Is it really you?'

'Yes.'

'How can you be here?'

A suspicious look around the room. 'It's complicated, and I will explain everything, but we have to leave now.'

'Are you real?' I asked, still stunned by his appearance.

'I have answers - real answers - just not here.'

'Wait. You said the police weren't looking for me. How do you know that?'

'I know how this place works. It's not like that at this stage.'

Did the dead constantly speak in riddles? It must make for a really confusing afterlife. 'Why can't we stay here, then?'

'Because of him. The one you see in the corner of your eye.'

'How do you know about that?'

He made his agitation obvious with another loud sigh. 'Right now, all I can say is that he's looking for me. The darkness, the wind - all this mess is down to him. If I don't get you out now, we're both going back to the beginning. Believe me when I say you can't be in anymore danger than you are right now, so take my hand, and for the love of God, trust me.'

It was only half a story, but I did what he said. It beat the alternative of sticking around to get nabbed my the plods hands down. The pain in my shoulder had eased off, but I felt another twinge when he grabbed on to me. 'Fine, let's go. Is your car outside?'

He laughed. 'I don't need a car.'

With one squeeze of my hand, my lounge and everything in it jerked and shuddered around us, furniture shimmering and glistening in swirls of bright lights shining all around. The chill of the room vanished, and a more bearable temperature took its place. My apartment was dematerialising in stages before my eyes. 'What's going on?'

'Hush, I'm concentrating.'

A few seconds passed and I found myself in a completely different room. It was small and bright, with a noticeably fresh atmosphere. Being there was like stepping out into a cool, autumn day and letting the breeze caress your face. There was no masking tape on the windows, either, which was a plus. 'What the hell was that?'

A cheeky grin. 'What do you think it was?'

According to Grandad I knew very little when it came to the ways of the dead. Not being a corpse myself and having little to do with the afterlife more than excused my ignorant behaviour, however. He told me there was no car, and after what I'd experienced, I must say I believed him. Why would there be a car? He was dead. How many ghosts have you seen that drive? They whizz from place to place at will, avoiding the hassle of petrol. To cut a short journey even shorter, the harebrained lunatic had teleported us to a brand new place.

'Beam me up, Barry,' he said, with a wink.

'I don't believe what I've just seen.'

'This is where I live. What do you think?'

There wasn't much to it. It was one room with a small sofa, a table and chairs, and a large window overlooking green fields. 'I didn't think ghosts needed things like this.'

'I don't *need* it,' he said, 'I maintain this little bundle of joy to keep the wolf from the door.' He checked under the sofa and out of the window. 'As far as I know, he's not even aware it's here.'

'Who's *he*?'

'I told you already.'

'Right, the mysterious black shadow, I get it.'

'He's much more than that. Don't underestimate him or his capabilities here.'

I pulled out a chair and sat down. 'You keep saying that. Where's *here*?'

His expression was conflicted, a mishmash of anger and elation. 'Here is where everyone has to go and be. You didn't get here by accident, but it was through no fault of your own. Millions of us are scattered around, but you'd never recognise them. *He* oversees the place. Think of him as a sadistic watcher.' He seemed afraid to clarify too much, fearing nastiness would ensue.

'So give it to me straight. Am I mad? Is all this just the end product of a fever?'

I saw sympathy in his eyes and a solitary tear rolled down his cheek. 'This bit never gets any easier. I'm not a ghost, Barry. Not in the way you think, anyway.'

'What then?'

'We're in the same boat, you and me. We're both dead.'

THIRTY-SIX

'Dead?'

'Yes.'

'Both of us?'

'Yes.'

'We're dead?'

'It's a shock, I know.'

'A shock? Not really, it's just one of the most random things I've ever heard. Are you joking?'

He sat down on the sofa and crossed his legs. 'Wish I was.'

I laughed. 'So that's it? Hi, Barry, it's me, Grandad. I'm dead and so are you?'

'No need to get cocky,' he snapped. 'Do you want to hear this or not?'

I never liked getting told off by Grandad. His stern voice always raised the hairs on the back of my neck. 'Okay.'

'Thank you. Now, give me a few seconds to get it clear in my head.'

Having a grown-up discussion with him was a whole new experience. He died when I was fifteen, and all our previous chats had either been about school, *Transformers*, or the drum kit I wanted for Christmas. I worshipped the man at that age; he and Grandma lived only a short walk from school, so I went to their house every day for lunch, instead of with friends in the canteen. At the end of the day, I'd go back and stay until Dad finished work and picked me up. I could have gone home to see Mum, but I preferred to spend my time with him instead. Being with Grandad was never a chore. Whatever we did together, I never grew out of wanting to be with him. From my first memory of him, to watching his health deteriorate and taking *that* call from the hospital, he never put a foot wrong in my eyes. He was my hero. He never let me down. He treated me like a second son and was always there for me. We had some unforgettable, irreplaceable times together, and to be reunited with him now was mindblowing to say the least, not to mention the whole *being dead* part. Yeah, that was weird.

He was deep in thought on the two-seater as I reminisced. I was stood in the kitchen watching Grandma put away the shopping. Grandad had been stirring a pot of homemade chicken soup on the hob, stopping occasionally for a sip of coffee...

Hang on a minute. Something hit the surface. The mug he drank from. I bought it. It was my birthday present for his sixty-fifth. Mum picked it out at the shop for me. On it was a sketch of a grandfather smoking a pipe, wearing a brown sweater with spectacles sat on the end of his nose. 'The notes.'

'Notes?' he replied, looking up.

'The ones you sent when you hid my Christmas present, y'know, the drum kit? You left a trail of small clues - a treasure hunt leading me all around the house. You signed them W.B.P.'

'*World's Best Pop.* It's what you always used to call me. It was written on that mug, remember?'

'You put the note in Kev's pocket.'

'Two out of two.'

'Why didn't you come yourself?'

'I didn't have the strength,' he said. 'It took everything I had just to utter your name. For a while, all I could do was write, so I left the note. I knew you'd have a tough time believing it was me, but I had to try. I couldn't let you carry on, oblivious as to what was really happening.'

I stood up and went to the window. 'Well, now I'm here,

so you can tell me what I need to know.'

He sat down. 'I'm so glad I got you out in time.'

'Are you ready to tell me?'

He nodded. 'I think so, but it's vital you let me start from the beginning, with no interruptions. Some of it will sound unbelievable – impossible even - but save your questions until I've finished.'

'I will.'

'You promise?'

'The floor is yours.' I peered through the window. Judging by the fields of green and yellow, we were in the countryside somewhere. It must have been a converted barn or shed. If Grandad was the one who renovated it, he did a fine job. 'Mind if I open the window first? Looks like a gorgeous day out there.'

'No!' He shot from the sofa and rushed towards me. 'Don't open it.'

It was too late. I'd unhooked the catch and the soothing, autumn breeze began to pour into the room.

'Oh no, no,' he cried. 'Barry, why did you do that?'

'What did I do?' I replied, baffled by his outburst.

He was banging his fists against the wall. 'No. It can't happen, not now. Not after all my hard work.'

'What do you mean? What can't happen?'

He dropped to his knees. Outside, the sun disappeared and a fierce thunderclap rocked the room.

I closed the window as jets of water tapped against the glass. 'Where did that come from?'

'No, no, no. It can't be. Stop it, please.'

He sounded in pain. 'Let me help you. What can I do?'

'I should have told you from the start. *"Don't open the window, Barry"* is what I should've said. How easy would it have been to tell you that at the beginning?'

'Is it such a big deal? Tell me what I can do.'

'What a stupid old fool. How could I be so thoughtless? There was so much to consider and I missed the most crucial thing of all.' He ran the palm of his hand across my face. 'Nothing, Barry, to answer your question. You can't do anything. It's too late. It's all going to happen again. I'll have to start over.'

I knelt down and squared up to him. 'Calm down. Tell me what's wrong.'

'It's found me.'

'What?'

'When you opened the window. It was enough to give away our location.'

'You mean the darkened figure?'

'Yes.'

I helped him on to the chair where he sat, crestfallen, head in his hands. 'I did my best for both of us.'

'I don't know what to say. I'm sorry, I didn't know.'

'It's not your fault. I should have taken more care.'

There had to be another option. 'Can't you teleport us to another place?'

'It wouldn't make a difference. When I first got here I was the same as you. Slowly, everything I owned and loved was destroyed. God knows how long it took, but by the end, I was the saddest excuse for a man.' He moistened his lips. 'Having learned how to travel between places, the time I spent in each location was limited. I had a few minutes at most before he sensed me. Then, I found this place. It was completely off his radar, somewhere I could haul up without the fear of him finding it. I thought it was too good to be true at first, but more time passed and he never found it.'

Hailstones were clattering at the glass and I was scared it would smash. 'And when I opened the window?'

'It was enough for him to catch the scent.'

Conversationally, we were going around in circles. 'Let's say he finds us. What happens next?'

He shrugged his shoulders.

'If we really are dead, it sounds to me like this is our hell.'

'That's one way to describe it.'

Part of me hoped he'd laugh and assure me it wasn't as bad as all that.

'At some point, you died. Like me, you probably had no idea it had happened. It could have been a blackout, you may have fallen over, lost your balance, anything like that. The point is everything seemed normal. To you life carried on, but in reality, you were brought here.'

I couldn't remember dying. 'Do you know when it happened?'

'No.'

'Oh.'

'You noticed it though?'

'Noticed what?'

'That for the last few years, no matter what you've done, where you've been and who you've met, everything in your life has gone wrong.'

It was hardly a revelation. The fakest of fake psychics could have figured that out after ten minutes alone with me.

'It's all connected. Everything is connected.' He sat up and turned to face me. 'This isn't really your life.'

'No?'

'No.'

'Whose is it, then?'

'Well, technically it's yours, just not the right one. There's only so much crap that can happen to one man, right? Beth, your flat, your parents, your job, your friends, Penny, your child?' He was counting them all on his fingers. 'They've all gone.'

'How come you know all this? Have you been watching all the time?'

'You're family, Barry. When you arrived I put all my energy into bringing you here.'

'I can't believe I'm in hell.' Saying it aloud made me feel like a nutcase.

'I prefer to call it a simulation. It doesn't sound as harrowing.'

'Right.' I said, thinking about Julian from the hospital.

'Like a video game, only bigger.'

'And it's all controlled by the man that's after you?'

He winked. 'You got it. The man in the corner of your eye.'

'You see that too?'

'All the time, and not only when I'm asleep.'

A chill cut through the room and I checked to make sure the window was still closed. 'You're absolutely sure there's no way to escape?'

Defeated, he shook his head. 'I've used every last trick I could think of. Maybe we'll get another shot next time.'

I understood the simulation part, but it was like trying to see far-away objects using someone else's glasses: the harder you focused, the more your eyes hurt. A couple of times he'd mentioned re-living things again. Were they throwaway lines, or did they hold a deeper meaning?

Before I could ask, I saw the dark shadow flutter in the corner of my left eye. If Grandad was telling the truth, which I now believed he was due to the lack of any sane witnesses, I was about to be introduced to the shrouded figure.

'Look at it,' Grandad said, 'it won't disappear this time around.'

In the corner of the room, illuminated by the light from the window, stood a brand new player in town. A mischievous smirk covered the lower half of his face and he was dressed head to toe in black, with the exception of a red scarf tied neatly around his neck. 'I gotta hand it to you, old friend,' he said, 'you made the search very entertaining.'

Grandad took my hand. 'It's time, Barry.'

THIRTY-SEVEN

'We meet again, Wilfred! I love what you've done with the place. Very homely, wouldn't you say, Barry?'

'Who the hell are you?'

'Quite an interior designer, your old Grandad. I should get myself a cushy little pad like this.'

Despite his charming exterior, he instilled a hefty amount of fear in me. It must have been the neatly trimmed beard and his bright, green eyes. Since his appearance, the wind and rain had picked up outside and the fresh atmosphere in Grandad's home was now sour and frosty. I guessed he wasn't the nicest man you could hope to meet at any time of day, not just in a dark alley after midnight.

'Did you honestly think I wouldn't find you, old friend?'

Grandad stood his ground. 'I'd be a fool not to try, and I'm not your friend.'

'Well that's not very nice, is it? We've known each other for such a long time.'

It was obvious they hated the sight of each other.

'That may be true, but if I had the choice, I'd never have known you at all.'

He brushed a little fluff from his lapels and turned to me. 'How very rude, Wilfred. Barry and I both think you need to work on your manners.'

'Don't bring me into this,' I said. 'Why don't you leave us alone?'

'It's not as straightforward as that. You see, your

beloved grandfather here has been flaunting the rules for some time now. It's something I just cannot turn a blind eye to.' There was a strong element of camp to his voice, like *Kenneth Williams*, only ten times as menacing. I couldn't be certain, but I swore I saw boot polish on his hair for added slick. 'His activities cannot go unpunished, you know.'

'You love the sound of your own voice, don't you?'

My smart mouth irritated him. 'Be careful, my boy. Lip like that will get you into trouble one day,' he said, snorting like a posh toff after the punchline. 'Whoopsy, my mistake, you already are in trouble. Tut tut, Barry Brooks.'

'Leave him alone,' Grandad said, with a snarl.

'To cut a devilishly entertaining story short, your Grandad here has been a very naughty boy. He's been evading me at every opportunity, using tricks of his rather outdated trade in an attempt to deceive me. But as he knows deep down, that can never be done, can it, Fred?'

That must have pissed him off; only Grandma was allowed to call him *Fred*. To his credit, it wasn't showing on his face. 'Apparently not.'

'What are you gonna do with us? Send us back somewhere?' I looked at Grandad. 'Isn't that what you were getting at before?'

'Well I never,' the man said, with mock surprise. 'You have been a busy boy letting him in on our secrets, haven't you? Here I was hoping I'd have the pleasure of breaking the news to him myself. And to think I trusted you.'

'Answer him. Why are you dragging this out? You do it every time. Don't you ever get bored?'

He cackled, a small jet of sputum landing on my cheek. 'Nope, it's as fresh and riveting as it always has been, but if you're gonna be a spoil-sport, I'll skip to the really entertaining part.' He walked over and draped his arm over my shoulder. 'You don't remember, Barry, but this is my favourite bit. I love all the teasing. It makes me go all tingly, like tea-tree shower gel first thing in the morning.'

'Enough,' Grandad shouted, 'just do it.'

He rolled his eyes. 'Fine, Mister Impatient, let's bring on the trumpets.' He pulled me over to the window and dipped his finger in a pool of rainwater on the ledge. 'I've changed my mind. I'm not going to get myself a place like this anymore. Do you know why?'

Neither of us spoke.

'Because I haven't been made to feel in the slightest bit welcome here. I sincerely hope you're happy with yourselves.'

'Somebody hire a professional mourner to cry on our behalf.'

'Sticks and stones,' he said, dropping the lighthearted tone. 'Thank you for your lack of hospitality, Wilf, but it's time for a change of scenery.'

He snapped his fingers once, and faster than the time it took to blink, we were all back in the debris-laden pigsty that was my front room. 'Group teleport,' he said. 'Pretty swish, wouldn't you say?'

I looked around and saw the photograph of Penny on the floor, separated from its frame. I bent down to salvage it.

'Isn't that sweet,' he said, watching as I wiped the dust away, 'a thought for the dearly departed?'

'What?'

'Penny. Let us all stop and reflect a moment.' He put his hands together to simulate prayer.

'Don't you dare. I don't wanna hear you say a fucking word about her, understand?'

'My, my, Wilfred, he is a feisty one, isn't he?'

'Have some respect,' Grandad spat, 'can't you see this is real to him?'

The insult hit a nerve and he gave Grandad a ferocious glare. 'You know, Fred, I've just had a thought. Why are you still here?'

No reply.

'I'll ask you again. Why are you still here? Or, put another way, why am I allowing you to still be here?'

'Do what you've got to do. I don't care anymore.'

'Barry does.'

I had a sinking feeling something terrible was about to happen. 'What do I care about?'

'I've had enough of your disobedience, Wilf. Enough of the rule-breaking and your blatant lack of respect for me. I think it's time we got rid of you.'

'Wait!' I shouted.

The man waved his arm, and before I could rush over to his defence, Grandad started to scream.

'What are you doing?'

His skin began to burn and dissolve. Red-hot liquid bubbled all over his hands, a pungent odour filling the room. Flesh ripped from his face and on to the floor, and not long after, all that remained was his skeletal frame, which collapsed in a heap. The sound of sizzling ended, and the bones crumbled into dust and disappeared as I watched in horror, unable to move. The lump in my throat grew, almost choking me as I saw the man I idolised fade into nothingness. When it seemed like my windpipe would explode, I vomited all over the floor. The acidic sensation in the back of my mouth sent a tight, shooting pain to my chest. Tears streamed down my face and I could taste salt on my tongue, mixing with the vomit. Strands of saliva hung from my mouth, dropping on to my foot. 'Why did you do that?'

The man was trimming his fingernails with a small pair of scissors on the sofa. 'What?'

'That. Killing him.' I crawled into the corner and tucked my knees under my chin.

'May I continue?' he asked, ignoring my question and popping the scissors back in his jacket pocket.

'What did he ever do to you? He was my Grandad, you maniac.'

'Come now, don't get yourself worked up.'

'He didn't deserve to die. Not like that.'

He sat back, showing no remorse. 'It's a little unpleasant, but necessary.'

'Necessary?'

'He did his utmost to disrupt my work.'

'What work?'

'My work in this place. This is my domain. Your grandfather thought himself a renegade within it.'

'Don't be so ridiculous. Do you know how stupid you sound? He wasn't a renegade. All he wanted to do was get away from you. Why couldn't you have left him alone?'

He wasn't sharing my pain, he was revelling in it. 'You can argue and insult me all you want, Barry. You could even resort to physical assault, but it wouldn't change the fact that he's dead now. You see, that's the constant, my boy. Set in stone, here to stay, no going back, done.'

I mumbled under my breath. 'If this is hell, I suppose that makes you the devil?'

'I actually prefer Boris,' he replied. 'Such a horrendous name, don't you think?' From the same pocket as the scissors came a compact mirror. He opened it and checked his reflection. 'Invokes a negative image.'

'What, the devil or Boris?'

'Perhaps I walked head first into that one,' he said, mid-preen.

'Why do I get the feeling you're toying with me?'

'Because I am. You're extremely perceptive, Barry. Have a gold star.'

'Don't patronise me.'

Confident that what he saw met with his approval, he tucked the mirror away neatly. 'Let me show you something.'

He pointed to the wall behind me. Projected on it were horrific depictions of Penny, Miles, Kev and my parents. They were clearly dead, stood in a line, decomposition disfiguring their features.

I jumped back in shock. 'No,' I said, trying not to look, 'turn it off. Why are you showing me this?'

'All part of the journey, my boy.' Standing by the images, he took a pointy stick from his trousers, as if about to give a business presentation.

'Get rid of it. I don't want to see anymore.'

'Calm down. You really want to hear this.'

As horrific as it was, I couldn't look away. I was connected to them all via my memories, recalling every event leading to their deaths, asking myself if it all could have been avoided. Asking myself if it was my fault they died in the first place.

He tapped Penny's decaying face. 'Let's start here. 'Yes, of course, Penny. What a lovely girl she was. Don't you agree?'

'Let's not start at all,' I said. 'You don't know shit about her or me. Switch it off.'

'Answer the question, unless you want to go the same way as your beloved grandfather.'

My defiance was getting on his nerves. It was the one thing that made me feel better. 'I agree.'

She was the best. A divine, kind-hearted soul who would have done anything for anyone, bringing happiness and warmth to every situation. Seeing her there, I looked past the gruesome image and pictured her smiling and healthy. I saw those loving eyes I longed to immerse myself in.

'Well, sweat ye not, for she never existed.'

'She never what?'

'She was all in your head.' He dragged the pointer to Miles, then Kev. 'So were these guys. Nothing but a figment.'

'What are you saying?'

'You know, I have always found the ability to listen one of the better human characteristics. Try grasping it, okay?'

'Fine, whatever.'

His jolly demeanour returned. 'Good, now, where was I?' He was pointing at Miles. He only had one eye and there was a large scar across his neck. 'Ah, yes. The chap you killed.'

'It was an accident. I didn't mean to.'

'Of course you didn't, but as I said before, he never existed. So answer me this, oh wise one - is it possible to kill someone who doesn't exist?'

More riddles. 'I guess not.'

'Exacto,' he yelled, 'so don't beat yourself up about it.'

'Is all this necessary? I'm starting to feel ill.'

He wasn't listening. It seemed *Boris* didn't take his own advice when it came to admirable human characteristics. 'Moving on. Your parents. Yes, I remember. They lost their lives in a tragic air accident. What if I told you that…'

'No you don't,' I interrupted, 'don't you dare tell me *they* never existed. I know for a fact they did, you demented fucker. Don't even think about taking that away from me.'

'Temper, my boy. I wouldn't dream of it.'

'Good.'

'They're not really dead, though.'

The thin piece of thread keeping my anger inside tore. 'That's enough. I've had it with your macabre *PowerPoint* presentation. I get that I'm in hell - Grandad told me as much - and my puny human brain also worked out that you're the devil, so congratulations. I'm sure the all-consuming power gives you a constant hard-on, but I'm not listening anymore. I don't wanna hear any of this.'

'Finished?'

'Am I bollocks. What do you want from me? What did I do that was so bad I ended up here?'

'Same speech, every time, without fail. At least you're consistent.' He thought for a second. 'Fine, if you want it spelled out to you like a five year old, sit down and shut up.'

He switched off the slideshow of death and I sat down in anticipation.

'This is your own, personally-sculpted hell, Barry. You have been here in my wonderful, magical fortress of pain, since losing your life near the summit of Ben Nevis.'

'Ben Nevis? You mean the *Three Peaks*?'

'Indeed.'

'That was ages ago.' Being so proud of my achievement that weekend, I could vividly recall the finer points of the trip from start to finish. 'Near the summit?'

A nod.

I thought back. It was the last hill we climbed. All had gone according to plan, except for the moment Dean and I got lost. We'd found the path again quickly, though. 'Nothing comes to mind,' I said. 'At what point?'

'You slipped and fainted, or so you thought.'

'At the top with Dean? That was my death?'

'It was.'

'But I woke up. Dean got me to my feet.' I finished the sentence and heard Grandad's words again: *"At some point, Barry, you died. Like me, you probably had no idea it had even happened. It could have been a blackout, you may have fallen over, lost your balance, anything like that."*

'No, no, no. You slipped, fainted and fell down a sharp drop. The very same sharp drop you were so afraid of. What a coincidence. Remember the cornice? I love that word, don't you? Rolls off the tongue beautifully. Corrrrrrrrrrrrrrrnice,' he purred.

'I can't believe it.'

'Believe it, fine fellow, because that *is* what happened. You died and I took your soul, creating your own alternative timeline. Aren't I generous? As far as you were concerned, Dean scooped you up and the rest of the descent was uneventful. You completed it in record time, too.'

'But really, I died?'

'Intriguing, isn't it? How reality can change so much under your nose without you suspecting a thing?'

Apparently, a full search and rescue operation was launched as soon as Dean realised I was missing. Given the hideous weather, I could have been centimetres away and he'd still have missed me. The dense cloud had also made it difficult to perform a thorough sweep of the area. My battered body was found six days later, a quarter of a mile down the mountain, in a secluded area not usually frequented by climbers.

'So that's that part out of the way.'

'There's more?'

'Of course there is. Because this is my domain and what

I say goes, I usually like to introduce a little spice into proceedings at this point.'

As I celebrated raising so much for charity, blissfully unaware of the new plain of existence I was a part of, a chain of cataclysmic events took place. Beth dumped me, and a few days later, my parents died. 'You're saying nothing was real from that point on?'

'It was real to you,' he said, fiddling with his shoes. 'What you experienced here affected you in the same way it would had you not slipped to your death.'

I couldn't think of a reply. 'Oh.'

'I have a question, though.'

'What's that?'

'I'm not trying to imply you're brain-cell count is perilously low in any way, but could you not sense something was amiss with the job?'

'How?'

'You went for the job of your dreams and got it. Then, when you started, everything that initially appealed to you had disappeared. Did you not find that a tad strange?'

'A bit.'

'Just *a bit*?'

Did he really expect me to figure out I was dead because a new job turned out to be rubbish? I occasionally had trouble with tabloid crosswords. 'Let me get this straight. The real world - the one up there - it continued after I died?'

He shook his head with a series of patronising tuts. 'You consider yourself so important that the real world would simply cease to be after your death?'

I took his point. It was a pompous question to ask. 'What I meant was...'

'Of course it did. It continued after you left and it continues now, which is very good news for me. I get a frequent intake of lost souls to shamelessly demoralise.'

No wonder the evil sadist was thrown out of heaven. He was loving his time in the limelight.

'It may interest you to know that I popped my head

around the door of your funeral. It was very touching.' He went on to describe the coffin, choice of music and cuisine at the wake. 'Beth was very upset. Inconsolable, in fact.'

'Beth?' I'd completely forgotten about her. Must have been something to do with the way she shredded my life so nonchalantly. 'Why was she there?'

'Oh, Barry, I'll never tire of our regular chats,' he said with a snort, pointing again to the wall. No doubt he was preparing another feast of blood-soaked imagery.

I was surprised to see it wasn't so harsh. On the wall, a video playback of a funeral was showing.

My funeral.

'Remember, events in your life are different to the ones in your precious real world. Up there, Beth never left you.' He was talking to me like a father would his baby son during a bedtime story. Every word was emphasised, every sentiment enhanced. 'She waited and waited and waited for you to return from the mountain, but you never came back. *Boo-hoo*. It smashed her perfect little world into smithereens. *Waaaaaa*.' He highlighted a figure on the wall. 'Look, there she is. See?'

I saw. She was dressed in a stunning, black outfit, weeping openly in the front row next to my parents.

I covered my mouth in horror. 'It can't be. She was there all the time?'

'She was indeed. While you were prancing around a mock-up version of your shared residence in bits, she was having the worst time of her life. You thought she'd abandoned you, after telling Will you'd had an affair with her mother, filmed a selection of intimate moments and emailed them to her Dad. All the time she was crying and wailing, desperate for you to return. She lost the only man she'd ever loved.'

I couldn't work out how I felt. At least it answered the question as to why Will was so upset with me that day. The intense adoration I held for Penny had been all-consuming, captivating in its passion, until now. Watching on as Beth laid a rose on my coffin was both soothing and disconcerting. 'She's alright now, though, isn't she?'

'Pardon me?'

'Beth. She got over me eventually?'

He rubbed his hands with glee. 'You know what? I lied before. *This* is my favourite bit. It always gives me goosebumps. Let me explain something to you about time. You see, up there, only a few days have passed.' He stopped to look at his watch. 'We're only on day fourteen.'

It couldn't be. I had lived the experiences of so many months since the freezing cold of the mountain. Physically, I'd aged. Only recently, I'd found a grey hair, surely proof of the passage of time? 'Two weeks?'

'Isn't it astounding?'

Not the first adjective that sprung to mind. 'Harrowing, more like.'

'Oh, come on, you can't say it wasn't entertaining?'

'How can you trivialise this so much? Can't you see it's eating me up?'

'There you go again,' he said, 'me, me, me. This isn't my fantasy, old chum, it's yours.' He prodded my head with his fingertips. 'It all came from in here. All I do is prepare the blank canvas. I give your nightmares the space they need to come to life. Think of me as an emotional landlord.'

'I feel sick.'

'I know, but it's what I do,' he continued, 'it's what I've always done. Try not to take it personally.'

It was hard not to. After battling through all the crap of the last eighteen months, to be told it was all a façade was unacceptable. Everything I did, regardless of the outcome, was meaningless. 'I think you've all about destroyed me,' I said.

'Sorry, lad, it's my job.'

'It's your job to be a sadistic bastard?'

'Yes.'

The street outside was still deserted. 'I know it feels real, but it isn't, is it? This is what my mind's created?'

'Yes.'

'What does it really look like?'

'Believe me, you don't want to know.'

I still felt sick, a combination of watching my grandfather die and the pain in my shoulder. 'So how come Grandad didn't get a slideshow like me?'

'He did.'

'No, you didn't give him the chance. You just waved your hand and sent him packing.'

'He had three.'

'When?'

'I'll answer your question with one of my own.'

I couldn't argue. He could do what he wanted. He was the one in charge.

'Given all you've discovered, what do you think happens now?'

It was the one unknown I was desperately trying to avoid. 'I'm guessing it's lights out?'

But I was wrong. I was so very wrong. He wasn't going to obliterate me into dust like Grandad. He was going to send me back to do it all over again.

I gasped. 'You're gonna do what?'

'That's how Fred got up to three, God rest his soul.'

'In English!'

'A re-run,' he said, 'a repeat. You know, like the *BBC* at Christmas.'

'You're gonna send me back to when I died so I can live this hell again?'

'Exactamundo. By Jove, I think he's got it. Give the man a slice of cheesecake. In a nutshell, you die, you come here and see your life fall to pieces in a truly spectacular fashion. Then, when it can't possibly get any worse, I take my cue and appear. I give you the slideshow of agony and torment, then whizz you back to when it first started.' He arched his frame and leaned in. 'Come closer, Barry,' he whispered, 'that's not everything. Do you want to know the real surprise?'

'Not really.'

'The real surprise, the belting, blinding, super-dooper,

piss your pants in shock clincher is that we've already done this four times before.'

'Come again?'

He gesticulated wildly around the room. 'This,' he shouted, 'all this you see. You've been in the loop. Every time I send you back, you have no memory of ever having been there. It's like a fresh start. A chance to balls it all up again in a new and exciting way. Isn't that just dazzling?'

'You're one twisted son of a bitch, you know that?'

'It was my idea, too. I came up with it all by myself and didn't look at *Google* once.'

Livid, enraged, seething. 'Dickhead. You're a class A, level one dickhead, Maurice.'

'It's *Boris*, but thank you, that means a lot coming from the mighty *Larry*.' He allowed himself a few moments for a personal pat on the back.

I surveyed the cluttered living room that didn't really exist. 'I thought I lived a pretty decent life, y'know. Paid my taxes, donated to charity.'

'So?'

'So, what do you have to do to get into heaven? Become a monk?'

A look of intrigue, as if I hadn't asked that particular question before. 'Heaven? There is no heaven, Barry. Don't believe everything you read.'

'There's only a bad place to go when you die?'

'No, Barry, there's only *one* place to go. I am merely here to provide you with the situations to create your own living hell. How you deal with them is completely up to you. A stronger man may not have suffered so.'

'But how can the devil exist without God and heaven?'

'You rely too much on stories. There was never a God. I didn't get banished from heaven. You can't get kicked out of a place that doesn't exist.'

'None of it is true?'

'*Noah's Ark* was just a glorified dinghy. I simply exist, here, in this little fantasy world, making sure folks like you have the most soul-destroying afterlife conceivable. Now, what's so wrong with that, hmm?'

Overall, it had been a truly miserable day. There was no hope, no redemption and no light at the end of the black tunnel. 'Fantastic. Thanks for all your riveting insights. It wasn't very nice to meet you.'

'I've been with you a long time. In your dreams, the corner of your eye... I've always been there.'

Was he expecting me to gasp in awe? Tough, I couldn't be arsed. Mrs. Winter would have been distraught to discover there was no God, especially after living and breathing the Bible for so long. I felt sorry for everyone whose faith kept them company throughout their lives, willing to sacrifice life on earth for the special reward in heaven. It was a swizz. There was nothing but this. Not even an opportunity to better yourself or form meaningful relationships, because this pompous twat had rigged everything to implode. You could work as hard as you liked to make things bearable, but they never would be. My whole life had been reduced to rubble, but I didn't even have the satisfaction of knowing it was finally at an end. I was going back to re-live it all over again.

'Right,' I said, 'what are you waiting for? Send me back.'

'Patience is a virtue,' he said, grinning. 'There's one more thing I want to tell you.'

'Don't wanna hear it. More boasting about your domain and off-key methods? Give me a break.'

'Someone's grouchy today. Why so grumpy, *Bazza-bear*? Time of the month? I was going to tell you how *you* can benefit from all of this.'

What was this, a way out? A loophole I could exploit? 'Me? Since when do you care about me?'

'I don't. You may not believe it, but I am a fair man, although I rather think you're leaning in the direction of not believing me.'

'What do you think?' I hoped this wasn't a kinky thing. I didn't fancy spanking his lily-white bottom blue and playing hide the bratwurst for an evening. The devil offering a lifeline? It went against every fibre of his malevolent existence. 'Fine. Tell me.'

'Throughout my administration of this quite faultless residence, I have tried to put myself in the place of those who come here. After all, there is no alternative, so what do people really think when they arrive at this stage?'

'They most likely think you're an obnoxious despot who gets off on the suffering of innocent people.'

'Which is what I thought,' he replied, without thinking, 'but I reckon it'd be even worse for me to cast you back with nothing to show for it.'

'I'm listening.'

'I'm going to allow you one wish. You can ask for anything you want. Think of it as my parting gift to you.'

I checked my ears for excess wax. 'You're joking?'

'No joke.'

'Any wish at all?'

'Any wish at all.'

'Does that mean I could wish to be sent back to the mountain, before I died?'

He smiled. 'Absolutely.'

There had to be a catch. No way the devil would allow someone leave his domain so easily. 'So, in theory, I could go back and prevent my own death?'

'In theory.'

It couldn't be that easy. His reply was too quick. If I was to use that option, he'd insert an unwritten clause designed bring me back somehow, possibly the same way. 'I don't suppose you can tell me what I wished for before?'

'I'm afraid that's against the rules.'

Use your brain, Barry. Come up with something spectacular to wipe the smug look from his stupid face. Knock him on his backside with the genius potential you have stored away in your head. You can do it, man.

I combed my imagination for a unique last wish, squeezing every ounce of energy into my frazzled thought patterns, desperately trying to recall how I might have played this before. Only thickos would wish to be sent back to Earth - too obvious - so I probably did during one cycle, maybe even two. He'd send me back to the top of Ben Nevis and I'd slip and fall again. I'd have no memory of the wish he granted, so why would I feel the need to be over-cautious?

Going back wasn't an option. Maybe accepting that could be the key to unlocking the perfect wish.

A high-speed joyride around a deserted London in a *Porsche*? A weekend with six *Playboy* bunnies in a tub of peach melba yogurt? The clever option: I wish for the power to destroy you and this reality.

That was a bad idea. He'd find a way to render it void too using complicated hell-speak. 'How about wishing for a lifetime of happiness?'

'Try it. But remember, a lifetime is just that. At the end of it, you go back to the beginning.'

Smart arse. 'Six lifetimes of happiness?'

'Barry, I'll happily grant that if it's what you really want. Don't think I'm going to help you, though. It has to come from you. No hints or little teaser trailers, understand?'

'There has to be a wish you haven't granted.'

'I'm sure there is. Take your time and try to think of it. I'm not going anywhere.'

My hands were sweating from all the hard thought. Wiping them on the front of my jeans, I felt something small with a smooth exterior inside my pocket. I delved in and took out a folded piece of paper. Taking time to straighten it out, I realised it was the message Grandad had sent to me via Kev:

This is the only way I can communicate. Diseased, unparalleled nonsense. I was found, but I wrote. They found me, but I still wrote. Imagine their frustration.

Over and over I read, before turning to the man in black. 'I think I have it.'

'Splendid. Come on then, chop chop, let's hear it.'

'I want to write.'

THIRTY-EIGHT

'An interesting proposal,' he said. 'What will it be about?'

Camping, felching and water births - what the hell did he think it was gonna be out? 'My time here.'

His cheeks flushed and he clutched his chest. 'I'm touched.'

I couldn't tell if there was a heart beating in there or not.

'You think so highly of me and my creation that you want to put it in print? You're so sweet, Barry.'

'Bugger off, it's not a guide book. If I wanted to do that I'd just wipe my arse with it.'

His smile faded. 'Harsh, but fair. What are your terms?' It was deviously said; his twisted way of letting me believe I was in control.

'You allow me to write about my experiences before sending me back. When I finish, you make sure the transcript is sent to my parents in the real world. I don't care how you get it to them, just make it appear somewhere they can find it.'

Was that admiration in his eyes? 'Fascinating. Just fascinating. You may have surpassed yourself this time, my boy.'

'I don't give two rats and a monkey's arse what you think. Do we have an agreement?'

'There is just one thing I need to know.'

'Yes?'

'What do you expect to achieve from this?'

None of his satanic business. 'You said one wish would

be granted unconditionally. Are you going back on your word?'

'I'm just curious!'

'Yeah? Well you can stay that way. I don't owe you a damn thing.'

He smirked and his teeth glistened in the light. 'No matter, I know anyway. You want them to share your plight, don't you? You think that by sending them a work detailing the ins and outs of your other life with me, they'll bridge the connection once again.'

'So why did you ask me if you've got it all figured out?'

'I just wanted to hear you say it.'

His abnormal glare sent a cold, spiking rush through my head. My vision was disturbed, and momentarily, I saw unabridged fear in the form of atrocious images, words and screams. By speaking, he revealed his true form - the way he really looked underneath the human exterior.

The culmination of all that was sinful, putrid and base.

The creature that soaked up every negative emotion, multiplied them a million-fold and unleashed them on all who passed helplessly through his wide-open door. This rabid, fetid captivator now had me in the palm of his hand, and I had no choice but to sit there, a puppet in his makeshift dimension.

He spat into his hand and extended it to me. 'You have a deal, my boy.'

'How do I know I can trust you?'

'I am many things, but not a liar.'

The peculiar thing was, I believed him. There was an unquestionable honesty in his eyes. For all the pain he caused, the unspeakable heartbreak I now knew was all inconsequential, I saw a glimmer of decency.

'Well,' he said, standing up to adjust his trousers, 'I'd better give you some space. Get the creative juices flowing, so to speak.'

I nodded. 'One last thing?'

'Hmm?'

'Now that you've granted the wish, can you tell me

what I asked for before?'

He reached the door and took hold of the handle. Staring into his eyes, I almost thought he would let it slip. 'A word of advice, Barry. Just be thankful I granted you this one. Do I look like the kind of man who shows all his cards?'

EPILOGUE

Evening Argus, 7 June 2002 - Final edition

Late mountain-climber's novel finally hits the shelves

An Hour with the Devil, a novel by the late Terry Cook, has finally been published today almost a year after the author's death. Terry fell to his death in June of last year close to the summit of Ben Nevis, during a charity hike with friends. His girlfriend Kath found the completed manuscript by accident a few weeks later at the bottom of the kitchen drawer, and decided to submit it to a publisher.

'I couldn't believe it,' she said, speaking at the launch. 'I was spring cleaning and saw almost four hundred pages of typed A4 sheets just lying there. I had no clue Terry could write so well.'

Horace and Elspeth Cook, Terry's parents, shared similar sentiments. 'It's a blessing to have something so personal we can keep close to our hearts. We're all so proud of him.'

An Hour with the Devil tells the tale of one man's ability to cope when his world is turned upside down by a horrendous pattern of events. It focuses on his state of mind throughout, and the way he is influenced by those around him. The book has been reviewed by a number of magazines and websites, attracting a wide selection of positive feedback.

According to the publisher, first week sales were looking very healthy. 'If Terry was here today, we're sure he would be happy with the book,' they said. 'In a delightful tribute, Kath also dedicated the book to their son, Barry, who was born after

Terry's death.'

Tearfully, she told us how Terry was unaware he was going to be a father when he died, and hopes her late boyfriend will somehow get to read his published manuscript, wherever he may be.

An Hour with the Devil, by Terry Cook, is out now, priced £7.99, published by *Tinkler & Tinkler*.

Acknowledgements:

Firstly, a big thank you to Paul Stayt and Kyle Robertson for the cover art. Guys, you're worth your combined weight in beer.

To my parents, who have shown nothing but love and support from start to finish, but will most likely gasp in horror due to the abundance of swear words. For that, I am sorry.

To Ted and everyone at *YouWriteOn* for their kind words, not so kind words, suggestions and sheer determination.

Finally, to Jim. He put the idea in my head all those months ago during a nondescript chat about baked beans. The best thing is, he probably doesn't even remember…

J.P. Ledwon lives in London with his fianceé, pet rats and framed, black and white print of a young Elvis, sat at a piano. He adores fish fingers, but has never been known to tell an inappropriate joke.

Printed in the United Kingdom by
Lightning Source UK Ltd., Milton Keynes
138432UK00001B/150/P